Original title!
"ONE THIN LOVE"

Murder in Mexico

Tom Larsen

2024, TWB Press
https://www.twbpress.com

Murder in Mexico
Copyright © 2024 by Tom Larsen

All rights reserved. No part of this story may be reproduced or transmitted in any form or by any means, electronic or mechanical, including photocopying, recording, or by any information storage and retrieval system, without written permission of the author, except in the case of brief quotations embodied in critical articles or book reviews.

This is a work of fiction. Names, characters, places, and incidences are either a product of the author's imagination or are used fictitiously. Any resemblance to any actual person, living or dead, events, or locales is entirely coincidental.

Edited by Terry Wright

Cover Art by Terry Wright

ISBN: 978-1-959768-44-9

Murder in Mexico

If I've learned one thing, it's that you can never really know someone. Really know him, I mean. You live with a man. You learn his ways and moods, his strengths and weaknesses. You come to count on him like you count on the sunrise. Then one day he tells you he's done with it. The work is too hard and the years have caught up with him. The ends no longer justify the means, not just for him, but for you, too. And you know he's been thinking about it. You've felt him toss and turn at night, and you've caught him staring into space. Maybe it's age or maybe it's envy, but he suddenly wants so much more out of life, more time and more excitement...but mostly more money.

So you tell yourself it's a mid-life crisis. Chalk it up to male menopause and let him blow off steam, but you can't help thinking what he says makes sense. It is a crazy way to live, trade your time for a paycheck and watch life pass right by you. You may think you're content, but you've spent your life in self-denial. If you could see how the haves live you'd hang yourself.

Then he tells you he has a plan. He's had plans before, some good ones, in fact, so you listen. But this plan isn't like the others. This one makes you wonder who this man really is. He says this plan will set you both free and give you back the rest of your lives.

All you have to do is murder someone...in Mexico.

A total stranger, one life for two.

And you see this man as you've never seen him before, but you find yourself wondering if his plan just might work.

Tom Larsen

CHAPTER ONE

Harry squints down Tasker Street into a smear of headlights, signals timed for stop and go, the crosstown mile in nineteen stops. He could walk to work in the time it takes, but for his arches and the fucking rain.

"See it?" Murrieta calls from the doorway.

"Not yet." Harry slips the hood over his head. "But that doesn't mean it isn't there."

"Oh, it's there, alright. Probably three in a row, now that we're soaked to the skin."

He joins his fellow commuter under the awning. The old Nails 'n Things gone bust long ago.

"How long we been doin' this, Harry?" Murrieta's all brown eyes under her yellow rain hat.

"Too long, darlin'."

"That's a fact. I remember you had a mean look then. And that moustache, you hippy dippy thing, you." She slaps his arm playfully.

"And you were gonna quit that job just as soon as your momma passed."

"Before she decided to live forever."

"Tell me something, Murrieta. When that alarm clock goes off in the morning, ever feel like you can't move?"

"Paralyzed, like?"

"Yeah. You know you gotta get going, but you don't have the strength."

"Every Monday through Friday. Knock on wood."

Harry reaches for his last cigarette. "How is momma, anyway?"

"She thinks we're livin' in Baltimore." Murrieta's eyes go all funny. "I tell her, 'momma, if this is Baltimore, how come the Philly cops keep comin' to pull your ass off the toilet?'"

"We'll be in her shoes soon enough."

"Look here." Murrieta pulls a handful of knobs from her pocket.

"What are they for?"

"Everything. Stove, oven, microwave, coffee-maker, Cuisinart, you name it."

"You have a Cuisinart?"

"I come home, everything's goin'." She flips open a purse full of remotes. "Oprah's on so loud I can hear her from here. Momma's deaf as a post and blind as a bat."

"So now what's she do all day?"

"Stares at the Bible."

"Jesus."

"Better than torching the whole damn block."

"It ain't right how life ends up."

"Amen to that."

Harry sees it coming, lumbering to the curb three blocks south, packing them in as the light turns yellow then blowing right through to a chorus of car horns.

He drops the half-smoked cigarette in a puddle. *Last smoke, never fails.*

The 5 rolls in with the usual cast. Murrieta sits with her sister's kids; Harry takes the wet seat by the guy with TB. The bus stinks of stale sweat and cheap perfume. Somewhere in the back, a baby starts yowling, and a bag lady at Washington takes forever to board. The cast changes as they head north, Asians where the Italians used to be, Filipino and Mexican everywhere else. Where the blacks ended up is anyone's guess.

"Say, man, help me out, will you?" White kid, fucked up, practically leaning over TB guy to put on the touch.

"What?"

Murder in Mexico

"Could you help me out, buddy? I'm hurting."

Harry looks around. "Why me?"

"C'mon, man, I see you around. Nelson's? The Candlewick?"

"You see me in a bar so I should give you money?"

"Okay, forget it. Okay?"

"No, I mean now we're ridin' the bus together, so what, I should put you through college?"

"Fuck it. I thought you was straight up."

"Straight up, what's that?"

The kid waves him off, turns away, and a strained silence settles in. The silence of two guys getting mouthy then having to ride another dozen stops together. The kid gets off downtown, flipping the bird as the bus pulls away. Harry sees himself pounding the kid's head to mush.

By Vine Street, it's standing room only. Harry squeezes out the rear door with a sharp stab to the small of his back and a wide stain on the seat of his pants. Wind ripples the puddles in Printers lot, pinning trash to the cyclone fence. Head bent to the gale, he passes through the trestle and slips into Janey's Café. Pauline, the counter girl calls to the grille.

"Cholesterol Special for Harry."

"And a large coffee, black."

"You want the IV bag with that?"

"You're a scream, Pauline." Harry looks across the street. "Paper come in yet?"

"Couldn't tell you, doll. You want me to put this on your tab?"

"Put it on Baldini's tab. Has Leon been in?"

"You see that Leon, you tell him he owes for two months parking. Janey got bills to pay, too, you know."

"Good luck, kiddo. Leon still owes me for the last Ali fight."

"And give this lite-lunch menu to Estelle." Pauline stuffs one in the bag. "She been sneaking salads at Mickey

~5~

D's."

"Anything for you, love. Throw a bagel in there, would you?"

He sees the delivery truck pull away and ducks across the street to the corner stand. The vendor sits behind the glass, leafing through the tits and ass.

"Daily News?"

"I don't open 'til seven."

Harry glances at his watch. "Yo, pal, it's five of. Cut me a break."

Fat fuck doesn't even look up. "I ain't open yet."

"It's fuckin' pouring out here."

The vendor looks to the heavens. "Might stop by seven."

Harry storms off half a block then doubles back for a whole bundle. A hard gust hits head-on at the trestle, and he curses the wind that blows both ways. Curses the crap piled to the arches and the gaggle of crack-heads burrowed therein. Spots Leon's pickup parked at the hydrant, tires showing thread but a brand new sticker on the windshield. Rounds the corner, climbs the stairs, and leans on the buzzer. Through the window he sees Leon shuffle over to let him in.

"What's that?" Leon thumbs the bundle of papers.

"Daily News. I got a deal on 'em."

Harry circles the shop, passing out papers. Everyone gets one, even Millard, though his is the top one, caked in pigeon shit. The bell rings, machines clatter to life, and eyes glaze over like lights going out. Harry clocks in, circles back to his press, and settles down to breakfast.

Minutes later, Baldini enters with an armload of the daily grind. "Hey, Watts, am I paying you to read the paper?"

Harry looks up. "Evidently, Ed."

"Let me tell you something, Watts." Baldini looks around. "These jigs see you readin' the paper, then they all want to read the paper."

Harry looks around. "And?"

Baldini steps in close. "You know something? You're a real smartass, Watts."

"Fuck off, Baldini."

"You think you're top dog around here, but I got news for you, smartass. You're expendable, just like the rest of them."

"So expend me."

"I got a better idea." Baldini smirks. "You know that personal day you put in for next week? Forget about it."

"I don't think so, Ed."

"You don't show, I dock you a day's pay. How's that, hotshot?"

Harry turns back to his paper. He usually gives as good as he gets, but the Baldini routine has worn thin. The whole fucking thing has worn thin.

"You hear what I'm saying, Watts?"

"You're in my light, Ed."

***

Morning passes without a thought. Harry runs the easy jobs first, saving the tough stuff for some other time. He can feel Baldini watching through the office window, gearing up for the noon go-round.

"Hey, Watts. What are you making, a career of this job?"

"That's good, Ed." Harry shoulders past him. "A pissant with a punchline."

Baldini flushes but lets it pass. "That Fidelity brochure has to run today and this—"

"First thing in the morning, Ed."

Baldini holds a beat. "So, now you make the deadlines?"

"Only in a real sense."

Tom Larsen

"You are *really* pushing it, hotshot."

"Hey, Ed. If I broke your nose, would you hold it against me?"

Baldini gives him his dangerous smile, at least one that feels dangerous.

"Let me tell you something, tough guy. You're not the only one from the neighborhood. You want to threaten me? I got family all over Southside. I got goombas and wise guys up the wazoo."

"Goombas?"

"You think I got where I am today by eating shit?"

Harry pulls a sheet right past Baldini's nose. "Where you are today is about halfway through running your old man's business into the ground. Your crew hates you to a man, and I, for one, would gladly break your nose. Although I gotta admit this goomba thing has me a little spooked."

"Okay, Watts. I don't have time to swap insults." He drops more work jackets on a banded stack of cartons. "I'm not kidding about the Fidelity thing. ASAP, like it says on the docket."

Harry turns back to the sports section.

"I swear to Christ." Baldini fumes. "You been working with the coons so long you're turning into one."

"Hey, Tyrone," Harry yells. "Boss says I been working with you coons so long I'm turning into one."

Tyrone chuckles. "Like hell. Man can't even hold a tune. Yo, Leon. You ever hear Harry sing?"

"Anglo Saxon motherfucker," Leon mutters.

And on into the afternoon. Harry sambas by the feeder to the tune on Manuel's boom box. Music to work by, leave it to the Mexicans. Baldini keeps coming by to check on the Fidelity job, and Harry keeps not getting to it. Leon dawdles at the sink as the time runs down; the rest mill around like they don't know what's coming.

"What are you doing, Watts?"

Murder in Mexico

"Washing up, Ed. Like it says in the manual."

"You ain't goin' nowhere. Not until that brochure's done."

"Screw that brochure."

Baldini sees them listening but let's fly anyway. "You want a job tomorrow, you finish today. Period!"

Harry rises to full height. The room falls silent, but the pissant stands his ground.

"Okay, boss. You win."

Baldini snickers. "That's better. In the end, money talks, right, hotshot?"

"That's right, Ed." Harry digs out the Fidelity job. "In the end, you do the right thing."

"Damn straight." Little shit struts off like the heavyweight champ.

And the right thing goes like this. Harry pulls an old flat from his workbench drawer, a flat he'd been saving for such an occasion. While the plate's burning, he throws black ink in the fountain and loads up the Fidelity stock, pricey stuff, sixty pound rag with a deckle edge. The bell rings as he's hanging the plate, and by the time he's inked up, the boys are shuffling by.

Leon stops on his way out the door. "Seen everything now, Harry towing the line."

"Life's a bitch, Leon."

"I don't get you, man. You played right into his hands."

"Hey, Leon, the Ali fight?"

Leon's nose wrinkles like the name smells funny. Harry claps him on the shoulder. "Forget about it."

"Hey, Harry. That ain't the Fidelity job."

"Take care of yourself, will you, Leon?"

While he's running up the press, he checks the classifieds: vacation rentals, Puerto Vallarta, three bedroom beachfront, maid included. He jogs a sheet through and rules it up, keeping an eye on Baldini's office. Sees the little bastard in there, telling the story, Watts bending to his iron will. Harry circles the machine, throws his stuff in a duffel bag and cranks up the speed. Ten sheets through and he's off and running, ten thousand impressions, three hours easy. Harry takes a last look around. The press doesn't miss a beat, cylinders chugging, sheets firing out in a blur, two lines running in endless sequence.

He ducks out the loading dock door.

Eat shit, Baldini. I quit.

***

He's halfway home when he wonders if it's Lena's day off. Not that she will hate him for quitting his job, but he doesn't feel up to the dance. Sometimes his wife has a short fuse. He pulls the cord at Ned Brennan's. No one's there but Ned stocking shelves and Fearless Fuller staring holes in the pig knuckles jar. He and Fearless go back to grade school, but Harry's into the little punk for a few bills and he doesn't feel up to that dance either.

"What can I get you, Har?" Ned's all smiles.

"I'll take a Bud Light..." *Instead of the bourbon I came in for.*

"Where you been, Wattage?" Fearless calls up an old playground tag.

"Around."

"Haven't seen you. Then again, I don't get out much. I heard there was a little scuffle over at the park."

Harry shrugs. "Beats me."

"Tong war, Crips and Bloods." Fearless moves a seat closer.

"I thought those Crip guys were Latino?" Ned sets Harry up.

"Not anymore." Fearless sets Ned straight. "Everybody's gettin' into the act. What is it, Cambodians over there, Wattsy?"

Murder in Mexico

Harry doesn't say.

"Yeah sure, and Vietnamese. You know how they copy everything. Skinny little gang bangers with the do-rags and the whole nine yards."

"Jesus," Ned says just to be agreeable.

"And what kills me...they can't even say the names right." Fearless pulls his eyelids all crooked. "We da Clips, Broods no good."

Fucker fairly dissolves in laughter. The door opens behind him, and Jack McCabe stalks in, throwing off meanness like heat from a bulb, nods to Ned, nods to Harry, ignores Fearless completely. Ned walks a shot to the corner as McCabe slips in behind it.

"Like I was sayin'," Fearless continues. "Cambodians, Vietnamese, it's like the freaking Ottoman Empire over there."

"Ass wipe," McCabe weighs in.

"What's that?" Fearless challenges him.

"The Ottoman Empire was in Turkey, seventeenth century, Islam and high culture."

"What do you know?"

"I know this. An ignorant fuck shouldn't run his mouth."

"Screw you."

McCabe rattles his stool, and when Harry looks back, Fearless is gone. Ned mutters something, and an uneasy silence descends, the silence of three guys contemplating violence.

"Well, you know what they say?" McCabe finally breaks in.

"What do they say?" Harry looks him in the eye.

"They say..." McCabe hunkers over his drink, "that the only place left in the world where they still speak the language of the Bard is in the deepest hollows of Appalachia."

Harry considers this.

"What do you make of that, friend?"

Harry huffs. "I think a little knowledge is a pain in the ass."

McCabe howls and hammers the bar.

"And what's your pleasure, pardner?"

Harry runs a hand over his face. "Maker's Mark."

McCabe slips from his stool, circles the bar and grabs the bottle.

"It's a funny thing about language, how it gets spread around." He settles onto the stool next to Harry. "Oh, the eggheads know the migration routes, how what tribes got where, but what they can't account for is the roustabouts. No one ever can."

"I wouldn't know."

"For instance." McCabe pours a round. "The coastal clans of Greenland and the head hunters of Borneo have the same word for fish."

"Fish."

"Fish. Of course it could just be coincidence, but I'm thinking some old Norsemen saw more of the world than anyone knows."

"Well, you know what they say?"

"What do they say?"

Harry smiles. "It takes all kinds."

"That it does. That it does. Take yourself, for instance." McCabe bobs his head at the door. "You hate the sight of that little blowhard, but it bothers you that I insulted him in front of you."

"Not that much."

The difference between me and you?" McCabe looks straight ahead like he's reading a cue card.

"I couldn't find Borneo on a map?"

"You don't like to be cruel."

Harry doesn't know what to make of this, so he says nothing.

McCabe slaps the bar and spins around. "Look at us!

Murder in Mexico

Sittin' in a gin mill watchin' the rain fall, just like our dads. Makes you wonder if there's anything to that theory of evolution."

Harry taps the big guy's Rolex. "What is it, Jack, you been dipping into the trust fund again?"

"You'll love it. I got hit by a Brink's truck over in Queen Village." McCabe holds the watch to the light. "They've been very sympathetic."

"You look okay to me."

"Tore up my shoulder." He holds his arm straight out. "That's as high as it goes."

"That's as high as anybody's goes."

McCabe shrugs. "Go figure."

They drink together until McCabe gets rammy. Harry can hear him laughing and breaking things in the pisser. Ned's nowhere around, so he leaves a few bills on the bar and steps out into the after dark. Spots a parked BMW with JackyMac tags and nails it with a nickel as he rounds the bend. He can walk okay, but no way will he fool Lena. Not that she'll bug him about knocking back a few, but twice in three nights is pushing it. Definitely pushing it. The upside is he won't have to explain coming home early.

The bus rolls in lit up like Walmart. Harry sits in back, staring at his reflection in the window. Septa, the last place to be on a full buzz with a dull pounding in the brain stem.

Jesus, I look like my Uncle Jimmy.

He sees an ad for Bally's and thinks, for the hundredth time, about cashing in and letting it all ride, one roll of the dice, as good a way to go down as any. He even pictures himself, what he'd be wearing, the gray slacks with the black silk shirt. Sees the chips sliding over the green. Go for the load, just to be done with it.

"You okay, Harry?"

"Pete...hey. I guess I was nodding off."

"You look like you were dreaming."

Tom Larsen

"Dreaming, right." Harry jabs his chin at Pete's plastic cooler. "Yo, Pete, what's the deal? Every hard hat in the city has one. The orange boots and the little cooler. What is that?"

"It's a fashion statement, Harry."

He points to an empty seat. "Take a load off, Pete."

"I'm just going a couple of stops. You still working downtown?"

"Yeah, yeah, three years now."

"Three years?" Pete goes wide-eyed. "That's a record for you, ain't it?"

"My fault, right? Three shops in a row go belly up, and I'm the bad guy. Half the places I worked are long gone."

"Must look good on the old resume, eh?"

"What about you, Pete?"

"Right now I'm at the new Marriott, but I gotta have surgery on my knee next week. After that I'm done for the year."

"Surgery? Tough break."

"Oh yeah, I get to lay around all winter while Lottie waits on me hand and foot."

"Still...surgery..."

"I get to collect unemployment and watch TV while Danny Blake lays tile in a hundred and thirty-seven bathrooms. Tough break, all right. If it was up to me, I'd have the doc lop it off at the knee, get permanent disability."

Harry smiles and shakes his head. "And they say American workers ain't what they used to be."

Pete leans in. "Yo, Har, you hear about Walt Sandusky?"

"What about him?"

"Died last Thursday. He was down at Margate, fishing and just slumped over dead." Pete shakes his head. "Forty-seven years old."

Murder in Mexico

Harry sits stunned. The Sandusky crew grew up on his block. He can remember the day Walter was born.

"Doctors say it was a blood clot. And he just bought that new boat."

"Jesus, I didn't hear anything. How's Sherry?"

"Not so good. From what I hear, Walt's insurance company went under. She'll have to sue, and even then it's first come first serve."

"They can do that?"

Pete huffs. "Hey, you buy a piece of the rock, they tell you to bend over."

"I can't believe it. The man was in great shape. You can see some guys, but not Sands."

"Hey, Harry..." Pete steps to the door as the bus eases in. "Take care of yourself, will you?"

***

The house is dark, and he has to light a match to fit the key. Lena's way of saying he's pushing it. Harry feels his way through the living room to the kitchen and stands at the window, drinking from the bourbon bottle. The news about Walt hit him harder than he would have thought, the front line boomers poised at the edge. And he's not kidding himself for a moment, either. It's his own sorry ass he's mourning. By the time he's Harry's age, old Walt will be five-years dead.

Blood clot. What would it feel like? The heart locks up and the lights go out. No time to even miss anything, just panic and pinwheels...maybe his head hit something on the way down.

CHAPTER TWO

The wipers beat the windshield like a drum, still Lena can barely see, just blurred taillights as puddles thud the floorboards, rain bouncing like pebbles off the roof and hood. The car ahead tails the car ahead all the way up the line. If the lead guy drives off a cliff, they'll all be along directly. Jaws of life, she can't stop thinking. Jaws of life doing whatever they do, ripping and prying.

Oh, spare me, Jesus. Spare me the jaws.

From the radio: >"So, those bozooms..."<

Shock Jacque pauses for effect.

>"They are real, no?"

"That's right. What you see is all me."

"Oh my."

"Do you like them?"

"I am madly een love with them. Especially thees one."<

Lena turns the volume up a tad. She's been listening to Shock Jacque for over a year, casually at first, but now she hates to miss him. It's not something she's proud of, but a little titillation seems to suit her in the morning, that there are women who will do that sort of thing. Somehow the radio makes it steamy.

>"And your husband, he does not mind that you bare your breasts for lecherous strangers?"

"On the contrary. It really turns him on."<

A trucker blows past in a rolling fantail; Lena bids him a fiery death. Another mile and she exits at the hospital. The old trees cut the rain to a trickle.

>"And when I get home? You know what's the first

thing he'll want to do?"

"Tell us, my leetle cupcake."<

Lena parks in her spot and listens until the commercials. Turning it off is like breaking a spell. As she stares out at the puddled grounds, a wave of weariness washes over her. Six years she's been at the nuthouse, and nothing she'd walk into would really surprise her. Then it's out the door, umbrella deployed and heels crunching across the lot. She tries to conjure a tranquil scene, but she's tried that before and it never works. Up the front steps at a perky trot, through the doors and into the bedlam.

"So you can march his black ass right back out of here." Alice goes hands-on-hips at a cop who looks fresh out of junior high. Behind them, two more cops wrestle with a huge, frothing guy. To their right, Big Dot yells into the phone, face knotted in fury. Patients mill around in varying degrees of agitation, and behind them, a maintenance crew gathers outside, looking in.

"Lutheran says they're full up," the young cop sputters. "What am I supposed to do, chauffer him around all day?"

"What's the problem?" Lena furls the umbrella and steps up to the plate.

"This one wants to kill his brother." Alice rolls her head to frothing guy. "Some hanky-panky goin' on, but I can't make sense of it."

"Get a hold of Doctor Herbert." Lena pushes through. "Tell him it's an emergency. Does he have a medical card?"

Alice breezes past with a snicker. "Piece of the Crock. You know, with the fool coverage?"

"Sentinel? Jesus, okay, call to clear admission and have his records sent over. Anyone know what he's on?"

"Had a pocketful of these." Dot holds out a half dozen crack vials.

Lena takes kiddie-cop aside. "Tell me, officer, what

exactly did Lutheran say when you brought him in?"

"The usual, short-staffed, no beds. Nobody wants the bruisers."

"And they told you to bring him here?"

"They suggested it. You're on the list."

"I wonder if you could do me a favor, in your travels today. If you should run into any more loonies..." Lena touches a finger to his wrist, "just look the other way. Could you do that for me?"

The kid swallows a grin. "Be a pleasure, ma'am."

Lena takes a clipboard from the desk and hands it to Dot. "Have them take big guy to the green room and stay with them until the doctor arrives. Alice? Get me Lutheran on the phone."

Lena drops her umbrella in the bin and checks the discharge board. A nervous little man approaches from behind.

"Nurse Watts? I hate to bother you...I know you're very busy."

"How are you, Mister Robbins." Lena forces a smile.

"I'm okay, I guess. It's about the lizards in my room?"

"Lizards? Are you sure they're not cockroaches?"

"Oh, they're lizards, all right." Mister Robbins wrings his hands. "Blue ones, about three inches long. At night I can hear their tails scraping the floor."

"Do you suggest we kill them?"

"They keep me awake."

Lena hooks his arm and walks him toward the common room. "But they *are* lizards, Mister Robbins, and quite rare in Philadelphia. Personally? If a family of rare lizards chose to live in my room above all others, I'd feel a little bit special."

"But their tails...scrape, scrape, scrape."

"Tell you what. The exterminator will be coming to check on the elves in Mrs. Tully's air conditioner. I'll send him over."

Murder in Mexico

The little man heaves a sigh. "Oh, thank you, Nurse Watts."

"No problem, Mister Robbins." Lena hands him off into psycho orbit.

"I have Lutheran on the phone," Dot hollers over.

Lena grabs the nearest phone and drops into the nearest chair. "Admissions? Yes, Freddie, hi. I'm calling about the ball-buster you dumped on me this morning—"

"You're welcome."

"Right...save it, Freddie. You're out of your league."

"You sound stressed."

"How about one fire alarm away from a wacko invasion? I got a guy who will chew your nose off. I got stalkers with no one to stalk. I got blowtorch killers, acid throwers. I got a freaking cannibal."

"Sounds like a fun party." He snickers.

"Do yourself a favor, Freddie. Next time make a few calls before you pile more shit on us." She hangs up, knowing she's wasted her breath.

Alice punches the speaker button. "Lena, line two. Sentinel Insurance Group. Girl, you are gonna love this."

"Hello?" a small voice says, clueless.

"Nurse Watts speaking."

"Is Mister Johnson available?"

"He's tied up at the moment..." *In a straightjacket.* "Is there something I can help you with?"

"Is Mister Johnson exhibiting suicidal tendencies?"

"He wants to kill his brother, so no."

"Um, what would you call that?"

"We call it homicidal?"

"I'm sorry. Homicidal is not on my list of coverages."

"Your list?"

"I have hallucination and hypertension but no homicidal."

"Try under 'N' for nuts."

"No...nothing. And it's a really long list."

~19~

"Oh dear. What shall we do?"

"I'm only authorized to approve things that are on my list."

"Tell you what. I'll just send Mister Johnson over to your office. See what you can make of him."

"Me?"

"Would you mind?"

"But we're in Atlanta."

"That way we can get him out of our hair and you can make your own diagnosis."

The voice gets even smaller. "In Georgia?"

"Let's just say you agree to take him."

"Maybe you should speak to my supervisor."

"That would make *you* suicidal. Now, look at your list there under 'S'. See it?"

"I'm new here."

"In that case, I'll need an okay from admissions...and Mister Johnson's medical history, including allergies. Think you can do that for me?"

"Oh, man, my boss is gonna kill me."

"That would make *him* homicidal. You might want to add that sucker to the list." Lena hangs up, hears something crash in another room.

Big Dot bellows from the hallway. "Yo, Lena, that creep Sanders just shit in the trashcan again."

She groans. "How lovely."

***

Six years, Jesus. It didn't start with the psychos. Juvee drug disorders had been Lena's first choice. At the time, it seemed to make perfect sense. She'd been a juvenile for years, and between school friends and her sister's crowd, they had the drugs covered. It would be just like high school only she'd get paid for the babysitting.

But these kids weren't like anyone she knew. They

came from crummy homes with moron parents, and it took all the drugs they could take to get them through it. Not so much recreational as occupational. Then came the crackheads, again a logical progression. Lena's first husband joined the junkie ranks soon after they were married, and she knows those ropes from top to bottom. But the crackheads proved so needy and obnoxious she dreamed of taking a hammer to them.

She lands back in the cafeteria, thoughts of better days behind her.

"And the woman is just flyin' around." Dot spreads her meaty arms. "What's wrong with my baby? Why is he in here? And I'm thinking, cause, honey, your boy's nutty as a fruitcake." The last line comes from the corner of Big Dot's mouth.

"Nutty as a god damn fruit cake?" Alice halves a donut in one bite.

"Crazy as a loon," Eddie croons.

Lena smacks her lips. "I have to tell you guys, those are really inappropriate comments. Where's your compassion? I mean, come on, crazy as a loon?" She looks to Eddie.

"Bats in his belfry does it for me, boss."

"Says it all." Alice bobs her head.

"How about that guy Harrelson, with the O.D.D.?"

Alice' eyes go funny. "What the hell's O.D.D.?"

Everybody just looks at her.

Tina floats by. "Harrelson? Didn't he have a screw loose?"

"That was Loopy Louie with the Supremes singing in his empty little head."

Lena thinks of Harry, for over a year now, fading away right in front of her. Twenty years of cheap hustles, punching clocks and pensions going south. Lena has her job and her own world to deal with, so what can she do? Anymore, living with Harry was like watching a real long movie with an unhappy ending.

"Lena had that guy, Morelli was it?" Eddie taps his chin. "She called him—"

"Mr. Punchy! Lookit, lookit!" Alice points to Lena and doubles up with laughter. "Like she's little Miss Nurse Appropriate."

"Or those twins she tagged the Twisted Sisters." Tina wags a finger. "I was never comfortable with that, Head Nurse Lady."

Lena checks her watch. "Okay, people, break's over. Time to let the animals out of their cages."

Eddie grunts. "I don't know 'bout this *people* shit. Could be we're the animals in this zoo."

***

Traffic going home is even worse. More rain, road turned to rivers, and cars spinning out like it's paved with banana peels. By the Acme, she sees a girl who looks like Marilyn standing on the shoulder, her car with a crumpled hood, Marilyn at twenty-one, a thousand years ago, well, at least ten since they found her frozen in the woods. So it couldn't be Marilyn, but Lena checks the rearview to be certain.

When she gets home, it's dark inside, and she heaves a sigh, scoops the mail off the floor, and sorts through it in the dim street light. Near the bottom, another traffic ticket for Harry, and under that, a cancellation notice from the car insurance company.

"Fucking moron." She storms into the kitchen, whacking herself in the head with the mail. "Why do I marry fucking morons? Joey Lats was a moron—"

"I thought Joey had a lot on the ball." Harry's voice from the table.

Lena pinwheels into the fridge. "Jesus Christ, Harry. Why are you sitting in the dark?"

"We have to talk."

She waves the mail at him. "Joey was a moron, but at least he had car insurance."

"Sit down, Lena."

"Just tell me, did you quit or were you fired?"

"Nothing like that. Come here and talk to me." Harry's hands are folded on the table, and he looks wrung out.

Lena takes the chair opposite, folds her own hands just to brace for bad news. "So?"

"I can't do it anymore."

"Do what?"

"This..." He holds out his hands to include the kitchen. "The fucking work-a-day wank, how 'bout it? It's not me, Lena. And it's not you, either."

"What are you telling me?"

"Look, we have, what...a couple of grand in the bank and a mortgage we'll never live to pay off? Not much to show for working our lives away."

"So?" Lena squeezes her fingers. "What do we do instead?"

"I'll tell you what." Harry leans in. "We live by our wits. We lay it on the line."

Lena gives her head another whack. "Now why didn't I think of that?"

Harry reaches for her hand. "Hey, listen to me, okay? The sad fact is that your current moron husband is worth a lot more dead than alive. A million bucks worth of—"

"This pipedream sounds familiar."

Harry settles back, arms folded. "So when I'm dead, things break your way, and you have nothing to worry about. You'll be set. Good for you."

"Oh, I hardly ever think about that."

"What about me? What do I get?"

"All that life insurance was *your* idea."

"I do it for you. It's all I can do for you, but what do I

get? Me."

Lena shrugs. "The satisfaction of knowing your widow will be rolling in dough."

"Come on, Lena. I want some, too."

She gets up from the table and turns on the ceiling light. "Harry, we've been down this road a hundred times. You can't fake your own death without a body. No body, insurance boys smell a rat."

"So..." Harry gets up and turns off the light, "we get a body."

"You know what? I'm going to hear you out, just to see how far your twisted mind has fallen. Start with the body."

"We go to Mexico."

"How nice...they got bodies lying around for the taking?"

"If I die in Mexico, you'll be the only one who can identify me. So you make a mistake, who's gonna care? See what I'm saying? Cremate the body instead of shipping it back. Come home, hold a little service, and Bingo...you're the rich, grieving widow."

"Get back to the body, Harry."

"Yes, well, that's the hard part. Only one way, really."

"Murder someone? You? The guy who catches spiders and lets them go outside?"

"Spiders have no insurance."

"You know the little rant of mine that starts with *you must be crazy?*" Lena does a little bongo on the table. "I'll save you the humiliation and turn on the TV."

"Sure, it's crazy, but my plan can't fail."

"Have you considered the part where I leave you for the next moron?"

"You don't have to make up your mind right away."

"Pay attention, Harry. Not only no, but fuck no." Lena gives him a pat on the back. "You just sit here and sulk, slugger. I've got soaps to watch."

CHAPTER THREE

The elevator opens to reveal an overweight patient with a goofy smile and a huge erection.
Alice locks on Lena's arm. "Mercy."
"That's very good, Dennis." Lena gives him a nod. "Go show Dot."
"Be still my heart." Alice fans her face with a clipboard.
"Charlie," Lena calls over her shoulder. "Get Dennis his Hustler before he impales someone."
Down the hall, Eddie sticks his head out. "Hey, Lena, Henry Walters wants to see you when you get a chance."
"Who the hell is Henry Walters?"
"The new CEO. Third floor, west, you can't miss it." He winks. "Big dollar sign on the door."
A pitiful moan rises from somewhere down the stairwell. Tish the Tramp shuffles past, clucking like a chicken. Across the hall, a TV blares to the beat of Lorenzo's head against the wall.
Lena looks to Alice. "You heard. When I get a chance."
"I'm thinking, September."
"2525."

***

The morning passes in a noisy blur. A maintenance man shatters a fluorescent light, setting off a spastic stampede. NASCAR roars all afternoon, and Larry the Lip stabs his shadow with a ballpoint: standard stuff, run of the mill.

"Anybody seen Dennis Carney?" Eddie queries the lunchroom. "Lena?"

"He was in the lobby this morning, waving his hard-on around."

"Forget what they say about white boys, honey," Alice purrs. "That one has the apparatus."

"Why Alice Long..." Eddie wags a finger. "I do believe you're smitten."

"Well, how crazy can he be? Maybe I could learn to live with it."

Lena stirs her coffee with a plastic fork. "Tell me something, Eddie. You've seen them do autopsies before. How involved is it?"

"What's the matter, Lena? The live ones starting to get to you?"

"I know they cut them up, but do they check dental records or anything?"

"You serious? Half these gomers don't even have teeth."

"How about fingerprints? DNA?"

"We already know who they are. Why make work for yourself? It ain't like anyone gives a fuck. Just slice, dice, and stuff 'em back together."

Alice swoons. "If they chop up Dennis, I know what piece I want."

"You nasty old thing." Eddie scowls. "What is it? Mr. Long not up to the job?"

"Between you and me, Mr. Long couldn't hold a candle to *that* one."

Dot squeezes past them, rolling her eyes. "They want you upstairs right away, Lena. Mister Powers-That-Be."

Lena looks to Dot. "How about this guy? What's he got, an early tee-off?"

"Be nice," Big Dot warns her. "Heads are rolling."

***

Murder in Mexico

Henry Walters studies the Titleist logo while picking off the lint from his pocket. He is tall and tweedy, richly tan and silver at the temples. He palms the golf ball as Lena enters and gestures to the chair facing him. "Ah, Mrs. Watts. Have a seat, please."

"That's okay, I can't stay."

Walters slips the Titleist in his pocket, gives her a once over: blonde, handsome...the small cleft in her chin says she's no pushover. "It's a pleasure to finally meet you. Tell me, how long have you been here at General?"

"Six years in February, and you?"

Walters smiles weakly. "Doubtless you are aware that the hospital has undergone a change in management."

"I'm aware, all right."

"It has been brought to my attention that certain staff members disapprove of these changes."

"I can't say I'm surprised."

"I'll come right to the point. There have been an inordinate number of complaints regarding, shall we say, the abrasive attitude of the nurses on the psych unit. Yourself, in particular."

"I wouldn't take them too seriously."

"I do take them seriously. In fact, I have no reason to doubt the veracity of these complaints. I might add that your confrontational reputation proceeds you."

"Think of it as a low tolerance for stupidity."

"Yes, well, as head of personnel, I've decided to assign John Strickland to oversee psych operations. Mr. Strickland and I feel that an alignment is necessary to ease budgetary constraints. This assignment will go into effect immediately and continue until such time as a determination can be made about the program's viability."

"Strickland?"

"That's right."

"With the pocket pal."

Walters squirms slightly in his chair. "Mr. Strickland

is the Efficiency Coordinator and Operational Liaison for the Metro Medical Group."

"Do tell."

"I sense a note of hostility, Mrs. Watts."

"Let me get this straight. Metro thinks that my unit is a money hole. As an *efficiency* measure, management will appoint a six figure bean counter to deal with malcontents. What else? Oh yeah, any confrontational or abrasive behavior will be dealt with severely. How am I doing?"

Walters taps his fingertips together. "I'm curious, Mrs. Watts. Do you like working here?"

"Is that a requirement?"

"According to your evaluations, your former superiors seemed to think quite highly of you."

"My former superiors were in the medical profession."

"Meaning?"

Lena shrugs. "Their primary concern wasn't turning a profit."

"Can I tell you a story, Mrs. Watts?" Walters drums his hands on the armrests. "Several years ago, a promising young surgeon applied for a position over at Mount Sinai. The hospital courted this particular doctor with the aim of setting up a first-rate cardiac program. It was a controversial courtship in that many on the staff believed the money could be put to better use. The hospital persisted despite a number of significant resignations."

Lena stares holes in his skull.

"But this doctor was a thorough young man. He looked into fiscal projections and concluded that, given labor unrest, the hospital couldn't afford him. In the end, Mount Sinai lost their doctor and, at last report, is now poised on the verge of bankruptcy."

Full bore lasers right between the eyes.

"You see, Mrs. Watts, as distasteful as it may seem, profit margins fuel the medical industry. This is a fact of life. Metro didn't invent the system, but we fully intend to prosper in it."

Lena holds her temper a few beats. "That's a terrific story. Now I've got one for you. There's a kid downstairs, Randy Hewitt? I don't expect you know him, but he's a good kid. A little paranoid sometimes, but he knows the program and he's making progress. In fact, he's doing so well his insurance company is switching him to outpatient."

Walters sneaks a peek at his watch.

"Now anyone familiar with his situation can tell you that Randy isn't ready, but tomorrow we have to discharge him. Another fact of life, but one that won't show up on your pie charts and bar graphs. This morning I found a note in my mailbox. Randy wishing *me* good luck, can you beat that?"

***

Lena comes home to find Harry digging through the file cabinet. She passes by him without a word and gazes out the kitchen window.

"Don't you want to know what I'm looking for?" he calls to her.

"Not yet."

"In theory, this cabinet is a repository for all our important papers. In truth, the sum total of our important papers could fit in a single manila envelope. But I like the repository idea. There's a measure of satisfaction in rolling back the drawers and perusing the contents. It's so, I don't know...grown up."

Lena crosses her eyes, makes her vision go blurry.

"So, let's see..." Harry pulls a pile from the drawer. "A random sampling of our important papers would include, but in no way be limited to, take-out menus, meter reader regrets, various catalogues, letters from your mother, unopened, a program for the Nutcracker, circa 1998."

"Here's an idea, Harry. Let's make believe we already had this out, and now we're giving each other the silent treatment. How about it?"

Harry sets the papers aside and joins her in the kitchen. "Bad day?"

"I feel like a human drain pipe. Everything swirling around, waiting for me to suck it down."

"Interesting analogy."

"I'm tired, Harry."

"In Brazil, everything swirls in the opposite direction."

"Remember when everyone was dealing drugs and living in nice places and nobody worked? We always thought we'd end up in Paris. How come we didn't?"

Harry shakes his head. "It was a combination of things. You were still married to Joey...then Gerry died. After that, I guess the years just flew by."

"I need rest, Harry. I need to crawl into bed and sleep for weeks."

"There, there." Harry rocks her in his arms until Lena goes limp. "Buck up, girl. Someday you'll look back on these days as the *good-old days*."

"sleeeep."

"So we didn't make Paris. There's always Atlantic City."

Lena shoves him away and grabs the vodka bottle.

Harry turns and stares into the sink. "Hey, we gave it a good shot, Lena. We kept our shoulders to the wheel and our noses to the grindstone, eh? Traded our best years for the small bucks, just like the rest of them. We did what we're supposed to do, and what did it get us?"

"Don't start, Harry."

"Look at your Uncle Ray, lying back in Lauderdale for the last twenty years. What are the chances we'll have that?"

"You hate Florida."

"That's not the point. Look at my pension, look at Social Security. We're the generation that gets screwed, and we sit back and take it. Unless..."

"Unless what?"

"Unless we screw them first." Harry looks out at the rain. "We're in a good position to pull this off, baby. Those policies are six years old now. We have good credit and pay our bills."

"Yeah, sure, I'm maxed out, and your car is a moving violation."

"Forget about that, will you?"

"Okay, let's pretend you've convinced me. Murder somebody and live happily ever after. Just how do we go about it?"

Harry takes a long pause. "It would have to look like natural causes, of course. Heart attack would be ideal, given the family history. One of those lunatic fringe websites could probably tell you how."

"I know a way."

"Or I could just ask my wife."

"When I worked at Mercy, we had this cardiac arrest, a woman with terminal brain cancer. Her husband did her in. The pain was driving them both crazy, and the bills were eating them alive. He used potassium chloride. Said it was painless and undetectable. Mr. Prince was his name."

"He confessed?"

Lena nods. "He would have gotten away with it, but he broke down and told me...in my office. I don't know why he picked me. He was a sweet old guy in a black fedora. A pharmacist."

"You never told me this."

"He injected her right there in the room then tossed the syringe in the wastebasket."

"What did you do?"

Lena looks away. "I told him he did the right thing.

His wife wasn't going to get better, and the pain would get worse. I told him to go home and get some rest."

"Then you took care of the syringe."

"I knew he'd never think of it."

"You let him get away with it?"

"I never told a soul."

Harry reaches around her for the bourbon. "This potassium chloride, where do you get it?"

"They sell it in the drug store."

"You checked?"

"What about our victim, Harry? Who is he gonna be?"

Harry pokes at a noodle in the drain. "This is strictly hypothetical, right? Okay, we need a guy who resembles me. Doesn't have to be a dead ringer, but in the ballpark, same hair, same body type. Say the guy's in Mexico by himself, cruising the hotspots, hoping to get lucky. And who does he see sitting alone by the dance floor?"

"Who?"

"You."

Lena knots her eyebrows. "That's the plan? That?"

"Oh, I suppose we could come up with something more complicated. But I think we should stick to what we know. We know bars."

"So, I sit by myself in a Mexican dive until some stranger who looks like you tries to pick me up."

"It's like riding a bike, baby. You don't forget how."

"When do you get to do something?"

"I'll be at the bar, keeping an eye out."

"And then, let's see...stranger takes me home and what, I slip him a mickey? Then when he's out cold, I shoot him up with potassium chloride."

"That's about it."

"Gee, we're a real team. Hey, why don't I turn a few tricks on the side, you know, for mad money?"

"Look, if it will make any difference, I'll do the injecting. You'll have to show me how."

Murder in Mexico

Lena smiles and shakes her head. "That's a first rate plan, Harry. I mean, what could go wrong?"

"You tell me."

"Well, for starters, injections usually leave a bruise. So your body goes to autopsy with a fresh puncture wound. No reason to suspect foul play there."

"So we inject him where no one will look, between the toes or under the scrotum. The guy had a heart attack. They won't go groping around down there."

"They'll do a tox screen. Guess what? The poor sap was dosed."

"So he was mixing pills and alcohol. Not advisable but certainly not unusual, or illegal."

"Can I turn the lights on now?"

"You're just being squeamish. And I can understand that. Fact is, the plan is foolproof. Worst-case scenario? The mark's a runt, or he's too hot to trot, I just get rid of him. We start over someplace else."

"What about the police?"

"They have no reason to suspect anything. You're a distraught American tourist in a tourist town whose husband just died. And remember, once they burn the body, you can't be proven guilty. Ever."

"You've given this a lot of thought."

"Years of thought. I've got it figured down to the last detail."

"So, if Harry's dead, who are you?"

"I don't get you."

"You can't be Harry anymore. You have to be someone else. How do you do that?"

"Easy. I've got Gerry's ID. I renewed his driver's license and his Visa card. Believe me, Lena, I'm way ahead of you."

"You always make it sound so easy. What about the local authorities?"

"Come on, it's Mexico. Wave a few bucks, and all

~33~

obstacles disappear."

"I'm going to bed now."

"You know it's foolproof. Admit it."

Lena yawns mightily. "I'm already sleeping. I'm dreaming this."

"Dream this while you're at it, a little house in the country, nothing to do, and a million bucks to do it with. Tell me you haven't had that one before."

"Lately, I dream about being single."

"We're getting up there, Lena. In ten years we'll be too old to pull it off. What do you think happens to us then? Think about growing old and never giving it a shot. If we get caught, I'll take the fall. No big deal. What's a life sentence to a fifty-year-old loser with a history of heart disease?"

"Sleeeep."

"Hell, the worst that could happen is you *would* be single again."

Lena starts for the living room stairs.

"It can't fail! That's what's bugging you, isn't it, Lena?"

She turns with an angry look. "Listen to yourself, Harry. You're talking about killing someone so you can be comfortable in your old age. It's insanity."

"One way or another, I'm getting off this treadmill. Little shit-balls like Baldini have no place in my life. I stay there and I'll end up killing *him,* and you won't get a nickel out of that!"

"You need professional help."

"Like I said, I can't do it anymore."

***

Later, in bed:

"What are you thinking about, Harry?"
"Who says I'm thinking?"

Murder in Mexico

"I can hear those squeaky little wheels turning."

"I'm thinking about your old guy in the fedora. You never said a word."

"I must have. You weren't paying attention."

"Uh-uh. That would have caught my attention."

"Maybe that's why I didn't tell you."

"Maybe, yeah...or maybe you were saving it."

"It's late, Harry. Go to sleep."

CHAPTER FOUR

Stevie follows the ripple of muscle, those shoulders of epic proportions, even the back, chiseled with the wing things spreading up from the ribcage. My God he's magnificent, the butt, perfect, the legs, ooh la-la! Twin tree trunks twisted in sinew, sculpted Adonis, diamond in the buff. Too bad it's all steroids and methamphetamines, and the poor pea brain will never see forty. Walking time bomb, primed and ready.

"You understand, Rolf. It's not anything in particular, just a general, well...incompatibility."

"Christ, Stevie, it's only been six days."

"Almost seven."

"And you were gone the whole weekend."

"So you had a few friends over. And my couch—"

"It was an accident."

"I know. It's unfortunate. Honestly, Rolf? It's as much my fault as it is yours."

"Oh sure, but you don't have to move back with your mother."

Stevie steps halfway to him. "It might work out this time. She needs you now, Rolf."

And that face, like something carved in marble, no, granite, the impossible jaw, the cheekbones like perfect little ledges. Like what's-his-name the football player. Howie Long, that's the one. Jesus. If you could just unplug them when you're through and stick them in the closet.

"What about my deposit?" Rolf grumbles.

"I told you. Your mother asked me to send it to her so you wouldn't spend it on drugs."

"You what?"

"I told you. You weren't listening."

"Fuck!" His muscles double then quadruple as Rolf bangs off the walls, calling up threats of death and destruction, coming down nose to Stevie's nose. "I ought to break you in half."

The meth-breath, have mercy.

"You don't want to do anything stupid now, Rolf." Stevie's voice goes all over the place. "Look, I can write you a check. Please, Rolf, my glasses."

He backs off to crunch a number. "Make it three bills. And I need to borrow a coat. It's getting chilly."

"How do you spell that last name again?"

"Just Rolf. They know me at your bank."

"Right. Okay then, look, no hard feelings, okay?"

"You never wanted it to work. I knew it that first night in the bar."

"That's not true. But we must be realistic, Rolf. The chemistry just isn't right."

"You're so full of shit, Stevie."

"I know you're upset. We'll talk about it when you come for your stuff."

"What stuff?"

"Well, your clothes and that chair."

"The chair? What the hell am I going to do with it? I got no where to put a chair."

"Of course, my mistake. The chair can stay."

Rolf continues to prowl the room, stuffing his stuff in a laundry bag, trying on Stevie's coats, pawing through Stevie's sweaters. When he has what he needs, he snatches the check and brushes past without a word.

Gone. Gone at long last. Stevie wanders from room to room, soaking in his absence, six days and nights of Rolf and his muscles. Mood swings and marathon phone calls. Weepy Rolf and his running babble on into the wee small hours. Lips smacking, tongue lathered in slime, Rolf and his relentless sweat, musky at first, but fading to stink. Mad Rolf gone from his life, at least until the check bounces.

A dumb idea, getting a *roommate* at this stage of the game, his daughter sick, his life unraveling, the latest in a long line of poor decisions, mercifully resolved. But thoughts of Lilly fill him with dread, and he sees himself running after the big lug, begging him to come back, at least for a few days. All the earmarks of a downward spiral, just the thing he doesn't need. He thinks to nosh, but he's already eaten too much today. He worries that worry will make him sick.

When he's sure Rolf's gone and not just out front, sitting in his car, Stevie goes out on the deck and watches the sun set, a real production with the swirls and streaks, every color in the crayon box. He watches to the end and into the darkness, slide shows rolling in his head.

Lilly. Poor kid's only five years old.

The phone brings him back, Dorie calling from the hospital.

"There's no change, Stevie. I know you hate to hear it, but that's all I can tell you."

"But did they say if the drugs are helping? I mean aside from killing her. I'm sorry, I didn't mean that."

"Have you given any thought to what Doctor Brymer was saying?"

"Any thought? What do you mean?"

"The bone marrow transplant? As a final option?"

"What, you don't think I'll go through with it?"

"I didn't say that, Stevie. It's just that you're the only compatible donor and you're in denial. You said so yourself."

"You have my word, Dorie."

Stevie hangs on as she fills him in on Lilly's day, the painful injections, the skin color, her words going in one ear and rattling around his head. He paces the kitchen, scanning the floor for food stains, squatting with the phone and a wet paper towel. Scrubbing and consoling, as is his way.

"And I'm praying for you, too, Stevie. Every day." Dorie's voice, frail and rubbery.

"I'll be down in a couple of days." He searches the cabinet for the Windex. It's disgusting in there, too.

"You know I think about us, all the things that happened."

"Dorie, honey—"

"Somebody should write a book, hey, Stevie? A heartbreaker in three parts."

Stevie toes a towel under the counter, scrubs at a spot on the oven door. "What's the third part?"

"I guess we have to wait and see."

"Jesus, Dorie. When you put it like that, it's sort of obvious, isn't it?"

"Did you deal with your roommate?"

"Don't remind me. It was like getting rid of a show cat that sprays."

"Spare me the imagery."

"Or a bad front tooth."

"My sister said he's a real hunk."

"He was okay, a little too *physique* for me."

Dorie goes on for ten more minutes, trailing off now and then as if she's been drinking. So what if she's been drinking? If he were there with her, they'd both go for the load. Poor Dorie, marries a fag then loses their daughter. Christ, what a thing to be thinking; Lilly's far from dead. The doctors give her a sixty-forty chance, or did last time he pinned one down. A while ago, now that he thinks of it. Even so, sixty-forty, for every two parents who bury a child, three will see theirs recover. Something like that, more than fifty-fifty. Better than even.

"Maybe you should give it a break for a while, Dorie. The hospital, I mean."

"Oh, that reminds me. I'm going to Mendocino next

weekend. Unless, of course—"
"With whom?"
"My friend Roger, from the city? The one in the photo I sent from Tahoe. The designer?"
"Oh, him. Well, yes, I think you should. It will do you good to get away."
 Balanced on a chair to wipe the windows, corners-in, three at a time. Then it's hands and knees for the baseboards and under the radiator, two rolls' worth when all's said and done. Dorie concludes her Roger rave with the weekend agenda. A quick go round with the Swiffer glove and Stevie bids her bon soir.

***

 Bone marrow transplant, God help him. The thing about living in Phoenix, there's no one he can ask about it, no one to give him the real scoop. As if he didn't hear enough the last time back, that it can be painful, what he remembers most. That you can feel pain *inside your bones!*
 He looks out on the inky desert, the light from some far off something beams comfort from the void. How he would love to lose himself in all that landscape, sun burned and wind chafed, a weathered, wizened man on the moon.
 Bone marrow, what it is and how they get it, scraping tools against raw nerves. It's never been a question of whether he would...only when and how on earth he will bear it. Not that he thinks it will work, even in the event, one of those last-ditch heroic measures. What you hear before you hear the worst.
 If only he could lose himself in some other worry, something serious but acceptable, open to options, a bad debt or legal problems. That money's never been an issue makes him feel guiltier, deserving of a cross to bear. Stevie searches for something else to brood about, anything to let the Lilly part of his brain cool down.

Murder in Mexico

Mexico! That's the ticket, still a few weeks off but out there waiting for him, bone marrow or no bone marrow. A real vacation not some butt fuck getaway, no one to nursemaid, nothing to do but relax.

Si, Mexico.

Tom Larsen

CHAPTER FIVE

By the time Lena gets there, the staff lot is full, pickups jammed in every direction, a plumber's van in her spot. She circles around to the visitor's lot and leaves her car under the bird-shit tree. Inside, workers and patients clog up the lobby. Down the hall she sees men removing tables and chairs from the nurses' lounge trailed by Alice, stoked and smoking.

"What's going on here?" Lena catches up to them.

"I'll tell you what's going on here." Alice hands her a memo. "Your boy Strickland wants us to squeeze in more patients."

Lena reads it, balls it up, and tosses it to a startled schizoid.

"He in yet?"

"Been in. It's gung-ho, honey."

"Hey! Hey, you," Lena barks at the flunky with the coffee machine. "Take that and I'm calling a cop."

Three doors down, Strickland mans the copy machine. There's a stool to the side, but he foregoes using it in deference to the crease in his pants. The first new suit he's had in a decade, the girls in housekeeping check it out. *Strickland's the name, efficiency's the game.*

And really, what could be easier. See which way the money goes then make sure it doesn't get there. Wouldn't need a degree for that even if he had a stinking degree. Start with the perks: the drug rep lunches, the concurrent vacations, the endless overtime. Just revamping the schedule should save a bundle. And when he gets himself mobilized and the unit softened up, he'll axe the whole program and save the freaking day! Oh yeah, shit-can the lot of them. Christ, Walters will *have* to give him the corner office with the—

"Mr. Strickland."

"What is it, Nurse Watts?"

"I'm just curious." Lena claims the stool by the copy machine. "When you decided to go ahead with these renovations, how did you think I'd react? I mean, considering my reputation and all."

Strickland busies himself with memos, anything. "Quite frankly, I didn't take your reaction into consideration."

Lena fingers the hem of her skirt. "Do you think that was wise? See, ever since I was little I've had this problem with my temper. You just wouldn't believe the trouble it gets me into. And it's not the kind of temper where I blow up and then forget about it."

"Nurse Watts, I'm extremely busy."

"It's the kind where I gotta get even. It's all about revenge with me, Strickland. You know, spreading rumors, plotting behind your back, stuff that makes for...well, inefficiency."

"Come to the point, Nurse Watts."

"The point is this..." Lena lets a shoe dangle. "If the nurses' lounge isn't turned back into the nurses' lounge by the end of the shift, the name Strickland shoots straight to the top of my shit list."

He goes with his smarmy smile. "This is an administrative decision. It's nothing personal. The unit needs a higher census to remain viable."

"Save it, suck up. I've got that crap coming out of my ears."

"That doesn't change the fact the hospital must have a solid plan of operation. It's my job to implement that plan. End of discussion."

"And the staff and I think it would be nice to have one

of those cappuccino machines in the lounge, the one with the espresso maker."

"Nurse Watts...I don't think you're behaving professionally. You'll find I don't respond well to threats and intimidation. I can assure you, the lounge will be restored when additional space is made available. Until that time you will take your breaks in the cafeteria."

"By the board room?"

"The patient's cafeteria. It will do you good to mingle with the other staff members. Might relieve that psych mentality."

Lena studies her nails. "You know, Strickland, a career is a funny thing. One miscalculation, a couple of bad decisions, and you find yourself being passed over."

He pivots to the window and heaves a sigh. "More threats I see."

"Look at it this way." Lena reaches for the car keys on his desk. "Alice and Dot have been here fifteen years. I've been here for six. You know how many pencil pushers we've been through?"

"That will be all, Nurse Watts."

"You might want to reconsider." She slips the keys in her pocket. "You have until 5:15."

He snorts. "Not a chance."

***

The kind of temper that sends Lena steaming out the front door, west on Tasker, into the badlands and up to the first broke down piper she sees. Not far, maybe three blocks as the bus flies.

"Julio, listen to me. Julio!"

"Hey, Nurse Watts, what are you doing out here?"

She dangles the car keys in his face. "These are for the midnight-blue Beemer in the executive lot. Think you can handle it?"

"Handle what?"

"Yes or no...okay, where's Manny? Manny!"

"No hey." Julio snatches at the keys, misses. "I can handle it. Got a guard in the big wig lot though."

"I'll take care of Marvin. Just give me ten minutes."

"So, what do I get out of it?"

She drops the keys in his hand. "I don't want to know anything. We never had this conversation. The next time you're in detox, you don't know me."

Julio's rheumy eyes light up. "For real?"

"Don't screw it up, Julio." She starts back the way she came.

"What's going on? You okay over there?" he shouts after her.

Lena turns and looks at him funny. "I'm sorry, do I know you?"

Julio grins and pockets the keys. "My mistake. I thought you was somebody else."

***

He hates the TV at Brennan's. From where he's sitting, Harry has to hold his head back to see it, and after a while, his neck starts to go. Of course, he could always sit on the other side of the bar, but this is his seat and he's partial to it. Harry swore to himself that he wouldn't hit the gin mills first thing, but what else is a grown man to do?

He still doesn't know how he'll break it to Lena, though he's been batting it around all day. Not quitting your job until you got another lined up suddenly makes more sense than it used to.

"Hey, Harry," Ned calls from the storeroom. "Did you see that gypsy wrecker cruising around?"

"I parked in back. Getting at it would be more trouble than it's worth."

"I wouldn't bet on it. This guy's hungry."

"When did you start getting so cautious, Ned?"
"It just comes over me, I don't know."
"Christ, we're all turning into sad old men."
"You're right." Ned backs out with a bag of recycling.
"I say we cuff him to the wheel and torch the fucker."
"Whoa, easy, partner."

One of those reality cop shows on the tube now, with the car chases and the hayseed accents, like we don't get enough of that on primetime. Maniac on a motorcycle, one of those sprint bikes he has to lie down on to ride. Kid's out of his fucking mind, all right, looping in and out, blowing through lights. The cops trail with radio chatter, flinching at the intersections but sticking with it. The bike opens up on the straightaways, pulling away in suicide bursts. It seems to go on forever with the two-way squawking and cars veering off into the bushes. They crest a hill and the biker's flat-out flying. No way trooper chases him down. But then the video slows down almost to a stop, and a red circle pinpoints out a jerky blur, frame by grainy frame as the biker T-bones a moving bus. Holy Jesus! They run it back once, twice, Harry can't make out the chatter, but the cops sound pretty hysterical. Then they show it once more at regular speed and the film keeps rolling. The cop car wheels up to the wreckage, and there's the rider in a heap on someone's front lawn. Broadside a bus, that's what becomes of you. Harry sees the cop walk into the picture and here comes the bus driver shrieking like a lunatic. Just as people gather and things are getting hectic, the biker scrambles to his feet and takes off running. The camera gets jostled for a few seconds then there he is sprinting a block away.

"Son of bitch." Harry works the kink in his neck.
"What's that, Harry?" Ned calls.
"Guy just hit a bus."

The door pushes open behind him, and Danny Smart stands blinking into the dimness.

Murder in Mexico

"Of all the gin mills in all the world." Harry can't resist.

"Harry Watts! Jesus, Harry."

"Shut the door, kid, you're letting the flies out."

Danny steps over and pumps his hand. "How you been, Harry? You look good, buddy."

"What's good?"

"I don't know. Everyone else is twice as big as they used to be."

"Where you been, Danny boy? I don't see you anymore."

"Been away. Anyone sitting here?"

Harry glances around the empty bar. "Go for it, pal. "

Ned makes an appearance, sets the kid up with a beer and a coaster. "What is it, Dan? You ain't been in since the last parade."

"He's been away," Harry explains. "Where is it, Jersey?"

"Vets hospital, up in New York." Danny flinches. "I been sick."

Ned looks him over. "You look pretty fit to me, compared to some."

"Not that kind of sick. Up here." Danny taps his head. "Can't keep it on straight."

Ned and Harry study their fingers.

"Don't worry, boys, you can't catch it or anything."

Ned shoves his hands in his pockets. "That ain't it. It's just everyone around here is a little off. What's the difference?"

"Maybe yeah. But most of them don't take a header off the bridge."

Ned's eyes go bulgy. "You?"

"Nah." Danny waves him off. "They talked me down. But I was up on the cables. Man, you can't believe the view up there."

"You're kidding," Ned sputters. "He's kidding, right,

Harry?"
"Danny smiles. "That's what I told them."
"So where's Kit?" Harry thinks to ask.
"She's at her mom's. I shoulda brought her along. You're the only one in here she could stand, Harry."
"I know just how she feels."
"How's Lena doing?"
"She's practically running things over at General. Queen of the not quite right." Harry plunks the bar.
"She's the best, Harry. If it wasn't for her, I'd still be in a rubber room."
"You were in General? She never mentioned it."
"I couldn't work. Everybody was making me nervous. Then I lost the house, and the next thing I know, I'm on the fucking bridge."
"How'd you lose the house, Dan?"
"My health insurance dropped me. I couldn't keep up."
"The VA dropped you?"
"Nah, that's the thing..." Danny shakes his head. "I didn't even know I was covered by the VA until Lena checked it out. Can you believe it? I forgot I was ever in."

Harry watches the kid cluck to himself. "Yo, Dan, you got shrapnel in one leg and a metal plate in your head. You forgot that?"

"The plate's plastic now." Danny grins. "The metal detectors were going through the roof. Anyway, it was so long ago it don't seem like the same lifetime."

Ned has a thought. "Hey, maybe the VA can get you a lawyer to help you get your house back."

Danny shakes his head again. "Too late, bank had me fair and square. But VA's been helping me get right, thanks to Lena."

"You think she would have clued me in."
"I asked her not to, Harry. The fewer people know you're crazy, the better off you are."

"Jesus."

"So..." Danny lifts his beer. "I can come around some time?"

Harry looks to Ned.

"You kidding?" Ned fumbles with a bar towel. "I got more nuts in here than Blue Diamond. Just don't be jumping off anything."

Harry sneaks a smoke from Ned's pack. "Yeah hell, you start acting up we'll just lock you in the storeroom."

Danny looks up at the TV screen. "Christ, how can you see that thing from down here?"

"Ned thinks it's a radio. Humor him, Dan-boy."

Ned kills the volume to a crunching sound from right outside. He checks the street but no one's out there.

"Wilson's got the funeral signs up," he tells them. "Maybe that'll get things rolling in here."

Harry grunts. "The thing about life. It always ends badly."

"You working, Harry?" Danny asks him.

"It ended badly."

"Reason I ask is I got a buddy painting lofts over in Port Richmond. He might need a hand."

"Painting?" Harry howls. "The last refuge of the unemployable."

"I know it ain't your line, but you could probably pick up a few bucks."

"And leave Ned here by himself? Who'd watch the radio?"

"I don't know, Harry." Danny shakes his head. "Sittin' in the bar all day."

"Come on, kid." Harry checks the clock. "It ain't even noon yet."

"It must be my medication. All of a sudden I'm worrying about everybody."

"Won't do a bit of good, son. Here, let me buy you another drink."

"Nah, I can't stay. I just stopped in to see if anyone wanted to paint a loft."

"I'd love to, Danny, but I'm off to Mexico." Harry claps Dan's shoulder. "Taking in the sights, don't you know?"

"Mexico? You don't look the Club Med type."

"Puerto Vallarta, three bedroom beachfront with a maid."

"Get out!" Danny gives him a nudge. "You'd pass up a paint job for that?"

"For Lena. She's been a rock."

"The best, Harry. The best there is."

"So they tell me."

Danny edges over. "I may be out of line here, but I heard something, Harry. The little tab you ran up with Billy D is due and payable."

Harry gives him a look. "Billy knows I'm good for it."

"The hoop season's been over a month."

Harry reaches for the remote. "It's taken care of, Dan, but I appreciate the heads up."

"Just something I heard, is all."

"I'm good, kid." The TV sirens kick in again. "It's all taken care of."

"Okay. Let me get going."

Danny taps him on the hand. "Stay off the bridges, cuz."

***

Harry sits through Maury and the Young and Witless, trying to nurse them but making a mess of it. Patrons come and go, mostly barflies and swing-shifters dropping in to kill the pain. By noon Ned and Harry have run out of patter, then the jackhammers make the point mute. Harry's coat catches the knob on his way out the door, and the Fletcher twins giggle as he bounces off the mailbox. It gets worse.

When he gets to the back lot, his car isn't in it.

"Fucking gypsy fuck." Ned comes up beside him. "Them wreckers get you every time. Anything with a registration gets the hook."

"What outfit?"

"How would I know?"

"You said you saw the truck, Ned. Give me a name."

"You kiddin'? If I could see that far I'd be in my twenties."

***

The door has a new nameplate. Henry Walters Esq. Corporate Executive Officer, in brushed brass framed by old screw holes. Lena shoulders her way inside, balancing med cups in either hand, a pair of manics in tow, whining at each other. Walters springs to his feet while Strickland sits scowling.

"Can we make this quick, fellas?" Lena skirts the desk and nods at the whiners inside. "We're short downstairs, and all hell's breaking loose."

"Mrs. Watts, what is the meaning of this?" Walters stammers.

"Not to worry. They're with me."

"But why are they with you?"

"Well, I know how these head-butting sessions can run on, and I figured I'd get some work done."

Walters marches to the door and summons his minions. "Mrs. Worthman, would you please get someone to return these patients to the psych unit."

Firm but polite, Walters thinks to himself, just like in the book. By God he'll take care of this. Firm but polite, that's the way. Walters returns to his desk and motions Lena to take a seat. Lena hesitates a moment then hands the med cups to Strickland. Strickland scowls and sets them on the windowsill.

Walters begins. "Mrs. Watts, I'm going to ask you a simple question. I want you to answer 'yes' or 'no'."

"Gotcha."

"Do you know the whereabouts of Mr. Strickland's car?"

"I could guess."

"Mr. Strickland has informed me that you've been harassing him with blackmail and threats of violence."

"I wouldn't call it harassing. Just laying some ground rules."

Strickland fidgets and Walters shoots him a look.

"Are you saying Mr. Strickland made it all up?"

"Sounds like him."

Walters strains to picture the book cover, the jaunty corporate raider with the chainsaw.

"I see. You're suggesting that Mr. Strickland fabricated these threats then stole his own car to discredit you."

"Brilliant, when you think about it."

"Have you been feeling all right, Mrs. Watts?" Walters tries another tack. Chapter Six, Changing Tack.

"Oh, I'm a little tired, what with the skeleton crew and inflated census. But, other than that..."

"Mrs. Watts, what would you say if I told you that you were seen driving off in Mr. Strickland's car yesterday afternoon?"

"I'll see you in court?" Lena calls his bluff.

"I beg your pardon."

"Watts versus General Hospital and the Metro Medical Group, defamation of character, slander, pain and suffering."

"It's no secret you disapprove of Mr. Strickland's appointment."

"Your choice of words."

"We are talking about a crime here! A legal and moral outrage! How petty professional differences could come to this is incomprehensible to me." He slaps the desk. Well-placed outburst, Chapter—

"Me too."

Walters wilts. "Mrs. Watts, just between the three of us, what are the chances Mr. Strickland's car turns up this afternoon? No questions asked."

Lena frowns. "I'd say not good. I gotta tell you, it's chop shop city around here, and the addicts know them all."

Walters wracks his brain for a chapter, but there's nothing in the book to cover grand theft auto.

"You're forcing me into a very awkward situation. You realize that don't you?"

Lena puts on her poker face.

"We're talking about a felony here. A serious crime you're unwilling to rectify."

Then it comes to him.

"Here's what I intend to do. As a last resort, I'm going to leave the room for a minute, in hopes that matters may still be resolved, in private, between two rational human beings."

"I wish you wouldn't," Strickland says.

"Strickland, please." Walters holds up his hand. "Nurse Watts is a reasonable person. I firmly believe this. I'm sure if you impress upon her your intentions not to pursue the matter. Not to seek recourse, as the case may be. Two clear thinking professionals should be able to come to a mutually agreeable solution. Mrs. Watts? I trust this is possible?"

"Never say never."

Walters hesitates then walks to the door, so quiet they can hear the nap in the carpet. He turns once on the way out then the door clicks closed behind him.

Strickland eyes Lena.

Lena pokes at a cuticle.

"That business in my office," Strickland leads off. "Very clever."

"That was nothing. Believe me."

"But you must be aware that, regardless of the outcome, your intentions have been revealed. That any further attempts to harass me would appear rather transparent, wouldn't you say?"

"Piss off, Bozo."

Strickland folds his hands like an altar boy. "Might I remind you that in the chain of command I am still your direct superior? Think about it, Nurse Watts. I'm in a position to make things rather difficult for you."

"You're history, pocket pal."

***

"Jesus, no one saw nothing! How is that possible?" Harry stares through the rain at the empty space.

"It's a vacant lot, Harry. Who's here to see?"

He walks a few steps closer, as if that might help. "And I got the precinct decal on the window, big as shit!"

Ned spits a foamy gob into a puddle. "Hell, every car in Pennsport has one."

"I gotta get outa the city, Ned."

"Russians, most likely. They own the impound lots too, so it's all tied in. By the time they send you a notice, you owe them half a grand. Not to mention anything outstanding, warrants, child support, alimony. It's a new world, Harry, nowhere to hide."

"What ever happened to the breaks evening out? Every so often you had a good day, remember?"

"Vaguely, yeah."

"I feel it, Ned. The walls closing in."

"I'll look in the Yellow Pages. Maybe I'll recognize the name."

"Fuck it. Let 'em have it."

"I don't know why you have to drive here, anyway. Hell, it's only three blocks."

"Four."

"Sometimes you gotta walk farther than that just to get to your car."

Harry blows raindrops off the tip of his nose. "Fuck the world."

"Don't take it so hard. Report it stolen. Insurance will cover it."

Harry barks a laugh.

***

"So, where to start?"

"I want my car back, bitch!" Strickland hisses.

Lena jumps up like she suddenly remembered something, the med cups, which she suddenly remembers to dump in Strickland's lap. Next thing he knows, she's screaming bloody murder.

"Mr. Strickland, don't!"

Walters and his minions charge in just as she's screwing herself into a corner bookshelf.

"He said he'd get me. Then he dumped those meds on himself." She claws a few volumes.

"That's a lie!" Strickland looks stricken. "I demand she be fired."

"Keep him away from me. He's unbalanced."

Strickland storms past Walters who makes no move to stop him. The rest stand wincing at the trail of expletives down the hall. When there is nothing left to hear, Walters turns back to the room and slowly closes the door. Lena and the minions huddle like there's a madman in their midst.

"Sarah Jane? Miss Worthman? Could you excuse us for a moment?" Walters nods them out. He turns back at the door, fusses at his bookcase then stares out bravely on the swayback roofs of Pennsport.

Lena smells a deal in the works.

"Now see here, Nurse Watts."

She can't believe he'd start with that.

"This is a disgraceful turn of events."

"Shocking, sir."

"Absolutely intolerable."

"I see you going far here, sir."

Walters pounds his fist on the desk then struggles to compose himself. "In a way, I suppose it's a good thing."

"How's that, Henry?"

"It makes it easier for me to make the decision." Walters shows his one true color. "To terminate the psych unit."

Lena rocks back half a step.

"Well..." The smirky bastard smirks. "It appears we've finally hit a nerve."

"The whole unit?"

"Efforts are being made to place the others."

"Alice Long is fifty-two years old. Where are you going to place her?"

"These are uncertain times, Nurse Watts. If it's any consolation, it was only a matter of when. Your unit was living on borrowed time."

There's a commotion outside the door, Strickland's return raising a ruckus. A sharp shriek sends Walters scurrying. The minions cringe as the men go at it, Strickland blubbering as he backs out the door. Walters returns with a spring to his step.

"There!" He smacks his hands together. "Now, where were we, Nurse Watts?"

"On borrowed time."

"Exactly, a simple matter of economics. The board had penciled you out even before the acquisition. It was only through my intercession that you shouldered on this long."

"You're a prince, Henry."

"It's a fact."

"How long do I have?"

"I'll allow you to close out the week, without incident, I trust. Oh, and I wouldn't bother about filing a grievance. By the time our lawyers get through with it, there won't be a unit to return to."

"I'll be gone after tomorrow."

"If you prefer."

"What about him?" Lena nods to the empty chair.

Walters' smile is a dental marvel. "Strickland's history."

***

Lena brings in muffins for the occasion. Raspberry and raisin for the crew, Ex-Lax marked with toothpicks for persons unnamed. She knows it's childish, that the whole thing is hopeless, but that's the kind of girl she is. Warm, fuzzy and out for blood, with Walters a long shot, but Strickland as freeloading favorite.

They gather at break time; she makes it official and the crew puts on a show of being dumbstruck. Staff wanders in from all over, and everyone rails against the injustice, head up and hang in there, the sad chant of the chronically clobbered. People she doesn't even know drop around, doctors to dishwashers, Haitians from housekeeping, the goons from security, half the loonies in the bin. Everyone but anyone from the third floor. If there's a better grapevine, Lena's never seen it. Word up on the toothpicks and no one goes near them.

"Aw hey, don't cry, girlfriend." Lena hugs Alice tight.

"I ain't cryin'. Must be these damn allergies."

"Come on, it's not like you'll never see me again."

"Yes it is. That's just what it's like."

"But we go shopping every other week!"

"Ain't the same." Alice turns away. "I know you from a thousand shifts. This is the Lena I know, right here."

"That's so sweet..." Lena's chin starts to quiver. "You guys..."

"Oh, baby, what am I gonna do?" Alice lets go a wail.

"You still got to the end of the year. Anything can happen."

"Five months of that man?" Alice does her floodlight eyes. "Now I know what they mean by aggravated assault."

Heart wrenching but strangely comical, what with cops taking statements and claims adjusters running interviews in the lobby. The stolen Beemer setting a tone tempered by the off-chance one of the bad guys nicks a muffin. The tone sparking the sort of badmouthing and finger-pointing usually reserved for contract talks and love triangles. Not that the brass had anything on Lena, hot cars in Cracktown being as likely to resurface as the Phillies in late September. It's a sad affair with the usual bluster and a faint but definite whiff of relief, the yet-to-be compromised counseling, the soon to be displaced. When it's over, Lena clears out her desk, hands in her keys, and grabs the remaining toothpick muffins to protect the innocent. Big Dot and Alice see her to her car, clutching at each other like the church girls they are. On her way home, Lena spots Julio on the corner, poking a pager and dripping bling. She glances over once but he looks right through her.

***

They watch TCM, an old Peckinpah he's seen before. Five times, at least. Their eyes fixed to the screen, but their minds going a mile a minute. For once in the game, there are secrets between them.

"Did you call about the car insurance?"

"I'm working on it, Lena. Today kind of got away from me."

"Where did you park anyway? You could fit a truck out front."

Murder in Mexico

"Did I tell you I saw Pete Malloy the other day?"
"Pete?"
"And his cooler. The day it rained."
"It's rained for forty days and forty nights."
"He told me Walt Sandusky passed."
Lena turns to face him. "You mean he died?"
"Heart attack."
"Oh my God!"
"That's what I said, 40-some years old."
"Poor Sherry...and the kids."
"Pete said the insurance is trying to weasel out."
"They can do that?"
"That's what he said. They're claiming bankruptcy. I'm thinking the bad things are starting to happen."
"Harry, don't."
"First Gerry then Bill Healy, now Sands. Wonder what they'd change if they could take back a few years."
Lena gnaws at her lower lip. "Stop it. You're scaring me."
"Oh yeah, and I saw Danny Smart. You could have said something, Lena."
"I couldn't. It was confidential."
Harry turns back to the show. "You haven't told anyone about our little scheme, have you?"
"You mean your little scheme?"
"Because if you tell, we can never do it. As much as the idea scares you, you don't want to rule it out."
"You're getting on my very last nerve."
Harry picks up the remote and turns down the sound. "Do this for me, Lena. Just come to Mexico. Think of it as a vacation. Who knows, maybe when we get down there the whole thing will seem ridiculous. Let's just pretend. See what happens."
"What do we use for money?"
"We've got the savings. Come on, let's live a little."
"But that's *all* we have."

"It's chump change. Old Sands owed more in bar bills."

"It's something."

"It cost that to bury my brother. What are you gonna do with it, retire to the Hamptons?"

Lena chews her lip bloody. "What about work?"

"Listen to you, Lena? What ever happened to the brassy blonde who was gonna see the world?"

"Last I heard she married a maniac."

"I gotta tell you..." Harry tongues a molar. "Those muffins you brought home tasted kind of chalky."

CHAPTER SIX

Stevie paces the parking lot trying to calm himself. Dorie's last call left a throbbing in his skull that over-the-counter won't make a dent in. Lilly's doctors are at an impasse. The drugs were a disappointment, but other options are still being considered. Time is a factor, but nothing will be decided before further testing and consultation, two weeks minimum.

At least the timing is right. Stevie's Mexico week is three days away, and his freelance load has been put on hold. The decks cleared for what's required, self-absorption Stevie-style.

"Lilly Winslow's room, please?"

The woman at the desk goes mushy at the name. "Such a hero to us. Right now that poor baby is the only thing holding this place together."

"I, uh..."

"You don't have to say a thing." She reaches for his hand. "You just follow me and see for yourself."

"Thank you." He tugs in reflex, but the woman's got a lock on it.

"Are you a religious man, Mr. Winslow?" She pulls him along.

"Not so much, no, but I am, you know, God fearing."

"Well, I'll tell you what. If prayers were popcorn, the Man Upstairs would be buried in the Big Bucket."

"Popcorn?"

"Course, the Lord works in mysterious ways, but I have to believe there are angels He just won't take from us. The special ones."

"I'm sorry, take?"

"Like your Lilly."

"Yes. Yes, Lilly."

And a somber group it is bunched around the bedside. Dorie, Dr. Whosits, Brymer, some couple he doesn't know, the fag designer, and now Stevie, trying his best to make his face work.

"Daddy?" His angel beams up from a thicket of pillows.

"Hello, sweetheart. How are you feeling?"

"Better, now that you're here."

Oh, the smile, haunted but heartfelt. As he leans over to kiss her, someone stifles a sob. One of the doctors, wasn't it? Jesus.

"I came as soon as I could." Stevie sneaks a glance around. "Mommy tells me you've been doing your drawings."

"Yep, I got lots of them now. Wanna see?"

"Maybe tomorrow, sweetheart. Daddy's got to catch up with mommy and the doctors."

"Okay. I got one of Randy too."

"Honey, Daddy's not with Randy anymore. But I still want to see it."

And the little arms, Jesus, so pale he can see every vein. How her eyes are sunken like a TV kid who won't make it to station break. Should they all be in here breathing up the air? Isn't it past her bedtime or are we at a point where it no longer matters? He hears clothes rustle around him. Someone's shoe scuffs the floor.

"Daddy? Remember when you took me to Disneyland and we stayed with Uncle Frankie?"

Dorie reaches to fluff a pillow. "He's not really your uncle, darling. You know that, don't you?"

"Try and get some rest, Lilly." Stevie takes her hands, ten little icicles in a sweaty palm.

"Are you staying with mommy tonight?" She gives a

light squeeze. "You could sleep in my bedroom, Daddy."

"Aw Jeez, that's so..." Stevie wells up for a second but bears down hard. "Thank you, precious. Daddy already has a hotel room."

"You could always cancel," Dorie pipes up.

"Oh do it, Daddy. Cancel it."

The designer sucks a tooth; the others do their best to blend in.

"But I didn't even rent a car yet."

"You can go with mommy. Please, Daddy?"

"It's not that I—"

"My Barbies are so lonely. You can keep them company."

He's come undone now, with the hands wringing and Adam's apples bobbing, every eye squarely on him.

"I...my bag..." He looks up but Dorie gives him nothing. "Okay...okay, sweetie, I'll stay in your room."

"Oh thank you, Daddy. You're the best."

Then the doctors herd them out the door and up the hallway. Stevie trails the pack into some dark paneled conference room, with photos of weathered European doorways, where they'll lay cards on the table along with every assurance and disclaimer. Risks are assessed, bases covered. They set a date, sign the papers for a bone marrow transplant, and it's off to Dorie's for God knows what.

***

"It's the bravest thing anyone could ever do. I mean that, Stevie."

"Dorie's right," Roger chimes in. "I can't tell you how much I admire you, Steven."

"I've got to tell you...I'm not really comfortable with the hero thing."

"And self-effacing to boot. Where did you find this guy, Dor?" The big homo drives like a motorhead with the g-forces and the downshifting.

"I told you, Stevie has the heart of a lion."

"Should we be driving this fast?"

"The whole verité feel of the thing. God, you could taste it. Gathered around, the shadows stretching, machines humming." Roger settles in behind a flatbed.

"Roger has a way with words. He's writing a screenplay about it. Dorie's Dilemma, we call it."

"Dorie's?"

"Well, it's about me and how life can just come apart at the seams, just by—"

"The Barbies line was a killer." Roger rims the shoulder.

Stevie stiffens. "I thought you were a designer."

"Strictly a sidelight. My agent says this is my breakout year."

Dorie's place, formerly their place, gone a bit to seed with the dead shrubs and the awful addition. Rumpus/Dance Studio with wall-to-wall rubber and matching isolation tanks. As he enters each strange yet familiar room, Stevie feels like an actor in a Roger film, something flat and painfully overwritten. A dark horse destined to shine.

"Nice tanks, Dor." He sidles up.

"Roger swears by them."

"Roger's a screaming queen."

"Keep your voice down. I won't have you insult him."

"Just so you're aware, Dorie."

"Oh, and just what agenda are we pushing here?"

"A gaping bottom or I eat the mortgage."

"I can't believe this. You of all the people."

"Look, I just don't want to see you get hurt again."

"Oh, just how fucking noble can you get, Stevie?"

Not that he isn't a tad relieved. No chance she's boffing this bozo, not while he can still dodge around it. The gay vibe is too well defined, though Stevie *has* known it to happen. And sooner or later it's bound to get messy, considering what Dorie's already been through. So confusing, this being jealous of something he never wanted. Relieved, too, that he won't have to spend time alone with either of them, as Roger seems to be settling in.

I can get though this. I really can.

"Dorie tells me you do some marketing, Steven. Fascinating field."

"Yes, well, it pays the bills."

"I mean, let's face it. The whole world runs on advertising."

"I don't know about that. It's just con—"

"Big bucks, for sure."

"Right."

"You should see Roger's designs, Stevie. The man is immensely talented."

"Yes, I'd like to sometime. Good design is very—"

"I mean I love what I do, don't get me wrong. I just don't have the ego for it. Know what I'm saying?"

Dorie nods along. "Roger's ahead of his time."

"The yes men and the lackeys and all the bullshit. It's not really me."

Turning tense when Roger takes his leave with a peck to Dorie and clumsy male hug at the front door. Stevie stands there until long after he's gone, listening to Dorie hum in the kitchen. Stands there with his nose to the glass, straining to feel *inside his bones*.

***

"I guess that's what attracted me to you. This way you have of seeing the worst in everyone. I thought you were so jaded."

Into the cognac now, Dorie's waving a framed photo of them on their honeymoon, hand in hand on the beach with boy chick leering from the breakers. As if the little shit knew it would come to this.

"If I'd let you have your little flings, would you have stayed?"

"Don't do this, Dorie."

"I just wonder... Couples have arrangements. I mean, it's just sex."

"There's more to it than that, and you know it."

"Sorry. I'm being maudlin, I know."

"No, just sentimental, but I'm in no shape for it."

"Okay...but can I tell you I love you?"

Stevie goes to her against all instincts. "You're the dearest thing in the world to me, Dorie. You and Lilly are the only family I have in the world. I have to believe we'll get past this nightmare. I have to focus on that exclusively."

"You're so good, Stevie, so wonderfully good and kind."

"I'd better turn in. I've got an early flight tomorrow."

"You can sleep with me, Stevie. No strings attached."

"I'd better not. Lilly made me promise."

Dorie sees him to the stairway, jasmine wafting in sad rebuke.

"When do you leave for Mexico?"

"Thursday, you're okay with it, right?" He touches her hand. "Anything happens, I can be back in a matter of hours."

"I wasn't, at first, but I know you, remember? If you stay you'll just obsess." She pulls him close. "Hold me, Stevie, just for a moment. I've been so lonely I could die."

No way out of it at that point, their embrace drawn out to nearly unbearable, dissolving slowly at Stevie's discretion.

"When you talk to Lilly, tell her the next time she sees me we're going to take care of this, once and for all. Will you do that for me?"

Dorie chugs away in his arm.

Murder in Mexico
***

And finally, there's Lilly's room. Pink with a stenciled border of bunnies, little desk, little dresser, little skirts and blouses in the closet. One wall is taped with drawings of people he can't identify. Black Beauty bedspread, Barbies aligned on the pillow. He scans the framed photos bunched on the dresser, him and Dorie, just him, Dorie and Lilly at Yosemite, some pre-pubescent boy band and the Tin Man from the Wizard of Oz.

Christ.

Stevie drapes his clothes on the little chair and turns down the blankets. He wants badly to brush his teeth, but can't bear the thought of running into Dorie again. Instead, he kills the lights and slips into Lilly's bed. Too small, mattress from hell, but now that he's in there he knows it's the right place for him, even if the pillows are foam rubber. Putting his nose into them, he smells for Lilly, and there she is, her very essence going right to his head. Stevie takes it in and holds it for as long as he can.

How many times he'd tucked her in, gazing at that angel face with genuine longing, the longing to be inside her heart and see things as she saw them, to *be* her, or close enough to feel what she was feeling. He used to think there had to be a way. The thought that it could never be was almost more than he could stand.

That was long ago now, two years but a lifetime of pain and humiliation, and then the move to Phoenix where he didn't know a soul. Had been there only once and came down with food poisoning, chose it for that very reason, not the food poisoning but the anonymity, the chance to start over. It had to be done and he did it, and it wasn't going *that* badly. The men in Phoenix weren't the greatest shakes, but at least he could be himself, if such a thing were possible in Phoenix.

Who was he kidding? He didn't care about his stupid

life any more than he cared about his business, or even Dorie, though he hates to admit *that*. He knows not caring about her, even secretly, is the cruelest thing he could ever do. But that's how it is and there's no way to change it. Nothing matters but Lilly, at least right now, surrounded by her surroundings. Stevie knows that will change to varying degrees as he mucks through the coming weeks. But tonight, here in his baby's cramped little bed, he's finally found a measure of contentment.

***

When he wakes, he doesn't know where he is. Then he turns to the nearest Barbie, and recognition hits him like a blow. He stares up at the bunnies and listens to Dorie humming in the shower, the way her hums never come together in a tune. Just a single note really, sort of peppy but mindless, though he can see where he might find it endearing in someone else. Can't recall her humming much when they were together. Could be it has something to do with Roger, but he can't bring himself to believe it. Plus the fact that she must know he can hear, must realize that she's sending a message. The wrong message, whatever it is.

Then he realizes that it isn't humming at all, something else, the dryer maybe. Just like him to jump to conclusions, the Maytag sounding a serenade.

Lord get me through this.
And then he remembers:
Mexico.

CHAPTER SEVEN

The big jet banks and she can see cars jockey on the interstate, the shape of the stadium, oddly pleasing, the movie complex three blocks over and finally Tasker Street, cutting in from the river. She tries to pinpoint the house, but it all runs together. Harry's probably home by now, or at Brennan's nursing his separation anxiety. Lena's gaze follows a tanker under the Ben Franklin then she settles back with her Stephen King and a gut full of troubles.

"Funny, from this angle it looks like we're hardly moving," the guy in front of her says.

"Look, Mommy, there's fire across the river." A kid to the rear stomps her seat back.

Mom glances out the window. "It's only Camden, honey. Not to worry."

"No matter how many times I do this, it still gives me a rush," her seatmate confesses.

"Pardone?" She gives him a Mediterranean look.

"Ah, quell coincidence." He grins like an imbecile. "Il y'est mon bonne chance."

She switches to a blank stare of unspecified origin then turns back to her book. Lena has set the time aside for disconnection, a reality respite that won't include this guy, in any language. But even their brief exchange has thrown things off, made her aware of this link-one in the chain of events. Events that have taken her out of her element and put her on a jet to Mexico, alone, under false pretenses.

"S'habla Espanol?"

She reads the same line over and over, feeling his

eyes, wishing him dead. And he gets the hint, finally, after a go at Italian and something Slavic. Gives up and starts pestering the guy in the aisle seat, attractive, well dressed, thin like Harry. Handsome stranger, that old fantasy, a man with a career and prospects, a skilled professional with an itinerary that doesn't include murder in the first degree with special circumstances.

Exactly what she doesn't want to do for the next how many hours. Think about the lunacy and the consequences and how they may just go through with it. Sit here and stew, but she can't seem to turn it off, the way the big things unfold just like in a movie. How many movies begin like this, jet lifting off, etc.

Lena let's herself go with it. The movie end of it, how it might just be a good movie with a happy ending. Woman gets on a plane, handsome stranger, Mexico, intrigue with a twist you can't see coming, something that changes everything, or at least the one thing.

"Hey, Mom, you know what Ricky told me?"
"Don't play with the buttons, sweetie."
"He said that jets are just flying funeral pyres."
"Ricky Talbott doesn't know his ass from his elbow."
"He said—"
"I don't care what he said. Play with your palm pilot."

What? What else did Ricky say? Lena shuts her eyes, counts to ten then starts the page over.

"He said the whole plane is loaded with fuel. Not just the tanks."

"Did you hear what I said, Walter? We talked about this, remember? One word to your father and you can forget about fencing lessons."

That shuts him up. No fencing lessons, a cruel if unusual punishment. No matter now, he's given Lena plenty to think about incineration as a plot devise, the killer twist any way you look at it. To calm herself, she thinks of Harry home alone, missing her. Then Harry selling himself on the murder, convincing himself he can pull it off. Not yet cruising altitude and she's into the untenable. Scenarios cued to the horizon, most of them worst-case, all of them unthinkable.

But then this is all uncharted territory, when she thinks of it. They've spent a few nights apart in their years together. Three she remembers, all in her absence, once to be in her cousin's wedding and again to attend a nursing conference in New Orleans. Harry handled both badly, calling the electrician when the circuits tripped, passing out on the couch with the beer opener in his pocket. The old Harry, around the house hapless, seen from this distance, the change is unsettling.

What it was about Harry was his knack for the angle. Before Gerry died, when a knack was all it took. Lena never cared for Gerry. She can admit that now, the know it all bluster, the sly flirtations, the harebrained schemes that never went anywhere. Like the Peppermint Patty machines. How he and Harry would stick one in every gin mill and clean up on the first of the month. Which one of the Ned's barflies sold little brother she'd like to know? Corner the Peppermint Patty market, as if anyone ate that crap anymore, even in Pennsport. As if nothing topped off an evening of boilermakers quite like a Peppermint Patty. Harry bought in on the off chance it might help Gerry out, put him back on his feet like the tanning salon and the water ice place were supposed to. How those stupid machines took up the whole living room until she finally called the company to take them away, and then De Sapios darkening her door. Oh yeah, Gerry was a loser, but Harry had a knack.

Even then it was insurance. Deep pockets swindle had that whiff of win/win Harry couldn't pass up. It started with car insurance, half a dozen fender benders spread out over two years. That's how he got them, Harry was patient, had a sense for suspicion, how patterns were tracked, knew who to use and who couldn't handle it. With Harry at the helm it went off without a hitch. Then it was personal injury claims with that doctor in the Northeast, the Russian with the list of accident-prone comrades. Talk about your poker faces. The KGB couldn't crack that bunch.

Yeah, Harry had it going for a while there. His end topped six figures two years running, even with the house down payment and his betting losses. But then the doctor got pinched and Gerry got sick and Harry simply stopped being Harry. Not all at once, but slow and steady like a disease. Lena saw it progressing, but what could she do? The wheels stopped turning, the hustles dried up, and it was down to a bad job and the Vegas line.

Which had to explain it, at least up to this point. Talking about it, she'd seen the old spark in Harry's eye, the pace picking up as the pieces fit together. So long now she forgot how she missed it. Like he'd come home from a long time away. So okay, this was different, even crazy, but she knew she'd do worse to have him back.

"Remember that movie where they sabotage the plane and the guy gets sucked out of the window?"

"Mommy's reading, Walter."

"He got stuck for a second and you could see his legs flop around and then, boom!"

"Shut up, sweetie."

Lena gives up on her book and looks down on a crust of coastline. She pictures a woman down there, catching a glint in the pale blue yonder, someone with hard choices to make taking something from the contact, the farthest flicker, a tremor of kinship. Lena sighs and wishes her well.

"Miss?"

She looks over the gap to a handsome stranger and a flight attendant.

"Would you care for something to drink?" The attendant smiles brightly.

"Red wine, please. Could you tell me what time we

land?"

"Three twenty." She works the top on a small bottle. "Captain caught a bit of tail wind."

Lena checks her watch. Three hours, plenty of time to mull things over. She takes a tin from her purse and pops a purple pill. Best to relax if she wants to think clearly.

"I hate to be a bother..." Handsome guy leans over. "You wouldn't have another book you could spare, would you?"

"I'm sorry?"

"I'm afraid our chatty friend has me at a disadvantage." He nods to the empty seat between them.

"Where'd he go?"

"Well, right now he's bothering the first class section, but he promised he'd be back."

"Here." She offers her Stephen King. "I can never concentrate on a plane."

"Bless you." He smiles at the heft of it. "If it comes to that I can brain him with it."

"I shan't raise a hand to stop you."

"The man spits when he speaks."

Lena takes the lead. "Are you going to Mexico?"

"Sao Paulo." He tosses the name like a native. "Ghastly flight, fortunately, this should be my last trip."

"Business or pleasure?"

"Neither, in fact. My sister married a Brazilian."

"You sound as if you don't approve."

His smile is rakish. "I've been assigned to pick up the pieces."

The contrast of teeth on deep tan trips an unfamiliar switch. Lena feels something here, a significance bearing directly on the story. Winging her way to the tropics, Banderas with a moustache, if she wanted this to happen she'd be stuck with Mickey Rooney.

"Is it perilous?" It just sounds so right.

His laugh is all crinkles and crow's feet. "Tedious

would be more like it. Brazilians can say the same thing in a million different ways."

"Like Rankin here?" Lena eyes the empty seat.

"Don't tell me you know the man."

She tries a smile she's never used. "No, that's just my husband's name for everybody. I don't know where he got it, but it always seems to fit."

Why would she do that, bring up Harry at the first opportunity? Not intentionally, but not by accident.

"Your husband, he is not traveling with you?"

"Ex-husband, continents removed."

Stranger shakes his head. "Messy business, matrimony. Just when you think you've got the hang of it, they throw in a new wrinkle."

"They?"

"The fates." His face goes slack. "My wife died three years ago."

"I'm so sorry."

"Oh, it's not like all that. We'd been divorced for years."

"Still."

"Yes..." He drifts for a second then looks over. "Recovery is a process."

"Quick, here comes motormouth. Scoot over."

Stranger grins and switches seats. He is Dominique, engineer of note and authority on everything from mosaic tile to mescaline. His voice is baritone deep and saxophone soft. Lena slips into her Bergman, and the cabin fills with chemistry.

"But that's enough about me," Dominique says. "What about you? What do you think?"

"About you?"

"Well, that would be a start. About me then."

"I think you are just what I needed. A distraction."

Dominique fakes a pout. "The story of my life."

What she might say to this, something ripe with

suggestion. Instead, she says nothing and the affect is similar.

He leans into whispering range. "Tell me something about yourself, your name, you never said."

"Estralita..." just to top his, "I sing."

And here she goes. Estralita prowling the stage, a life on the road and an ex husband down for the count. Lena's story and she's sticking to it.

"That's fascinating." Dominique's eyebrows come together. "Of course, you could tell me anything."

"And you can choose to believe it, of course."

"How perfectly delightful. I wish I'd known the ground rules. I would have made myself more interesting."

"You're doing quite well."

"What about him?" Dominique nods to third wheel.

"Rankin? Middle management. Can bore you breathless in three different languages."

"A man who spits."

"But a loving father."

"Of daughters, six and ten."

"Three and five."

"We could always find out, you know."

"What would be the point?"

The rest is all giggles and elbow jabs, running down the ranks like high school hipsters or housewives on whoever's missing. By the time they touch down they've cobbled an epic and pissed off half the people on board.

"Pity we must leave them in the lurch." Dominique watches the cast disbanding. "Somehow, I feel they need us."

"You could always stop over for a night." She opens the overhead.

"I would love nothing better. But this thing in Sao Paulo is at a crisis stage." His eyes flash regrets. "You believe that, don't you...Estralita?"

Lena's smile is pure Garbo. "I guess it just wasn't in

the script."

He puzzles it over.

She touches his arm. "You've been a dear, Dominique."

He reaches in his pocket and hands her his card. "Do one thing for me, whoever you are. Keep this with you. If you ever tire of life, you can reach me anytime."

"Why thank you." She closes it in her dog-eared paperback. "It will be a comfort to know."

He sees her to the gate with a nod to the uniforms. Claude Rains clearing customs.

"Remember..." He turns her by the elbow and she sees herself in his eyes. "Any time, day or night."

"Farewell, Dominique."

"Until we meet again."

Sigh.

***

Puerto Vallarta. So like she pictured it, she has to pinch herself: dusty streets, open cantinas, day-glo buses packed to the rivets. She moves along the sunny side, swinging her purse like there's nothing to it, another day, another country. One of a handful to get off in town, the rest heading on to the hotel complex, out by the airport, five miles easy. This is where she wants to be, right here in the middle of things, sidewalks buzzing, the day shaping up. Lena crosses to the real estate office and strolls in like she owns the joint.

"My name is Lena Watts," she tells the man gazing sleepily at a computer. "I'm here to pick up a key?"

The man doesn't answer. Looking closer she sees that his eyes aren't really open, just slits of wet like a cat dozing in a window. Moving behind him she sees a poker hand on the laptop screen, pair of sixes, king high.

"Hey." She gives a poke.

Murder in Mexico

He bolts upright in his chair.

"I'd fold 'em if I were you." She moves to a board tacked with Polaroids, listings for rent, most new and uninviting.

"Forgive me, I didn't hear you come in." He swivels to face her. "My name is Louis. You have a reservation?"

"Watts." She studies an overhead shot. Some compound carved out of the jungle. "We rented the Casa Luna."

"Ah, Casa Luna." Louis rifles the drawers, piling up keys on the desk. "Our prize hacienda. Lovely setting."

"Quite a building boom going on here." She scans the last row, mobiles and modulars cashing in.

"Yes, senora. Puerto Vallarta is one of the oldest resorts, but the last few years have been—"

"A real mess, looks like. Next they'll be putting in a Starbucks, eh, Louis?"

"Starbucks, si, we have two actually. I am partial to the double latte."

"Tell me, is there a liquor store nearby?"

"Yes, senora, two blocks that way." He nods to the window.

"And a pharmacy?"

"Si, around the corner."

"Excellent, now, the key?"

"Of course, my apologies." He fumbles faster. "Our filing system is in need of updating. You are staying alone?"

"My husband will be flying down tomorrow. The house is in town, yes?"

"Oh yes, not far from the beach. At night the sound of the waves is hypnotizing."

"No jet skis I'm hoping."

"Not after dark." Louis tries a second drawer. "There is an ordinance."

"Or drunken cruise ships?"

~77~

"Not so many. We try to discourage...ah, here they are." He holds up a ring shaped like a sombrero. "Casa Luna, mucho grande."

***

Lena steps over the ditch running through the lot next door. Big lot, bordered in backhoes and frontend loaders, bricks and lumber stacked in the middle. Casa Luna's cordoned off in hedges, a shock of salmon on a field of green with an arched stone gate and a shrine to the virgin. Lena balances the bag of bottles on her knee and fits the key to the back door lock.

Inside, it's el magnifico: pastel rooms, open and airy, floors of marble and terra cotta, walls inlaid in mosaics and stained glass. Lena sets the bottles on the counter, runs a bagful of limes through the cast iron squeezer, and breaks the seal on a fifth of vodka. Mucho fantastic!

"Buenos dias," a woman calls from upstairs.

"Hello?"

"Hello." She appears at the landing. "I am Rosa. I'm just making up your room."

"Hi, Rosa, I'm Lena. Can I fix you a drink?"

Rosa doesn't answer. Lena takes her second drink out the front door and across the street. Backhoes aside, the casa is a jewel box, half sun-drenched, half swallowed up in palms, street-side trimmed in wrought iron with bay windows opened onto the work site. The shrine wall trellised in roses and bougainvillea, the rear sculpted in gardens framing the pool. Above it, the main deck, and above that, a cozy bedroom balcony, both facing out on the town and the wide Pacific. Lena throws her head back and laughs out loud. Here's to Harry's knack on the rebound. Worse comes to worst, they'll be flaming out in style.

"Will you be needing anything?" Rosa calls from the doorway.

"No." Lena raises her glass. "I'm okay now."

"I left some snacks for you in the refrigerator. See you tomorrow?"

"You mean mañyana?"

"Right, mañyana. Your husband, he will be here tomor- eh, mañyana?"

"Si, in the evening."

"Should I stop over and fix you something? Pizza, maybe?"

Lena nearly chokes. "Pizza? You're not Mexican are you?"

"Guatemalan." Rosa shrugs. "But I make a mean pizza."

"That's okay. As a matter of fact, we'd kind of like to be alone for a few days."

Rosa frowns and lowers her eyes. "I'll stop around on Wednesday."

"Hold it." Lena crosses over and slips the girl a little something. "Make it Thursday. And call first, okay?"

"Gotcha." Rosa pockets the fifty and dances down the hill.

A servant, no less, not that Lena goes in for that sort of thing. But she's never had one and could see where she might get used to having one. Harry hadn't mentioned a servant, but he hadn't mentioned the pool either. Lena wanders through the house, taking in everything. A soft breeze catches the curtains, and a trumpet plays somewhere down the hill. Music, that's what she needs. She finds some CDs and a box of scented candles and by drink #3 the casa's lit up like a backstreet bordello.

Oh, Harry, wait 'til you see.

She hadn't given much thought to this, her night by herself. They'd decided it was best for her to arrive first, pick up the keys and deal with incidentals, Harry, sneaking in under the cover of darkness. With any luck, no one here will ever see him.

"And even if they do it'll just be a tall man getting out of a taxi." He'd turned his palms up like it went without saying.

"But what if something unexpected happens?"

"Hey, it's just a precaution, no big deal. Who's gonna say the dead guy isn't me?"

"I don't know yet."

"I'll be Mr. Invisible."

"What about when we're out trying to get me picked up?"

"They won't know we're together. Anyway, it's not like they'll be rounding up suspects. It's just a heart attack."

The Pickup. The way Harry sees it, men will be lining up to get a shot at her, that MILF thing, a lead pipe cinch. Whatever it takes, she'll see it through, if just to prove that he hasn't got a murder in him. Not a total stranger, in cold blood. Explode that notion for once and for always. Lena's even managed to work herself up for it. She sees the way men still look at her. Might be a hoot to rub Harry's nose in it.

And what if he *does* have it in him? Wouldn't going along only force his hand? Lena can usually tell what Harry will do, but not always and not lately. She's almost certain he's quit his job, but he hasn't said so. Of course, she hasn't told him she's been fired, but that's not the same thing. Telling him would give him that much more incentive. How much would be enough?

It was different when Gerry was alive. Brother-deep-end was no picnic, but he gave Harry something to fuss over. Without him, there's too much time to brood. It was after Gerry died that Harry started in with the life insurance, more to hedge his bets than provide for Lena. She complained, but it's not such a bad idea when she thinks about it. And she's been thinking about it.

Lena soaks in moonlight, drunk enough to follow her

thoughts anywhere. Closing her eyes she calls up Dominique. What life might be like without Harry's problems, so much different she can almost feel it. No storm clouds, no more rocks in her stomach, so much better it makes her ache. *Save your own life*, her head tells her, but her heart holds the key, deep in that soft spot where Harry lives.

***

"Hey, hey, hey!" He's at the front door in a loud Hawaiian shirt, cargo shorts, flip-flops, and a Phillies cap.

"Harry?"

He throws his arms wide. "Takes low profile to a whole new level, don't you think?"

"Weren't you cold on the plane?"

"I changed in the cab. Come on, it's funny." He squeezes past and heads for the refreshments.

"That's okay, you can kiss me later, Harry."

"First things first. I got trapped in coach with the Wilson twins. It was a nightmare."

"The who?"

"The Wilsons?" He pours vodka on ice. "I took names and addresses so I could look them up somewhere down the line."

"When you get to the W's."

"Right." Harry turns without spilling a drop. "Casa Luna! Nice, or what?"

"It's better than nice." She grabs the bottle and leads him along. "Wait 'til you see the view."

It's all the way to the bedroom balcony before Harry finally pulls her to him. Lena holds on tight, hears his heart beat through that godawful shirt. Loves her Harry and it makes her crazy.

"I know what you're thinking." Harry crooks her chin and searches her eyes. "You're thinking old Harry really has something here."

"I was, yeah."

"You're thinking this is it. Am I wrong?"

"This is it, Harry."

"Did I mention the pool?"

"There's a girl who comes in to cook and clean. Rosa."

"Get rid of her."

"I already did. Too bad, though, she makes a mean pizza."

"Though that might look funny. Maybe—"

"Let's sit a while." She leads him to the table for two. "It's our first night. I want to just chill."

"It was raining when I left." He takes the corner chair. "I always get a kick out of that. How was your flight?"

"Oh...uneventful, you know."

"Aren't you the cool customer."

"I travel well." Lena smiles. "Not like some people."

"You never traveled with Roly and Poly."

"They were fat kids?"

"Not just the fat, they had nostrils like tunnels. You could see way back, and there was stuff in there."

"Porcine."

"Exactly."

She sniffs a tear.

"What is it, Lena?"

"What is what?" She reaches for the bottle.

"Your problem."

The Garbo smile again. "I let people talk me into things. Dumb things usually. The wrong hairstyle, the wrong car, you name it. I've always been like that."

"Wrong husband?"

"No, Harry. I'm talking things, not people. But I'm thinking it's a little late in the game to make another mistake."

Harry's seen this coming. "What better time? At this

Murder in Mexico

point you can't wreck your whole life. Not even half of it. Worst that can happen, the state nurses you through those golden years. Can't you feel it, Lena? The way out."

"But it's murder, Harry. You can't take it back."

"You can't take anything back."

"To throw everything away.

"G'bye." He tosses a hand.

"If you're dead set on the idea." Lena leans into his field of vision. "I mean if your life is so unbearable."

"Come on, baby, not every button."

"I won't stand in your way."

"If it makes you feel better, you couldn't stop me. How's that?"

Lena settles back. "And when everything goes wrong and someone's dead and we're rotting away in some Mexican hellhole, I want you to swear you'll blame yourself, Harry."

"My right hand to God."

"Because come what may, I have to be able to look at myself in the mirror and say, 'You're good, Lena. You just let people talk you into things.'"

"Burn in hell, gotcha."

"Okay?"

"Okay." Harry shrugs. "Anything else?"

"Yeah this." Lena reaches in the mini bar, pulls out a small bottle and sealed plastic bag and hands them to Harry.

"Potassium chloride." He reads the label. "Baby, you're the greatest. And this?" He waves the tiny bag of powder.

"Secanol. They keep some at the hospital."

"Right. So the song and dance?"

"I meant every word."

***

In the morning, they take a walk around town. The houses shine in the sunlight, and the people move with the ease of natives. This will change within the hour as tourists shuttle in, but for now, they seem to be the only outsiders, lean and leggy, half a head taller. Not really tourists, but not from around here. They stroll the ocean promenade, watching from the palms as a cruise ship passes.

"We're not the cruise ship type are we?" Lena shields her eyes with a hand.

"Sadly no."

"I didn't think so."

"Too much getting there. We're more fixed destination."

"Like Paris?" She looks over. "A real vacation."

"We do this right and we can be there for Christmas."

"You mean it?"

"Absolutely."

Sure sounds like the old Harry, but something else, too. An edge she's never heard before, a note of certainty that's a shade too certain, too focused, as if still trying to sell himself. And, of course, he still would be. Harry's way with the hard things, box himself in until he has to, now that they're down here, now they've spent the money. Not her way, but strangely effective. What she hears in Harry is a note of resolve, or his take on what resolve might sound like. And this, parading around like actors pretending to be tourists, Harry getting into character, not exactly nervous, but strung a little tighter, locked into ends instead of means, so that they're no longer on the same wavelength. Last night when he told her what she was thinking, she'd felt something change between them, a slip of the grip. How someone like Harry would go about this. Murder. He'd have to change himself. Become someone who could. That would change her too, and then where will they be? It's a way to lose him she's never considered. That's what really scares her. That, and the thought she could still talk him out of it.

"Harry?"

"Hmmm?"

"I've been thinking. Venice would be nice."

"Venice, Rome, the Riviera. You name it, kiddo."

"The Riviera." Lena sighs.

Harry sits beside her. "I remember I was in Janey's Café one morning. It was in the winter, cold snap, snow all over, the city a mess. There was a paper on the counter, one of Janey's tabloids. On the cover was a picture of Richard Gere romping in the surf with some dreamboat. That's what it said, 'romping in the surf.'"

"In Cannes."

"Wherever, and I'm thinking, look at this guy lying back in some tropical paradise while I'm on my way to work. For the next eight hours I'll be breathing fumes and butting heads with Baldini while old Richard is boffing some Bimbo and ordering room service."

Lena doesn't know what to say. Richard Gere?

Harry turns to her. "There's only one way to make it when you really think about it. It's either screw or be screwed."

"If you say so, Harry."

A strained silence falls between them. Harry flinches first, walking out to the water with his hands in his pockets. Lena sits watching, toes curled in apprehension. She sees a small boy approach with a fist full of sticks, souvenirs or something to eat. Harry takes one and turns the kid her way. They stand side by side, waving, and she feels a small weight dissolve in her stomach. By the time he returns, Lena's mind is made up.

"What is it?"

"Grilled fish." He hands her one. "Wait 'til you taste it."

"My God, that's incredible."

"Gerry would love this." Harry scoots in beside her.

"He wanted to live where it was always warm. I remember we'd watch football games from the coast, sitting in the cold and dark, the Raiders or the Rams in sun-drenched stadiums. Half naked fans dousing each other with beer while out the window it's ten below. Gerry would stare at the TV and say, 'someday I'm gonna live there.'"

"Gerry? Football?" She tries to picture it.

"He was just like me before the heroin. That guy you knew? That wasn't Gerry." Harry draws in the sand with his stick, a jet plane with two faces in the window.

"You quit your job, didn't you, Harry?"

"Don't worry about it."

"Because I got fired."

Harry keeps his eyes on the water.

"Did you hear me?"

"I heard you." He turns with a grin. "Guess we'd best get busy."

CHAPTER EIGHT

The cab pulls up to Chico's Place. Harry goes in first, takes a seat at the bar. Lena enters, looking pale and anxious. With a quick glance to the bar she circles the dance floor and settles in a corner table. Chico's is half full, but it's early yet, Friday night the world round.

"Roses, Senior?" A girl in the mirror cradles an armful.

"Sorry." He doesn't turn to face her.

Lena looks straight ahead, as if daring any man to come near her. Sure enough some do. Harry watches in the mirror, a beefy forty-something in a loud Hawaiian shirt. Jesus, what did these guys wear before Jimmy Buffet? Shirt tries his line, but Lena sends him off with a sniff. The music starts up and along comes half her age, impossibly bronzed and blonde, whispers in her ear, and Harry hears a Lena laugh. Next thing he knows, she's out on the dance floor, Jesus, with the hips going—

"Get you another?" The bartender steps into his view.

"Make it a double."

They dance into the next song as Harry fidgets, kid's hand almost where it shouldn't be. *Light My Fire*, the long version, and Harry's got two cigarettes lit. Doors, for Christ sake as they slow to a grind, Lena's beaming like the queen of the hop. The kid leads her back to the table then hustles to the head. Harry slips off and slices through the crowd.

"What the fuck, Lena? That kid won't look like me for twenty years."

"He's sweet. Besides, what am I supposed to do all night? Sit by myself?"

"Get rid of him."

"How?"

"I don't know. Tell him you have grandchildren."

"Why Harry Watts. You're jealous." Lena bubbles up. "Oh, this is priceless!"

"Everything okay, Meredith?" boy toy calls from the stairway.

"It's okay, Romeo. I'm her husband."

"It's alright, Tyler."

"Ty-ler?" Harry recoils visibly. "You know, Ty-ler, you should be ashamed of yourself. This woman is old enough to be your mother."

"I know." The kid leers. "Guess that makes you old enough to be my dad."

"Get rid of him," Harry snaps at Lena.

"I'm sorry, Tyler. He threatened to jump off if I didn't talk to him."

"Do you want me to stay here with you?"

"I'll be fine."

"Yeah, she'll be fine," Harry snarls. "I saw an old lady in a wheelchair on the deck. Go get 'em, Tig...I mean Tyler."

"Careful dad, blood pressure." The fuck shoots a finger.

***

"Here's one. The Silver Sombrero, Sea View, Dancing and Dining." They sit poolside, sipping Margaritas. *"Where those who rate congregate."*

"So what, we're gonna spend the whole time in discos?"

"It's Saturday night. Tomorrow we can do whatever you want, but we can't miss date night."

Lena smears sunscreen on her legs and moves into the shade.

"Hey, Harry, what if we like him?"

"Who?"

"The victim. What if he's an okay guy?"

Harry looks to see if she's kidding. "Middle-age, single, traveling alone? People end up like that for a reason, Lena. He's either cheating on his wife or divorced so many times only a stranger can stand him."

"Maybe the bar is the wrong place to look. I never met anyone in a bar but Joey."

"This guy will be just like Joey."

Lena sucks on a slice of lime. "You and Joey sort of look alike."

"A weeper. A guy who puts four sugars in his coffee."

"I wish I never told you."

"A farter in bed."

***

The Silver Sombrero, your standard meat-rack, Led Zeppelin loud and lit up wall to wall. A crowd has the bar boxed in, but two couples leave just as Harry gets there.

"To the seventies!" He salutes them. "Wherever they went."

The bartender grunts. "Easy for you to say. Try listening to the Bee Gees four nights a week. This is the high school reunion that never ends."

"Always a down side."

"It's the air guitar guys that get you." Barman leans in. "With the big gut and the little ponytail? Christ, I hate that shit."

"Leave it to the boomers to bow out gracelessly."

"And the veterans, an hour of them and you see why we always muff it. And potheads, Christ! Try running a tab with that bunch."

Harry watches Lena work a too-tall cowpoke, all boots and belt buckle. She flutters a lash, and the guy's all over her.

"Cruise ships are the worst." The bartender shakes his head. "They get drunk then they buy the sombrero then it's Mexican hat dance time. Out there flopping around until one of them pukes or falls down. Take my word, it's an ugly business."

"Ever see that big guy over there with the blonde?" Harry nods their way.

"Sure, Bo Mitchell? He runs a charter boat out of San Pedro. The ladies really go for Bo."

"Is that right?"

"Word is he's hung like a horse."

"Get me a pack of smokes there, would you, pal?"

The bartender moves off and Harry catches a face in the mirror. Male, thin and fine featured, something about the face.

"Cruise ships and Club Med." Barman circles back. "They love to get up on stage. Some pencil neck pinhead doing Hendrix on his knees. Painful to watch, man."

"Middle age." Harry smacks his lips. "Wasted on the wasted."

Lena pulls up her sleeve to show her tattoo, the small butterfly winging in from the sixties. Cowboy gawks in dadgum wonder. Harry gives him ten minutes, tops.

"Excuse me..." The face in the mirror bellies up beside him. "Is this seat taken?"

Harry looks him over. "Be my guest."

"Bartender? May I see a wine list please?"

"Red and white friend." Barman shoots Harry a get-him look.

"That's it?"

"Hey, it's the seventies." He shrugs. "What do we know from vino?"

Harry raises a bottle to Barry White. "1978, to be exact."

His face falls in a frown. "But then shouldn't we be

younger?"

"Go with red," Harry tells him. "The white comes in a tanker truck."

They watch a quartet of Cornhuskers mangle the mambo. The spirit is willing but the flesh makes a mess of it.

"Just pray they don't play YMCA," the bartender mutters.

Meanwhile, Bo's at that point in his sagebrush saga where he pokes the table repeatedly. Lena wears a smile he could hang his hat on.

"Yeah..." Barman follows Harry's line of sight. "Old Bo does alright for himself."

"Twenty bucks says your goober doesn't get the girl."

Barman looks to New Face then back to Harry. "You know her?"

"Never saw her before in my life. My guess is Bobo's out of his league. The lady's just amusing herself."

"Make it fifty and you've got yourself a bet."

"Can I get in on this?" New Face wants to know. Something about this face.

"What's your name, pilgrim?" Harry asks.

"Stevie, uh, Steve Winslow."

"Gerry Green." Harry shakes his hand. "Looks like you're in, Stevie-boy."

"Just Steve."

"By..." Harry squints at Stevie's watch, "eleven, long tall will be singing those lonesome blues."

"I think you're half right." Stevie fingers his chin. "She's definitely slumming. But the cowboy has a certain swagger. She might indulge him."

They watch as Bo unveils *his* tattoos, then another cowpoke stops by to swap lies and stare holes in Lena's blouse.

"See?" Harry nods to the mirror. "She's bored shitless."

Stevie turns to watch. "I'm not so sure. Note the slight flair to the nostrils, the smoky gaze. Soon she'll be running a hand up his thigh."

Barman leans in. "Be brave, little lady."

"You guys." Harry shakes his head. "First mistake, you think he can get inside her head. I'm here to tell you it can't be done."

"Who said anything about her head?"

"Mistake number two. You assume he's calling the shots. She's just yanking his chain."

Stevie checks the bartender. "Shall we go for a hundred?"

"One hundred it is." Harry smacks the bar. "Barman, where's that red wine for Steve?"

Cowboy springs for a second round then settles in for the siege. He wrangles a laugh every now and then, but on the whole, it's going nowhere.

"So I rented a jeep, if you can believe it. Me in a jeep." Stevie giggles at the thought. "I drove out of town and up into the mountains."

Barman flinches. "Wouldn't do that if I were you."

"Why not?"

"Banditos."

"You're not serious."

"The old ways die hard."

"See anything interesting?" Harry asks him.

"There's a town up there. San Lucas. I found this strange little store, a junk shop, really. Poor people's junk, at that, tools, car parts, old appliances. Way in back, she had this display case."

"She?"

"The girl that runs it. She followed me back. More junk, some costume jewelry. But on the bottom shelf I saw a small black case, matchbox size. I asked her to show it to me."

Harry studies Stevie's profile. "We've met before,

haven't we?"

"I don't think so, I'm from Arizona."

"What about the case?" Barman butts in.

"It was amazing. The lid was really a magnifying glass. She held it out to me and I looked and—"

"Ever been on television? Maybe that's it."

"No, well once, but that was a crowd scene."

"The case, man, for God sake!"

"You'll think I'm crazy, but I saw it with my own eyes. Through the glass, a pin sticking straight up and on the head of it was The Last Supper! Painted!"

Harry nearly swallows an ice cube. "You know the air's pretty thin up there, Steve."

"I'm serious! Right there as plain as day. Jesus and the Apostles, or were they disciples?"

"Painted on the head of a pin."

"Yes," Stevie insists. "Oh, I knew no one would believe me. A collector's dream, stumble into some backwater trading post and make the find of a lifetime. It sounds impossible, but I know what I saw."

"So why didn't you buy it?"

"She wouldn't sell! She said they used to have more but the old man who paints them died. It was the last one. I offered her $200."

Harry catches cowboy scribbling something on a napkin. When he looks to Lena she's staring right at him.

"Maybe she was insulted, Steve." Harry tears his eyes away. "Maybe she gets ten grand for them."

"It was in the bottom of a display case. There were dead flies."

"I'm just wondering..." Barman runs his towel through a puddle. "How would someone go about painting The Last Supper on the head of a pin?"

"He used a hair from his arm," Stevie tells him.

"Oh, right."

"She told me. The old man was her uncle. He used a

hair from his arm and painted between the beats of his heart."

"Come on, nobody could do that."

"Nobody *you* know. This guy lived in the jungle."

Harry gives Steve a long look. "Did I mention the bridge I'm selling?"

"Look, there she goes." Barman nods to Lena heading off to the ladies room. "A quick tinkle, a little makeup, and Bo's on his way."

"Says you." Harry fumbles for a smoke.

"Money in the bank. I've seen it a hundred times."

"Is there a window in that bathroom?"

Lena rejoins cowboy minutes later, but they make no move to leave. Harry checks Stevie's watch. Quarter of and time's a-wasting.

"My ex-father in law to my left," Stevie babbles on. "I forget what I was telling them but the mouth is going and the hands are going and everyone's sitting with tight little smiles. It was a nightmare. And I'm leaving things out, important things, and I know I'm losing them. Suddenly, my hand hits my wine glass, not hard, but just hard enough. Everybody watches as it goes over. Suddenly the old reflexes kick in and my hand shoots out and—"

"You catch it?" Barman hopes against hope.

"More like I whack it. The glass flies across the table and takes out two more glasses. The old man's covered in chardonnay. The whole place falls quiet as a tomb."

Barman sees Lena gather her things. "Okay, guys, Showtime."

She pushes away from the table, gives a little girl wave and turns for the door. Cowboy sits there shaking his head.

"Gentlemen?" Harry lays a hand across the bar. "It appears we have a winner."

Barman reaches for the tip jar. "Now *that* is uncanny!"

Murder in Mexico

"Let that be a lesson to you, men. Never put your money on a man named Bo." Harry wiggles his fingers as the losers tally up. He pockets the bulk of the money, stuffs a ten in the jar and leaves two twenties on the bar.

"Another round for my man Steve, one for yourself and one for Lover Boy there."

"Hey, where you off to?" Stevie grabs an arm. "Stick around for a while."

"No can do." Harry slides from his stool. "Whenever I find myself in a bar at midnight I always wake up in the slammer."

"Listen, Gerry," Stevie hems and haws. "I'm uh...how about having dinner with me tomorrow night. You pick the spot."

"Tomorrow?"

"Why not, a couple of bachelors out on the town? At least meet me for a drink."

"Let me get back to you, Steve. You have a number?"

Stevie jots it on a matchbook. "I'm at the airport inn. If I don't hear from you I'll drop by here tomorrow evening."

"I'll try to make it."

"Excellent!" Stevie smiles. "We can talk about that bridge you mentioned."

"Take care of this guy, would you?" Harry winks to the bartender and wades into the crowd. Cowboy looks right through him as he passes, out the door and into a curbside cab.

***

"He's the one, Harry." Lena taps him on the knee.

"The cowboy? Come on, Lena, everybody knows the guy."

"Not him. Your bar buddy."

Harry's cigarette snaps in two. "I didn't get that."

"Of course he was, Harry. The man couldn't take his eyes off you."

They're in the kitchen hashing it over. Harry waffles; Lena spells it out in three letters.

"Forget it, Lena. You think everyone is gay."

"Me? You're the guy who won't use a urinal."

"That's a health concern."

"You think everyone wants to look at your weenie."

"Well? You seem to think *he* does."

"Believe it, he does. Which has the strange ring of el solution perfecto! Oh come on, even you must see it."

"You're delirious."

"Don't play dumb with me," Lena snaps. "Same game, different players."

Harry paces the length of the counter. The switch up hits him like a safe full of anvils.

"You're not suggesting..."

"That's exactly what I'm suggesting." Lena taps a finger on the table. "There was nothing in the plan that specified gender. What is it, Harry? Suddenly you don't look so good."

"But he can't think *I'M* gay! I mean, look at me."

Lena looks. "So what, you think it was any easier for me fending off Bronco Billy?"

"Barman said he's hung like a horse."

"Hmmmm."

"They were positive you'd leave with him."

"You swine." Lena misses with a kick to his shins. "How much did you soak them for?"

"I don't know. Couple of bills."

"Gimme." She holds a hand out. "Come on, boy. Momma's done her bit and now she's on vacation."

Harry tosses the bills on the table. "This really lights your bulb, doesn't it?"

"Have dinner with him, Harry. What could it hurt?"

"Don't push it, Lena. You're in no position."

"Keep it up, sweetie. You just might scare me."

Harry stares out at the lights of town. "I might figure I don't need you."

"Figure what you want." Lena gets up and eases past him. "Right now Momma needs a bath."

***

They're in bed. "Okay, I'll call him." Moonlight frames the window and laughter floats in over the water.

"Atta boy, Harry." Lena curls into his side.

"It's just dinner. I'll find out what I can about the guy. Could be he's too good to pass up."

"What about the bartender? You three were pretty chummy."

"No problemo. Anyone asks, I'm just a guy named Gerry."

"Why does that worry me?"

"Funny thing is I felt more comfortable as Gerry. I mean I was swapping jokes like a traveling salesman. It's amazing how constricting your own personality can be."

"Well, if it works for you."

"It's like you're a prisoner of yourself. Act a little different and everybody notices. I need to be someone else for a while. I'm sick of being me."

"Oh, it can't be *that* bad."

"I'm serious, Lena. This is our chance to start all over, reinvent ourselves. I'll be more sociable. The guy that lights up the room."

"I'll be a cat person. We'll need a cat."

"We can pick up new habits. I'll work the crossword puzzle over coffee in the morning. Maybe whistle a little tune."

"You can't whistle."

"I'll learn. You'll lie in bed listening and you'll know I'm working the puzzle. Jesus, it's like the dawn of a brand new day."

"The new, improved us."

"I'll call him. What the hell."

"And then you'll kill him."

"Come on, the guy came on to me in a bar. It's a gift horse."

"Ever wonder if you're losing it?"

"Diminished capacity. There. I even have a defense."

***

Stevie's on his second drink when Harry gets there. They take a table on the deck and watch a fat guy strap himself to a kite ski.

"Thanks for coming, Gerry. I didn't think you'd show."

"I would have been here sooner but cabs are scarce."

Stevie sits back and takes in the view. "Great place. Are you a regular?"

"Never been here before. I saw it coming in from the airport."

"By the way, that was some entrance. Every eye followed you across the room."

Harry picks at the corner of a menu.

"The way the sun was reflected in your shades. The easy stride."

"My life, Steve. Like a cheap novel."

"I want to hear all about it."

Harry gives him a sidelong look. "This morning? I walk into the bathroom and there's a monster in my bathtub. No lie, Steve, a five-pound cockroach just lying there."

Stevie's takes a guess. "You smashed it."

"Not me. Something that big is gonna make a mess." Harry drains his drink. "I ring the maid. She picks up the toilet plunger and starts beating the thing, Christ, it was

~98~

horrible. Must have nailed it a dozen times, but I could still hear it scrambling around."

"My God, how gruesome."

"It was the *way* she went at it. Like she does this every day. When it was over, she just handed me the plunger and waltzed off. The thing is covered in gore, just dripping with it, and I'm not getting near that tub. Uh-uh."

"Not very vacation-y."

"I want to know how this thing got into my house."

"They come up through the drain," Stevie explains. "Tragic really, all that way to get bludgeoned in the bathtub."

"The *drain*? Yo, Steve, I know plumbers smaller than this thing."

"Pity the poor plunger."

Harry shudders. "I tried running it under the faucet but it wouldn't wash off."

"One more thankless task."

"I'll tell you one thing. I fell in love with her."

"The maid?"

"The way she wasted the thing. God, it was thrilling."

"Interesting."

The crowd swells for sunset, but the show's a bust, just a ball of red dropping like a rock. Harry orders the oysters while Stevie quizzes the waiter on the salads.

"So anyway, Steve, this..." Harry points to their place settings, "you and me having dinner. That's what this is, right?"

Stevie stifles a smile. "Let me level with you, Ger. I'm a 48-year-old queer who just came out of the closet. Right now I'm trying to get through a nasty medical crisis. I won't bore you with the details but, let's just say the prognosis isn't good."

"I'm sorry to hear that."

"Which part?"

"Well the prognosis."

"The gay part, you're okay with it?"

"Two guys having dinner, that's all it is."

"Because I couldn't get a sense with you, Gerry. Last night. Usually you can pick up on something, but with everything going on..."

Harry lets him twist.

"You're not, are you?"

"Not what?"

Stevie blushes furiously. "God, I have the worst gaydar."

"No problem." Harry waves him off. "I get that all the time. Must be something in the stride."

"I bet wishful thinking has a lot to do with it."

"Know what I think? People make too much of sex. I prefer to deal on a higher level."

"Well, *that's* a relief. I must say you do have a way, Gerry."

"So..." Harry holds a beat. "You're traveling alone?"

"I had to get away from everyone. After a while the concern becomes suffocating."

"Odd you would pick Mexico."

"My first time, would you believe it? No one even knows I'm here."

Harry takes note. "This condition, is it..?"

"Terminal? They say 60-40. That is, if the procedure doesn't kill me. I'll let you in on something, Gerry. When I first booked the trip, the idea was to come down here and end it all."

"But now?"

"Now I just want to relax and enjoy myself. And you know what I enjoy more than anything?" Stevie arches his eyebrows. "Good conversation. What separates us from the animals. And I must say, Gerry, last night, well, I haven't had such fun in years."

"You seemed in good spirits."

"That's just it, I *was* in good spirits. Thanks to you.

Murder in Mexico

You couldn't know it, but you were drawing me out of my shell. I can't describe how wonderful it felt."

Harry shrugs. "Pleasure's all mine."

"I'm serious. It was worth every cent. What do you do, Gerry, if I may be so bold?"

"Restaurant supply." Harry wings it. "Grim but profitable."

"East coast?"

"Jersey, South Dullsville."

"I grew up in Bozeman. Montana."

"You big sky guy, you."

"Predictable nightmare childhood. My dad was a rancher, my bothers were jocks, and I was the family punching bag."

"So you walked away from it. Good for you."

"More like fled, screaming into the night."

"Works for me."

"After cutting the brake lines on the family station wagon and stabbing my bother with a fork."

"Hey, you do what it takes."

"My shining hour to this day. Alas, they were too drunk to chase me."

Harry has to laugh. "I once drove across Montana in a VW bus with flowers painted all over."

"And lived?"

"It was brutal. Three miles in, someone took a shot at me."

"Typical Montanese."

"And the cops...the way they kept pulling me over you'd think I had a body strapped to the hood."

"The Angry State. What made you do it?"

"I had a carload of Jersey seashells. I wanted to scatter them on the beach in Malibu."

"What on earth for?"

Harry shrugs. "I wanted to have an effect, screw things up. Plus I had a car."

~101~

"I find driving long distance painful," Stevie winces, "the boredom, the confinement, the excruciating passage of time."

"Oh it's agony, but addicting." Harry taps a swizzle stick. "You develop a road personality, a self you didn't know was in you. Then one drizzly evening you find yourself passing over the refineries, wired on caffeine and cigarettes, thinking *this* is somehow essential."

Stevie blanches. "The seedy side does nothing for me."

"Drive three hundred miles inland and it's all underbelly. East to Midwest will break your heart. Past the Rockies it's even worse. Out there it's another planet."

"Okay, I'm sold. When do we leave?"

Their food arrives and they hop through topics, mostly Stevie's life in the closet and his coming out travails in Phoenix. Funny stuff, really, and Harry laughs out loud. Other patrons are drawn to their banter, and good cheer spills over the room. By dessert, Harry's picked around enough to piece it together, big heart and a quick wit, playing out a shitty hand. The guy already misses himself.

"This treatment you mentioned. What about it, Steve?"

"Oh, let's not talk about that. I made a promise to myself not to dwell on the bad things."

"I'm interested. Humor me."

Stevie makes a face. "The procedure is strictly last ditch. The thing you do before they throw in the towel. Like sandbagging. One day you're manning the barricades, the next day you're living on the roof."

"I might be out of line here, but that sounds like the wrong way to approach it."

Stevie reaches for the champagne. "I reserve the right to my melodrama."

"When will you be leaving here?"

"I have to fly to LA next week. That's where she

lives."

"Who?"

"My daughter, of course."

"Must be tough on her."

"Please," Stevie holds a hand up. "Happier subject."

"Sorry."

"Now then..." Stevie fills both glasses. "Where are you staying, Gerry?"

"I've got a little place in town."

"How nice. The hotels are a nightmare, you know. Bussing us in like cattle, wandering the streets like Sebastian in 'Suddenly Last Summer.' I keep waiting for the children to pounce." Stevie forces a laugh. "So, are you with anyone?"

"I'm a firm believer in separate vacations."

"Ah, a kindred spirit."

"The thing is, when you travel with someone you feel compelled to fill the time. I like to sit back and do nothing."

"Now see? I have to get out and see the sights. So much work. This morning I wanted to lay there and watch TV, but I couldn't let myself."

"Try some of the local reefer," Harry jokes. "Two hits and you won't leave the room, I promise you."

"I'm afraid my psyche is too fragile for that. I'm the sort who has bad Tylenol trips."

"Too bad. Under the proper influence, Mexican TV can be mesmerizing."

"I'm curious, Gerry. Do you think we share a certain resemblance?"

Harry doesn't flinch. "I suppose, now that you mention it."

"Yes, we're a definite type." Stevie wiggles with delight. "Same build, same jaw line. I bet these people think we're brothers."

"You think?"

"The irony is my *real* brothers look like Dan

Blocker."

"You've held up well, Steve, for a 48-year-old punching bag."

"Thank you." His eyes shine over the rim of his glass. "I'll take that as a compliment."

Harry tosses his napkin on the table. "Come back to my place with me."

"Hmmmm."

"For a nightcap. I've got something you might like."

"How can I be sure your intentions are honorable?"

Harry grins. "We can walk. It isn't far."

"I warn you. Any funny business and I call the federales."

***

Lena watches the Gila monster locked in a square of moonlight.

"Go away."

The lizard retreats into the shadows. She sets the ashtray on the table, fingers an ice cube from her glass and bounces it across the floor. The damn thing doesn't budge. Lena turns to the mirror and searches her reflection.

"You will not go through with this."

***

Stevie stumbles on a cobblestone, knows he's rambling but can't help himself. "My mother's bras made her tits look pointy. The Jayne Mansfield effect, real pointy and defiant. When she hugged me, which was rare enough, I could feel the underpinnings."

"Hold up, Steve. This clown has a headlight out."

"A fortification. That's what it felt like. Naturally I thought the female breast was hard and solid, like a muscle."

"Okay. We can cross here."

Murder in Mexico

"The first time I was intimate with a girl? I was dumbstruck. These soft things, almost gooey, I thought there was something wrong with her. I tell you, Gerry, I couldn't stand to touch them."

"You'd like the new ones. Tough as shoe leather."

"But what really killed it for me..." Stevie clutches Harry's sleeve. "Menstruation. Every month an open wound. Explain to me how you process this?"

"That's easy. I'm Catholic."

"I was grossly unprepared. Oh, I'd seen Playboy, but there was no porn in Bozeman. I'd never seen *it* before. And when I finally *did*, it scared me half to death."

"A nasty business, this sex."

"I had male crushes, but they weren't physical. I wanted a Spin and Marty thing, but even *they* were too, I don't know, furtive. I was sexually ambivalent. I loved my wife and I loved my lovers. What about your wife, Ger?"

"I worried she would kill me in my sleep."

Stevie glances up the road. "You didn't tell me you lived on a mountain top."

"We're almost there. Another block."

***

Lena moves like a shadow through the dim rooms. Harry should have been back long ago, dinner and drinks, four hours now. She wonders what this means, but it could mean anything. It's a good sign, she decides. They've hit it off and now Harry sees the whole thing for what it is. A bad idea run amuck, a fatal mistake they won't have to make.

She passes into the kitchen, freshens her drink, picks an orange from the bowl on the counter. The room rings in silence, the house so still she can hear breakers in the distance. It was a mistake to let Harry go off on his own. Something bad always happens when she's not there to watch him. This man, Steve, what do they know about him? Who does he know here? Where the hell are they?

"Come on Harry," she whispers at the window. Cool air filters in from the terrace and her arms pebble in goose bumps. Then she's back in the bathroom, looking at herself, looking at the death drugs. She breaks the seal on the syringe and touches it to the orange skin. As the tip pierces the surface she hears voices down the hill.

***

Harry enters bearing drinks. The Gila monster flicks his tongue.

"A platonic nightcap, could there really be such a thing?" Stevie takes the dosed one and settles back in the sofa. "Here's to you, Mr. Lizard."

"I've grown quite attached to him, actually." Harry returns to the kitchen. "Like sharing your house with the distant past."

"My brother had a tarantula when we were kids. He got it to terrorize me, but my mother's shaky grasp made that dicey so he soon lost interest. For months it just lay there pining for the desert. Then one day I came home and found the terrarium on the floor in a million pieces. The cat must have knocked it off the shelf. My heart stopped when I saw it. Of course, the tarantula was nowhere to be seen. Where are you going, Gerry?"

"Go on," Harry calls from the hallway. "I can hear you."

"It's the classic nightmare, when you think about it. You know it's somewhere, but where?"

Harry pushes into the bedroom. Lena looks up from the bed, arms folded, needle pointed out.

"Oh man, we've got a live one," Harry whispers. "Get that thing ready."

"Who is he, Harry?"

Murder in Mexico

"He's nobody. He's our ticket out."

Lena looks at him like she's never seen him before.

"I used your measure of Seconal. That should do it, right?"

"I'm shaking, Harry."

"That's enough, right?" He goes to her. "Lena, help me out here!"

Nothing. Harry ducks out and hollers down. "So what did you do? About the spider."

Stevie laughs to think. "Mother and I spent the summer in a tent in the living room."

Harry rejoins him. "That's pretty resourceful."

"It was a living hell! Every time I picked up a towel or opened a drawer I'd expect the damn thing to leap on me."

"What, no plunger?"

"Plus the close quarters, my mother's gastrit..." He breaks off in a yawn. "Coldest winter on record."

"Killed it?"

Stevie's eyes glaze over. "Must have, killed everything else. Ooh, that chocolate mousse is killing me, Gerry."

A dog barks deep in the night.

"How was San Francisco anyway?" Harry pushes.

"Elitist, self-imp...a shnotty little town."

"You forgot cynical."

"Hmmm?"

"Cynical? San Francisco?"

"Bah." He waves a hand. "Rank amateurs. San Frisco still wants to be loved. For true cynicism you must go to Paris."

"France?"

"Ab-so-loot..." Stevie rubs a hand over his face.

"Paris, France, Steve?"

"Paris, yes." He curls in a ball. "All the European pretensions... plus...it's in Europe. I got mugged by a Paki near Clingan...the flea market."

"How exotic."

"The man spoke perfect French." Stevie hiccups once and fades out.

Harry leans forward. "This condition of yours. Tell me about it."

"Lilly, oh God please help."

Lilly? Or was it liver? Something about his liver?

"Steve?"

"Just a few days, then...then they can..."

"Steve?"

"No cure...hopelesh."

"Can you hear me, Steve?"

***

Lena hasn't moved a muscle. Harry blows in then out, then in again.

"He's out cold." He pries the syringe from her hand. "We can't pass this up, Lena."

Her name sounds somehow different.

"Wait," she whimpers.

"Listen to me." Harry takes her by the shoulders. "He's dying, Lena. The man came here to kill himself."

"What?"

"We'll be doing him a favor. Don't you see?"

"Dying? Of what?"

"Something, I don't know, AIDS? He said the prognosis is hopeless."

"He told you he has AIDS?"

"Yes." He gives her a shake. "The man is suicidal. I know it's sudden, but we'll never get a chance like this again. It's fate, Lena!"

"Oh, Harry."

"Look, we said we'd see how it goes. Well, now it's going and look what we've got. It's over for this guy. He's already a statistic. And he's suffering, Lena. You saw

Gerry. You know what happens in the end, the wasting."

Lena buries her face in her hands.

"I know it's a nightmare. Until he told me there was no way I could go through with it. What you said before, I do like the guy. But he's a dead man looking for a way out. We'd be sparing him the worst."

"You can talk yourself into anything."

"What do you mean? Instead of dying piece by piece, he'll go a little earlier, before the bad stuff. We can live with that, Lena. I know we can."

"How?"

Harry pulls her hands away. "If we don't, he'll soon be just as dead, and we'll get nothing."

"What about the autopsy?" She grabs at anything.

"What about it?"

"Whatever's wrong with him, they'll find it. How do I explain my husband having AIDS?"

"You don't have to explain. First of all they may miss it. If not, you say you didn't know, or you suspected he was gay or on the needle, or anything."

"Anything? Hey, Harry, when you're getting away with murder you want to have your story straight."

"See, now you're making problems for yourself. If you don't know anything you don't need a story."

Lena moves away. "It's madness, Harry."

"Madness? What's left for this guy? If he were a dog they'd put him under. If I offered, he'd probably insist." Harry turns away. "You don't have to do anything, Lena. I'll take care of it, just like you showed me."

He walks away and she sees him clearly, head down, shoulders hunched, syringe in hand. Something comes over her, warm and visceral, the drag of time running down. She hears the clink of a belt buckle and shoes hitting the floor. Harry's gone a long time and she grips the mattress to keep from going to him. Then he's there in the silence, a shape in the doorway.

"Lena?"

***

She wraps herself up to hold it together, chews the edge of the blanket to keep from shivering. Harry rushes from room to room, switching on lights then switching them off again. Then he's gone for a while and she hears him in the bathroom, feels the dead presence in the other room.

"Wallet, wallet," Harry mutters. Lena moves to the doorway, sees Stevie naked and spread eagle, Harry going through his pants, piling things on the table. Finds the wallet and a hotel keycard, checks the driver's license and the cash.

"You okay, baby?" he asks for the tenth time.

She makes herself ask, "Did you feel for a pulse?"

"I couldn't feel anything. Help me get my pajamas on him."

She crosses over and takes Stevie's wrist. Nothing.

"What are you going to do?"

"Check him out of the hotel." Harry stuffs Stevie's arms through his sleeves. "There's a bus leaving in ten minutes."

"You're leaving me with *him*?"

"One hour." He pulls a foot through the pant leg. "Maybe less. Don't do anything until I get back."

"But why?"

"Guy checks out, who cares where he's going? We don't want anyone looking for him until we're done."

"I can't stay here with him."

"Then *you* go! We should have rented a car, damn it."

Lena looks to Stevie staring up at the ceiling. "All right, Harry. I'll stay here."

"One hour." He pulls on Stevie's jacket. "Think about what you're gonna tell the cops."

"The cops."

"When I'm gone. Lena, don't go to pieces on me now."

***

He takes the bus to hotel row, caught in the crush of swing shift and last call stragglers, windows opened wide but the air thick with semi consciousness. They take the coast road curving south and out to the point. The hotels gleam like apparitions.

"In and out." He matches hotel logos to Stevie's keycard. Wind whips the saplings lashed to the median. Walls of bedrooms glassed up and sealed in stainless steel, nothing native but the latitude and the faint smell of shit. Harry stands and watches, a lone figure in the thin vapor light. A kid snoozes at the desk. A couple exits the elevator past a black man pushing a floor polisher. Harry rolls up his collar and closes in, through the door and straight to the stairway. Cables clanking, TV's mumbling, three flights up in half a minute. His lungs wheeze as he tiptoes down the hall. The card trips the lock and he pushes in without a sound.

He runs down his mental checklist, first the rubber gloves then the drapes then the bathroom light. A suitcase lies open on the bed. Harry moves around it, scooping things into the travel bag. He checks the desk and dresser, the closet shelves, under the bed. When he's finished he forces himself to do it again, then once more in reverse order.

"Medicine chest, check, cabinets, check, bath tub check."

Last on the list, a call to the desk. Harry punches up the number and the snoozer answers.

"Front desk."

"Hi, yeah..." He checks Stevie's Visa card. "This is

Mr. Winslow in 3E. I forgot what day I'm supposed to leave. Could you please check my reservation?"

"Let's see, 3E, says here you're paid up through the weekend."

"Thank you so much."

Four days before the cops get involved, time enough to wrap things up unless Harry's missing something. He flips through Stevie's picture ID, assorted smiles and hairstyles. Ducks into the bathroom for comparison, not exactly twins, but close enough for the barely interested. Grabs the bags, starts for the door, locks in his tracks as a knock sounds.

"Stevie?" a soft voice, almost feminine. "Hey, you in there? It's Roland."

The knob turns and Harry presses to the wall, thinks body slam and blunt force trauma, anything he can get his hands on.

"Come on Stevie. You can't still be mad at me."

The knob jiggles, the voice grumbles, the footsteps slowly recede. Harry can't move, can't breathe, knows only that he must get out without Roland seeing him. He puts an ear to the door, forces himself to count to one hundred, then fifty, twice. Tugs it open and bolts down the hall to the exit sign. He stumbles at the stairs, and the travel bag crashes to the landing, crap spilling out, tubes and sprays, pills in every direction. Harry scrambles after, catches a strap on the stair post and quick glimpse of his feet flying, suitcase flapping open, clothes raining down in an avalanche of evidence. He lies in a heap for a good half-minute listening for the rush of footsteps. A full minute, no one comes.

Somehow he manages to stuff everything back together. Crosses the lobby, sees floor polisher gabbing with a trucker at the delivery entrance. Harry wills them to turn away then hobbles past when they actually do, out the door and across the parking lot, stopping at the dumpsters to bury the bags.

Murder in Mexico

***

"And don't volunteer anything. The less you say, the less you have to remember. Just act like you're in shock." Harry pockets both wallets.

"Act?" Lena's voice comes from the shadows.

"Don't try to help them. If they don't ask you for something, don't give it to them."

"I'm cold."

"Never underestimate the power of incompetence, Lena. It's what made the Third World what it is today."

"What about that?" She points to the syringe on the counter.

"I'll get rid of everything. Wait a half hour after I'm gone then call the police."

Lena dabs her nose with a tissue.

"Hey..." Harry kneels down next to her. "Don't come apart on me now, Lena. Listen, you don't have to lie. You don't have to remember anything except *that's* your husband and he's dead."

Lena can't bring herself to look.

"Don't forget. When you get home you place an ad in the Catskill classifieds, like we said. One of those thank you God messages with a PV for Puerto Vallarta so I'll know everything's okay."

"But which paper?"

"All of them. How many could they have?"

"When will I hear from you?"

"I told you." Harry wipes down the glasses. "I'll call you on the first...at the market. Twelve noon, the pay phone on Christian."

"That's two weeks!"

"Has to be that way, Lena. Any contact will trip us up."

"That's crazy. Get a burner cell phone. They're untraceable."

"That's just what they want you to think. We call, we get caught."

"By the first I might be in the slammer."

"Don't think like that, Lena. The only way it works. No contact."

Lena's eyes fill with tears. "I don't think I can do it, Harry."

"Okay, fine." Harry wags a hand at Stevie. "We'll just tell them he forced his way in and killed himself on our couch."

"I never thought you'd really go through with it."

"No problem, just a little miscommunication. Hey, my fault completely."

"Don't hate me, Harry."

"No, hey, we go on just like always except for the jobs and the rosy future."

Lena says nothing.

Harry shrugs and reaches for the phone.

"Who are you calling?"

"I had no right to get you involved in this. I must...yes, give me 911, please."

"Hang it up, Harry."

"Hi, yes, I'm sorry, 9—"

Lena pushes the button. "Stop."

Harry moves her hand and dials again. "It's okay. I'll tell them you weren't even here."

"It won't change anything." She takes the phone from him. "He's dead no matter what we do." They look to Stevie, head cocked, eyes still locked on the ceiling.

"Well, yeah, but now you've got to deal with police and then you have to pretend to be a widow. I don't know what I was thinking. It's way too much to ask."

"We never talked about this part of it. What it does to us?"

"We'll just tell the truth. We came home from the bar. We had a drink and the guy had a heart attack. They'll go for it."

"No, no, I'm okay."

"You're not okay." Harry pulls out the stops. "I've done this to you and I'll never forgive myself. Hell, I spent three days trying to peddle your ass and now I've finally killed somebody. You should get as far away from me as you can."

"It's almost like we owe it to him."

"You think?"

"We've come this far."

"Yeah..." He looks again to Stevie. "It would be a shame."

"Be careful, Harry." She hugs him to her. "You got enough money?"

Harry sneaks a peek at his watch. "Not a problem. The guy had a wad."

CHAPTER NINE

Once when Lena was a girl, her parents left her behind in a restaurant. It was a family gathering, the grownups had been drinking, and somehow no one missed her until they got home. Lena sat alone in the restaurant lobby, trying not to attract attention. She can still remember cars pulling up outside, the well-fed look of families going home. Someone finally noticed and she was taken to the manager's office. They were nice enough, but when no one came to claim her, talk turned to the police.

"No, please," she begged them. "Someone will come soon."

"Don't worry," the manager told her. "The police are your friends."

Lena was young but she had watched TV. Cops were always the worst thing that could happen. Her father showed up before it got that far, but she never forgot the chill.

"Are you cold, Senora? I can get you a wrap."

"I'm okay."

"Again, our condolences for your misfortune." The lieutenant nods to the medics circling the body.

"Thank you." She forces her hands between her knees. "I guess it hasn't hit me yet."

"Mrs. Watts, you say your husband had a heart condition?" the man in the suit asks her.

"It ran in the family. But Harry never went to the doctor."

"I see, so we can assume."

"I suppose so, yes. Please, could you cover him at

least?"

The lieutenant smiles sadly. "I'm sorry, the lab team will be done soon. If you like we could use the other room?"

"I don't want to leave him."

"Of course. We understand what you're going through. Tragedies like this are rare in Puerto Vallarta, but not unheard of. We'll try to make this as painless as possible."

There's a commotion outside, and a third cop enters with a silver haired man in a burgundy bathrobe.

"What is it, Morales?" The man stops when he sees Stevie. "Oh my goodness."

The lieutenant sighs. "Heart attack, apparently."

"I saw the police cars from my window. Can I be of any assistance?"

The lieutenant turns to Lena. "Mrs. Watts, this is Mr. Santos. He's with the Chamber of Commerce."

Lena smiles weakly.

"Poor thing. She's freezing." Santos shrugs out of the robe and wraps it over her shoulders. "Can I get you anything?"

"I'm sorry, I really can't think straight."

"Of course you can't. This is a terrible thing. Sergeant Morales is a good friend of mine. Excellent man."

"That's Lieutenant," Morales grumbles.

"Right, and in light of the circumstances, the late hour, the traumatic—"

"Please..." Lena sniffles. "I don't think I can stay here tonight."

"Don't worry about a thing. I'll book you a room in the hotel. Would you excuse us for a minute?" Santos takes Morales by the arm and guides him outside. They huddle by the pool in quiet discussion, returning moments later with a plan of action.

"My heartfelt sympathies, Mrs. Watts." Santos stands

beside her. "Please, allow me to speak frankly. As head of the Chamber of Commerce I am not without influence in official circles. I would be grateful if you would allow me to represent you in this unfortunate matter."

"Mr. Santos is also an attorney," the lieutenant explains.

"I can assure you that you will not be inconvenienced any more than is absolutely necessary."

Lena lets a tear roll down. "Oh, how can I thank you?"

Santos takes her hand. "I am at your service. I've persuaded Sergeant Morales to forego questioning until tomorrow. If you have no objections I will call a taxi to take you to the hotel."

"Thank you so much."

While he's on the phone, a team wanders in from the coroner's office. Lena watches as they empty Stevie's pajama pockets, sealing things up in a clear plastic bag. The lieutenant flips through the wallet without an expression, so far, so good. If she can latch on to this Santos, he might just waltz her through the investigation.

"A taxi will be here shortly," he calls over and signals someone for a pencil. Handsome in his slippers and pin stripe pajamas. The way he seems to be taking over, cutting through the bullshit like he always runs the show. Sometimes what you get is exactly what you need.

"I'll have to pack a few things." She forces herself to her feet.

"Take your time. I've got a few more calls to make."

Calls to make, a lawyer, by God. Just popping up like that. An hour into it, and the whole mess is out of her hands. She smiles to herself and heads for the bedroom. One of the cops falls in behind her, but Santos heads him off.

"A little privacy, captain, if you please."

Mover and shaker, puller of strings, oh, if Harry could

only see this. She grabs her new dress, some shorts and tank tops, the ones her nipples show through.

"Forgive me for interfering." Santos escorts her to the waiting cab. "I know you must be in a state of shock. It will be better for me to stay here. I am accustomed to dealing with the authorities, and my presence will serve to expedite matters."

"I don't know how to thank you."

"Nonsense. It's the very least I can do. Is there someone I could contact for you? Family?"

"I'll have to do it. I just can't believe this."

"Be strong," Santos says. "Just remember you are not alone."

"I'll never be able to repay you."

"Repay me? Don't worry yourself. Try and get some rest. I will call for you tomorrow. Say, nine-ish?"

***

He arrives on the dot in a seersucker suit and Panama hat, native son, patriarch, a man who commands attention just walking down the street.

"My friends call me Carlos. May I call you Lena?"

"Please."

"There are a number of details we should discuss that might strike you as, well, intrusive. I trust you will bear with me."

"I'm okay, really, Carlos."

"Do you have children, Lena?"

"No. Too selfish, I guess. That must sound terrible."

"Not at all." He presses a hand to the small of her back. "I, too, am childless by choice."

"Harry worried about dying young, like his dad."

"A noble sentiment, though children can be a comfort at times like this."

"I was the only family he had."

"He could do worse, I assure you."

The widow Watts goes to work. "Harry really loved this. The tropics, you know, especially Mexico. Ever since we were kids he'd say, 'someday I'm gonna live there.'"

"I'm afraid I would have liked your Harry."

"Afraid? Why?"

"Well, I just mean it's a pity we'll never have the chance to be friends."

"Yes, you would have liked him. And he'd be grateful to you for what you've done, terribly grateful."

"I'm sure in my position he would do the same."

"Truth is, I'm no good in a crisis. Things go wrong and I fall to pieces. Harry knew that."

"You've done no such thing. Considering the circumstances your composure is quite admirable."

Lena swings her arms like a schoolgirl. "Viva Mexico, is that how you say it?"

"Viva Mexico, si."

"Yeah, Harry was nuts about it. He had a saying 'when it's time for me to go, lay me down in old Mexico.'"

"I never heard this expression."

"The cold really bothered Harry. He worried about it."

"Cold?"

"And what happens to you after, you know. That's why he wanted to be cremated."

"He discussed this with you?"

"Oh sure. He had this big thing about dying. Sort of an obsession, death and decomposition, he never shut up about it."

"Forgive me. Americans have such peculiar ways."

"Now I have to ship him home in February. God knows what *that* will cost me. I swear Harry never had any luck."

"Tell me, Lena, do you have any relatives here in Mexico?"

"No. Why do you ask, Carlos?"

"Well, sometimes arrangements can be made."
"Arrangements?"

Santos flashes his can-do smile and takes Lena by the elbow. "Let's just get this business with Morales over with. Then we'll see what I can do."

***

Harry still can't get over it. Passive aggressive never works with Lena, but it was the only thing he could think of. The 911 call clinched it. Do they even have 911 in Mexico? Actually dialed the fucking number and pretended to speak with someone, fast on his feet just like the old days. Lena's a whiz at matching wits, but this time he pushed the right button.

Too fucking much, yeah.

Just killed a guy, now he's sitting on a plane laughing. What a sick fuck he's turned out to be. Cold blooded killer with a shit sense of humor. Never thought his conscience would be a problem, but laughing about it? That's disturbing. And then he thinks of something else, something hard to express, but painful to realize. Harry's always considered himself a decent sort. Not a saint maybe, but someone you could trust. That part of him has changed forever. A decent guy doesn't take out a stranger. A decent guy doesn't let you grab the check before he kills you.

Steve was a class act, Harry has to admit, a tad faggy but clever. Best back and forth he's had in years. Now he's dead and it's on Harry's head.

But he was going to die soon, anyway! They really did spare him the messy part, the pain and suffering. Steve wouldn't have handled it well would be Harry's bet, as if his bets ever paid off. Might have handled it like a trooper, for all he really knows. Not that he's going to beat himself up about it, but a heavy load is nothing to laugh about.

He *did* say he was going to die. Harry distinctly

remembers. Not in those words, but that was the inference. Hopeless, that's what he said. Hopeless means without hope, that simple. But what if it wasn't that simple? What if hopeless really meant incurable or inoperable? Steve might've lived with whatever for years before it killed him.

The last ditch something, the stuff about the sand bags, it starts to come back to him. Whatever treatment Steve was getting wasn't working and that meant curtains. It *had* to, otherwise why come down here to kill yourself. He *did* say *that*. Absolutely said that in the restaurant, or maybe it was the bar, either one. But if he can't even be sure of which one, how can he be...

For Christ sake, think about something else. Think about what Lena's going through and how he could leave her in the lurch like that. But, of course, that's even worse. And it's not her end that really worries him. Try to relax, read a magazine. He leafs through the In Flight in half a minute.

"Excuse me, miss?" He hails an attendant. "Do you happen to know if Mexico has the 911 Emergency response system?"

"No, sorry. Maybe I can find that out for you."

"In Mexico?" a guy three seats up hollers back to him. "No way, Jose, they can't count that high."

Harry gives him a fuck-off wave.

Why get worked up about nothing? What he couldn't plan for, the disorienting effects of killing somebody. The plane doesn't help with the weird acoustics and all that sky. Maybe shut his eyes, try to catch a nap. By nightfall he'll be in the Catskill Mountains and Harry J Watts will cease to exist. Takes nerves of steel to do what he did, steel nerves and a strong stomach, fumbling around with a dead guy's dick. But he did it, and the checks will soon come rolling in. Think about *that* for a while, why don't you? What you can buy!

They should top off at over a million with the

insurance. A million bucks, how 'bout that? They'll get a nice place in the country, one of those log cabins they're building now, deer and the antelope playing on the hillside. Quit the city for once and for all. Still nice in the Catskills, scenery to die for and low taxes; he had checked into it. They can get back to the land and still be a train ride from Times Square. A cabin, an SUV big as a bulldozer, the rest Lena can spend as she pleases. All of it, until death do them part.

Yeah, the 911 call was brilliant. To quit when the guy's already dead, Harry's play put it all on Lena. More of that cold blood, but what choice did he have? She's in it now, that's the key. The grieving widow better be good; Lena was born to the role. If the fake phone call hadn't worked, he would have threatened to kill himself. When there's no turning back you do what it takes. What's emotional blackmail compared to killing someone for no good reason. Right now, on a slab at city morgue, Steve is stitched up from stem to sternum.

He tries to find something on the headset to distract himself, a bluegrass channel, NPR, classic rock, as if we haven't had a belly full. He finds a spot on the band that's just static, the low hiss of ambience, the whitest noise...

And who the hell was Roland, anyway? And why was Steve mad at him? Steve never mentioned the guy, but why would he? Did they know each other, or was Roland just another homo cruising the hallways. Harry shouldn't think about him, the one fly in the ointment, if he doesn't count the snoozer at the desk. Which he is definitely not counting, since the kid never looked up from the console, or whatever it—

Console! Good Christ, the whole thing must be on security tape! Oh Jesus, don't do this, don't, just think, *think*, what would they see? A tall guy in Steve's jacket and tie. So they see his face, what could it tell them? But what if there were cameras at the restaurant? And is it standard procedure to review security tapes? What the hell does he know, anyway?

    Okay, all right, there's bound to be doubts in this sort of thing. Murder, what it does to you, the ways you can trip up, give yourself away. They've written a thousand books about it. Harry couldn't name one, but it's a theme. How the crime consumes the criminal. Never thought of himself as a criminal, but how else to put it? Capital crime, at that, the big one, homicide, how they put so much into catching the killers. Always some gumshoe mad to get to the bottom of things, at least on television. Might try and figure a defense, now that he's got some time on his hands. Just in case. Getting caught isn't always the end. Diminished capacity, like he said to Lena. He's seen them pull the fast ones on television. The daily cop show bombardment, watch enough and you'll consider it. The Dick Wolf defense, he could see that working, hears the grumbles from the gallery as they read the verdict. Tough luck, Jack, can't win 'em all.

    He orders a drink as they roll the movie, something Cusack with that girl who used to be on ER. What's her name, Lena would know, can't really get into it, petty intrigue, office romance or some shit. Cusack going for the cheap laughs, stupid stuff, Hollywood drivel. Harry closes his eyes, thinks of Lena back at the casa. To walk off and leave her, how to square that, left to face the cops and questions, the dirty work, almost all of it. Anyone can kill. Okay, maybe not everyone, but what's whacking a guy compared to that whole show? Jesus, it's unconscionable. If they suspect anything they'll put her through the wringer. Lena's a tough nut, but who knows what tricks the federales have up their sleeves? Dumping it on her, who would do that? If he could only see what she's doing right now. See what she's up against and how she's handling it.

***

"Thank you both for coming." Morales waves them inside. "I trust Mr. Santos has been of assistance?"

"He's been wonderful." Lena gushes. "I don't know where I'd be without him."

"Please, sit down." he gestures to two chairs facing the desk.

"Mrs. Watts is anxious to make her arrangements." Santos settles Lena in. "I've explained to her the formalities involved here."

"As the law requires."

"And the bureaucracy." Santos nods sagely. "I would take it as a personal favor if we could make it brief. My client has a rough enough road ahead."

"Of course. What we need to establish is an approximate time of death. I wonder, Mrs. Watts, when was the last time you saw your husband?"

"You mean alive?"

"Yes. Understand it's just standard procedure."

"Well, I went to bed around midnight. Harry wanted to watch the ball scores."

"Ah, baseball, he was a fan?"

"Big fan, baseball, football, you name it."

"So you heard nothing, a groan perhaps?"

Santos drums his fingers. "I'm sure Mrs. Watts would have mentioned any indications of distress."

"The memory is a peculiar thing," Morales counters. "Sometimes one does not realize what one remembers until later."

"I was out like a light," Lena tells him. "I didn't hear anything."

"You discovered Mr. Watts around three AM, did you say?"

"It was still dark out. I didn't see a clock."

Morales looks to Santos then jots something in his report. "So we can estimate your husband died between midnight and three AM."

"Yes, I woke up and I could hear the TV. I thought Harry had fallen asleep. He does that a lot."

"Did your husband suffer from any food allergies or immune system problems?"

"Like I said, Harry didn't go to the doctor. He wasn't allergic to anything that I know of."

Morales makes a longer notation. Santos clears his throat.

"You were in Puerto Vallarta on vacation, correct?"

"Yes, our first in ten years."

"Mr. Watts was quite enamored of the area," Santos interjects. "He expressed great admiration for the climate and culture."

"Oh, Harry loved Mexico. Wore you out with it."

"Please excuse the suggestion, but was your husband ever convicted of a felony?"

"Oh no. He was a straight shooter, Harry. Ask anyone."

"And your marriage, it was satisfactory?"

Lena looks to Santos.

"My clients were childhood sweethearts, Sarg...Lieutenant," Santos snaps. "They've spent virtually their whole lives together. It's understandable, your official inquiry, but this is obviously a case of natural causes."

"Very unfortunate," Morales concurs.

"And, of course as a guest of our country, an American guest in good standing, I think we can dispense with questions of Mrs. Watts marital situation."

"Forgive me, yes." Morales wilts. "We can waive that information."

Santos gives Lena a wink. "An incurable gentleman, my friend Morales, it's one of the reasons I supported him in his campaign. In a town like this, you need someone with a sense of compassion."

"You're too kind." Morales blushes.

"Nonsense. I was just telling Victor that the

department has an air of professionalism of late, so important for a resort town, very important. And Victor agreed."

"Who's Victor?" Lena wonders.

"Jose Victor, our mayor," Morales explains.

"Let's do this, Lieutenant..." Santos leans forward. "I'll take these papers back to my office and go over them. I'll get Mrs. Watts to comply with everything essential and get them back to you tomorrow."

"I suppose we could—"

"It would be a shame to waste such a beautiful day on grim details. After all, Lieutenant..." Santos gestures to the window. "It's what these people come here for, eh?"

"Yes, yes indeed." Morales shuffles papers into a folder. "There are some forms that have to be signed, and the certificate will have to wait for the Medical Examiners report. But given the shock of this tragic ordeal, I see no reason to delay you further."

"Excellent!" Santos springs to his feet. "Oh, by the way, given Mr. Watts' fondness for the area, Mrs. Watts has requested that her husband's remains be interred here, in the country he loved. I trust that won't be a problem."

"It's an unusual request." Morales sets the folder down. "But I think arrangements might be made."

"Very good, Lieutenant." Santos claps him on the back. "I must say I like the way you get things done."

"Yes, thank you very much." Lena fights the urge to hug. "I'll never forget you, both of you."

The men stand side by side, grinning like idiots.

***

Harry stares out at the lights of New Jersey. He knows it's New Jersey because the pilot just pointed out Newark airport, lit up like Vegas off the starboard bow. Actually called it the starboard bow, and Harry makes a note of it.

Set to touch down in fifteen minutes. He hears the whir of landing gear, feels the sinking dread as they lean into a turn.

From Newark he will fly to Albany then rent a car for the last leg. Wishes he was in the car already, sealed off with miles ahead of him, time alone to reflect. But that's still hours away, doesn't even know why he's looking forward to it, since brooding makes the bad thing worse. But he's been around people all day, and he's weary of the contact, the bored detachment of the non-homicidal.

But he couldn't know about that. Just as likely one, or even several *have* killed, in passion, for gain, or simply by accident. No, an accident isn't murder. Accidents are accidents. Okay, so if you divided the number of people by the number of murders you'd get a percentage of murderers to general population. Get a feel for how common it really is, or how uncommon. Harry has no way to determine these numbers, but a ballpark figure is easy to come up with. Twenty thousand US murders a year sounds good. It might be way off, but he'd bet it's close. Divided by, say, 300 million, to keep it manageable. That would be...let's see...

Never Harry's strong suit, math. Lena would have it down to the decimal in seconds, but he doesn't want to think about Lena now. What's happening to her, whether they've gotten to her, so he just picks a number out of a hat, one in a hundred, say. Out of every hundred people you get one murderer. Then he forgets why he's trying to figure it out, what number he was trying to come up with. To get a feel for how many killers are out there. That's it, the chances of coming in contact with one. How to spot them is the problem. Do they have a look? There must come a time when it doesn't weigh on you. Eventually you forget, or at least don't dwell on it so much.

So there's a murderer on board, according to that equation, possibly two, which doesn't seem like a lot. Two murderers, all these people, their combined years on the planet. Turns out murderers are few and far between, when he thinks about it. And now he is one. And then the equally plausible chance he's the *only* one, just him.

***

"You've been a life saver, Carlos. You must let me repay you."

"I wouldn't hear of it." Santos looks up from his menu. "You've been through a tremendous ordeal, Lena. I'm just happy I could help."

"No really. Your time must be valuable."

"My duties at the Chamber of Commerce are not so taxing." He sets the menu down. "Quite frankly, Lena, I'm grateful for an excuse to get out of the house. Since my wife died, I'm afraid I've become a bit of a recluse."

"I'm so sorry."

"It is I who should be thanking you." Santos smiles. "To be quite frank, I've been feeling fairly useless of late. This will get me back in the swing."

"I just wish Harry could have met you."

"I'm quite sure if our positions were reversed, your husband would do the same for me."

"Oh, in a heartbeat." She smiles but has her doubts.

***

"What do you mean you don't have a car?" Harry fumes.

"They closed JFK yesterday." The geek in the glasses shrugs. "We had a real run."

"But I had a reservation."

"I'm sorry, sir. Regulations require us to make vehicles available in emergency situations."

"In New York City? That's a hundred miles away."

"You should have seen it on 9/11. There wasn't a rental car in the state."

"I didn't need a rental car on 9/11. I need one right now."

The kid shrugs again, and Harry wants to rip his head off.

"I'm really sorry, sir."

"Okay, hot shot, what do we do now?" He feels like Baldini facing a deadline.

"I could call around, see if anyone has something. I wouldn't get my hopes up, though."

Harry feels the weight of the world come down. The terminal has that slapdash look of renovation and scattered passengers huddle like refugees.

"So call."

"There is a bus that leaves every hour on the hour."

"I don't want a fucking bus. Call around, Gomer, I'll wait right here."

***

The bus is standing room only. Harry managed to grab a seat, but the guy standing next to him reeks of cologne, and the one next to him keeps searching through his pockets, over and over in the same sequence. As if his chance of coming up with whatever he's looking for is related directly to the effort to find it. Harry's certain something sexual is going on, a way to rub up against him, all that grunting and squirming around. And the cologne guy, Jesus, he'd wring both their necks if he could get away with it. His eyes throb and his mouth tastes like metal. He gets off at Hudson. The platform is lit but the station doors are chained and padlocked. He walks to the end of the parking lot, drops his bag and stares down Market Street, 5 AM, nobody home. A foghorn sounds downriver, and seagulls swoop in over the trees. Seagulls? The Catskills? Harry sits on a bench by a row of bike racks. The first step is going badly. Just damp enough to seep through his sweater and cold enough to chill to the bone. He hears the snap of branches in the shadows, and seconds later, someone stumbles from the bushes. Coming at him from across the parking lot, last guy he wants to see.

"Hey, bub, wouldn't have a buck you could spare, would you?"

Harry looks around for something to smash him with.

"A quarter, maybe." Wino eyes the travel bag. "I gotta eat something."

"Piss off, ass wipe."

"Hey, you got no right to talk to me that way." Wino taps himself on the chest. "I'm a human being, you know."

"No, you're not."

"Am too."

"Are not."

"You're talking to Jake Spitzer." Says it like he expects an argument. "There was a time I could buy and sell you."

"Here..." Harry throws some change on the ground. "Now beat it."

"The hell with you." Wino backs away. "This here's a free country, by God. I go where I please."

"Yeah, yeah."

"I don't know what made you the way you are, mister, but it ain't nothing compared to what I been through."

"Tell it to the seagulls, Sparky."

"Had me a nice house and a good woman." He looks around as if they must be here somewhere. "It was the devil that done me in."

"Look at me." Harry frames his face with his hands. "Do I look like I give a fuck?"

"Something bad is gonna happen to you, buddy. You'll see."

"It already has." Harry holds out his arms to include everything.

The wino squats and scoops up the money. "Yessir,

got a real strong hunch about you, pardner."

"No you don't."

"Do too." Wino heads back the way he came. "Feller like you always comes to a bad end."

"Have a nice day." Harry waves.

An hour later, he's sitting in Eva's Place, got your truckers, guys in bib overalls, fat-ankled waitresses schlepping chow. Harry wipes a hole in the sweat-smeared window and watches school bus kids lined up across the street. Real shit hole this Hudson, houses crumbling, streets puddled over, businesses boarded up. The lot behind the bus stop is choked in weeds and littered in car parts. No high end, nothing much to brag about, as far from Mexico as he can get.

"More coffee?" his waitress chirps.

"Thanks, yeah."

"The special today is SOS. Gus just made up a bucket."

"Sounds tempting."

"Oh, he's known far and wide for it."

"I'll take the eggs over easy with ham."

"Suit yerself."

The guy in the next booth leaves without his newspaper, and Harry grabs it when nobody's looking. He pages through from cover to cover, pausing at the tit bar ads, settling on sports. Seems odd to see the same old names in the Phillies' lineup. The same world hotspots, the same movies playing, calming in a way, like nothing really happened. Time still passing. Life going on like it's supposed to.

Dead for a day now, almost two, the grim hereafter well under way. Not yet sunrise in Puerto Vallarta, Lena sleeping who knows where. What will she face in the coming days? Why the first of the month to call? Here he's going bonkers and it's just the fifteenth. Lena was right. He should call her. Who cares if they can trace it? Why would they trace what they're not even looking for? How did he think he'd be able to stand this?

Must get in touch. Must be a way.

But Harry can't think of one. He could call the hotel or the Mexican police, but he's not sure of the risks and knows he'd never dare it. He could call one of the numbers in Steve's wallet but what good would that do? Whoever answered wouldn't know a thing unless it all went wrong. He could just fly back, who'd be the wiser? Then he flashes on Chico's barman and it scares him silly.

"Here you go, hon." Waitress sets his eggs in front of him.

"Do you know if there's a hotel nearby?"

"Motor Lodge right up the road." She nods at the window. "The Sleepy Hollow, can't miss it."

***

By the time he pays the check, the mist has turned to drizzle. Pickups pass in a steady rush, faces set in the rustbelt light. No sidewalk so he takes the shoulder, dragging the bag along, teeth chattering until his jaw aches. Six blocks, it turns out, passed Mickey's Brakes and Mufflers, a sad stretch of row homes, two Laundromats and a Christian Science reading room. The woman at the motel desk doesn't hear him come in, so he stands there jiggling change in his pocket.

"Goodness! I'm sorry." She clutches at her collar. Wattles hang like draperies, pushing eighty if she's a day.

"Any vacancies?"

"Oh my, yes. Only one room taken, in fact." She pats at her bun. "Off season, you know."

"Right." Harry signs in. "And the season would be when?"

"Summer, of course. Come July the place is all a-bustle."

"I'm sure."

"Well, folks don't come like they used to, but we still get the campers and the Jesus crowd."

"Is there a phone in the room?"

"Yes, but you have to use a credit card. Will you be with us long?"

"That depends, a few days, maybe."

The room faces out on a trio of dumpsters, the walls paneled in wood grain, the furniture early American seedy. There's a badly framed print of a schooner between the windows, a bedside Bible and a desk calendar from 2012. Harry cranks up the heat, checks the phone for a dial tone and turns on the TV. Soaps, Oprah and on into the afternoon. He lies on the bed, smoking and thinking. Rain rattles down just like in the movies.

***

Santos signs the voucher and hands the tickets to Lena. "So your flight leaves at 11 on Thursday morning. I'll have a cab come for you at your hotel."

"Seems like all I ever get to say is thank you."

"Don't be silly. I wish there was more I could do." He guides her past the sidewalk vendors. Voices call out in greetings, hands reach to take his hand.

"Thursday. That gives me three days."

"Time enough to arrange a service for your husband. May I make a suggestion, Lena?"

"Yes, of course."

"My nephew is a parish priest. I could have him preside."

"Aww gee, that would be wonderful. Harry's Catholic, born and raised."

"Well, here we are." Carlos takes her arm and leads her down a stone stairway. The Chamber of Commerce is in an old movie theater; the lobby covered in murals, peasants working the bean fields, leaders in uniforms. They cross the dimly lit basement to a door marked Director. His office is bright and cheerful. French doors open to a small courtyard, sun dappled trellises teem in roses.

"How lovely." Lena puts her nose to a petal. "I was expecting something more..."

"Institutional?"

"Well, hardly so serene. It's like a backyard paradise. How do you get anything done?"

"You'd be surprised. At times it can be quite frantic."

Lena peruses the plaques and photos, Santos cutting ribbons, Santos dining with dignitaries, Santos dancing with a stunning brunette.

"Your wife?"

"Aida, yes. Taken three years before her illness."

"She's beautiful."

"Miss Jalisco Province, 1972. The year we were married."

Some of Santos in a moustache, ends drooping Zapata-style. Across his desk more pictures of Aida. The younger ones in languorous poses, almond eyed and swimsuit slim. Poor thing smiling like it's forever. Lena offers up a prayer.

"I'm curious, Lena." Carlos turns from the photos. "When Morales wanted to know about your marriage."

"Yes?"

"What would you have told him?"

She runs a finger along the desk. "Honestly? I have no idea."

"If I asked you?"

"Harry was a good man, but, I don't know, for the past few years he hasn't been himself."

"Poor health perhaps?"

"No, not physically, but he seemed to lose the spark." She takes a breath. "My husband was unhappy. It's hard to explain."

"But you stayed with him."

Lena meets his eye. "I could never leave. Harry needed me."

"You were wrong about your husband's luck." Carlos holds her gaze. "He had what every man wants in life, loyalty, devotion, things that are rare in the human condition."

"You say the nicest things."

Lena knows she should watch herself here. With all that's happened, it's easy to forget she's in mourning. She turns away and moves into the square of sunlight. "Harry had big ideas when we were younger. He was going to be somebody."

"What sort of ideas?"

"We were going to travel. Have adventures and see the world. He was in a band then. You know, rock and roll? They were good too, but it didn't break for them."

Partly true, at best.

"Sometimes dreams die hard, Lena, especially American dreams."

"The print shop jobs were supposed to be temporary, and I guess that's what they turned out to be. He'd work a few years and the place would go under. And he hated the work, and the years just kept going by and, well, we never got there. This trip? Mexico? It was the first time either one of us ever left the country."

"Every marriage has regrets, I know."

"And then his brother turned into a junkie and Harry had to look after him. And then Gerry got AIDS and, I don't know, something changed in Harry."

Carlos pours a pair of brandies and takes one to her. "But he had you."

"There's something else. For the past few months I'm pretty sure he's been using. You know, drugs?"

"Was it serious?"

"I don't know. Harry was good at hiding things from

me."

Carlos rests a hand on her shoulder. "Listen, Lena, whatever your husband was doing, I'm sure he had good reason."

"I guess it doesn't matter anyway. Not now."

"That's the best way to look at it." Santos raises his glass. "Here's to Harry Watts, a good man gone to a better place."

***

The remote doesn't work; Harry has to get up to change the channels. Someone keeps sneezing next door, the other guy, what's *his* story? Some sad little peddler with a backwater route, coming down with something nasty. Probably stays here whenever he's in the area. Probably a regular at Eva's, crazy about the SOS. Harry has the sudden, wild impulse to go chat him up. Just knock on the door and see what makes the peddler tick. He knows he never would, but sitting here watching one bad rerun after another is a hard way to go. He managed to get a few hours sleep but he's getting hungry again. And it's raining harder and now it's dark. Maybe the guy has a car. Of course he has a car, it's a freaking motor lodge.

He watches the news for the third time. The script, so familiar he could quote whole segments and does. Bush mangling syntax, the senator's lawyers denying allegations, feel good story, behind the scenes report. Then he stops when he realizes other guy can hear him. Sixteen rooms and they jam them together. Save the maid a couple of steps.

Okay, Jesus, enough with the TV. Semi-darkness, that's the ticket. Should have bought a bottle, go for the load and sleep it off. Kill the time while events unfold. A couple of days would do the trick. Sleep until he's sick of it, holed up in the off-season, gloom, doom and nothing to do.

He thinks of Steve, those dead eyes, then another impulse, truly alarming. Turns his head and looks at the ceiling, let's his eyes go dead. Stillness, total and complete, limbs lifeless, holds the pose for a minute, then two minutes. The room seems to fill with silence, the traffic in the distance, the thin snip of the digital clock, death stare, the final fixed point. Takes it to the limit, ten minutes, fifteen. Imagines the scene when they finally find him, the old lady, the lazy maid, Sneezy next door.

And then he notices up in a corner, a smudge of something vaguely familiar. When was it? Years ago now, a similar smudge, not on the ceiling but wedged in a windowpane. A crisp Sunday morning on Christian Street, Harry in bed, sizing it up but too sleepy to investigate. Another hour until curiosity got the best of him, then getting up and going over. Not a shadow or a gob of caulk, the shape failing to conform, even at close range. He gave it a poke then jumped back as the damn thing dropped to the floor, red beady eyes, wingspan like the movie logo. Fucking bat! Then scrambling from the room when it sprang up at him, legs tangled in bed sheets, the last of it on hands and knees. And then the best part, swinging the door closed behind him! Shutting Lena in. That sudden squeal and bounce of bedsprings, the suck of air as she ripped it open, that he'd do that, leave her in there. How he choked under pressure, how Lena never spoke of it. Did it open her eyes or was she already resigned to that side of him?

When he finally gets up, there's a sharp stab between his shoulders. He pushes himself to the edge of the bed, rolling this and rotating that. It's okay, nothing really, his stairwell pratfall weighing in. Harry sits there looking out on the dumpsters, the clunky shape, the stenciled phone number.

Sits there.

He trapped the bat in a colander. It was easy enough.

Murder in Mexico

By the time he came to face it, the poor thing had flown himself into a heap. Harry slid an album cover underneath and took it outside. Watched from the street as it fluttered up, turned in a circle then bee-lined back to the house. Same thing happened the next night. Harry put him in the car and drove him to Jersey.

If only he could rewind back to that time. Forfeit the years if it came to that, write them off and take it from here, this very morning, everything intact and nobody missing. Push the button and watch the years fly.

Harry turns on the TV.

***

They hold the service high on a hillside, just Lena, Santos, Father Esteban and Morales. It's a fine day with a light sea breeze, little cotton clouds and a single vulture circling overhead.

"Dear Lord in Heaven." The priest looks to the vulture. "We pray you will accept the soul of this, our fallen friend and your humble servant, Harry Watts. And while I never got to meet Harry myself, in speaking with Lena, his lifelong companion, I feel I've come to know him well. Harry was a good man, Lord. True to his faith and bound by holy tenants of the Father."

Lena clutches the urn to her waist. She never pictured a sendoff for Harry, but if she had it would go like this. A few more in the mix, maybe, but quiet and dignified.

"Lena told me of a time when Harry played music." Father looks her way. "The guitar, was it?"

"Drums," she whispers.

"The drums, that's right, a time when the message was love, when peace was the credo of the young. Lena told me that on a night when Harry was scheduled to perform, his brother fell ill and was rushed to the hospital. On a night, that night, when he might have triumphed,

Harry went instead to his bother's bedside. Stayed with him, gave him comfort. On this night and many like it, Harry proved, beyond doubt, his worth in God's eyes."

In fact, Gerry fell through a skylight on a B&E. Of all the stories she'd told the young priest, Lena never thought he'd go with that one.

"And we ask you, dear Lord, to have him prepare a place for Lena, and all his friends and family, and for ourselves as well."

Morales dabs his eyes with a tissue. A laugh carries up from the lowlands and the buzzard starts his downward spiral. The thing Lena can't figure is why no mention of AIDS in the death certificate. No tumors, no lesions, no sign of the virus. Either Steve was lying or Harry got it wrong.

Or Harry's lying.

"Lena?" The priest signals for the urn and she hands it over. He removes the lid and closes his eyes. "Dear Lord, we commend to you our brother's spirit."

Father hands it back and gestures to the hillside. Lena walks a short way down and shakes out the contents, turning in a circle for the full effect. Instead of scattering, the ashes pour on the ground and she feels them crunching under her shoes.

"Is that all right?" She squints up at them.

"That's fine." Santos goes to her. "Now you've done your best for your husband, and Harry's where he wanted to be."

***

He should shave. He really should. What looked okay at thirty comes off Gabby Hayes when it's gone to gray. Three days he's been here. Two since he's stepped out the door, and then only for provisions, beer, the chunk of boloney and loaf of bread he keeps on the outside windowsill. Or did until something got at them last night. Didn't hear a thing, but when he looked this morning, the bag was torn to pieces. Three days watching the tube and nothing about a murder in Mexico. No missing tourist or widow's arrest. He should take it as a good sign, but for all he knows, a dozen tourists disappear every day in Mexico. Could be bodies popping up all over, widows cued up for the firing squad.

Nine days until he hears for sure. Nine days.

He spent Day Two doing battle with the telephone. Not the phone itself, but the urge to use it, couldn't even risk directory assistance to see if the Mexican cops or hotels were listed. Any call at all would come back to haunt him. He didn't know how, but neither did half the guys on death row. He soon grew to hate the sight of it, beckoning. Okay, not beckoning, just there, beside the bed, waiting for him to hang himself. Finally, he disconnected it, stuffed the phone in the dumpster under an orange mess in Styrofoam. Not that *that* made any sense, since he knew where it was and could go get it any time. Which he did, more than once, nacho stains on his sweater to prove it. Finally, he returned the phone to the desk, saying it kept him awake. Didn't say how since he'd gotten no calls, but then again, she didn't ask.

Now it's time to go, and he looks like a guy who wouldn't need to fly all the way to Mexico to kill somebody. Wouldn't even have to leave the building. So he shaves, quickly with more than the usual nicks and gouges, then has to wait for the bleeding to stop, watches the end of Oprah while his stomach growls in protest. Oprah with a girl who rescued a family trapped in a car wreck. Four lives saved, and she's not even ten. Talk about getting a leg up in the karma column. Kill a few down the line, and she'll still be in the black.

Time to go, but where? The plan never had a Catskills agenda. In his head it was always just a block of time to be gotten through, like the movies with clocks spinning and calendar pages tearing away. What he did with it hardly mattered. It was all about what Lena did.

But it matters now. Now he has to go. Right now while he still can, before Oprah and the dumpsters and the thing up in the ceiling and the guy next door suck the heart right out of him.

Halfway into town he spots the car rental. Harry's got Gerry's license and credit card, kept them valid for the unforeseeable. They might balk at the photo, but then they might not. So he walks in, goes through the motions and drives off in a brand new Caddy. The sporty model, fully loaded, and just like that he's human again. A new car, that's the ticket. Nothing pulls it together like a brand new ride. Takes the Rip Van Winkle Bridge across the Hudson and just drives, winding roads, postcard country. Stops at a diner in Athens and gorges himself on hotcakes and coffee, watches out the window as the sun breaks through. On the way out of town he passes an old hotel facing out on the river. The Stewart House, Food and Lodging. It's the "Lodging" that does it for him.

"Can I help you?" The sweet young thing at the desk wants to know.

"I'd like a room for the night."

"We have four singles and the Meryl Streep suite."

"Meryl Streep?"

"Ever see the movie *Ironweed*?"

In fact, Harry has, a grim little gem about Depression derelicts. The scene where Meryl sings had him sobbing into his shirtsleeve. Everything Meryl did made Harry blubber.

"You don't mean?"

"Yep." She beams. "Shot it right here."

"No!"

"The death scene. Where she finally scrapes enough money to rent a room. That's the room."

"I'll take it."

"It's got a great view and we keep it furnished like it was in the movie."

"The same bed?"

"I don't know about that." She pokes her chin with a finger. "Say, that's an idea."

"A marketing goldmine, if you ask me." Harry chuckles. "Share a bed with Meryl Streep."

She laughs. "I like it. You in advertising?"

"Not me. I'm retired."

"Wow. On a road trip or something?"

"Always wanted to check out the area."

"Well then, you've come to the right place. One night, you say?"

"Maybe longer, depends on how it goes."

She signs him in and hands him a key. And such a key, solid iron with gap teeth and a ring on the end, like whatever it opens will change everything. Meryl's is a corner suite, big and airy, wainscoting, brass sconces, floorboards creaky underfoot. At first, Harry couldn't recall the death scene from *Ironweed*, but the room brings it back to him, Meryl at the end of her rope, Jack, the bastard, running out on her. Right goddamn here!

He leans out the window and takes in a lungful. Just south of town, the river makes a turn, and he sees an old lighthouse midway to the bridge. There's an intersection right below him with a strip of businesses running along the bank, a gauntlet of gaslights, an old-time bandstand in the square, small town down to the barber pole and the dog sleeping in the street. He shoots a wave to a shopkeeper on the corner. If he'd come here to begin with he wouldn't be in the shape he's in.

Kim and Uri own the place. Kim, the chef, is blonde and boyish, flushed from the kitchen and the cooking sherry. It's Uri who runs things, ponytail bouncing as she flits from floor to floor. Once again, Harry's one of a weekend pair, Jenks is the other, freshly widowed and up for the foliage. This he learns from Uri on his way out for a ride around.

"They used to come every autumn." She hugs an armload of folded linens. "Last year we had a party for them. It was their fiftieth anniversary, can you imagine?"

"I'm afraid I can," Harry tells her. "My wife and I are halfway there."

"No kidding. Where is she?"

"Out of the country I'm afraid."

"Too bad. The fall is the best time up here. Seems a shame to see it alone."

"Yes, well..." He twinkles an eye. "It was an opportunity I couldn't pass up."

Still feels the tingle an hour later, climbing the cutbacks to Hunter's Mountain, human contact just when he needs it, that and the weather. It's what threw him coming in, the fuck-up at the airport, the bus-ride from hell, and the weather. Christ it was depressing. Hudson in the rain, shades of gray, steam ribbons rising off the mountains. So not what he expected it's a wonder he survived it. Everything's good now. The caddy purrs like a kitten. Sun shining, sky scrubbed clean and the foliage. Hadn't even noticed until today. Flame reds and yellows layered in gold. The fucking wonder of it. Wood smoke, winter coming, and just last week he was sitting on the beach.

And then Steve's face floats into the picture. A bit fuzzy after a week, the shape of it mostly, then Lena in some Mexican standoff, crying in a cell while the bull dykes gather. It takes all Harry's got to shove these thoughts aside where they circle at the edges, refusing to fade.

On the way back, he stops at a stand for a jug of cider. The old man makes his change, cackling at the scene across the way. Harry turns to a big house set off the road on a yard-size square of blacktop.

"I get such a kick out of it." Old-timer chuckles. "Feller hired a crew of landscapers, but the deer gobbled up everything they planted. Dropped a bundle, he did. Even had 'em fence the yard in, for all the good that did. Finally just paved the whole thing over. Funniest damn thing you ever seen."

Harry stands there scratching his head. "Does look pretty silly. I guess in the end you do what it takes."

"Go tell *them*." He points over Harry's shoulder. It takes a few seconds to see them. Deer, in assorted shapes and sizes bunched in the shade at the edge of the yard.

"Jesus!" Harry counts half a dozen. "What are they doing?"

"That's a matter of speculation?" Old-timer shakes his head. "Some think they're plotting something. Looks that way sometimes."

Harry sees three more coming out of the trees. "You mean they're there all the time?"

"Some critters don't have the brains they were born with." The old man leans in as if they could hear him. "You ask me, they're just wondering what the hell they're supposed to eat."

CHAPTER TEN

Lena sees brother-in-law Mel beaming like a runway beacon. The doofus, as Harry calls him, Rita at his side looking ten years older. Lena's been over this part a thousand times, but as they draw close, she feels exits sealing up around her. The phone calls were bad enough. Every one breaking off in stunned disbelief. Harry dead? Oh no, not Harry.

Ned Brennan was the worst. She could hear him sobbing over the bar buzz. The first two to Alice and Rita and the one to Father Mac were hard enough, but Ned was the killer. By now the news is all over Pennsport.

She sees Rita chew her lower lip. It would be like this in the weeks to come, the questions, the lies, the playing on sympathies. For the first time Lena feels something harden inside. Harry left her to carry the weight, all of it, all the way.

"Oh honey, we've been worried sick." Rita wraps her up while doofus takes her bags.

"You didn't have to both come." Lena forces a smile. "Who's watching the kids?"

"They're at mother's." Rita blinks away tears. "My baby sister just lost her husband. How could I not come?"

They hug and something hard presses to Lena's heart. Rita bawling, Mel staring at the terminal carpet, strangers shooting looks of concern, the hard part breaking like a tidal wave.

"Oh Lena." Rita holds her at arm's length. "How could this happen?"

"Like Harry said, it all ends badly."

"Minna's a wreck. Everyone's a fucking wreck. Mel's just sick about it."

"I hope you don't mind, but I placed an obituary in the Inquirer," doofus tells the carpet.

"He composed it himself." Rita brushes Lena's collar. "Stayed up half the night."

"I'm sure Harry would be touched, Mel."

They start down the concourse, and Lena sees herself reflected in the window, the widow Watts coming home.

"You okay, sis?" Rita keeps asking.

"I don't think it's hit me yet. Right now I'm just numb."

"I know sometimes it was hard to tell, but we really thought the world of Harry." Rita dabs her nose with a hankie. "I just can't believe we'll never see him again."

"Harry loved you too."

"He did?"

"He said you were the best in-laws a guy ever had."

"Hear that, Mel? He wasn't serious when he said you couldn't come over anymore."

"That was a joke," Lena assures him.

And the lying begins.

"I've packed a few things." Rita holds up a plastic bag. "Let me stay with you for a while."

"No please, thanks, but I want to be alone for now."

"I don't mind, Lena. You might need someone to make arrangements, answer the phone, you know."

"It's all been taken care of. We scattered Harry's ashes the other day."

Mel and Rita exchange looks.

"I better warn you, Minna's a little upset with the cremation business. It's the Catholic thing. She's worried Harry will have trouble in, you know, the hereafter?"

"There was a priest. It was lovely, really. Much nicer than being lowered into a hole."

"Oh, we have no problem with it. Spare yourself the

melodrama, and all."

"Not to mention the expense," Mel weighs in.

"But you know mom. A death without a funeral doesn't sit right."

"She'll have to get used to the idea," Lena tells them. "Harry's where he wanted to be."

"Anyway, we were thinking you could have a service or something. It doesn't have to be religious or anything. Just a gathering of Harry's friends, you know, in a week or so."

"I couldn't go through it right now."

"You poor thing."

On the drive in, Rita goes on about nothing, Mel speaks when spoken to, ear cocked to the hockey game. Lena tunes them out and draws into herself, staring out at the city skyline. Where is he? What's he doing? If there's any justice, Harry's driving himself crazy. She could be in jail. The cops might be looking for him and he must see by now, this phase of the plan is strictly wing it.

"Lena?" Rita taps her leg.

"I'm sorry, what?"

"Harry's family? At least you won't have that to deal with."

"Oh, I forgot to call his Uncle Ray. Remind me, will you, Reet?"

"I didn't know he had an uncle."

"Ray's not really related. Harry was the last in line."

It isn't easy thinking of him out there somewhere, not dead. One thing for certain, he'd be glad to miss this, Rita rambling, Mel gloomier than ever, a flurry of condolences but everyone adjusting. Before you know it, time will pass, things will come up, and the space that was Harry will fill in forever.

"Benny and Diane are at Minna's," Rita tells her. "They want to see you. Mrs. Levitsky practically lives there now. Oh, and Carol wants you to call."

Murder in Mexico

"Okay, just stay by me, would you?"

"Count on it, baby."

She could tell them everything. Just blurt it out and end the whole charade. Lena feels the words form on her tongue, and it scares the hell out of her. Would it always be that way? Harry insisted once the body was gone there'd be no way to catch them. But Lena's no fool. They never stop looking for the murderers.

Mel turns in the driveway. Rita's children gather at the door while Lena's mother throttles a dishtowel. Mel kills the engine and turns to Lena. "You sure you can do this?"

"Do I have a choice?"

"Just say the word and we're outa here."

"Thanks, Mel." She squeezes his arm. "I'll be fine."

Someone herds the kids away, and out steps her mom, shading her eyes against the porch light, smaller and thinner than ever, the spitting image of her own mother when they were growing up. Lena sags for a second then squares her shoulders and steps right up.

"Hello, mother." She bends to kiss her.

"I promised myself I wouldn't cry," Minna says without a trace of a tear.

"I'm sorry I didn't call. It was hectic."

"Hectic, yes. You stay for a while. I'll make coffee."

"Sure, okay." Lena follows her up the steps. "The block looks wonderful."

"Yes. It seems we've been 'discovered'. Live long enough and anything can happen."

"Are they nice? Your neighbors?"

"Nice?" Minna leads her inside. "I have no idea."

The house smells of Pine Sol and canned ravioli. There's a built-in microwave above the stove and a Mister Coffee on the counter, other than that the kitchen is unchanged. The same pictures and knick-knacks, the same cabinets, the same table and chairs. A woman turns from the sink as Lena enters and the kids stare in from the living room.

"Lena." The woman opens her arms and Lena steps into them. "I've been praying I wouldn't miss you. You have my deepest sympathy."

"How are you, Mrs. Levitsky?"

"Oh, I never change. Sit, I'll make you a sandwich."

"Thanks, no, I'm okay."

"You have to keep your strength up, Lena." The old girl wags a finger. "I've got some nice boiled ham and olive loaf."

"Really, I couldn't eat."

"Bennie? Diane? Come say hello to Aunt Lena," Rita yells in. There's the squeak of vinyl, and in they shuffle, trailed by Father McIntyre.

Lena smiles at the old prelate. "Still at it, eh, Father Mac?"

"My child." He hugs her to him. "It's been too long."

"Hi, Aunt Lena." Diane waves a finger.

"Hi, Aunt Lena," Bennie mumbles.

"My God. You kids are all grown up. Look at you." Lena hugs and kisses them. Grown up all right. Diane must be a size 14 and Little Doofus is all belly and butt. The kitchen seems suddenly much too crowded.

"We're sorry about Uncle Harry," the kids say as one.

"Thanks, you two. Really. It means a lot to me." What it means is she'll probably have to see them on a regular basis, something Harry would never put up with. Lena lets them fuss and fidget, feeling herself dwindle to family size. She's grown apart from them over the years, partly because of Harry but mainly due to lack of interest. She and her mother were never close, and Rita's changed so much that Lena hardly recognizes her.

They speak fondly of Harry, some of it genuine, Lena's sure. The years changed all of them, but only Harry cancelled his membership. He hadn't been joking when he put the ban on Mel, and Rita was as close to non grata as could be and still get a foot in the door. This show of support was just that, a show, sincere in its way, but for all the wrong reasons. For her, not for what she was left with, a hole as big as Harry to fill. Lena had expected to feel shame in the deception, but it feels more like let me out of here. Luckily it's late and no one objects when Mel announces it's time to go.

"I'll call you tomorrow." She kisses her mother's cheek.

"I go to mass at eight. Maybe sometime you can join me."

"Not yet, Minna. Right now I'm not speaking to Supreme Beings."

"You shouldn't be alone at a time like this. I know it doesn't mean that much to you, but a mother worries."

"I know. I love you moth...uh, mom."

As he walks her to the car, Father Mac covers the bases. "I know it's none of my business, but did Harry have a chance to make his confession?"

"I'm afraid not, Father. Harry wasn't big on religion."

He pats her hand in a pastorly way. "I wouldn't worry too much. He may be a while in Purgatory, but there was goodness in Harry. I must admit he was a favorite of mine."

"Say a prayer for him, will you, Mac? Wherever he is, I'm sure he can use it."

"You can count on it, Lena. Did I tell you the sisters have started a novena? Sister Muriel took it pretty hard."

This one cuts deep. Every Catholic kid from Tasker to Tree Street owed a debt to Sister Muriel. When Gerry broke his nose in a playground fight, Muriel carried him all the way to Mt. Sinai. The old girl came to both Lena's weddings and saw Harry's mom once a week before she passed. They didn't make them like Muriel anymore. When Lena thought about getting over, she hadn't thought about Sister M.

"Tell me something, Father. Say you did something wrong and you were truly sorry, but there was no way you could fix it. Can you ever get over something like that? In your head, I mean."

"There aren't too many things that can't be fixed, Lena. At least in the eyes of God."

"But say there was. Could you ever be yourself again?"

The old priest turns her to him. "The human spirit is tougher than most people think. Look at your mother. When your father died she could have caved in completely. But look at her now, Grandma Minna."

"But she's a rock. The bad things only make her stronger."

"Don't burden yourself with guilt, my dear. It won't help Harry and it can only hurt you."

***

The house looks the same but different, flatter somehow, the bricks a shade lighter. Streetlight is mirrored in the bedroom window, something she never noticed before. She closes the car door as softly as she can, but before Mel's halfway down the block, the outside lights are popping on. Then doors swing open and neighbors tumble out, phones beeping and kids bunched at the windows. Aw, Jesus.

"We couldn't believe it when we heard." It's Sally, next door in bunny robe and slippers. "We thought Ned had fallen off the wagon."

Mary Perkins shoulders in. "You okay, Lena?"

"I'm tired."

"Somebody take her bags," Fireman Jack barks from his stoop.

"Lena?" a voice calls over the blather.

She turns to Ned in his grungy apron. Ned's never

been much to look at, but Lena's never seen him like this, unshaven, red-eyed, lower teeth missing.

"You look awful, Ned."

"I'm so sorry, honey." His eyes well up. "Harry Watts was the best man I ever knew."

"Thanks. You were always a good friend to him."

"You need anything, you let me know, right?"

"I will, Ned."

"Anything, Lena, I'm serious."

"Bless you, Ned." She kisses the top of his greasy head then turns to the crowd. "Thank you all. I know this has been a shock, and I'll always love you for being here for me. I just want you to know that Harry always considered this the best block in the city. And if we know one thing it's that Harry was rarely wrong."

"The freakin' best," someone bellows from a window.

"Harry rules!" some kid pipes up.

Lena smiles bravely. "Now, if it's okay, I just want to decompress. It's been a long week."

"Get some rest, Lena." Sally leads her to her door. "Duffy will get your trash in the morning. I'll call you around lunch time."

"Thanks, Sally, everybody."

Alone in her own home, she feels his presence. The walls close around her, silence hangs like a shroud. Their things arranged just as they left them, mail piled on the foyer floor, the phone machine blinking impatience. She stands there taking in shapes and sizes, Harry's jacket on the coat hook, the dark frame of a picture, his life-size wooden Indian with a fistful of stogies. A wave of sorrow breaks over her, and she crumples to the stairs in a sobby heap.

"What have we done?" She groans into the banister post. "It went just like you said, so how come it feels so hopeless? It's more than you bargained for, isn't it, Harry? And you can't ever take it back."

Tom Larsen

***

Nothing in the Greene County Gazette, the Hudson Mirror, the Albany Post, though it's probably still too early, or she picked a paper nobody reads. But there are no others, except for a few local rags she'd never track down and even those he checks, standing at the convenience store rack so he won't have to buy them. School board meetings, police blotter, lots of livestock photos. Nothing from Lena, the answer to every question, the last stop for all trains of thought.

Until this morning, while shaving, like a lightening bolt to the brain. The rich Widow Watts rides off into the sunset. What he's doing now, pretty much floundering, might be how she leaves it. Now that Lena's on her own, what does she need Harry for?

This one chilled him. Not that she might, that it would occur to *him*. But it had, and now he keeps going back to it, unconsciously, like teeth grinding. He knows Lena better than he knows himself, but their frame of reference has been scrambled. They're murderers now, not to be trusted.

Harry drives aimlessly. Something about the country scares him a little. The way the clouds bunch against the hillsides, the unpeopled mass if it. He stops at a joint in Cairo, Lou's Cork and Crown, empty but for Lou and a plumber working on the bar sink. Two shots of bourbon and the grip of panic loosens, three and Harry hasn't a care. The idea of Lena pulling a fast one, Jesus, he can take these things to extremes.

"From around here?" Lou wants to know.

"Just passing through."

"Didn't think I'd seen you in here before. I got a head for faces." Lou's own being pinched and pale to the point of bloodless, see-through hair raked straight back. It's a type Harry's known his whole life.

"Tell me something. You get the OTB up here?"

"Place over in Coxsakie, mebbe three miles," Lou tells him. "You a betting man, are ya?"

"I dabble." Harry flaps his hands.

"Don't gamble myself. Not that I don't have my share of vices. I'm a feller who likes to get something for his money."

"Amen to that."

"I mean at least with liquor you get something to drink. Your bettin' money just disappears into thin air."

"My bookie, notwithstanding."

"My sister's husband, now there's a man who would wager on anything. Won $300 right here in this taproom, betting on the QVC."

"What's that?"

Lou looks at him like he must be kidding. "The home shopping network. He hit the price of zircon necklace right on the nose."

"Some guys have all the luck."

The plumber pulls something long and hairy from the sink drain. A tangle comes loose, and the pipes cough up a soupy mess. Lou steps away as the guy goes up to the elbows in it. Greasy and foul smelling, sewage related. Christ Jesus. There may be worse things than being a plumber, but Harry can't come up with one.

"Scratch my nose, would you, Lou?" Plumber's eyes cross as he points it at him. "Right there, that's it."

Back on the road as the lunch crowd filters in, the mountains and the bourbon working their wonders. Once they're living up here, it will all come together, once the pace changes and they can relax. Just yesterday he passed a trio of log cabins right on the interstate, models for a custom builder, solid and handsome, big front porches. Harry felt a deep and sudden craving for porches. The look of them, so inviting, porches and rocking chairs, there ya go! Buy a piece of land with a view and rock away those golden years.

Which reminds him of a place they rented in Lake Tahoe, back when he still had a hand in, North Shore in the snow, looking out on the lake and the high Sierras. Harry couldn't get enough of it. The view was like a living thing, changing every time you looked. For a week they had their meals delivered and never set foot out the door.

Good times, that's what they were missing. Harry feels like he's been locked up for years and someone finally opened the door. They were at the point where he had to do something, now that it's done there's no going back.

"Beat yourself up if you want to," he says out loud. "It won't change a fucking thing."

And it makes him feel better, it really does, for a good ten miles, maybe twenty. Then the buzz flattens out, the clouds roll in, and then it's raining again, wipers keep the beat. He thinks of the Sleepy Hollow motel, how rain will always remind him of it, lousy weather and how it can work on you.

"After Steve was dead the weather turned lousy," he hears himself say. What the-? Oh man, this can't be good.

***

Lena runs a finger over the photos. Within the hour, they're scattered across the sofa, memory lane leading back to high school. A Polaroid of Harry and her first husband Joey, opening a concert in the park, heads joined at the mike, sweat slick and hair to their shoulders. The Church Street Four set to hit it big, wasn't that how the papers put it? She pages ahead to the brown newsprint sheathed in plastic. "Poised on The Edge of Stardom," above a solemn group shot begging for an album cover. It was Joey's band, the sixties, but they never really cooked until Harry joined up.

In the end, they went with Lena's dog for the record cover. The album never happened, but for years she kept the covers in a box, moving it from place to place until a leaky pipe welded them into a solid block. One yapping Barney after another, peeling in shreds as she pried them apart. When the deal fell through, Joey slipped over the amphetamine edge. A year later, he was in the slammer and she and Harry were set up on Two Street.

Summers on the beach in Wildwood, the trip they took to California, a dozen different Christmases, names and faces long forgotten. It's been years since Lena's gone down this road, but instead of bringing things into focus, the pictures hint of the trouble to come, Harry getting older, the good times fewer and further between. There's Lambertville Frank fresh off a rehab, Butch Fellers with puppies at his feet, Marilyn Miller vamping in a halter, gone longer than they were here. Lena sees them as if for the first time, life losing steam as the years begin to blur. The photos span the decades, a measure of when and who had a camera. Harry's goatee, a winter's affection, Lena in the cloche hat she lost less than an hour later. She's almost to the end when the telephone rings.

"Lena? Did I wake you?"

"No, mom, I couldn't sleep."

"I had an idea you might be up. That's how I was when your father died. Everything looked different."

"Like I've been away for years."

"Like the life has been drained out." She can hear the words catch in her mother's throat. "Oh, Lena, how could this happen? Harry was a young man."

"He didn't suffer," she thinks to say. "It was just like going to sleep."

"And no children...no one to carry on. How many times did I tell him? Give me grandchildren."

"There's still Bennie and—"

"I even offered to pay for their college. You two, so irresponsible. And who ever heard of not having a funeral? No grave, no headstone. How will you visit him?"

"I won't have to visit. I brought a little of Harry home." Lena flips a photo page. Minna at their loft on Race Street, younger than Lena is now.

"Who ever heard of such a thing? Your father bought our plot the second year we were married."

"A little morbid, don't you think, mom?"

"People took care of things in those days. They didn't leave a mess behind for others to deal with."

Lena beams in on the image, the Minna she remembers. "Look, mom, I'm sorry I don't have a brood of fatherless kids and a dreary graveyard to visit, but that's the way it is."

"You have it there with you?"

"Have what?"

"Harry."

Lena glances at the matchbox on the coffee table. "Right here."

"It would be a comfort, I suppose."

"We're looking through old photos. There's one of you in a loden coat."

"Good heavens. I remember that thing."

"With the bangs, Harry said you looked like 'The Sound of Music' meets 'Mary Tyler Moore'."

A strange noise comes over the line, and suddenly Lena's six years old again, telling knock-knock jokes at the kitchen table. Decades now since she's heard the sound, her mother's laugh, brittle with neglect.

"That Harry, he always knew how to get my goat."

"You liked him, didn't you, mom, behind all that Catholic indignation?"

"I did, yes." Minna's voice softens. "At first I didn't approve, but he worked on me. Your husband knew his way around women."

"He liked you, too. Harry said you were the best straight man he ever had. One time he bet a long shot named Mother 'N Law and bought me pearl earrings with the winnings."

"Your father was a lot like him when we first met, always a laugh at someone's expense."

"Dad? A joker?"

"Once, oh I shouldn't tell you—"

"No. I want to hear it. Please?"

"This was before you were born. We were still in Olney. You remember Kelsey, the neighbor?"

"The postman? Big guy, nasty."

"My goodness, you were an infant. I must have told you this already."

"Never. You didn't tell stories."

"Anyway, your father entered a contest, you know how he was always entering contests."

"No, I never knew that. Contests?"

"Yes, you know, twenty-five words or less on why you like Babbo over Arm and Hammer."

"Oh, this is priceless. Babbo?"

"They were clever. Not poems or anything, but well written. Your father was an excellent speller."

"Okay, ten minutes, three major life revelations. You should call more often."

"Well, I have had a bit to drink."

"Oh, Minna I love you for this. What about the contest? Tell me."

"He won a new set of tires, but it turned into a nightmare. Other prizes never arrived. Your father was convinced Kelsey was stealing the mail."

"Jesus, Min, how many contests did he enter?"

"It was his hobby, not so much after you kids came. So he decided to send himself a package. He even wrote the word 'PRIZE' under the address. Inside was a brand new toothbrush in a handsome carrying case.

"What'd he do to it?"

"Do you remember Mr. Jeffries' Labrador? The one that always did his business in our yard?"

"He didn't."

"After that, we picked up the mail at the post office."

***

Harry hops from bar to bar, knows it's a bust but just can't stop himself. It's like when he was a kid and they'd do something crazy, climb the water tower or run the railroad trestle, risking it all for a cheap thrill. The same mix of madness and melodrama, the rite some poor schmuck doesn't live through. Lena must never know of this. Not ever.

He checks himself in the rearview. Not so bad if he shuts one eye. Oddly enough he's driving okay, speed steady, curving smoothly. Spots a roadhouse in a grove of evergreens.

***

"'That time of year thou mayest in me behold, when yellow leaves, or none, or few do hang.'"

"Can it, Casey, the guy's not interested," The bartender, Willie, calls over.

"No, hey..." Harry holds his hands up. "Really, I don't mind."

"You're sure? Drives most people nuts."

"'In me thou seest the twilight of such day as after sunset fadeth in the west.'"

"He'll run out of steam pretty soon."

"Shakespeare?"

"In his dreams."

"'In me thou seest the glowing of such fire that on the ashes of his youth does lie.'"

"Hamlet, I think, or Macbeth."

Willie shrugs. "I don't know dick about poetry."

The old ham, Casey, pauses for a snort. With the moustache, the nose, and the elbow patches he's Colonel

Schweppes gone round the bend.

"Give our learned stranger a round on me." He jabs a finger at them. "Tis so seldom we drink at the trough of enlightenment."

Harry gives a nod. "So it is Shakespeare."

"The same..." Casey nods, "and not without a certain level of interpretation, I trust."

"I thought it was terrific. Best I've heard in, oh God, months."

Casey seems to consider this then fades to barely breathing.

"I'm Gerry."

The left eye pulls open. "Hats off to you, friend. Willie? Gerry's drink?"

Willie turns to the bar, losing himself in his own reflection.

"The thing about poetry?" he tells the mirror. "I never know what the fuck they're talking about. Where I come from you say what you mean."

"If we said what we meant, the streets would run with blood," Casey counters.

"It's like what's his name, Dylan. I mean, what the fuck is that guy talking about, anyway? And how come poets are so freakin' whiney? Explain that to me, wouldja?"

"If only there were time."

"Chrome horse with your diplomat? I mean, what's up with that?"

"Are you of the local citizenry, Gerry?" The name sounds funny when the old man says it, like what it is, bogus.

"I'm thinking about it," Harry tells him. "Try and sell me."

"Well, I can get you into Fairview Cemetery. Just had two lots go up for bid, perpetual care included."

"That *is* a tempting offer."

"Handsome view of the Con Ed towers. We offer a

pet-free environment and the added benefit of soundproof crypts."

"Pet free?"

Casey's head wobbles visibly. "Felines in particular, ghoulish creatures, cats. The grounds are patrolled at three-hour intervals. Our dogs are trained to chase, not kill."

"I'm impressed."

"Most importantly, we are well above the water line and we use no motorized grounds-keeping equipment. No power lawn mowers or leaf blowers, no chemicals or pesticides."

Harry holds his palms up. "That's it. Count me in."

"Also poems should rhyme." Willie beats the dead horse. "And they shouldn't look like, I don't know, a building or something. The shape of them, you know what I'm saying?"

"I gotta go with you on that." Harry belches. "If it doesn't rhyme, we got no time."

"And no way 'shown' rhymes with 'born' or any of that. A rhyme's gotta rhyme. Rule number one."

"What about 'thous' and 'seests?" Harry wonders.

Willie thinks a minute then shrugs. "I'm okay with the 'thous'. They don't bother me."

Casey makes his way to the bar, not far, but it's touch and go, in his eighties, easy, tacking slightly, chortling to himself. Harry braces to catch him, as if he wasn't as drunk, or drunker.

"'Bout time for you to head back to the boneyard, ain't it, Case?" Willie checks him in the mirror.

"You live in the cemetery?" Harry has to ask.

"It was a dream of mine when I was a boy. The only one that was realized, sad to say."

"Must get kind of creepy sometimes."

"He reads 'em poetry," Willie snorts. "That's how come he knows all that stuff. Been up there for years, howling at the moon. The kids call him the Grim Reaper."

Casey paws through the beer nuts. "When it comes to children, the dogs of Fairview go for the throat."

"I mean, on foggy nights, I'd go batty." Harry can almost picture it.

"Not to worry." Willie laughs. "Everybody knows the dead just stumble around like robots. A good head fake and you blow right by 'em."

Casey shakes his head. "I'm afraid in my case it would be the tortoise versus the tortoises."

"Just don't let 'em corner you," Willie warns him. "That's when they get you, every time."

"Reading poetry to the dead, what about that?" Harry strains to focus.

"Reciting, please," Casey corrects him. "My audience can be quite demanding."

Willie barks a laugh. "Yeah. They hang on your every word."

The door opens. A woman circles to the bar without giving them a glance. Willie and Casey ignore her.

"Every time I go into a bar, lately, Shakespeare comes up," Harry tells them. "Like he just died and he's on everyone's mind."

"Shakespeare will never die," Casey proclaims. "All hail the Immortal Bard!"

"That's the other thing." Willie gets a puzzled look. "This immortal crapola, what's it been, like, three hundred years since Shakespeare? Four?"

"Don't tax yourself, young Willie."

"Who's to say a thousand years go by and all kinda stuff happens, and before you know it, nobody ever heard of the guy. Hey, it happens. Look at the Aztecs."

"Must we?"

"How do we know they didn't have this super poet? Guy could make you laugh or cry at the drop of a hat. And rhymes? No 'moon in June' stuff either."

The woman clears her throat and Willie loses the

thread. He looks to Casey then heads off to take her order.

"That's my cue." Casey slides from the stool and steals a look down the bar. "My granddaughter, Louise. Right now she's unhappy with me."

"How come?"

"I won't permit her to escort me home. I've explained to her that when the time comes when I can no longer navigate the way, it will be time for me to die."

"She's probably worried you'll fall and break a hip."

"I can think of no finer fate. He was found frozen stiff in a Hudson Valley snow drift."

Louise is in her thirties, handsome but severe with no makeup and streaked hair tucked in a wool cap.

"Does she follow you?"

"It's only two blocks. She has one drink then drives past to make sure I made it. I find it extremely motivational."

"Well, you take care of yourself." Harry lifts his glass. "I'll look you up when I get settled in."

"Please do...Gerry." He wrinkles his considerable nose. "Something about that name doesn't suit you."

"You get used to it."

The old man looks around in vain for Willie. "It seems our philosopher king has run out. Tell him I will see him on the morrow."

Casey toddles off and Harry turns back to his drink. His reflection blinks back like an old crony. This place certainly fits the hideaway bill, open country, cozy watering hole, not to mention primo burial plot. People live in places for worse reasons. He'll have to think it through when he's sober, but Harry's got a good feeling about this place, whatever it's called. The matches on the bar lettered in branches, Pine Needle Tavern, Owl Hollow, NY.

He pushes to his feet. Really should wait for Willie but he's got it going, steadies himself against the bar, fumbles with the zipper of his jacket.

Murder in Mexico

"Do not go gentle into the good night."
Harry turns. "I'm sorry?"
The woman stares straight ahead.

***

It's nearly dawn when they say goodnight, the longest she and Minna have ever spoken, by far. Lena stares up at the ceiling, filled with thoughts of her father, the house she grew up in, dogs and neighbors long dead. Mindful of the night's connection, linked to a Minna she never knew. For years she's envied Harry's freedom from family. Now, as with everything, it feels all wrong.

Her mother reaching out after all these years, only something drastic could do that. Sister M taught them that tragedy brings out the best in people, even when the tragedy is a sham.

She waits for the sadness to hit, but when it does the impact is minimal. As if her wounded spirit has finally scabbed over, still there but firmly encased, the hard thing sealing up.

***

His eyes snap open, and he knows something happened, smells her in the bed sheets, the woman, Louise. Remembers the name but the face is a blur, streaked hair, missing bicuspid. He lies perfectly still, trying to detect her presence. Recalls the pitcher and washstand from his room, but nothing about how they got here.

His foot inches past the point she would be and he grunts in relief. Lying here like this, he can pretend he's okay. With Harry, hangover is a full body bummer, total recoil, light, sound, movement. As long as he's still, his body won't know. But it takes some effort and his bladder beckons. Ears, eyes and brain pounding, body primed to a hair-trigger touch. Feels it come as if from a distance. One good sneeze and Harry's head explodes.

***

Chef Kim peers in close. "You've been a bad boy."

"Please, I need aspirin."

"Relax. I will bring some for you."

"You're a lifesaver."

A whole fistful, it turns out, plus a platter of deviled eggs, a pot of coffee and half a fifth of Wild Turkey. Harry passes on the eggs.

"Salud, my friend." Kim settles on the radiator. "Have you seen her yet?"

"Seen who?"

"Meryl, she's usually made an appearance by now."

"Meryl Streep?"

"Yes." He bobs his head. "In the dressing gown? Many of our guests have seen her, though most won't admit it."

"But Meryl Streep is still alive."

"Well, yes, in a literal sense. But the spirit of Helen Archer is right here in the Stewart House."

Harry looks him over. "Who?"

"That was her name in the movie."

"Okay."

"My wife, Yuri, cannot see her. People too earthbound cannot see her. But you can see her, can't you, Gerry."

"A few more of these and I'll be seeing three of her."

Kim laughs warm and friendly. The kid's a trip, Harry must admit.

"I have to ask you, Kim. Did you see anyone come out of my room this morning?"

"You mean, Louise?" He smiles and shakes his head. "I didn't think anyone could get to Louise."

"I don't think we got too far."

Murder in Mexico

"We could hear you. Yuri had to phone your room."

"Oh, right, I forgot."

"Louise's grandfather owns the cemetery," Kim tells him.

"Owns it? How can you own a cemetery?"

"Oh, there's some sort of arrangement. Casey's what you call a colorful character."

"I met him. He sold me a plot."

The kid moves around Harry's room, handling things, bud vase, alarm clock.

"Our specials today are the flounder stuffed with crab, London Broil in a béarnaise sauce, and osso buco with Vidalia onions," he announces out of nowhere.

"No food, please, my stomach is a wreck."

He rolls his eyes to the door, and Harry hears a floorboard creak.

"On, uh, second thought it might do me good to eat something. I also wanted to ask you about the area, your take on the people and places."

"Ah, the people, bona fide salt of the earth." Kim checks himself in Harry's mirror. "Of course, scenically, the Catskills are world famous. We have an abundance of natural attract...okay, she's gone. You must forgive Yuri. She worries about me."

"Maybe you shouldn't go on about Meryl. I mean why make trouble for yourself?"

"She thinks I drink too much." He pours another round.

Harry gives him a look. "We both got some red flags waving here, don't you think?"

"I suppose I do have a problem...definitely, now that I think about it. It gets lonely up here, especially in the winter. Those old mountains..." He gazes off.

There's a tap at the door. "Kim? Can you come help me with the ham?"

"Oh yes, and ham." He moves to the door. "Virginia

baked, with an orange glaze, yum."

"Bless you, kind innkeeper. Oh, and hang that Do Not Disturb sign, would you?"

But Harry can't sleep so it's back to the tube. Watches a tennis match, two guys in dreads and perfect teeth, the sweatbands, the stupid ball boys scampering around. Stuck between drunk and badly hung over, every little thing fraying the nerves.

Shortly before noon, a Sousa concert kicks in over at the band shell. Tennis gives way to golf on TV, guys in hats and dorky clothes, some of them fat, none of them familiar. He gets an overwhelming urge to call someone, anyone, and before he can stop himself, he's dialed the pay phone at the market. A week early, but what the hey.

"Yo."

"Hi, uh, is Lena there?"

"Who?"

"Is this the Italian Market?"

"Off the phone, punk. I got fucking bidness here."

Click!

Not a good sign, Lena sees a banger and forget the whole thing. So he calls again.

"Yo yo."

"Yeah, listen, homey, Winslow here. Narcotics. You're anywhere near that phone next Sunday and I'll personally deliver your ass to every donkey dick in the roundhouse, capice?"

Click!

Winslow, Winslow, *where did I come up with that*? Then it hits him, dead Steve's last name. Winslow, from Phoenix. Steve Winslow. Looked enough like Harry he can no longer recall the differences, shorter, but just slightly. Had a slightly rounder chin, too, or was that the barman's? What the hell was *his* name?

Never did get rid of Steve's wallet. Thank God he left it here when he went drunk driving around. Put it...in the...

Murder in Mexico

He knows he's searching in places he will search again and again, cursing himself every time it isn't there. With finding, it's all about the effort. In minutes, he's looked everywhere in the room, again and again, saving the car for later, when he's frantic, another place to look, even though he knows it's not in the car. Distinctly remembers *not* taking it, as a precaution. Sticking it...

The luggage takes longer, poking and patting, ripping and tossing. The anger doesn't help. The anger and the panic building as the wallet refuses to materialize. Finally the car, so new and clean there's no place to look besides the glove compartment, door pockets, under the seat.

Only one thing can explain it. The girl, Louise, must have taken it while he was sleeping. Which explains why she snuck off without saying goodbye, unless some other stuff happened that he doesn't remember. She fucking stole it.

Then a timid knock and there she is with take-out coffee and a bag of something, oranges?

"Feeling better?" She drops the bag on the bed.

"Hi, yeah..." Her name evaporates. "Whew! We really tied one on...I guess."

"Mostly one of us."

"Listen..." Christ, he knew her name a minute ago. "I have to ask you something."

"That's funny. I have to ask *you* something, too." She looks younger than he remembers, pretty, in a randy aunt sort of way. "Did you really see the Last Supper painted on the head of a pin?"

"I said that?"

"You said you saw it in Thailand, during the war."

He feels his way to the bed and stretches out on his stomach. Outside *Maple Leaf Rag* rises up from the band shell. Puts him in mind of the movies, the bad thing happens when the happy music plays.

"I've never been to Thailand. I was drunk. Don't

believe a thing I told you. What else did I tell you?"

"That you played for the Phillies and once dated Grace Kelly's niece."

Jesus, that old fantasy! What next, lampshades on the head? "Did I mention that I'm a pathological liar?"

"No." She smiles demurely. "You did say you were good in bed."

"About that—"

"You needn't apologize. I'm a big girl, Gerry."

"Still, I feel like a dope."

"You're sweet." She smiles again. "So, what did you want to ask me?"

"I uh...nah, it's nothing."

"Come on. What did my grandfather tell you?"

"No, it's not that." Harry rotates his head to face her. "Look, don't take this the wrong way, okay? I had a wallet here yesterday and I can't find it. Did you see me stick it somewhere?"

Her face grows a scowl. "What, you think I stole it?"

"No." Harry tries to roll over but it's too much for him to manage. "No, of course not. I just know how I get when I'm shitfaced."

"You had your wallet at the bar."

"A different one. Black, with—"

"I didn't steal your fucking wallet, okay?" She glares at him.

"Please, I just need to find—"

"And about last night." She crosses to the door. "You were right, we didn't know what we were doing. It happens. But when it happens again..." She swings it open. "Try to remember her fucking name."

Slam!

CHAPTER ELEVEN

The kids stop by on their way to school, Tina from across the street, the Delluci twins, Eddie, and the Feeney boy, blinking up from the sidewalk in their Sacred Heart uniforms and Flyers gear. They tell her how sorry they are, from the heart, not as instructed. Harry was good with the kids, telling jokes and giving them nicknames. Eddie was The Destroyer after his Big Wheel head-on with the lamppost: "D-man" since to everyone but his grand mom.

"You're not gonna move away, are you, Lena?" What she loves about Pennsport, the first name basis.

"I hope not, Tina. Things are kind of up in the air."

"You could live in our house. We have an extra room."

"Oh, baby, that's so sweet. We'll see what happens."

"Father Stapleton says that Harry's in heaven with Pope Paul and Larry Wilkerson."

"Who?"

"The kid from 4th Street." Eddie clues her in. "He got leukemia."

"Okay, you guys." Sally sticks her head out her front door. "Time for school."

The kids bunch up in mumbles then break into a sprint as the bus pulls in.

"How you doin', hon?"

"Better now, Sal. I slept a little. What's the number?"

"648, I wasn't in the ball park."

"648? That's my mother's address."

"You should call her."

"She doesn't play."

Sally looks stricken. "How can she not play?"

The phone rings, and Lena's day begins, Rita and her mom pop over, the grannies visit after mass, and the morning unwinds over coffee and condolences. Doorbell runs the old girls ragged. Neighbors Lena knows by name and by sight, Harry's boyhood pals, their City Council rep, assorted mummers and stevedores. Of all the rituals Harry managed to dodge, this is one he wouldn't have missed, old friends telling his story and paying their respects. By the time it's over, she's run out of vases, and the counters are choked in cakes and casseroles.

"Have you thought about what you're going to do?" Sally asks as she loads the dishwasher.

"First, I have to see about Harry's insurance and Social Security. God, I dread it."

"I'll help you. It seems like a lot, but it's pretty cut and dry."

"It just makes it so final though, closing the book on twenty-five years."

"Just remember, you got friends, Lena. These people would do anything for you."

"I know that, Sal. Sometimes it's the only thing that keeps me going."

Sally pecks Lena's cheek and gives her hands a squeeze. "Okay then, let me get outa your hair. You need anything, call me, yeah? Oh, hey, street sweeper tomorrow. I'll get Duffy to move your car."

"I can get it. Duffy's done enough."

"Are you kidding? It's the only exercise he gets."

So goes her day. What she never could imagine played out in hugs and Tupperware. Death marks her as something special. Lena's seen it happen. In a world of survivors, the widows move above the fray. Now that it's official, she feels strangely empty, a nothing left but the money funk. All of it had her worried at first, but this was the lump that was hardest to swallow. If you live a lie, hearts can turn on a dime, Lena's seen that happen, too.

First thing tomorrow she'll call in an ad to the Albany paper. She already got the number for the Catskill edition. By the week's end Harry should get the message. On Sunday she'll take a stroll to the market.

***

"Yes!" He pounds his fists on the table. The Albany Herald, St. Jude kudos for an answered prayer. The initials PV under heartfelt thanks as Harry's worries circle the drain. He folds the paper and sets it aside. The buzz of Eva's Place warms him, and his heart swells with love for his fellow man, these kickers of shit with their gap teeth and cholesterol levels. Only yesterday he'd have switched shoes with any of them. Well, maybe not that one with the walker, but most of them. Good old boys without a clue.

"What can I getcha, luv?"

"The usual... No, make that steak and eggs, medium rare with home fries."

"Special occasion?"

"Something like that. You believe in miracles, Libby?"

"Miracles? I don't know. Seems like for every good thing that happens, something bad will be along."

"Pretty cynical for a country girl."

"Well, I'm Baptist. We got the jaundiced cyc."

Miracle, hell, this is just everything turning out like it's supposed to. Not that *that* isn't miraculous, but the way he set it up only something minor could go wrong. The major things are easier to keep track of; it's the details that kick your ass. From the time Harry drew it up he was convinced the plan would work. Hard to recall what that felt like now, but he wouldn't have done it if he wasn't dead certain. No way, not in a million years, he's pretty sure. But here in the first flush fortune, it's hard to recall how he felt about anything. The last few days in particular, the thing with Louise, Steve's wallet in his shoe, right where he put it, Casey snubbing him last night at the Pine Needle, Harry's new life a mess already.

St. Jude, patron saint of hopeless causes, his mom's lifelong last resort. Hard to believe the old boy would back something like this, but then who really knows the score? No one, that's who. The world is sick and twisted and nothing's what it seems. This Steve, who was he anyway? Could be Harry rid the world of a monster. Not that it's likely, but anything's possible.

A classified ad as prelude to the good years, Harry feels what it feels like when dreams come true. So good he can hardly stand it.

"Here you go." Libby lays out his breakfast. Filet mignon it ain't, but Harry digs in, chewing and humming along to the muzak. Scanning the front page, dum dee dum, right to lifers on a rampage, three dead in a row-house fire, American businessman missing in Mexico.

"You okay, handsome?" Libby waves a hand in front of his face.

"I, uh, have to..." Harry stuffs the paper under his arm and thumbs some money on the table.

"Hey, where you going? You didn't touch your eggs."

***

He reads it in the car, hands locked to the steering wheel, short and sketchy but with the ring of more to come. American authorities announce the disappearance of Phoenix software developer while vacationing in Puerto Vallarta. Sources say Steven Winslow checked out of a hotel in the seaside resort and hasn't been seen since. Investigators tracking him through credit card receipts and airline reservations, references to similar unsolved Mexican

Murder in Mexico

mysteries. Front page, under the fold, but just barely.

Harry turns up the heater but it doesn't stop the trembling. He stares at the trucks idling, the wet asphalt and grainy sky so real it could kill you. He tries to think of what to think, but the trembling blurs his brain and those birds swooping in over the lot. Seagulls? In the Catskills? All of a sudden the Caddy feels conspicuous, sitting off by itself, running, driver trembling. He puts it in gear and exits the lot, in one end of town and out the other. Follows the curves up into the foothills, ugly houses, gutted vehicles. Crosses a bridge, makes a left back to Athens, the Stewart House, the side lot empty save for Yuri's Civic. Harry slips in without being seen.

The evening news shows a picture of Steve hunched over a little girl in a knit cap, wisps of blond trailing in the wind. Then the daughter alone, a recent school portrait as the newscaster tunes in, oozing concern. Harry listens to it all, the daughter's illness, the risky transplant, the only donor presently missing. When it's over he shuffles to the bathroom and vomits into the sink.

He dials home, but wimps out at the final digit. Listens to the hum, pictures telephone lines stretching to South Philly, beefy detectives huddled in his kitchen. For years he's felt Lena slipping away, that look she gets like his stock is slipping. How is it she's stuck with him *this* long? Then the big question bobs to the surface, what would make her agree to it? Small stuff, sure, but cold blooded murder? You just can't force that on someone.

"Mr. Watts?" Yuri raps at the door. "Will you be dining with us tonight?"

Harry doesn't answer, stands braced at the sink, eyes wide and desperate. If she could see him, she'd run screaming from the building. Truly disturbing with his shirttail hanging, his sweater splattered in bile, the thin slab of door all that stands between them

"Mr. Watts?"

"Yes, Yuri."

"I'm sorry to disturb you." She sounds all out of whatever it takes. "I need to know if you'll be having dinner here this evening."

"I hadn't thought about it. Is there a problem?"

Something catches in her throat. "It's Kim. He never came back from the farmer's market. I don't think—"

"What time did he leave?"

"Early this morning."

Harry opens the door, and she falls to pieces.

"I never should have come here with him."

"Hey, don't. Here, come sit." he leads her inside. "Take a deep breath...that's it."

"I don't know why he's so unhappy? I don't know what more can I do?"

Harry gets the bottle and pours a stiff one.

"Drink this, Yuri. It will help, I promise."

She turns her head away. Harry throws it back and pours another.

"Try this one."

Damned if she doesn't, every drop without flinching. He sees her color slightly, and the tension slips a notch.

"Better, am I right?"

"Thanks. I'm so sorry." She really is lovely with those buggy eyes he goes for.

"Where's the market? I'll go find him."

"No, thank you, no. I couldn't ask you."

"I don't mind, really." Harry squats down next to her. "Listen, just tell the other guests that Kim's sick. People get sick, it's no big deal."

The eyes go even buggier. "There are no other guests. There were two dinner reservations, but I already cancelled them."

"Then just sit tight. I'll find him, don't worry."

"How can I thank you, Gerry?"

"Try to relax." Harry counts the ways.

Murder in Mexico

He takes the road to Cairo, humpbacked Catskills rolling to his right. The crash of events has him churned up, talking Yuri down, putting himself out like this. It's what he needs, a different road to go down, someone else's troubles as a distraction. He's been so caught up in his own it's like getting back in touch, the old Harry, solid type, a guy who goes out of his way for a pretty girl.

He stops at the Quick Way for a pint. This drinking and driving has to stop, but for tonight, to level the playing field. Yuri gave him the names of two taverns north of town, ten miles of switchbacks into timbers, deer grouped in fields of haystacks, geese winging in a ragged V. Harry takes comfort in the dashboard lights, the wrap around feel of Caddy containment. He finds a country station on the radio and settles back.

The daughter, Lilly her name was.

***

"Hello?"

"Hi, uh, my name is Ed Baldini? Harry might have mentioned me."

The midget maniac! Untold hours on the maniac!

"Baldini? No I don't recall the name."

"I was his boss at the print shop."

"Ooooh, Okay. Harry didn't talk about his work much."

"I just heard about it. Geez, it's just...he never mentioned me, no kiddin'?"

"Oh, he may have. Harry worked in a lot of places. I couldn't keep up."

"I just wanted to say your husband was a good pressman and a good, uh, person. I mean, we had our differences, sure, but we were up front about it. Know what I'm sayin'?"

"Thank you, Mr. Baldini. I'm sure Harry would be

touched."

"I could always count on him for the big jobs, the process work, the tight registration. There's an art to that stuff, believe me."

"I'm sure there is. My husband was a man of many talents."

"Right, I mean, we had our differences but, you know."

"I know, and again, thank you."

"My brother too, talk about differences, ho-boy! But man to man like, well, like men."

"Yes."

"So I just wanted to pay my respects. I uh..." She hears muffled wheezing. Crying? No he's laughing. The maniac is laughing!

"Mr. Baldini?"

"I'm sorry, whew! I was just thinking...no, I better not."

"Please tell me. I'd like to know."

"Oh Christ it was funny. I don't know, that brother of mine. Harry and him were going at it. I forget about what, about the exterminator, that was it. We had a guy come in once a month..." More laughter, deep and phlegmy. "Harry didn't want the guy spraying around his press. He had a mouse over there, didn't want the mouse to, you know."

"Die?"

"Well, yeah."

"Harry never said a word about it," she lies. But now she thinks of it, he never told her how it was resolved.

"Right. So what happened is the mouse, well, he *did* die, I guess. This was a few years ago. We had a lunchroom back then. You sure he never told you this?"

"About the lunch room?"

"Yeah, my brother's lasagna?" Wheezing and something pounding. "Oh Jesus, just thinking about it."

"Lasagna?"

"Leftovers..." wheeze, "big container..." wheeze, wheeze.

"Are you all right, Mr. Baldini?"

"The mouse...buried, inside. Ohgod, ohjesus...my brother...crunching..." wheeeeze, stomp, "baaahahahah!"

***

Harry kills the bottle in the parking lot, Kim's truck listing badly by the front door. Dew Drop Inn, if you can believe it, a fake Tudor mess with diamond paned windows, neon letters glowing on the roof, the thing about neon, how it blurs at the edges. He feels the cold seep up through the floorboards, but he doesn't feel up for this anymore. Really should have eaten something, fucking bourbon wreaking havoc. How redneck bars creep him out, the air of hostility, nowhere to point your eyes. The night he drove home from the Apple Jack at a hundred miles an hour, Christ, where'd that come from? Last call watching the bouncing beer signs, ten minutes to fit the car key.

He crosses the lot without stumbling, finds Kim slouched in a corner booth, a bit foggy, but not surprised to see him.

"Yuri said you'd be here."

"You talked to her?" His smile is warm and sleepy.

"She called."

"She's worried." Harry slides in facing him. "You okay?"

"I'm afraid I've crossed some lines. Those flags you mentioned."

"Drink up, pal. Show's over."

"Have one with me, Gerry. We've miles to go before we sleep."

Harry eyes the bartender working crosswords by the register.

"One drink and we're gone."

"I never got to the market." Kim slips a cigarette from his pocket.

"No one gives a shit. Forget about it, Kim."

"Yuri does. It's something of a regular occurrence. You see, Gerry, it seems I've ruined her life."

"Don't flatter yourself. Yuri's a survivor. Believe me, I know the type."

"Doubles, right?" Bartender sets them down, more like triples but what the hell. They clink glasses and down the hatch. Whatever it is isn't bourbon.

"You should have seen her when we started up." Kim slumps back into the corner. "I really sold her on the program. All talk, that's my style."

"Seems like it's going pretty good to me."

"Her parents lent us the start-up capital. We limped through the summer, but the locals never warmed. The place was a real watering hole back when men folk gathered to stoke their ignorance." Kim taps the table. "The Stewart House, a family sore spot going back to the steam wheelers. As it looks now, we'll be bankrupt by May Day."

Harry grunts. It's a damn shame, sure, but try murder for something to unravel over. Murder and a death sentence for the little ski bunny, go on, live with that. And dragging your wife into it, for Christ sake, hounding her until she'd agree to anything. You want regrets? Try forcing her to face the music alone. Bankruptcy? Divorce? He'd give a kidney for Kim's problems.

"That's rough, I won't kid you. But it isn't the end of the world."

"You don't know Yuri. Last year she had a miscarriage. Nobody said it was my fault, but nobody tried to convince me otherwise."

That's more like it, life, death, the real stuff of meltdowns. Turns out the miscarriage was Yuri's second, the first following a car wreck the year before, a rear ender on the 9W, you-know-who behind the wheel.

Murder in Mexico

"Kara Mia, we'd already picked a name."

"Kara. That's nice."

"We couldn't wait to have her running around the hotel, growing up there, meeting different people. My grandmother was raised in a boarding house in Austria. It's all she ever talked about."

"It was an accident, nobody's fault," Harry says, as if he has the faintest idea. "Things you can't control, Kim. Knocking them around is a waste of time."

Two kids on his conscience, it's a wonder the guy's not in worse shape. So much shit goes down in one lifetime, it's hard to see how it's worth the effort. Kara Mia, can you beat that? Harry waves for another round.

***

"Hello?"

"Oh, Lena, I just can't believe he's gone. It's me, Sue Anne. We've been crying all day."

"We?"

"Me and Laurie, she heard it from Diane. Everybody's in total shock."

Lena rolls her eyes. "Diane Petrone? I thought she was living in Florida."

"She's back. Her mom's in a nursing home. God, it's all starting to happen."

"What is?"

"The dying. Once it starts it doesn't stop. First it's people you hardly know then...oh why did it have to be Harry?"

"I wish I knew." Lena counts the floor tiles.

"He had everything, looks, brains, the moustache."

"Harry shaved that years ago."

"I used to have such a crush on him." Sue Anne sighs. "Once he kissed me at a Who concert and I nearly creamed my jeans."

"That's so sweet."

"Me and Laurie have been going through the yearbooks. God, we all look like children. You had that Twiggy thing going, remember?"

Lena butts her head against the doorframe. "How is Laurie?"

"She's doing better since the divorce. My kids call her Auntie L. Here, say hi."

"No, that's—"

"Lena?"

"Hi, Laurie." Hotpants, the enduring image. "It's been a long time."

"I'm really sorry for...you know."

"Thanks. I think."

"I just want you to know that I never meant anything to Harry. When he was with me, all he talked about was you."

"Really."

"And that time I had the hickey on my neck? That was from Gerry."

"I haven't thought of it in years." Fucking Gerry, dead for years and still stepping in it.

"Anyway, Lena, I hope you're okay and that this doesn't change anything between us."

"Not at all, we were kids," Lena assures the stupid bitch.

"Here's Sue Anne, Bye."

"Goodbye, Laurie," *and drop dead, could you?*

"Lena, hey, listen, we were thinking. Me and Laurie joined the gym, and for a third membership you get a discount. I know you're probably busy right now, but later, if you ever feel like working out, I don't know, it would be great...all of us back together."

"Sounds good, I'd like that," *not a chance.*

"Well, I'll let you go, oh wait, here's Harry with the band. Geez, I didn't even know I had this picture. There's you, Lena, with the go-go boots."

"Let me see," Laurie whines in the background.

"God, he was hot, like Jim Morrison only skinny. Look."

"Who's that guy next to him?"

"Move your finger, Oh, that's...oh, what's his name."

Lena lugs the phone down the hall, reaches outside and pushes the doorbell.

"Oh hell, someone's at the door. Listen, Sue, I gotta go."

"Started with a 'P' Peter?"

***

"Your sister?"

"Maddie. She had cystic fibrosis. I used to lay in bed at night and smell her pain."

"Christ, that's awful." Harry's glass misses the table on the down stroke, clanking to the floor then rolling under the booth behind them.

"And when she died?" Kim's head moves with a life all its own. "My dad put a padlock on the door to her bedroom. No one's been in there in twenty-three years. Now do you see, Gerry?"

"Know what I think?" Harry gives him the eye that's working. "I think on Judgment Day... Oh man, I can't wait for that fucker."

"Judgment Day?"

"Yeah, when they tally up the score and everybody gets what they deserve."

Kim slams the table. "That's what I've been telling you. It doesn't matter what you do when the Man upstairs has it in for you."

"Fucking justice, man."

"Okay, that's it," Barman barks. "You two are flagged."

"One for the road, Ray," Kim wheedles.

"Forget it. I should have cut you off hours ago."

Harry pushes to his feet, but by the time he gets there he's forgotten why.

"In that case..." Kim struggles to join him. "My friend and I will take our business elsewhere."

Ray shakes his head. "Come on, Kim, no one's gonna serve you in your condition."

"We'll see about that." Kim hands Harry his coat. "Shall we?"

They take the Caddy, keeping to the back roads at Kim's direction. The liquor store is still open so they stop for a bottle, something sweet and scorching, whatever. Half moon bright above the mountains, the mile wide Hudson streaked in silver. They end up in the old town cemetery, high beams on headstones going back to the colonies. Kim calls off names and dates, Harry blows lunch out the window.

"'Sarah Jane, wife to Orrin, resting in the sleep of peace'"

"Uunnnngh..."

"Sort of clumsy, hic, resting in the sleep?"

"whooooaaa..."

"Old Casey might have something, you know? Reading to the dead. I mean, what could it, hic, hurt, right?"

"Reciting, oooh."

"Let's see, there was a young girl from Nantucket."

Harry's head comes to rest on something, the ground. Blades of grass curl under his cheek, the smell of dirt, a good smell from long ago.

"You look a sight, Gerry." Kim belches. "I'll have to ask you to let me drive."

Dewdrops glisten at eye level, and Harry touches his tongue to one.

"Gerry?"

Murder in Mexico

Something teensy scrambles over his eyelid.

He wakes to the noon whistle, a vacuum above him thumping walls. For a second, Harry thinks it's Sunday, that he's missed calling Lena, but playground racket makes it a school day. Which one, he couldn't say. Harry runs down the blackout checklist, keys and wallet on the nightstand, bridgework in place, insides in order, no bleeding or broken bones. His clothes stacked and folded on the bureau, coat hanging from the hook on the door.

Okay.

***

"Sister Muriel. What a surprise." My God, there's nothing left of her.

"Hello, my dear. Yes, I don't get around like I used to. But I had to come see you."

"Come in, come in." Lena steps out to help her. Stoop salt crunches underfoot and a stiff wind catches the old nun's habit.

"You're by yourself?" Lena takes her elbow, knobby as a walnut. "You shouldn't be out in this cold. I've been meaning to get over to see you."

"Now I've saved you the trouble. They think I'm in chapel. It's the only time I can get anything done."

"Come, sit." Lena guides her into the kitchen and offers Harry's chair. "Can I get you something, some coffee, tea?"

"If it's no trouble." She fusses with her habit and Lena hears the rosaries rattle. "Coffee please, black."

"Father Mac said you'd started a novena. I wanted to thank you."

"We're into the third week. Somewhere around seven we tend to lose track. It's no fun growing old, Lena."

She really did intend to drop in on Muriel somewhere down the road. Now that she's here, Lena feels a fresh stab of guilt. Lying to the world is one thing, lying to Sister M is something else entirely.

Lena sets two cups on table. "So how are you, Sister?"

"I'm well, Lena." The old girl takes one in both hands. "Oh, I've cut my activities down to the nub, but I still have my moments of usefulness. The question is how are you?"

"I keep waiting for it to hit me, but there's so many distractions."

"They say a mother's worst fear is to outlive her children. You were all my children, and I've buried four of late. Now Harry. I believe my faith has been shaken."

"Don't say that, Sister M. It's the last thing Harry would have wanted."

"I admit it bothered me as a young girl. The pain we all endure. I must have thought I could do something about it, but in the end, the bad catches up with you. Harry was a fine boy."

"Now he's in heaven. We'll see him again."

Sister Muriel takes off her glasses. "I used to block all of that out, the afterlife, the eternal reward, but the day comes when you must make your peace with it."

"What do you mean?" Lena pulls her chair around.

"You learn a lot as you get older. You start to see things differently. When the Sandusky boy died I couldn't make sense of it. It's not my place to question the way of the Lord, but certain things demand an explanation."

"I..."

"Spend your life in the classroom, and it's easy to spot the special ones. I remember when Harry first started at Sacred Heart, the kids just seemed drawn to him."

"Mac says Harry will be okay," Lena tells her. "A stretch in Purgatory maybe."

"Purgatory?" Muriel's scoff is pure Harry. He saw Purgatory as a medium security prison with conjugal visits.

"You don't believe in Purgatory?"

Murder in Mexico

Sister gazes off. "Just the name, like some small country in the Soviet Union."

Lena takes her hand. "You taught us that the Lord works in mysterious ways."

"Too mysterious for my taste, and cruel to the point of criminal. Fifty years explaining God to children. Will it ever make sense?"

"I don't know."

"Of course you don't." Sister sips her coffee. "And since we teach the children not to question, the answers become meaningless. Take yourself, Lena."

"Me?"

"Your husband is taken and you're resigned to God's will. No anger, no bitterness. If it wasn't for the church making His excuses you'd see it for the outrage it is."

Whoa, the unthinkable, Patron Saint of Pennsport having her doubts? Lena always thought faith was something you had or you didn't, like freckles or a fear of heights. Muriel's spent her whole life in the convent. If she loses it now she loses everything.

"Can I be honest with you, Sister?"

Muriel just looks at her.

"Harry had a vision right before he died."

"A vision." sister frowns.

"I know, it sounds spooky, but he said Gerry came to him and told him heaven was everything you said it would be."

"Gerry? In heaven?"

"I know, right? But Harry said Gerry said that they didn't keep score. Not like a permanent record thing. God just looks into your heart and sees your true worth."

"And Purgatory?"

"He didn't say. But I'm sure there's nothing to worry about. It's like out patient therapy. You're not really in the hospital but you're pretty close."

"A vision." Muriel mulls it over. "It doesn't sound

like Harry to me."

"He was really getting in touch with his spiritual side towards the end."

"I have to tell you, I never put much stock in visions."

"Well, I'm not saying he really *saw* Gerry. Not physically."

Muriel studies the logo on her coffee mug.

A vision? Jesus, what kind of crap is that to hand her? The old girl's in a crisis, and that's the best I can do?

"Sister Muriel, don't you see? It's what you do with your life that matters." Can't be happening, *me counseling Sister M.*

"Yes, but—"

"Look at what *you've* done. There's a wing named after you at Mt Sinai, you're a member of every New Years club on Second Street, and half the girls in Pennsport are named after you."

"Middle names, mostly."

"Still."

They sit through a moment lost in thoughts.

"What will you do now, Lena?"

"I'll be okay, Sister M."

The old nun fingers an empty ashtray.

"You wouldn't happen to have a cigarette, would you, dear?"

CHAPTER TWELVE

The Caddy takes the curve out of town, and Harry feels the load lighten. Okay, so the Catskills didn't cut it, plenty of burgs up here to get lost in. Next time he'll go about it a little differently. The liquor is out. Harry's always been a boozer, beer man mostly, but this? Days lost to hangover, nights veering into sloppy moves and hard feelings. Drink enough and something bad always happen. He runs through the images, Louise and Casey turning on him, Yuri's deep freeze when he paid his bill. No doubt about it, the booze is out.

He takes the interstate north, Cooperstown bound, Hall of Fame baseball to take his mind off things. Something he's dreamed of since he was a kid, knows the names by heart, seen the plaques in photos a million times. It was all wrong in Athens, no sense kidding himself.

Hall of Fame came to him at Eva's, a placemat map of the upstate attractions with a smiley baseball beaming on Cooperstown. A day made to order, Harry, the Caddy and a grand destination, the hand of God showing the way.

Thinks of Kim, that death warmed over look. Should have known better than to mess in his mess, drunks and their problems, who fucking needs it? From now on it's strictly beer. And reefer if Harry can find some. Wishes he had a joint now, as a matter of fact, toke a buzz to enhance the trip. How it makes the wheels turn so almost anything's interesting. Driving especially, long distance, follow your thoughts anyplace they lead you. Reefer would be perfect for this, the mountains, what's left of the foliage. Ease whatever's kicking in his stomach, fucking bourbon eating at his guts. Checks what's left of last night's bottle, peach schnapps, if you can believe it. Harry takes a pull and turns up the radio.

"*The Defense Department has lied to us for decades. Look at Rumsfeld. He's just MacNamara with a better haircut.*"

"*You mean a different haircut?*"

"*Right. And more pie charts.*"

Harry hits the buttons to distant static, then "seek" stopping at a rockabilly station, then "seek" to a show about floral design.

"*Of course listeners can't see it, but the arrangement is simple yet elegant, with the holly and the baby's breath rounding off the shape.*"

Then more classic rock, boomers stuck in the rut, like the old man with his Glenn Miller.

"*Sat- tis-faction, Du dunt dunt.*"

Near the Finger Lakes he stops at a rest stop. Nathan's Hot Dogs lit up like Coney Island, same crowd as always, sweats and windbreakers. How the fatsos love that shit, waddling over to the queue, lined up for their nachos and chilidogs. Americana in blubber and butt cracks, nothing like the road to put you back in touch. Takes his order back to the Caddy and watches the parade. The hot dogs mix with the schnapps and breakfast, bubbling up like something toxic.

Peach schnapps, who would do that?

Back on the road, he thinks of Lena. Feels like years since he's seen her. The classified ad told him what he had to know, but he's dying to talk to her. Try to explain the fuckups. How Steve made it sound like *he* was sick, not his daughter. Barely mentioned her, except that last bit when he was going under, the stuff about the operation, desperate measures, long shot odds. All true, more or less, but coming across lame when Harry puts words to it. Okay, what you can't fix you live with. The money will make it

Murder in Mexico

right. The main thing now, the million bucks.

Steve as headline news, that's a worry. That's what *should* be on his mind, but the last few days, with the drinking, Jesus. Harry doesn't know much about Puerto Vallarta, but two Americans casualties in two weeks might raise a fuss. Not such a small town, but not like Philly. Forget about it. Two stiffs in the same room maybe, but otherwise...

Coming into Rockville, it starts to snow. Ice really, pinging the windshield, hardening to a crust around wiper fantails. The road turns slick, and Harry slows to well below the limit. The last thing he needs is a fender bender or speeding ticket. By Mitchellsville, the bottle's empty so he stops for another, back to bourbon for the home stretch. Last one, positively.

Serious snow now, wet and heavy, radio warns of a winter storm due in from Canada. *Yo, pal, try looking out the window.* Harry wonders where he'll spend the night, someplace warm and cozy to ease into it. A lodge would fit the bill, with a lake view and a mini-bar for emergencies. A lodge or an old inn, stone and timber like Bucks County. He and Lena used to go in mid winter. The Black Bass Hotel on a snowbound weekend, the carriage suite, if memory serves him. A hundred thousand years ago.

Signs for the Lake and the Hall of Fame. Harry can't recall anything about a lake, but there it is, wide and white-capped, curving around to Cooperstown. Hey now. Like a slide show with the downtown and the fucking lake, all brick and storefronts, perfect for an inn or lodge. An unlikely setting for baseball, but comfy in that high-end way, antiques and more antiques, restaurants and galleries, an upgrade from anything Catskill. Harry passes a few motels but nothing rustic. Turning back, he parks at a boutique strip, walks off the woozies to the corner Starbucks.

"Let me ask you something." he chats up the counter

girl. "My wife and I are in town for the weekend. I'm looking for a place with, you know, atmosphere."

"That's so romantic," she croons. "Try the Willows, half mile out of town. My husband and I stayed there for our anniversary."

"The Willows. Romantic, right?"

"Ver-ry romantic. Get a suite with the lake view." She winks. "You won't regret it."

The Willows, right where she said it would be. Nestled into the hillside, wood and windows, smoke curling from chimneys, just what Harry had in mind. He checks in with Gerry's card and takes the escalator to the third floor, deep wood paneling, fresh flowers, violins lilting in the background. His is the Ives suite, late of Courier. Brass bed smothered in comforters, fireplace, flat screen, lake view from his private balcony, all the comforts of a rich man's home.

Harry puts it off for a while, but with the snow falling and the fire roaring and the crab cakes from room service, it's not long before he's into the mini-bar, all those bite-size bottles, chocolates, peanuts. It will set him back a bundle, he knows, but how many times do you Hall of Fame? Here's to Cooperstown, so much nicer than it had to be.

Later, TV to die for, a thousand channels, the premium package with an X-rated option. Harry feels like he's gone to heaven, just for one night, but it makes all the difference. In the morning he'll take in the town, save the Hall for the afternoon. Or maybe vice versa, see how he feels.

Forget the Catskills, this is holing up in style.

He awakens late, dry mouthed and groggy. Little empties line the coffee table along with crumpled candy wrappers and a saucer piled in butts. On the TV screen, a redhead writhes in silent ecstasy. Harry groans once, buries his head in the pillows and dozes into the afternoon.

Murder in Mexico

***

"Can I get you more coffee?"

"Please." Harry shoves his cup over. "What's the word on the snow?"

"The radio says it's supposed to stop this evening. Plows have been running all night."

"Beautiful day for a ballgame, eh?"

"Snowball maybe. You know I may be out of line here, but you don't look so good."

"Flu. Must have picked it up on the plane."

"Also, you have your sweater on inside out."

"Thanks. I'll take it up with my valet."

Harry fights down breakfast then throws it up back in his room. Famished again, he finishes off the chocolates to a Thin Man sequel then orders up a ham on rye. Christ, he's gonna regret this, three figures easy on the room service tab. Plus the mini-bar, plus another night here, since it doesn't look like he'll get anything together today, snow up to the knees out there and getting deeper. Hall of Fame will have to wait. Less than 24 hours until he can talk to Lena, tomorrow, provided the phones don't go down.

He meant to rehearse his end of the call last night, but for something on the TV, what was it? The fight! Ali versus George Foreman, Christ how could he forget that? A remastered tape, clean as a whistle, mid seventies, wasn't it? Ali, thick in the chest and shoulders, but still cat quick, Foreman with hair and looking mean, not that smiley fathead with the indoor grille. The two of them as they once were. God, it was glorious, and endless with the clutching and slugging, way beyond exhaustion.

Harry wonders who won.

Now he's watching some geezer building a cabin in the wilderness, all by himself with primitive tools. The guy's meticulous. Christ, chopping and scraping, filing and smoothing until everything fits just right. Watches him build the fireplace stone by stone, lugging squares of moss for the roof, things Harry would never dream of doing. Hapless, that's Harry, and proud of it, though the cabin idea has a certain appeal. And this guy's no spring chicken either, craggy and buzz cut, a man's man, no doubt about it. Drop him in the woods with a penknife and he'll carve out a kingdom. Not Harry, not come winter. And now it *is* winter, and the guy's punching holes in the ice for water, fucking hell! Can't tell how cold it is since the sound is turned down, but it looks, oh no wait, woodsman checks his thermometer. 25 below? Jesus pal, you've made your point.

Harry drops off, dreaming the dream he had as a kid. The weird one about living underground, his own private bunker, air conditioned with a trapdoor hatch and a wrap-around view through a hidden periscope. He gave a lot of thought to the details back then, so this dream features a fully stocked bar and satellite TV. Can't recall much else when he wakes, but that old feeling of safe and sound.

The sun breaks through in the afternoon, bouncing off the lake in jagged slashes. He watches ducks in a clumsy landing, steam rising over patches of asphalt. The storm's end deflates him like it always does, part of him wishes it would never stop. That he could just stay here forever, downing shots and stuffing his face. How everything is suspended in silence. Always quiet when it snows. Quiet and eerie, calm descending, the soft, muffle made for blowing off the day.

He downs a short one to shake off the doldrums, quick shave and shower and he's off to the Hall of Fame. What he's here for, right? Those boys of summer duly enshrined. He bundles up and takes the escalator to the lobby. The Caddy's plowed in so he heads off on foot. Farther than he remembers and slow going with the sidewalks half shoveled and the wind picking up. Not the right shoes and no gloves, but he shoulders on. Better than holed up with the stupid porn and the mini-bar. The longer he's gone the

Murder in Mexico

better he'll feel. And it will be a while when he factors in the whole mess freezing up when the sun goes down. Turning back would be the smart thing, but he just keeps going. If anything will get him back in gear it's baseball.

But it's closed. He can see from blocks away, nobody there and the lights low inside. Slogs to the finish anyway and stares through the door at the turnstiles, the floor wide and empty. A life-size Ted Williams, he'd know that stance anywhere. Now that he can't get in, Harry wants to more than ever. To lose himself in baseball, see the old names again and the plaques and whatever else they have. Like what's that, by the hallway leading off to the right? A room full of monitors for watching film, and this exhibit, The Story of the Bat, where they come from, how they're made. Hell, he'd settle for *that*, though you'd think they'd have something more interesting right there, by the entrance, something to get you in game-mood, a picture of the Babe or Ebbett's Field. Harry stands there until his toes and his fingers throb with the cold.

"What can I get you?"

"Shot of Jim Beam and a Heineken."

"You got it, Hell of a thing, snow this early, right?"

"They closed the Hall."

"Hah! They could burn it to the ground for all I care."

"You live in Cooperstown and you don't like the Hall of Fame?"

"It's a tourist trap. Pushing merchandise, that's all it is."

"That's funny, like hating cleavage and living in Vegas."

"And your average fan? A real cretin, I can tell you."

"Come on, it's the Hall of Fame. There must be some good things about it. What about the plaques?"

"What's good about it? Let's see..." The bartender pretends to think then holds up a finger. "It ain't the Football Hall of Fame. Oh yeah, and the plaques? Have you ever seen them?"

"Not in person."

"They're plastic! And the faces? They don't look nothing like the real guys. I mean Yogi looks like Bella Legosi, for Christ sake."

"Plastic? Can't be."

"And like this big." His hands make a little box. "We're talkin' el cheaperoo."

Harry always pictured a large room with arched doorways and vaulted ceilings. Brass plaques mounted around the perimeter like Stations of the Cross.

"So..." the bartender leans in, "who did it for you?"

"Did what?"

"Which player? When you were a kid, let me guess." He steps back and sizes Harry up. "Willie Mays, right?"

"Koufax."

"Kou-fax! LA? I never pegged you for the west coast."

"Just Koufax, not the Dodgers. Best ever, for those few years."

"Yeah, Koufax is a whole other level. The curveball alone would have gotten him in."

"Like dropping off a table. I can still see it."

"Me? I don't even follow the game anymore. These guys with the steroids, they *poisoned* the record book. Ripped the heart out of the game, if you ask me. I mean the game is *built* on numbers. Now they don't mean a thing."

"You're angry."

"Damn straight, I'm angry! 70-75 homers a year. It's *obscene*."

"And the money."

"It's not about the money. Money's money, it can ruin your life but it can't ruin baseball. It's the *numbers!* Screw with the numbers and it stops making sense."

"I don't know, there's other con—"

"Numbers. Don't you get it?"

"Yeah, okay, the numbers, right. Listen, any cabs in town?"

"I mean, look at Barry Bonds. Do you mean to tell me his numbers are gonna stand up, huh?"

"No, I—"

"They *can't* stand up. No one will ever be able to touch them, and they don't mean a thing. You're *always* gonna be up against that, that *travesty*!"

"Okay, whew. That really hit the spot. Listen, good talking to you."

"Or *Canseco*! Christ, he better pray I never get my hands on him!"

Back into the cold and wet. The wind has died down, but the sidewalks are slick and drifted in stretches. Not a cab in sight. Harry takes to the street where the footing is better. Not much traffic so he makes good time. Sure the guy had a point about the numbers, but going postal over it, not healthy, not healthy at all. Put a kink in the old Hall of Fame plan, though. Might not even bother depending on the price, plastic plaques, that can't be right. A blowhard, that guy. A moron, like this guy here, big smiley face in a knit cap, what's he waving at? Move the fucking car, pal. Hey!

The window goes down, something jazz on the radio, this face—

"Harry? It *is* you. What the hell are you doing up here?"

"Frank? Holy shit!"

"I *thought* that was you. What are you doing walking around in the weather?"

Head spinning. What to say? What the fuck? "How are you, Frank?"

"I'm good. Listen, you going far? You look cold."

"Just up the road."

"Get in." he pushes the passenger door open. "I'll give you a lift."

Harry gets in. What now? This is so bad in so many ways. This is the world blowing up in his face.

"I can't believe it, Harry Watts up here in the boonies. I didn't think you ever got out of Pennsport."

"I, uh, always wanted to see the Hall."

"So what, you schlepped the wife and kids up here and now they're driving you bonkers, right?"

"Something like that, yeah."

Frank...Lavin! From Fairmount, they worked a job together back in the nineties, good pressman, hockey freak.

"Good to see you, Harry. Wait 'til I tell the wife. All the way up here."

By all means, tell the wife and the whole damn universe. Just like that, out of nowhere and no way to fix it. Frank's seen him and Harry can't change it.

"What are you doing here, Frank?"

"I had business in Albany, and I always wanted to see the Hall. Of course, I didn't know there'd be a blizzard."

"She's up here? Your wife?"

"No, hell, Sandy hates baseball. That was the whole point! Now the danm thing isn't even open!"

They pass the Willows, taking a long curve to nowhere. Harry can't think what to do.

"I think we passed it, Frank."

"That place back there? Nice, Harry. I'll turn around."

Buy some time, can't let him go. Think! "Listen, Frank, you doing anything right now?"

"Not really. I have a meeting in Rochester tomorrow, but—"

"You hungry? What do you say we grab a bite?"

"Yeah, sure, I could eat something. Let's do it." He swings around and heads back to town.

"You know what, Frank? I passed a little place out by the interstate. Shrimp, all you can eat. I've been thinking about it all day."

"The interstate? Okay, why not?"

Keep it going, something will come to him.

"Ever see any of the guys, Har? Herman? Jimmy Fours?"

"Not for years. I lost touch."

"The last time I saw Jimmy he was in the hospital. Diabetes, I think it was. What's it been, six, seven years?"

"Long time, Frank. So what, you're out of the trades?"

"I got into the jewelry business. Importing. I haven't run a press since Fairmount."

"Good move, pal. The industry's dead. Kind of a stretch though, jewelry, Frank?"

"Diamonds mostly. Get this, I was in Albany as an expert witness."

"What, a robbery?"

"Smugglers. Real cloak and dagger, I'm telling you. How about you, Harry? You working?"

"I'm on sabbatical, Frank. Set a year aside to do all the things I wanted to do."

"Hence, the Hall?"

Harry smiles for the first time all day. "Hence, the Hall."

Shrimp Shanty, loud and crowded. They take a booth and order all you can eat. Frank turns out to be pretty much all about diamonds. Harry tunes out most of it, feels himself watching from overhead like a film director. He doesn't like the feeling, but he can't seem to shake it. And the shrimp comes but he can't eat. He can drink okay, three Bloody Marys to Frank's glass of wine, but then he starts getting a weird feeling about Frank. And this place, something wrong with it.

"Cold, Harry?"

"What do you mean?"

Frank shrugs. "You look cold."

"I do feel a little funny."

"Maybe the shrimp?"

"No, no I'm okay." But he's not okay. His heart is

~199~

pounding, and everything Frank says scares him to death. What the fuck is he doing here and what the hell's happening? Harry can't seem to catch his breath.

"I gotta get out of here." He gets up, starts walking, has to get away. Frank throws some money on the table then scrambles after him, catching up in the parking lot.

"Harry, hey, what's wrong? Are you okay?"

"I gotta go, sorry, Frank."

"Okay, listen, I'll drive you, Harry. Come on, you're having a reaction or something."

Too cold, so he goes with Frank back to the SUV. They drive back toward town, Frank yacking but Harry doesn't hear him. Scared to death but at least it's warm.

"That's probably it, Har. An anxiety attack, my brother gets them sometimes."

He's thinking it's no accident Frank turned up. He knows about Mexico. They're after him, and now Harry will have to go to jail. And Lena too. He misses Lena so much. They've gone through hell and now this.

"Where are you taking me?"

"To the hospital, Harry. They'll fix you up, don't worry."

No hospital, couldn't stand that. Once he's in he'll never get out. He's going crazy, that's the only explanation.

"Let me out."

"You can't do that, Harry. It's bitter cold. You'll freeze to death."

"I'm serious, Frank. Let me out."

"Okay, look we'll pull in here. It's all right."

Frank turns into a picnic area half plowed, big lot with benches and stone barbecues piled in snow. Harry's out the door before the car stops, slipping on his side and into a plow bank. Then he's up and running past the benches and tables towards the woods, Frank calls after, but Harry keeps going. So hard running in snow, but he makes it to the trees, stands huffing in a clump of pines as Frank shouts his name. Oh Christ, here he comes, picking his way along Harry's footprints, with a flashlight and something else, what? Oh shit!

"It's okay. Everything is going to be all right. Can you hear me, Harry?"

No, nothing will ever be right again. All over for Harry, just like that. He presses up against a tree, watching as Frank draws closer, the flashlight sweeping over the snow between them. Harry hears his heart thumping through his jacket, searches in the snow, finds a fat branch.

"No, Harry. Hey!" The first blow catches Frank's arm, then one to the forehead, and he goes down hard.

"Unnnh, no, Harry, *Please, no!*"

Another to the back of the head, solid, like Ted Williams, then a few more. Frank lying still now, blood everywhere, that second one, solid. Harry knows he's dead. Oh Jesus, can't catch his breath, head hammering, stands bent at the waist, gripping the club in both hands, steam clouds blowing back in his face, this is no dream, this is happening. He's killed him, Frank Lavin, from Fairmount. But then, oh God no, he's moving and Harry has to hit him again, then again. No other choice. The branch shatters at the end, jagged shards dripping and Harry's wailing now. Head thrown back, arms wide and turning in a circle. Screams it all out then lets fly. *FOOM!* The club windmills off in a crash of branches.

Has to get out of here, all he can think. Hears a truck downshift miles off, the SUV running in the parking lot, Harry starts for it, bloody hands, no good, turns back and squats by the body, just does it before the idea can freak him. Washes his hands in the snow and wipes them dry on Frank's scarf. Takes the scarf. Takes his wallet. Move. Think. Running through the snow then he's in Frank's SUV. Warm, oh God yes. Get going. *Move!* Harry puts it in gear and swings around, pausing at the entrance to hit the lights.

Not a car on the road back into town. Empty now, everything closed. Harry parks in one of the strip mall lots and wipes down the wheel and the knobs, anything he might've touched. He finds a gun in Frank's glove compartment. Not a big gun, but nasty looking, and Harry takes it, wraps the scarf around to cover the bloodstains on his jacket. Locks the SUV and crosses the lot, the gun, solid and heavy in his pocket. A long haul back to the lodge but he forces himself, left, right, stepping off into shadows when a car passes, not many, thank God. Couldn't face anyone in this condition. What happens now? Who has he turned into?

Nearly walks right past the Willows then can't bring himself to enter, stands in the lot, looking in through the windows. Can't decide what to do, then just opens the door, no one at the desk, thank you Jesus, bypasses the elevator for the stairs, some trouble with the key card then he's in his room, cleaned and straightened, bed made. The front of his coat smeared in blood, his pants, some on his shoes. What a mess! Wraps the gun in his pants, wraps his pants in his jacket and stuffs it all in one of the drawers. No good. Takes them outside and sticks them in the trunk of the Caddy. Stumbles to the mini-bar, claws the door open, grabs one, any one, tears off the cap then guzzles straight from the bottle.

***

"Hello?"

"Lena? You're okay?"

"Jesus, Harry, it's freezing out here. Where are you?"

"God I've missed you." Harry can't stop crying, holds the phone away.

"You don't sound so good. What's happened?"

"I've been a wreck here."

"I know. I miss you too, Harry. You saw the ad?"

Murder in Mexico

"Yeah, I saw it, yeah. It's okay, then, right?"

"It worked," she says in a whisper. "We did it, Harry. You wouldn't believe all that's happened. Where are you?"

"Some little town, I don't know. Lena, I feel so bad leaving you down there. I don't know what I was thinking."

"It's been crazy," over vendors hawking produce. "Oh, Harry, the neighbors have been so sweet. Everyone's—"

"They're looking for the guy. Steve. On the news, it should have taken them longer. The thing about his daughter, I didn't know, Lena. You gotta believe me."

"We can talk about that later, Harry. I'll be meeting with the lawyers this week about the insurance."

"When can I see you?"

"Not for a while yet. If I went off somewhere, people would wonder." over Sirens screaming Doppler. "I'll have to set up an excuse. Oh, and about the insurance, Harry, I can't find one of the policies. It wasn't in the drawer of important papers."

"It must be on my workbench. Look down there."

"Also, I need the key to the safe deposit box."

"What safety deposit box?"

"Oh, I thought we had one."

"Listen, forget about that. Lena, I'm...Jesus, I'm a mess without you. Just tell me you don't hate me."

"I don't hate you. I love you, Harry. You know that."

Aw, what the...snot all over, fuck it.

"You sound sick, Harry. Now I'm gonna worry."

"They're looking for him, Lena. I can't get it out of my head."

"Well, gee, it's not like they're going to find him."

"But they're *looking!* They'll find something."

"What'd you think, no one would ever miss the guy?"

"He told me the operation never worked. It was like sandbagging."

"What?"

~203~

"The prognosis was hopeless, his words—"

"What's done is done. Try not to worry, Harry."

"You're magnificent, Lena. You know that. You carried the whole load."

"Yeah, well—"

"The money's all yours, baby. I wouldn't know what to do with it."

"Is there something you're not telling me? Anything I should know?"

"No!" He bites his tongue." I, uh...no nothing."

Poor Frank frozen stiff under a fresh layer of snow. God help him.

"Someone wants to use the phone, Harry. I gotta go now."

"No wait!"

"Call me next Sunday, noon. And send me an address where you're staying."

"I'm sort of moving around."

"Then rent a mailbox. Call me Sunday. Don't forget."

"Okay, but—"

"Love you, Harry."

"Love you, Lena."

***

She hangs up and heads down Christian, hugging herself against the wind. Harry's all fucked up, crying, it sounded like. The whole thing has him wrung out, the dead guy, the daughter working on him. He shouldn't be up there by himself. Only something bad can happen.

An odd phone call, short and jumpy, not what she expected after so long apart. Nothing really got said, and Harry sounded like he's falling apart, not that he doesn't deserve to suffer. But it chills her to think, Harry all alone in the mountains, like The Shining, Jack Nicholson slipping into madness. Whoa, don't want to go *there*.

Murder in Mexico

Lena stops for a Sarcone's loaf since she's down here, in line, staring into space, drifting to the buzz of Harry.

"Hey." A big hand waves. "Anybody home?"

"Riley?" She feels her face spread into a smile. "Oh my God!"

"Come on. Can't be that bad."

"No, I, it's just so good to see you." *Real good.* Riley Prentiss from the dancing days, a little beefier with those wrinkles around the eyes. *Geez, it's been years.*

"Geez, it's been years, Lena." His kiss lands on her lips.

Yum. "I can't believe it. You?" She gives him a shove.

"Looking good, kid. How do you do it?"

"You don't look so bad yourself. How's Kathleen?"

"Same as always. She should be here. Listen, about Harry, I can't tell you how hard it hit us."

"Thanks, Riley. Harry loved you guys."

"He was the best. Look, you in a hurry?" He takes her arm. "Come have coffee with me."

"Make it a cosmo and you got a deal."

Riley leads her a block up Ninth Street then down a stairway, through an unmarked door to a private club. Tiny place, guys at a table, nods to Riley. They sit at the bar, how nice just the two of them, mid Sunday, football blabbing in a back room.

"The thing is, some guys..." Riley shakes his handsome head, "you don't ever think about it. It can't happen to them."

"Then there are other guys."

"Right! Kathleen's got an uncle...has a stroke every three weeks. Just turned 80."

"You look good, Riley. You really do. What did I hear about you? Something in the papers."

"My fifteen minutes of fame, old news, Lena. I was going to get in touch with you, but I wanted to let things die down. You must have your hands full."

"It's leveling off. Sally's nursing me through it, and my friend Alice from work and really, everyone. I think about people who don't have that. How do they survive it, Riley?"

"Harry was special, and so are you." He leans in. "I know it's none of my business, Lena, but you're okay, right? Financially?"

Lena smiles sweetly. "I'm okay. Thanks for asking, Riley."

"You know I still remember the first time I saw you. Wagner's Ballroom, the old line dance, Maurice Williams and the Zodiacs."

"God, it's almost embarrassing." Lena hides her face. "Don't look at me."

Riley pulls her hands away. "Please, I want to. You don't know how good it feels for me."

"Me, too." Lena blushes. Creaming her jeans, what Sue Anne said.

"Just remember one thing. I'm serious about this. If you ever need anything...anything, Lena—"

"I know that, Riley. Where is Kathleen?"

"Right now she's next-door at Mary's," Riley tells her. "We came up for Marissa's confirmation."

"Up? From where?"

"We bought a place on the Chesapeake. Little Cape Cod on the water, the golden years, right?"

A fat man bellies through the swinging door and cocks his head their way.

"Cosmos, Tiny." Riley shakes two fingers. "The Stoli's, not the rotgut."

"Cosmos? What do I look like Joe the Bartender?"

"That's all right, I'll get them." Riley slips behind the bar. "Who's up, anyway?"

"We're getting clobbered." Tiny shoots Lena a wink. "Why do we do it, Rile? Every year like the flu, like we don't remember last year, or the year before. It's a sickness,

I tell you."

"Hey, Eagles Fever." Riley shrugs. "Catch it and die."

"I can't understand it." Tiny bounces back from whence he came.

"Harry was a big fan." Lena smiles to think of it.

"Tell me about it. We were at the snowball game back in the 80s. Bad call on a last minute drive and a million snowballs coming at ya. The freaking mayor leading the barrage."

"Tough town."

"Boo-bird, that was Harry. He liked it when they stunk up the place. Wins? That was bandwagon stuff."

"Tell me about the Chesapeake Bay."

"You'd like it, Lena. The Island's a different world. The slow pace suits me."

"Sounds good."

"You'll have to come down and visit. Kathleen would love to see you. Jesus, we go back, Lena."

"Yeah, way back." Lena tears up a little. "God, the years get away from you."

"Here's to the baby boom." Riley clinks her glass. "May we bleed the children dry."

"Oh, Riley, remember when you and Harry..." And off they go into the sixties. Another round, and Lena let's herself forget about the phone call, Harry and whatever he's doing, Mexico. This is what she needs, a chance to unwind.

"Aw Jesus, look at the time. I should be getting back, Lena."

"Me too. Gee, Riley, you don't know how much good this has done me."

"Hey, memory lane. It's what geezers do." Riley grabs a matchbook and jots down his phone number. "Here, I want you to go home and write this in your book."

"Okay."

"You need anything, you call that number. Promise

me, Lena."

"I promise, Riley. And thanks."

"Come on, I'll take you home."

"That's okay, I have my car. Walk me over, would you?"

Then it's warm and fuzzy until she gets home. Cop cars at the far end bursting that bubble. How easy to picture Harry cuffed in back, wide eyed and sputtering. What he's like on a bender, listening to him slur, waking late at night to things crashing. Harry face down at the table or passed out on the bathroom floor.

Lena parks a block over. Stillness settles like a last note played. Cat's eyes shine in a front window. The cops drive off to worry someone else.

***

Harry drives north, away from the Willows and the mess, past the SUV parked in the lot, right at the light to the lake road. New snow light and fluffy, sky so blue it hurts to look at. His hands shake so bad he can't light a cigarette. Get out of town before he does something crazy.

The long night and the minibar, three bills worth at final tally. The phone call still chills him, blubbering like he did. Sunday will be different. She did say Sunday, right? The more he tries, the more he can't remember. Monday sounds just as likely, now that he says it to himself. Okay, it's all right; he'll call both days.

"Fuck it," he says aloud. Shakes so bad he can barely work the screw cap, half of it dribbling down his chin and through his jacket. How crazy is *this*? Drinking and driving, bloody clothes and a gun in the trunk, dead men's wallets, *two* in case one won't hang him.

He drives all day, coming into Albany at sunset. Albany, for no good reason, because that's where road goes. He stops for a bottle and checks into a Motel Six.

Murder in Mexico
***

"Lena?"

"Who?"

"I'm looking for Lena? Blonde? Fortyish?"

"Honey, what *you* need is some young pussy. Ain't no Nina got what I can give you."

"She's supposed to be there. Could you look around?"

"I'm looking, but I ain't seein'. Bitch musta stood you up."

Okay, so it *was* Sunday

***

"Harry?"

"Lena?"

"Did you get a mailing address?"

"I couldn't. I've, it's been..."

"Okay, Harry, listen. I'm coming up there. I want you to sit tight and wait for me. Can you do that?"

"Here?"

"It's okay. I told everybody I want to get away to think things over."

"I'm not, uh, settled in yet. The weather—"

"Tell me where you are, Harry."

"Lena? Let's go to Paris."

Silence.

"Did you hear me?"

"We'll talk about it. First, let me come up there."

"It's what you always wanted, baby. I've been thinking a lot about it."

Lena feels suddenly woozy. "You don't have a passport, Harry. We'll have to figure out a way to—"

"I have Gerry's."

"Gerry had a passport?"

"He wanted to go to Amsterdam. Bow out in a blur, you know? By the time the damn thing came, he was too sick to go."

"All right, we'll go to Paris. But I have to see you."

"Why? What's happened?"

"Nothing's happened." Lena fights to control her voice. "I'm worried about you, that's all. Tell me where you are and I'll be there as soon as I can."

"Really, Lena, I'm okay."

Oh yeah, never better, in a rumpled heap at a Midas Mufflers' pay phone with an unbroken view of the Albany incinerators.

"Please, Harry."

Click.

"Hello?"

***

Lead in news, you couldn't miss it. In a pink dress with a bow in her hair, cameras flashing and a phone number scrolling at the bottom of the screen. The first time he'd been too distracted by the photo insert of Steve to catch the gist, little Lilly jerking tears from coast to coast. So sweet and sad, the phone lines sizzled, money pouring in and a Mexican manhunt underway. Pink dress and the close up clincher:

"I miss you, daddy. Please come home."

Then back to the news team for the details. Police keeping a lid on but Steve rumors flying, a business deal gone bad, drugs and sex, then Lilly's prognosis, donor matches and success rates, all of it added to the things he mustn't think about, the ever growing list of horrors. Harry watched without moving a muscle, nothing to be done for Steve or Lilly, nothing to be done for Frank either, or *his* daughter, if he has one.

So unnerved he hasn't watched TV since, leaving him hours to drink and think, but not shave, shower or change out of his pajamas. Painfully thin now that he's stopped eating, gaunt and hollow eyed. No way can Lena see him like this, evil looking, now that he is evil, a mug shot mug if ever there was one.

Has to pull it together, but that won't happen, not today with a new bottle to while away. And the irony isn't lost on him. A week ago he would have given anything to see Lena. Now she wants to come and he's scared stiff. What she'll see in his eyes, the worst thing he could do, lock himself in and drink the night away.

Thinking crazy, get out of the country, Paris and no extradition, that killer, Einhorn, fled to France, lived like a prince for thirty years. Then it fades and it's all he can do to inhale and exhale, sick to death of the drinking. Never been a lush but what else is there? Hates the stumbling around and the drapes drawn, trash all over, Jesus.

And it's not over yet. They'll be finding Frank soon, if they haven't already. Definitely no TV for a while, though he knows he'll be glued to it, as if you can sit alone in a room and not watch television, or drink. He keeps the gun in the car so he won't play with it.

***

"Hello, Carlos?"

"Lena! So wonderful to hear your voice! How are you?"

"I'm not interrupting anything, am I?"

"Not at all. I've been hoping you'd call."

"How are you, Carlos?"

"Up to my ears in lawyers, at the moment. You've heard about the American who disappeared?"

"Yes, it's terrible, his poor little girl."

"Yes, a tragedy, and bad for business, if I may be so crass."

"The poor man. Is Lieutenant Morales investigating the case?"

"Morales? Oh no, I've got my top people on this. Also the FBI sent a medical examiner, just in case."

"Have they found out anything?"

"Of course, I'm not supposed to say..." Santos lowers his voice. "But yes, it seems there's a gay angle involved. Possibly a tryst gone bad, if you follow me."

"How tawdry!"

"Yes, and quite a PR problem when you factor in the daughter. A witch-hunt while she wastes away."

"I never thought of that."

"But enough of that. Tell me what you've been doing, Lena. I've been anxious for news of you. Are you holding up okay?"

"Right now I'm just trying to keep warm. I keep thinking about those balmy nights in Puerto Vallarta. It's funny, I thought I'd never want to go back there."

"Come see me, I insist! I've got a big house and everything you could ever need. Say the word and I'll make the arrangements."

"Right now?"

"Right this minute. Think of it, Lena, something wild and spontaneous. Please believe me, my intentions are above reproach."

"You are an angel, Carlos, but I couldn't. Not yet."

"In the spring, then. Promise me you'll consider it. The village is lovely and you couldn't find a better guide."

"Oh, Carlos, I'd love to, in the spring, when things have died down. For both of us."

"Fantastic! I'll book a flight today. Why, I feel like a boy on the last day of school."

"Someday I'll repay you for all you've done for me."

"I won't lie to you, Lena. I live for that day."

"What happens if you don't find him, Carlos?"

"The American? Don't worry, if he's down here he'll turn up."

"I'll let you go now. Say hello to Father Esteban for

me."

"Ah, the rascal! He talks of you endlessly. He'll be delighted to hear my news."

"Goodbye, Carlos."

"Farewell, dear lady."

***

"Lena?"

"Oh, Harry, thank heavens!"

"What's that clacking noise?"

"I'm shivering, Harry. It's twenty degrees."

"Have they found him? Steve?"

"What? Harry, how could they find him?"

"Right, I keep forgetting."

"Oh Jesus, please tell me where you are. Do you have someplace to sleep? You're really scaring me, here."

"Forget about me, Lena. You'll be better off."

"What are you saying? I want to help you. It's okay, you'll see. Just tell me."

"It's no good. I can't think."

"Then come home. We'll work something out."

"That's crazy."

"Where the fuck are you? Harry, please."

A commotion then: "Hello?"

"Who's this? Where's Harry?"

"Dude you was talking to booked up. Left the phone dangling."

"Please, that man, what did he look like?"

"He be all shaky and shit. You know, tore up."

"Oh Jesus, oh, please, tell me where you are."

"Who? Me?"

"I need to find him, that man."

"I seen him cross the street to the Motel Six."

"What city? What's the address? It's an emergency."

"Life or death, yo?"

"Please, the Motel Six, where?"

"Route 62 and the interstate. Exit 8. Albany New York."

"Thank you, God bless you, oh thank God."

"You're welcome."

***

Slick roads and Lena fishtails to the inside lane. An hour in and knots in her neck and arms. Almost wishes she hadn't gotten an address so she wouldn't have to do this. Now she has to, can't just sit there while Harry goes down the drain. All night it takes her, so buzzed on caffeine she can't think straight, thinks of nothing but Harry and all the miles between them. Every one adding to the pressure, her bladder bloated but she never could pee in a public bathroom, especially on the interstate, forget it. Thinking this is what real trouble feels like, the roof caving in, shit hitting the fan.

How could she not see it coming? Harry can't be by himself, even in ideal conditions. He just doesn't know how. And the warning signs, coming home to find him huddled in the bathtub. The falling down and that night he plowed through the cornfields, blowing the horn and howling like a loony. Signals everywhere she looks, especially after Gerry died. Keeping his accounts open, not for down the road, not in the beginning. As long as Gerry got mail, the book wasn't closed for Harry. Even those insurance policies, some months he had to scramble to meet the premiums. *Most* months, unless he worked overtime, which was hardly ever once he and Baldini started knocking heads. And wasn't *that* a tipoff? Every guy Harry worked for, like he's never wrong and they're never right.

Husband on the rocks, wake up Lena! A thousand pysch shifts and she's fucking clueless!

God!

Murder in Mexico

Up the Thruway she sees signs for Albany. Why would Harry go there? Why would *anybody* go there? The mountains probably spooked him, what did Harry know from mountains? Just as likely he kept moving until he came to a city. Thank God it wasn't Buffalo or whatever stupid cities they have up here. She doesn't want to think what she'll find at the Motel Six. If she thinks about it she'll scare herself, and then she'll have to pee. But just touching on the subject has her squirming. She turns off at a rest stop, pads the seat with toilet paper, straddles the bowl and dribbles a thimbleful.

"Let me get a pack of Newport Lights."

"Yes, ma'am. That's eight dollars even."

"Forget it. Never mind."

"Got these for $6.50."

"Gimme."

Just south of Exit 8 she sees a car pulled over, state cop, storm trooper hat, jodhpurs, Jesus, Harry wouldn't stand a chance. The motel is right off the exit. A dozen cars ring the lot. She checks at the desk, Gerry Watts, room six.

"Who's there?"

"It's me. Lena."

Silence.

"Let me in, Harry. Please."

"Who's with you?"

"Nobody. Harry, it's okay. Just look through the window. It's cold out here, honey."

Sees the drapes pull away and she fakes a smile. The drapes fall back, then a rattle of locks.

"Oh, Harry!"

Haggard and somehow smaller, and drunk, the room reeks of it. Trash everywhere, fast food, pizza boxes, empty cans and bottles.

"I've been sick."

"Oh, baby." She takes him in her arms, skin and bones, three-day growth, all bourbon and body odor. And

~215~

Harry's crying like a baby, then they're both crying.

"Lena."

"It's all right now, baby. I'm here, okay."

Okay, maybe, but she's never seen him like this, not even when Gerry died, and that was bad. Harry didn't leave the house for weeks. And she had help then, everybody coming to rally around. This is nothing like that, alone in Albany and sinking fast.

"Here, Harry, sit down." She pushes him toward the bed. "Just let me clear this," shoves all the crap to the floor. "Sit."

"How did? Wait, am I dreaming this?" He looks like he really doesn't know.

"Let me get my bag. It's in the car. Just sit until I get back."

"Don't leave me, Lena."

But he's still there when she returns. Ten years older, at least in a sweater she's never seen before, something spilled down the front of it. She sets her things down, kneels by the bed and holds him, tapping his back like she can't help doing it.

"Harry, what happened in the mountains? What made you come here?"

"No questions, Lena. Not now."

"You're burning up, Harry. You should be in bed." She grabs a blanket and tries to wrap it around him. "Oh, my poor baby."

"Jesus, I'm tired." He burrows into the pillow. "Turn the heat up, will you?"

"It's turned up all the way. Harry, it's sweltering in here."

"Flu, or something."

"Lie here and I'll fix you some tea."

"Tea, yuck."

Lena tucks him in and fills the coffee pot. By the time she figures out how to work it, Harry's snoring softly. Even his snoring is different, ragged and heavy with significance. She makes tea for herself and slides a cigarette from the pack. Six years since she gave it up, now a thousand in the past month. Funny how she always knew some Harry crisis would reel her back in.

"Look at you, Harry. What am I gonna do?"

Fix the room, for starters. Lena thinks more clearly in the neat and clean. For the next hour she sorts through Harry's mess, a whole drawer set aside for dirty laundry, his socks rank and stiff, his shirts, some inside others for layers. What's this? A scarf with more stains on it, shoes ruined, a belt? Since when does Harry wear a belt?

When it's all straightened up she pulls a chair around and watches Harry sleep. More cigarettes while someone storms around in the room above. Thinking back to better days, when they lived on Morris Street, Harry still in the game. How he looked in those days. Cocky, her mother said, but it wasn't that. You just knew Harry could get over, and he knew you knew it. Not this Harry. This Harry looks all done in.

He's still not awake when the sun comes up, and she let's herself think all this sleep will help. Sober him up, give him strength, get him in the shower then make him eat something. She's never seen him this skinny, and Harry's always been skinny.

Maybe she should wake him? What *is* she going to do?

Morning turns to afternoon. She fiddles with the remote, finds a movie, *Holiday Inn* with Cary Grant, oh no. Lena knows what she can stand and she could never stand that. Not Cary Grant and that great snowed-in cottage in the country with what's her name, Harry would know. They watched it not so long ago, during a snowstorm, the real deal right outside the window. The day she called in sick and they lay around watching old movies. Didn't even dig the cars out, when the plows socked them in. Harry

between jobs, their lives ahead of them.
She flips it to a TV preacher.

***

"Harry? Can you hear me?"

Grinds his face into the mattress, one eye half open, makes the connection then closes again. "What time is it?" he croaks.

"A little after ten. In the morning."

Rolling onto his side, both eyes open now, blinking like a man coming out of a coma. "What day is it?"

"Monday. They're calling for more snow."

"I'm so thirsty." He struggles with the blankets.

"Let me." She heads for the bathroom. "I think your fever broke over night."

"Not water."

"Then you'll have to get dressed and go get something." Tough love, all's she's got, really. "And I wouldn't go looking like that."

"A beer. It can't all be gone."

"Yes, it can."

"Christ." Harry groans in disbelief. "Where..." He picks up her pack of Newports. "You're smoking again?"

"Ain't it grand?" Lena hands him a glass of water.

Then more TV preacher as he retches in the bathroom. Leave him alone when he's puking, best thing for him at this point. Purge the system then get him some breakfast. Harry's always hungry after he's been puking. Should switch motels too, no sense making people wonder. Maybe get him some clothes, this jacket, what a mess, and the pockets, Jesus, what's with the wallet. What—

"Give me that." Harry grabs it from her.

"Where did you get—"

"Some guy left it on the bar. I waited around but he never came back."

"Get rid of it."

"I was going to."

"Who leaves their wallet on the bar?"

"Some salesman, he was drunk." Something flickers in Harry's face.

"Harry?"

"I'll get rid of it. Okay?" He grabs his pants.

"Aren't you going clean up a little?"

"Just take a minute." He throws on the jacket, slips on his shoes.

"Harry, wait." But he's out the door, then back for the keys and out again. Lena doesn't try to stop him. Listens to tires crunching ice. Then he stops and fumbles with something in his lap, the car running and voices on the radio. Then he's gone for a few minutes, then he's back.

"You could have waited."

"You were freaking me out, Lena."

"All right. Let's just get out of here."

"Right." He moves around, opening drawers.

"Don't you want to shower first?"

"Right." He drops everything and pulls at his clothes, the pants, oh man look at him. Like he lost the rock fight, like he just crawled through the desert. Skin and bones, scrapes and bruises. Then the shower's running, more thumping upstairs, Lena zaps to an old ER, mid Clooney, guy gets his hand caught in a garbage disposal, Christ!

"Get me some underwear, would you, hon?"

Good, he's shaving, that will go a long way. Poor Harry. The weight she can see but how do you get smaller? And shaky, like the phone guy said. Maybe not such a good idea, shaving, but he's already at it. And it goes okay. He comes out looking semi-human, with the puny arms, pubic hair all scraggly and gray.

"How are you feeling?"

"I'm all right," he says without conviction

"Can you eat something? I think you should eat."

"Not now. Help me with this, will you?"

Lena works his shirt buttons. "Listen to me. We have to think about what we're doing here. Find some place on the Thruway with a restaurant. We'll eat and then I want you to rest. Your resistance is low, Harry. I'm a nurse, remember?"

"Okay." He struggles to rise then starts to sag.

"Harry!" She props him up, heavy somehow, like there's rocks in his pockets.

"Oooomph," and onto the bed, lies him down as best she can, but half sliding off.

"Oh, baby, help me, could ya?" Wrapping him in blankets, feeling his head, pacing and smoking with the snow starting up again. She thinks of going out for food but decides against it. If he wakes to see her gone, who knows what might happen? He needs to eat, though. Harry's fainted before when he drinks without eating, unless it's something else. The fever's gone but that could mean anything. She'll go when he comes around.

Or leave a note! Run out for food and a pharmacy; saw one at the rest stop coming in. Get aspirin and cold pills. Go before it's too late. Leave a note.

Harry, be right back. Lena

But she can't do it. He could die; Lena's seen it happen. Or he misses the note, or can't make sense of it, thinks it's a trick. So she stays instead, and now she's starving.

***

"Eat the peas."

"No peas."

"But it's beef stew, Harry. Peas are good in beef stew."

"Brown. I need brown food."

"You look a lot better. So we'll stay here for a day or

two."

"This guy on the pay phone, it's not right that he fingered me. What if you were gonna kill me?"

"He wanted to help. I was hysterical."

Harry smiles and Lena's heart breaks a little.

"Hey, this might even be fun." She's trying her best. "What the hell, Harry. We don't have to be at work tomorrow."

"You saved my life, Lena. I don't know what I was going to do."

"Yeah, well, just something I picked up from Sister Muriel."

Harry looks away. "How'd she take it?"

"She was devastated. Everybody, Harry, you don't know."

He does look better. The shaving mostly, but clean and the eyes look more like him. Except the teeth, the front one discolored when the light hits it right. How long since he's been to a dentist? But his color is better. Hearing about all this probably helps, neighbors and friends pulling together for him.

"I mean it, Lena. It was over for me."

A new low, too drunk to know he was sick. When he first saw her through the motel window he thought he'd lost it. Lena? Here? Nothing could account for it, unless he was hallucinating. But he knew that wasn't it. The drapes were too tacky, the parking lot way too ugly. It wasn't possible but there she was.

"I don't know what made us think we could do this, Harry. Stay separated for so long, when I think back on it."

"This other guy in Puerto Vallarta." Harry stares off. "Just taking over like that, Jesus!"

"Carlos. God, Harry, there was nothing he couldn't do. We really owe it all to him."

Stay on track, Harry's thinking, Mexico, the aftermath. Steer Lena clear of what's been going on with him. Stick with the flu and the liquor to explain the mess. Focus on Mexico. They'll be okay if they just stay off the daughter, all that. Nowhere near that, or anything Catskill. Thank God he managed to ditch the wallet and those bloody clothes in the car. Stashed them in a dumpster behind the motel office, a miracle Lena wasn't watching.

"Our one lucky break."

"Yeah, but one we had to have. Think of it, no Carlos and I'm on my own."

"That's why it had to be you, Lena, American widow in distress."

"Carlos said the FBI is there. The local guys are out of it. That means the cops and anybody who worked on, you know, Steve?"

That scratch under Harry's ear, how'd he get so banged up, anyway? Not that he's nimble when he's on a tear, but under his ear? Unless he was crawling or crashing around outside, that would explain the shoes, but it's been so cold up here. And that wallet left on the bar, though that kind of thing does happen to Harry. Wallets and money lying on the ground, she's seen it herself. The guy was drunk, he said. She's better off not knowing.

"I'm serious, Lena. I want to go to Paris."

"Okay." Good enough until she can think of a way out of it. "I'd love that too, when you're back on your feet again."

"Soon, Lena, I want to go soon."

"We don't even have the money yet. And I have to get my passport renewed. I'll do that when I get back."

"Go for a month, maybe. Stay under the radar."

Better to go now, this week, have Lena meet him when everything clears. Hard to believe they haven't found Frank yet. Unless they have and they're keeping it quiet. But why would they? Really have to be zeroed in to put the two together, Mexico and Cooperstown, no fucking way, unless he's missing something. Is he missing something?

For all he knows they've pieced it together. For all he knows they're closing in, the sort of hot on your heels that ends in SWAT teams and battering rams.

Lena reaches for his hand. "Look, this is really hard for me. I know you don't want to hear it, but I need to tell you. About the girl, Lilly."

"Lena, please."

"I know you didn't mean it. What we did? It was wrong, we both know that, but it's done and we have to live with it."

He stares at the peas on his plate.

"Did you hear me, Harry? Thinking about it will drive us crazy."

Us? Despite all she's been through, Lena looks better than ever. Slimmed down and the clothes are new, he's pretty sure. Getting over on all those people, straight faced and cool as a cucumber, Harry knows he never could. That sense of betrayal, he can feel it in his gut. Any way this turns out he'd never be able to face them again. "I feel like a shit for Sister M."

"She came to see me. God, she must be a hundred. They're holding a novena for you."

Lena skips the rest, Muriel's doubts, the cigarettes. It will just make Harry feel worse, guiltier, if that's possible. He's always had a soft spot for the Sisters and soft spots are not the way to go here. Give him some good news. The way the claims are sailing through and, okay Paris, if it helps. Lay off the daughter and whatever he's been doing, unless he brings it up.

They take a room for two nights. Harry seems all right at times, but mostly fades in and out. Lena tries to make him focus. He can't live in motels forever. He needs to connect, make an effort, save himself. But except for a promise to settle somewhere, Harry just lets her go on.

***

"Hold still, would you?"

"I can feel it eating my scalp."

"It's just hair coloring, Harry."

"It looks bad. I can see already."

He's right about that. What it looks like is a guy with dyed hair. A detail you might remember once you've noticed, so in the end they just shave it off, a living skull, like those holocaust survivors.

"Don't worry. It'll grow back. Maybe a beard would help."

He just sits there looking at himself.

"See Harry? Your own mother wouldn't recognize you."

It's a struggle, but with Lena pushing, a plan takes shape. She finds a short-term rental by the airport and books a week in advance, Executive Suite, with a kitchen so he can cook, though it's hard to picture it, Harry and supermarkets, that whole thing. So she goes for groceries, mostly nukeables, then the video outlet for movies, long ones, the whole Sopranos, anything to keep him out of the deep end. She thinks of it that way, the surge of panic when you can't find the bottom.

"Maybe there's a library in town, Harry. You could get some books. You know how television burns you out."

"I'll be all right. You don't have to worry."

"I know." Lena smiles bravely. "It's all gonna work out fine."

She leaves in the morning. Harry watches her car turn out of the lot, and it all falls apart and he knows he's in trouble. Spends that first hour pacing, hands on his hairless head. Puts the liquor store off for what seems like a long time. But being time it eventually runs out and midnight finds him blacked out in front of QVC.

***

Murder in Mexico

They plow Frank up the following Wednesday. At first they think a bear got him, but the missing wallet shitcans that theory. By Thursday the consensus is murder, which revs things up, and by Friday they have the bloody club and a motive. Robbery, though Frank turns out to be strapped for a diamond guy, and what about his SUV parked in town? It comes to Harry in dribs and drabs, further details, this just in. A terse no-comment from police and a plea to the public with a scrolling phone number. Anything you might have seen, only no one saw a thing. A waitress remembered Frank, but he was by himself, nothing to implicate Harry beside the club and whatever they might be hiding. And the club can't be traced to him, even if they find fingerprints. Harry's never been fingerprinted in his life, that he can remember. And you'd remember being fingerprinted, he's pretty sure.

The newscasts end the same every time, a shot of Frank's home in Fairmount, bigger than you'd think, new siding, drapes drawn tight, two kids and a wife who refuses to be interviewed. Harry met her once when she picked Frank up at work. All eye makeup in a Flyers sweatshirt. The TV says Frank was a roofing contractor and this starts to work on Harry. Frank may have faked the diamond business, but he was no roofer either. Harry grew up with roofers, and Frank didn't have the mouth for it, something going on here.

And since he still can, he throws on his clothes and walks over to the rest stop. Rows of big rigs and cowboys talking on cell phones, more women than you'd figure. Harry cuts through the restaurant to a bank of pay phones.

"Central Hot Line, can I help you?"

"Yeah, hey, I'm up here hauling pipe to Buffalo and I seen the news. That dead guy they found in Cooperstown?"

"What about him?"

"Right! I seen him a few days before it happened. Or maybe it was the day before, I can't remember. But it was him."

"You saw him."

"That's right. We got to talking and he told me he was moving diamonds."

"Sir, can I have your name please?"

"Whoa, this is a hotline, ain't it?"

"You're aware of the reward?"

"I ain't interested in no reward. I keep seeing the news and nobody says nothin' about diamonds. Might wanna look into it."

Click.

Harry's ruse works like a charm. The tip's passed on and by the morning newscast motive has been firmly established. Turns out Frank really was in diamonds, not a player, but a courier, the guy you rob, meaning he was probably connected and almost certainly armed. His brag about the trial testimony, also true, in a smuggling case, with a grant of immunity, more to old Frank than met the eye. And like most tips that pan out, this one will take on a life of its own, people turning on other people, old scores settled etc. And since a lot of guys would kill for diamonds, suspects emerge and the whole investigation steams off in the wrong direction. A real stroke of genius, if Harry could only see it. But his little tip takes a day to get rolling and by then he's way too blitzed to care.

CHAPTER THIRTEEN

Alice wipes her fingers on a napkin. "Girl? You would not recognize the place. All those crazies? Gone. No crack-heads, no junkies, just old sick people. And you *know* how I feel about sick people, shriveled up white folks lookin' dead already."

"Sounds awful."

"Awful ain't the word. You know how sick people smell? It's like something goin' bad inside 'em, and the bedpans and sponge baths? Say what you want about those crazies, at least they can wipe their own damn selves."

"Now they're on the street."

"Street, hell. They all livin' in the subway. I saw Crazy Daisy on the B line."

"Wait 'til they start finding them frozen in the bushes. Walters will pay." Lena pushes her salad around her plate. The endives taste funny. Everything tastes funny lately.

"Don't ever see dat man no more. President of the god damn golf course is what he is."

"What about Strickland's replacement? What's he like?"

"Testy, but manageable. We call him Snidely. Snidely Whiplash, you remember Snidely?"

"Rocky and Bullwinkle."

"Yeah, always skulkin' around and twirling that moustache."

"He's got a moustache?"

"No, but that's the name we give him."

"Good to hear the unit hasn't lost the touch."

"You gonna eat that, or you just playin'?"

Lena hands her plate over. "I keep thinking of the Hewitt boy. The kid deserved better."

In fact, she's thinking of Harry. All she thinks about anymore, what he's doing up there, a fuzzy picture in her brain. As if thinking about him will keep him safe. The last time they talked he had that foggy affect the patients get, short answers, long pauses.

"Yeah, I miss those crazies. Dot too! They got her wrasslin' big fat sick people around like she's Hulk freakin' Hogan."

"I guess it was time to get out. But I miss it sometimes. You guys."

She thinks a lot about Harry blowing it, in a bar somewhere, running his mouth. Half believes that by imagining what it would look like, she cancels out the possibility. What happens instead might be just as bad, but that one thing won't happen if she pictures it. Other factors come into play and it can get pretty complicated, but it's a line of logic that's hardly ever failed her. So she pictures Harry on a bar stool, slurring.

"Speaking of crazies, you see they found that Fairmount fella murdered up in New York? Dogs got him, ugggh." Alice shudders at the thought.

"In the city?"

"No, way upstate. Near a psychiatric facility, wouldn't you know."

Lena can't help but laugh. "Nutty as fruitcakes."

"I mean, killing somebody's bad enough. But lettin' the dogs get 'em! 'At's evil, you know what I'm sayin'?"

"I hadn't heard about it. Lucky for our crazies the subway only goes to West Oak Lane."

Alice does that choke-y laugh with the legs bouncing. Lena laughs along, and a wave of relief washes over. So long since anything's been funny, and a laughing Alice is something to see, the chins jiggling and those big apple cheeks... But the wave passes and the cloud blows back

Murder in Mexico

over. Not thinking of Harry makes her think of Harry.

"That Hewitt boy, he really got to you, huh, Lena?"

"He was making such progress."

"You know, I'm worried about you, girlfriend. I called your house over the weekend and you weren't there. What's up with that?"

"Oh, uh, Harry has some relatives up in Jersey."

"You should let me know when you're going out of town."

"I'm sorry Alice, I—"

"What is it, honey? You feelin' okay?"

Lena makes a face. "I must be coming down with something. I think maybe I better go."

"Stay at my place for a few days. Jake can take Tamika's old room."

"I just need some sleep."

"You've had a hard time, girl. I don't want to see you get sick on top of it. Come on." Alice gathers her things. "I'm taking you straight home."

***

Frank Lavin. The name doesn't ring a bell. Lavin, Lavin nope, nothing, his picture in the paper, younger guy, crooked teeth, Lena's never seen him before. It's okay then, just coincidence. Not even that *much* of a coincidence, two guys from Philly in upstate New York. Big deal. Cooperstown, it says, where the baseball Hall of Fame is. Harry didn't say anything about the Hall of Fame. And he would have mentioned that. Lena folds the paper and shoves her hands between her thighs, Jesus, always freezing anymore. Her ears like ice and the tip of her nose, cold and wet like her old dog Barney. Dogs, oh man what they do sometimes. His picture in the paper, the relief she felt when the face was unfamiliar. Her unspoken fear, murder as a recurring theme.

So it's okay, but she checks the news anyway, again at eleven for good measure, more coincidence than she's comfortable with, but nothing to tie in Harry. Nothing. And he didn't know she was coming so she would have seen something if there was something to see. What did she see, the wallet, the belt, Harry's shoes, what could it mean? Does it mean anything? All his talk about the Catskills and he ends up in Albany?

Then she thinks of the scarf, something was on it, could it be blood? Lena checks the dead man's picture but, of course, he isn't wearing it. Nothing about a missing wallet, but they don't always give all the details, leave stuff out to trip up the killer.

Unless it was Harry's scarf, an old one she's forgotten. He never said and Lena didn't ask. She didn't recognize it, but sometimes he'll come in wearing something she hasn't seen before. Not often but once in a while, a shirt he's had for years or a sweater. They have a closet full of scarves and hats going back for years. Or maybe he bought the scarf while he was up there. That would make sense, except it didn't look new. What was on it? And where is it? She's looked around but hasn't seen it since.

She's up all night, back and forth, adding it up and sorting it out. Been through so much lately it's hard to trust her instincts. What *are* her instincts, anyway? Does she really believe Harry killed Frank Lavin? Can she convince herself he didn't? Oh Christ, what it could mean! Harry's up there *killing* people!

***

"Hello, Carlos?"

***

Guns, right? How easy, just point and pull the trigger.

Murder in Mexico

Harry curls his lip, as close to badass as he can manage, stick thin and hairless, like he is. Leans in until his nose hits the mirror, pores like drainage ditches, blackheads and the bushes in his nose, plucks until his eyes water, how fucking old he looks! The web of wrinkles when the light is right, and that front tooth, less than attractive when you throw in the wrinkles and the ears. Look at him. Fucking Dumbo, pinhead fuck! His new look, old bald guy with a gun.

"Stick 'em up."

Took a while to figure out how to unload the damn thing, not so big but heavier than it looks, a gun that could do damage. What did he read? That getting shot doesn't hurt, not like you'd think. It hurts later, but not right then. Like a punch to the face doesn't hurt, just impact and stars going off, but no pain. Until later.

Harry pokes himself in the face, just can't resist. Not that hard but, oh Christ, now he's bleeding. Stumbles to the bedroom, grabs a towel, sits on the toilet, gun in one hand, towel to his nose. Soaks it in bourbon and ouch, bad idea! The taste of blood like when he was a kid, always in one scrape or another, all of it wreaking havoc on his stomach, oh man, an ulcer or something in there, eating him alive.

And then he's heaving yet again, turned inside out, nothing coming up but battery acid. The drinking! It's *killing* him! Slumped with his head on the toilet tank, knees popping when he tries to stand. Sort of shoves himself up the side of the shower then turns to the mirror, *God. Jesus!* Run some water here; *clean yourself up, for Christ...*

Good. Oh, that's good, cold water splashes his face, getting warmer, then hot. Then too hot, whoa, then cold again, until he's wide-awake for the first time in days. Like a layer of something peeled away, and he can breathe again, gulping mouths full until his head gets fizzy. Feels like he's floating, then it's head down in the sink when the next wave hits, the world's weight, the whole mess. Hours until he feels a little better. Pale from puking, but the bleeding stops and he's okay. Why people splash water on their faces. Because it works. Not that he's sober, Harry's not kidding himself, a fifth of Jim Beam and it's not even dark yet. Makes another drink, stretches it with water, what's left of the ice, passes another mirror, full length, wasted and naked like that. Why is he naked?

Porno! That's where he was going when he saw the gun in the bathroom. Where he left it last time he was playing with it. Fucking gun.

"What the fuck are you lookin' at?"

***

Lena meets once with the lawyers in a posh downtown office close to city hall. So close she can see the pigeons living on Billy Penn's hat. Now that it's come, Lena likes this part of it. The men defer to her, the view is terrific, and the coffee! She can't help asking where they get it, Cherry Street someplace. They sit around a polished wooden table, and the men tell her what to sign and where, like in the movies when they meet with their lawyers. And she knows it's silly, but Lena likes having a lawyer, likes the idea of meeting in a posh office to sign papers relating to large sums of money. And it goes off without a hitch. The papers get signed. They take in the view and finish their coffee. The rest is all faxes and registered mail.

Road crew finds another body on a Thruway pull-off, and the media goes with serial killer. But this one's solved quickly, a hitchhiker it turns out. They charge him with Frank's murder too, but drop it for lack of evidence. Meanwhile a nationwide search is launched to find a donor match for Lilly Winslow's transplant. Oprah gets in on the deal and Ellen and all of them, pushing for her. Even Shock Jacque takes a turn, offering to donate his *own* organs to transplant listeners with the saddest story, a sort of Queen for a Day with strippers and sound effects. Lena stops listening.

***

"What's that noise?"

"There's a fire on Washington Avenue. You sound funny, Harry."

"Broke a tooth..." on the toilet seat, caught his chin last night on the way down.

"Not the front one."

"That's the one."

"Harry, where are you?"

"Albany."

"You're still in Albany?"

"I'm leaving soon. Tomorrow."

"Did you hear about Oprah? Harry?"

"Oprah?"

"They're searching for a donor for the little girl. Lilly?"

He stops breathing.

"And they'll find one, too. I just know it, Harry." A chance in a million but, hey. "Did you hear me?"

"Donor?"

"For her transplant. You'll see. Oprah can do anything. She'll find one."

And damned if she doesn't, some no neck welder in Texas. And the media loves it, brave little Lilly and the welder with the goatee, part-time football coach and instant celebrity. The procedure is scheduled for three weeks and Oprah's transplant team looks like they could handle anything, best in the business, hang the expense. And Harry follows closely and soon he's cleaned himself up and starts eating, cuts down on his drinking then stops completely, just to see if he can. And he can.

He gets his tooth capped, nothing to it. Picks a dentist out of the phone book, Indian fella, laughs at every thing

Harry says. And since Lilly's in the news a lot, they daily update the search for the father, the lack of progress on *that* front not escaping anyone's notice. Ditto on Frank's killer, though the diamonds keep 'em guessing, no one near hooking A to B. So that's good, and Harry can feel the pressure ease a little, and then it's a week until the operation and he's really zoned in, the kid's chances, the high drama. The kind of story that could really grab the country, only there's another tsunami somewhere, and Oprah gets distracted, and the momentum doesn't build quite like it should. Though it's still news, Page B, but hanging in, and as the day draws near, Harry feels the scales come into balance. He's done some very bad things, but he's not a bad man, and he's certainly suffered for what he's done. Feels genuine remorse for Steve and even worse for Frank, and he's been through bloody hell over it, really. No excuse for murder, but there *was* a reason. Not a good reason, but not like this, a little girl.

So he gets caught up and it helps him. He buys some new shoes, eats regularly and stops playing with the gun fifty times a day. But not carried away or anything. He's back to the beer and still smoking, but in control, nothing crazy, his old self, more or less. Gets good at shaving his head and the look starts to grow on him. Scholarly, especially with the glasses, good with the turtlenecks he picked up in town.

"You sound better, Harry."

"That kid's a trooper, Lena. It's gonna work for her, I know it."

"They said the operation was a complete success."

"It'll be weeks before they know, for sure."

"Well, yeah, but they think it looks pretty good. I mean, there's real hope."

"Are you coming up next weekend, Lena?"

"With bells on. I told everybody I was going on retreat. My mother thinks I'm getting religion."

Murder in Mexico

***

They meet at a chalet in the Adirondacks, nice place with a view and a hot tub. Harry looks better than he has in months. *Years*, really, once you get past the skinhead. And *such* a head, with little ridges and fissures running through and so shiny.

"You look like Mel without the fringe."

"I like it. Gives me an edge."

"So the first check should come this month, two hundred thousand after taxes. Can you believe it, Harry? We're freaking rich."

"Did you get your new passport?"

"It's coming. Are you still hot to go to Paris?"

"Definitely. Get away from this circus for a while. Aren't you?"

"Yeah. In the spring, like you said."

"I never said spring. We should go right away. Why wait?"

He's right. It's Carlos who was spring. Lena can't think of a reason why Paris should wait, so she sticks with the standby, the neighbors wondering. But Harry's tired of worrying about the neighbors and shows her brochures from fancy hotels on the Champs d'Elysee. Makes her watch a video of a walking tour with a jolly Parisian guide, Harry found it in the library. Lena doesn't know why she doesn't want to go, but she doesn't, not just yet. Too many things up in the air, and the neighbors *are* a problem. And her mom. What would she tell her? But Harry's psyched about it so she lets him go on, yessing him to death. Flips through the stupid brochures, sits through the video and tells herself it'll never happen.

Other than that, the weekend goes well. Harry's funny and attentive and doesn't get drunk once. They make love a few times, dine out every night, and even shop a little. She leaves Monday afternoon and the long ride gives her a chance to think. For the first time since she flew back from Mexico she's thinking they might just get away with it.

***

He takes up jogging in the morning. Not to get in shape, but to forge a routine, something to get him out of the room every day, a regiment. Jogging, then a big breakfast at the local House of Pancakes, the two canceling each other out for the most part, but that's not the point. The point is to get involved in the world again, re-establish contact, put some god damned weight on and clear the lungs a little. Afternoons he reads. Updike novels, Stephen King, old New Yorkers filched from the barbershop, anything he can get his hands on about Paris. Tracking the sun's progress from the bed, head propped in his hand until his wrist starts to hurt or his fingers lose feeling.

And for some reason - who knows why - he gets hooked on nature documentaries, watches a few on PBS then starts renting them from the video place, the whole National Geographic catalogue, no commercials or pledge breaks. The Vanishing Wilderness it says on the box, and Harry can't get enough, loves the camera work and celebrity narrators. Movie stars, mostly, some deadly serious, others sad or whimsical. Costner and wolves, like he invented them, and Willem Dafoe with the Indian elephants, Susan Sarandon and *plankton,* for Christ sake! One after another, evenings on end, all creatures great and small. Who knew the lowly ant could lift fifty times his weight or that monkeys kill for sport? Why *is* it only the pig will eat while he's being eaten? Harry learns something every day, starts a list for when he sees Lena. And the babies! Cutest little buggers every one. Cubs, kittens, pups, even things that will soon be ugly, even *snakes* when they're wriggly and all balled up.

So he watches then watches again, and he comes to

know a marsupial from a mollusk, what a gestation period is, the importance of fungus, and the threat to the barrier reef. Laughs out loud at the courting dances, sobs at the carnage, the dwindling habitat, the relentless encroachment of man. It's a learning experience, much better than porn, though some of that to break things up, a bare minimum.

A healing effect, no doubt about it.

**

When the first check comes, Lena leaves it on the table unopened for three days. She gets a kick out of all that money waiting for her to get around to it, like she's too busy for money. Though she really *has* been busy visiting Minna and her sister, neighbors and friends. And phone calls, the paperwork of dying, a red tape process like getting divorced. But winding down, she can feel it. People still call or drop in but the shock has worn off. Some funny things she wouldn't have expected. Ned stops by every Friday with steamed mussels, and the kids come around to dodge their parents. Almost always someone here except in the evening, just her then, but not so bad anymore. Not that they're out of the woods, she knows that. But Harry coming around like he has, it's a huge load off Lena's mind.

He's been sending her letters, or poems, really, two last week with a Christmas card and again yesterday. In an envelope marked Hadley's Grain and Feed, Martinsville, GA. God knows where he got it since the postmark said Poughkeepsie, long letters about the mountains and Paris and growing old with plenty of money. Harry always wrote good letters, and she's glad to get them, though writing back is a chore.

Dear Lena,

In my dream we're old and gray, but we have a fine house in a small town, and you can usually find us on the front porch. Friends gather in the evening, cats and dogs stop to visit. It's a good life, and we sleep like babies. Some of the neighbors wonder about us. Oh, we're pleasant enough, even sociable, but we volunteer little and that makes us mysterious. I suspect it's the berets but I could be wrong...

The weather makes me miss you, the rain here, so cold and lonely. When you close your eyes, can you feel my love? Just know that everything I did, I did for us, so that we can be together, on that front porch, in that small town.

Forever, Lena,

Harry.

I mean, really. What do you say to *that*?

***

Once the money's in the bank, Lena starts to spend, a little here, a little there. Gets a new couch and that antique end table she saw in New Hope, some clothes, okay, lots of clothes. Three times what she'd planned to spend, though it hardly makes a dent. And it's okay to spend it. Everyone knows Harry had insurance and no kids and the mortgage whittled down, so she has the rugs taken up and the floors refinished, hires a handyman to fix the million things Harry couldn't. A dry coat on the roof, gutters and caulking, bricks pointed, the sort of things you do with a windfall. Christmas rounds the corner; the neighbors help her deck the halls. The whole block lit up, the kids giddy and the whole of Pennsport putting Harry behind them.

CHAPTER FOURTEEN

Lieutenant Flatfoot is giving Pittman the third degree.
"How tall?"
"I don't know. He was sitting down the whole time."
"So, white guy named Gerry, you don't know how tall he was but he had a thin face. Thing is, for a bartender you're not very observant."
"He was middle age. They looked like brothers, maybe. I wasn't wearing my contacts, okay?"
"Then how do you know the guy with him was Winslow?"
"It was him, I know it, gay, I'm sure. He said he was from Phoenix."
"Sure you're not just sniffing around the reward money, Mr. Pittman?"
"Look, where's Morales? He knows me."
"Lieutenant Morales has been transferred. If you want to deal, you to talk to me."
Fuck you, Flatfoot. He never should have come here. Swore to himself he wouldn't, but this is Oprah, for fuck sake. They've jacked up the reward to a hundred grand, and Pittman could sure use a hundred grand. Now this fucking guy going all hard-ass and him, Pittman with warrants out in Vegas and Atlantic City. Probably ship his ass back to Jersey, unless he can get a rise out of flatfoot.
"We were just talking, that's all. I don't think the guy was hitting on him, but what do I know?"
"Not much so far."
"We had a bet going. Some cowboy was hustling a

blonde and the guy, Gerry, bet he wouldn't score. It was funny."

"Sounds hilarious."

"You had to be there"

"But you *were* there and so was Mr. Winslow. At least that's what you say."

"Look..." Pittman starts to get up. "Let's just forget I came in here, okay?"

"Sit down, Mr. Pittman. We're not through."

Fucking shit, now it's going to cost me money. He's supposed to be at the club in an hour, and once those warrants come up...what the hell did he think would happen here? It's been weeks since Pittman saw the guy. He's got no head for faces to begin with, and the next night's cruise ship melee scrambled his brains for a week. Besides, he was paying more attention to the *other* guy, the one who's missing, Winslow. Try as he may, Pittman can't recall a thing about the bettor but the shape of his head, and even that's iffy. Could have him confused with someone else entirely. How many faces does he see in a month?

"Listen, Lieutenant, I know it sounds lame with the reward and all, but this is legitimate. I swear to you, I'm not lying."

"Then why wait until now to come forward? That's withholding evidence."

"It's the way you guys work. I mean, look at this. I come all the way down here to help, and now I'm looking at the rubber hoses."

"Tell me about the blonde."

"There's nothing to tell. She was way across the room. She didn't even know we were there."

"I'm going to ask Sergeant Rosario to help us with this. Rosario's our sketch artist. He'll help you put together a composite."

"But I have to be at work."

That flatfoot smirk. "It shouldn't take long. I'm sure

you wouldn't want to walk away from all that reward money, would you?"

Composite? As if *that* will do any good. How do you describe a head with no features? Where are the mug shots they always make you go through? Pittman was counting on the mug shots; maybe one of them would click. No mug shots, that's when he realized. They've got no suspects, nothing, which means the reward is all his if he can just convince somebody.

Flatfoot's gone for twenty minutes, and Pittman thinks to walk away, just go home. Forget about that night like he should have in the first place, and *would* have, if not for Oprah running that street-smart game. Looking him right in the eye like it was just she and him and not every split-level and trailer park in the Western fucking hemisphere. Oprah appealing to his *greed,* for Christ sake, close enough to see the sweat on her upper lip.

"If not for the money—one hundred thousand—for that sweet little girl," Oprah teased. *"If you know something or saw something get it off your chest. Do the right thing."*

That's what kills him. Not that it worked, but that Oprah can do that, plug into whatever she wants and just take over.

"Maybe you're all jammed up. You don't want trouble and I can understand that. But, honey..." All sass with the hands to the hips. *"Oprah's here to tell you trouble ain't gonna happen."*

Jammed up, like some hip-hop old hippo, Jesus.

"I will see to it personally." She screams to the faithful, flailing and foaming at the mouth. Nobody should have that kind of power. It's *obscene!*

Flatfoot returns with an older man in a suit, and if this guy's a cop, Pittman's Popeye the Sailor. The Rolex alone puts him way up the food chain. The suit gives a nod and takes the only other seat.

"This is Mr. Santos," flatfoot tells him. "He's been helping us out on this. I told him you were just fortune hunting, but he's very interested in what you have to say."

The two men exchange looks, and Flatfoot steps back outside.

"Mr. Pittman..." Santos fiddles with a cufflink. "I want you to think back to that evening. You say the man proposed a bet?"

"That's right, it was Bo Mitchell with some blonde. Bo's the local ladies man."

"I see."

"The guy bet Bo would strike out. And Bo never strikes out."

"Let me guess. He did that night."

"Big time, to the tune of two bills. 'Never put your money on a man named Bo' is what the guy said."

"And this woman..." Santos prods him. "She was American?"

"I never talked to her, but yeah. She was American, all right, older but still a looker. We don't get that type much in the Sombrero."

"And the man at the bar? American?"

"Him, too. But they never got near each another."

Santos brushes at his sleeve. "Of course not. I'm just trying to get a picture here. I'll be quite frank, Mr. Pittman. The Lieutenant is convinced you fabricated this whole tale, and I'm inclined to agree with him. However, we are obliged to follow all leads in this matter, and since overlooking even suspect information might prove regrettable. We are prepared to give you the benefit of the doubt."

"Now that Oprah's on it, you mean."

Santos gives him a weary smile. "Please, Mr. Pittman, some respect for our beleaguered brothers in law enforcement."

"You think I'm talking through my hat, but I'm telling

you the truth. The guy you're looking for...Winslow? That was him. Listen, I've got to get outa here."

"You're free to go, Mr. Pittman. But please, leave us your phone number in the event we have to contact you for the reward?"

Pittman stands to leave. "You know where to find me, if I still have a job."

"Oh, and one more thing." Santos holds up a finger. "The ladies man, what was his name, again?"

"Bo Mitchell, Mitchell's Charter Boat Service. But you're wasting your time with him."

"Procedure, Mr. Pittman. Cover all the bases."

"Just don't tell him I sent you, okay?"

"You may rest assured."

***

Lena's walking home from Sacred Heart when she hears a car roll up behind her. Turns to a black Benz with Jersey tags and a faint but familiar sneer above the steering wheel. The Benz idles up and the window slides down.

"Lookin' gooood," says Billy De Pastore, Billy D to the initiated.

"How are you, Billy?"

"Can't complain. Well I *could*, but who wants to listen, right?"

"Right, so see you around." Lena walks off with a wave. The Benz trails at half a length.

"Let me give you a lift," Billy calls to her. "We have things to talk about."

Something clenches in her stomach. Talking with Billy is tricky business, and Lena doesn't feel up to it. They dated for a while years ago, and if she could take back one thing it would be that.

"It's not a good time." Lena steps up the pace.

Billy guns it and the Benz bucks past. "I'm serious,

Lena. About Harry."

Even worse, Billy's a bookie so it's about money. More of Harry's shit coming down.

"Take it up with my lawyer, Billy."

"Five minutes, Lena." He reaches over and opens the door. "Honest, just talk."

"We can talk right here." Lena checks the street. Empty.

"Don't be like that, girl. I might be able to help you."

"Oh sure, the wise guy with a heart of gold."

"What wise guy?" Billy whines. "Geez, where do you get that? I'm a businessman. Here's my card."

"D's Dromat? What's a dromat?"

"Laundromat! I got a string of 'em. You need something laundered, you come to me."

"So, it really *is* who you know?" Lena stuffs the card in her pocket. "I feel so darned connected."

"Take a ride, Lena. No funny stuff, I promise."

Reluctantly, Lena gets in. In the years since their fling, Billy's worked the fence both sides. That he's managed to survive is a measure of the current criminal element. Not that he's a moron, but Billy couldn't spell Mercedes.

"First, let me say that your old man was a standup guy and a pretty good horse player." Billy eases away from the curb. "Sadly, basketball was not Harry's game."

"Shaking down widows?" Lena tsks. "And they said you'd never amount to much."

He looks truly horrified. "That's cold, Lena. I was sick when I heard about Harry. You think I enjoy this?"

"You're the bookie, let's see the book."

"Come on. I can't do that."

"Why not?"

Billy looks away. "It ain't ethical. I got my reputation to think about."

"See, it's your reputation that concerns me, Billy. You

stole the March of Dimes money, remember?"

He whacks himself in the forehead. "That was in the fifth grade. We're adults now, Lena. This is grownup stuff."

"Oh?"

Billy looks over, and Lena has to laugh, silver ring through an eyebrow, Betty Boop tee shirt under an Armani jacket.

"This hurts me, Lena." And he does look hurt.

"How much?"

"Three grand. I told him he was nuts to cover Tennessee State."

"I'll write you a check." Lena fumbles in her purse.

"Lena, don't insult me."

"It's good. I promise."

He reaches for her knee.

"Easy, Billy-boy. Harry would break your arm."

"Aw, don't be like that. You know I've always had it for you, Lena. It's just something I can't control."

Lena jabs his hand with a ballpoint.

"Yaaah! Fucking..." Billy cracks her in the face.

Lena goes for his neck, but he pushes off and pins her to the door.

"Bitch! Now you've made me mad. Remember how I get when I'm really mad?"

"Get off me, you piece of shit!"

"Guess what, I'm still like that, baby." A hard shove into the window. "Mean as a junkyard dog."

He scoots back behind the wheel and steps on the gas with a giggle. Lena thinks to bail but Billy's all over the road. They sprint down Second Street through two lights and onto the freeway.

"Go ahead, say it, bitch! You think I'm a loser, right?" Shove. "Right?"

"Where are you taking me?"

"Where nobody can hear you scream. Look at this.

Look!" He waves the stabbed hand in her face, and she leans in and takes a bite.

"Yoowww!" He nearly sideswiping a minivan. "Owyowyow!"

Lena can taste him, sweat and garlic, and when he looks over, she lets fly.

"Fucking cunt!" Billy wipes spit from his face. "Okay, that's it. I was gonna just scare you, but you *had* to push it. You know what I think? I think you had this all planned, right? You know I like the rough stuff, and you wanted to push my buttons."

Lena stomps him into a cross lane skid; they nearly whack the rail but Billy wrestles it back together.

"You're crazier then I am, I like that."

"Lookout!"

The Benz swerves around a pickup and spins off the shoulder in a cloud of smoke. Lena struggles with the door, but Billy yanks her back.

"Okay, Lena, game's over." He shows a knife. "If I have to kill you to get off this fucking freeway I will."

Lena nods.

Billy puts the knife to her ribs. "It's okay, I'm not gonna hurt you, baby." He pokes around. "Might have trouble riding a bicycle for a while, but that'll pass."

Lena forces a laugh. "And you might just live, if you get to a hospital."

"What are you talking about?"

"Blood poisoning. I'm a nurse, remember? It's an ugly way to die, Billy."

He just laughs. "What, you think I've never been stabbed by a ballpoint before?"

"Listen to me, Billy, Harry's alive. He'll hunt you down and cut you to pieces."

"Jesus, just how stupid do you think I am?"

"The whole thing is an insurance hustle. Don't do this, Billy. Take me home now, and Harry will never know. I swear it."

Instead, he exits by the airport and takes the ramp for the cargo terminal.

"What is it, Lena, I'm Italian? You think all dagos are stupid, right?"

"I'll pay off Harry's losses and keep my mouth shut. He's crazy, Billy. He'll figure it out, you know he will."

"I ain't listening, Lena. Dead or alive, Harry don't scare me."

They cross railroad tracks and turn into a warehouse parking lot. Billy circles behind a row of empty flatbeds, kills the motor and slips something from his jacket pocket, a square of tinfoil. Lena watches him pick at a corner, hears an inbound freight and trucks idling by the front gate. She makes a grab for the door, but he's at her too fast, pressing the blade to the point of her chin.

"How far you think you'd get?" Billy sweeps a hand at the lot.

"Okay, Billy. You win, I won't fight you."

"Maybe just a little, eh?" He snickers and snorts up a fingernail full. "Oh, that's good. Some for you?"

"Yeah, okay."

"Atta girl." Billy chops more lines. In coming train catches his profile and he turns to look. Lena barks a cough while pressing the dashboard lighter, four...three...

"Fucking teamsters." Billy tees up another nose full.

The train rumbles in, and the snap of the lighter is lost to the racket.

***

Harry takes the back roads south, starved for the city. How he thought he could hack the hinterland, just another flaw in the plan. Like getting Steve's story wrong and having to kill Frank. Mind blowing fuckups any way you look at it, and Harry's looked at it every way there is. He needs to be around people and cut the distance to Lena. Manhattan for the sheer numbers, one more needle in that freaking haystack.

He knows they've been lucky and wants, desperately, to believe their luck will hold. Really *does* believe it for long stretches, unbelievably lucky with Frank when you consider. How you club a guy to death and just walk away is a testament to something, shoddy police work or divine intervention, or both. Not to mention Frank's luck, all bad, has to count for something. The press floats their motives, cops in the crosshairs, but any strong leads have fizzled by now. All the evidence in the world won't help if you don't have a suspect. What good is the answer if you don't know the question?

So back to civilization, but round about it, via old roads with their postcard views, hills, dales, sleepy towns no one would miss. He listens to Poppa Hayden, humming along to the cello solo, thinking about the money, what it would look like banded in bundles. Around noon he sees a sign for Larry's Bar-B-Cue 1/4 Mile hand-lettered and cut from cardboard. Last thing you'd expect out here in bucolia, but a quarter mile later, like the sign said, a tin shack at the edge of a parking lot across the road from a by God pig-pen. Harry parks and heads inside.

"You Larry?" he asks the old guy at the counter.

"Yes, sir. Got a yen for some barbecue, have ya?"

"You got that right. What's on the menu?"

"Today we got garlic sausage and onions. And chips and whatnot. Doctor Pepper, if it's cold."

"That's it?"

"Come again?"

"That's all you have? Garlic sausage and onions?"

"Had some kielbasa but we're out of it."

"That's quite a selection, Larry."

"So, what'll it be?"

"Let's see...know what? Give me the garlic sausage

Murder in Mexico

with onions and peppers."

"No peppers."

"Hold the peppers, thanks."

Larry ducks through a curtain, and Harry listens to him knock around the kitchen. Not much to the place, a few picnic benches and a short counter, but the smells drifting in go straight to his stomach. Pork and garlic, onions and coffee, food, the way it should be. He hears real pigs grunting and a tractor way off and something high and lonesome on someone's radio. Larry brings him a big sandwich on a paper plate with chips and whatnot. Harry digs the fuck in.

"Truly delicious, Larry, but I gotta tell you. It isn't barbecue."

"Well now, *barbecue* is what you call a catch phrase. Gets folks thinking pork."

"You're a pork man?"

"Forty years. Tell me something about pigs I don't know."

Harry pauses for dramatic effect. "Did you know that a pig is the only animal that will eat while he's being eaten?"

"I won't ask you how you know that, young feller, but it has the whiff of horseshit to me."

"I saw it on television."

The old man chuckles to himself. "Pigs and show business."

"It's a little known fact. Honest, Larry."

"Fact is eatin's all a pig knows to do. But *getting* eaten involves a fair amount of discomfort. Not the sort of thing to work up an appetite."

"They couldn't say it if it wasn't true."

Larry looks to see if he's serious.

Back on the road and into the mountains, snow capped Catskills draped in evergreen. He listens to a program about restless leg syndrome, how it ties in with chronic fatigue syndrome and other figments of the medical imagination. Lets his thoughts run to the money, what to do with it, bankroll something, put it to work. Harry's no math whiz, but he can see where a million might not last. Best to look into investments, maybe real estate or those storage places. Ned owns one, and Christ, they make a mint. And it's time to start thinking of where they'll resurface. And forget the country life. Those sticks run him up the freakin' wall.

***

Lena ditches the Benz in the ShopRite lot and walks the two blocks home. There's a cut above her nose, and her wrist is burned where the lighter fell after she jammed it into Billy's thigh. Other than that she's okay, has to hide her face when she passes Gus Lane smoking on his stoop, but reaches the house without incident. In and out in a flash with an overnight bag, her down pillow and Harry's ball-peen hammer.

Drives her own car to the airport and checks into the Ramada. Knows she should be scared, that she was lucky Billy bolted from the Benz without the key. That she should go to the police and get dragged into some Billy D mess, no thank you. Knows for god damn sure she should never have told Billy about Harry. Not that he believed her, but sew a seed in that mushy head and... Knows that Harry must never learn of this, any of it. Wants, right now, to do nothing more than pound something with this hammer, something glass, or solid and splintery, a skull, maybe. Two skulls.

She settles for the hotel pillows, flailing little round dents until the hammer flies from her hand and crashes through the ceiling tiles. That done, she gobbles some valium and sleeps like a baby.

In the morning things look better. Not her nose, swollen now and gruesome, but her slant on things. What her options are and how she should proceed on this. Unless he's all the way psycho, Billy will lay low for a while, lick his wounds and see what happens. Sunday, when she talks to Harry, she'll make some excuse to come see him, get out of town for a few days, let the dust settle. When he figures out she didn't go to the cops, even a pea-brain like Billy will surmise he got lucky, a few burns and abrasions, nothing felonious.

She'll tell Harry she hit a pole. Shit happens when you're not around.

Lena checks out and drives back to town. Raining now and it's backed up going into the city, and even though she fights it, she can feel her resolve crumbling. It's just as likely Billy's waiting for her. No way does he let something like this slide. And just like that the fear rolls over and she slips off the exit and back to the airport. Sheraton this time, two nights, cash in advance.

***

Past Rhinebeck, Harry stops for gas and a paper. His eyes are gritty and his mouth tastes foul, but he's making good time and should hit the city by daybreak. Get a room and a bottle, lose a day or two to cable, put this upstate behind him and chill for a while.

Takes the tunnel into midtown, and after weeks of isolation he feels suddenly alive. Crowded streets, noise and motion, all the people he'll ever need. Harry loves the mid-town mess, nothing like it in Philly or anywhere. Full-length mink stepping out of a limo, old Asian lady trailing old Asian man, shift the eyes, focus on anything, the wrought iron storefronts, the stoplight parade. Here and now at the highest level, just what he needed, just in time.

"I'd like a room high up, with a view."

"How's the forty-fifth floor, East River side?"

"Perfect."

Harry watches from his window, taken by the contrast. Streets set in perpetual motion, Manhattan millions to swallow him up.

"Room service."

"I'd like to order steak and eggs, coffee and a cheese croissant."

"We got latte, double latte, cappuccino, espresso, double espresso—"

"Regular, black."

"How you want that steak?"

"Medium well, eggs over easy."

"Some orange juice with that? We got pulp, no pulp, extra pulp—"

"No pulp, large."

"What kind of cheese croissant? We got—"

"Surprise me."

"You got it."

And on into the afternoon, bourbon and TV talk shows, Seinfeld reruns. Dozing through a John Ford epic, dreaming of Mexico, a dusty bus ride, the cluster of hotels out by the airport. Something tugs at his subconscious. He awakens to a voice outside the door, two voices then a lock unlocking, none of his business, doesn't concern him. Shadows stretching to the river, bourbon and Oprah, God, how he loathes her. Falling out again, voices in a hallway, trapped in a hotel room, Roland at the door.

Then he's sitting up, blinking into the TV light.

***

"You okay, pal?"

"I'm sorry, what?"

Bartender leans in. "You want I should call a cab?"

"'At's okay. What do I owe you?"

Harry settles up and stumbles outside. Jesus, look at this, would you? One in the morning and the streets are packed, clubs still swinging, bars and cafés all a-buzz. Night-wired and hopelessly hip, a crowd no one could ever stand out in. Maybe stop somewhere for a nightcap, but Harry's feet are a problem, slapping the pavement even when he concentrates. Fucking feet.

"Coke, reefer, ex."

"So how do we do this?"

"Step over here, my man." Black guy leads him under a stairway.

***

Fashions a pipe from the cardboard core of a toilet paper roll, a hippy trick from way back when. The first hit nearly kills him, scorched tracheal recoil, slobber spew, bits of lung. Smoke cloud billows to the corner while he thrashes into the cushions. Smoke spreads and catches on currents, cast in TV colors as he writhes in aftershock.

Then he's up and at the windows, clawing at the locks and yanking them open. Grabs a towel from the bathroom and fans the air. Christ, like a bomb went off in here, cold air washes over as he kills the lights, the volume. Harry huddles at the door. No Smoking signs plastered everywhere, one right here on the fucking door, lettered in red and trailing exclamation points. What the fuck?

***

Lena works the remote. She slept until the jets woke her, now she's just lying there wondering how she could sleep with Billy out there. Now that she's convinced herself Billy's crazy and not just a blowhard, like Harry always said. And he is crazy, pulling something like that, even if he wasn't going to kill her. She's never heard of Billy killing anyone, but she knew about the rough stuff. Not personally, but through the grapevine, his thing with the handcuffs. Never murder, though there's always the first time.

By now he knows she's gone into hiding. A smart guy might check the airport hotels, but Billy's a cretin when you get past the blather. Still it chills her. He was going to hurt her, though she won't dwell on that. Not right now. She's earned the right to pass that over.

More likely the bastard can't even walk. Lena got him good. She could smell it. Billy tried to dodge her, but there was nowhere to turn and a lot of him to go for. By the time he tumbled outside, she'd branded him forever. He must have known she could just drive off, but he just kept rolling around, screaming and grabbing at his leg.

Oh yeah, he's pissed.

Test pattern, snow, snow, snow, cute guys running off a football field, a car crashing through a plate glass window, a woman in need of a vaginal deodorant, snow, cartoons, a commercial for Arkansas, pharmaceuticals and more pharmaceuticals, a few minutes with Larry King, now this, "Animals of the Serengeti."

"The gazelle is a master of escape, usually tiring his pursuer with his broken field acrobatics. But midway through the chase this gazelle will panic, foolishly abandoning his evasive maneuvers he will try to outrun the leopard."

Lena's finger hovers over the button.

***

Harry springs from the bed. "Run, damnit!"

The camera zooms in, the gazelle, insanely frightened now, a blur against the brush. Behind it, nothing, nothing, then something, gaining, the single swipe of a big cat paw, then two. Then four as the camera pulls back and the stride lengthens, rear legs actually cycling over, ripping chunks of earth as it closes the distance. My God, he's beautiful, locked in a pure, mad contortion of speed.

Murder in Mexico

"With all the diversity and complexity of life in the Serengeti; the evolutionary leap-frogging of predator and prey, one fact will always hold true. No animal on earth can outrun a leopard."

Harry jabs the remote.

***

"When it's over, the leopard settles in for lunch with a wary eye out for thieves and interlopers."

Lena winces as the big cat tears off big bloody hunks, tossing his head playfully then bearing down, ughh. And *it's still alive*! Rolling over in surrender, offering up, aw, for... Lena turns but not quite out of peripheral range. Ripped open and now, spilling out, bloody sacs and what the hell? Sausage links or some—

"But here in the last great refuge of nature, death is never the end. For the creatures in the lower links, the gazelle's misfortune is only the beginning."

In the background at a gallop, something awful through a shimmer of heat.

"Enter the jackal, first in a long line of scavengers and opportunists who will dispose of the evidence and consign the gazelle to the realm of non-existence."

Lena sits through the whole thing. The jackals and the buzzards to maggots and flies. All of it, down to things microscopic, until there's nothing left but a clump of fur and a wide swath of crimson. Watches 'til daybreak, one after another. A PBS marathon she can't break out of, even with the valium, even with the vodka chasers. Watches bears chomp salmon and wolves mangle a baby moose. No escape from the carnage, nothing to do but bear witness, snakes swallowing, spiders poisoning, sharks tearing up anything that moves. The more she sees, the less it affects her, until she's anxious for it, doesn't care about the mating crap and the babies, though they're cute as all get out.

Wants only to see how they buy it in the end, what it looks like, real violence.

When the sun comes up, she pulls the drapes and watches some more. Always hated the eating-things-alive documentaries. Always wanted to scream at the camera crew to help, for God sake. Just to stand there and film it? What kind of heartless shit is that? But something about this is different. Maybe it's the buzz, or stress, or the thousand variations of ripping and mauling, but she feels a change come over her, something that will help, if she can fit into it. The natural law where everyone is a victim and there's always someone after you.

CHAPTER FIFTEEN

Lena calls Sally and the girls on the block, tells them she's at a nursing convention and will be home in a few days. She tells Alice she's staying with her mother, tells her mother she's going out of town with Alice. As she's packing to leave she sees something on the television, a photo just left of the anchorman's ear, the little girl, Lilly. Lena paws through the blankets and finds the remote.

"Doctors are unsure what is causing this reaction, but a spokesman for Children's Hospital described a rare infection that appears to be serious."

"Oh no, please, oh no!"

"The spokesman stressed that the condition may be treatable with a new strain of antibiotics. But this reporter could detect a note of resignation in his voice."

On the way to the market, Lena prays he hasn't seen it. That sweet little face, Harry just couldn't take it. She thanks God it's telephone day, and she won't have to wonder. The real issue, what Harry might do and what it means for her. Makes her nuts, and she's driving too fast, trying to make the Washington intersection, whizzing past a westbound cop car. Lena turns on the tears, but they write her up anyway, and though she doesn't know how, she knows it's an omen. Forces herself to park and walk then wait for the Chinese kid screaming into the pay phone, God, Jesus.

"Harry?"

"Lena."

"Oh, Harry, I miss you so much. Where are you? I'm

coming up."

"You'll love this. I'm in Manhattan."

"What?"

"Yes, and I want to see you, too."

He hasn't heard, she can tell. And she can get to him soon, an hour, if she pushes.

***

Harry sends down for more coffee and picks through yesterday's paper, sees a small headline, boxed off with other small headlines. Man Questioned in Thruway Killing, homeless hitchhiker, Christ, who hitchhikes these days? Only a paragraph, but it doesn't sit right, and Harry starts pacing. How he's still got Frank to worry about, and how it scares him. Blind luck that no one saw him with Frank. So wound up now he goes for a walk, across Avenue of the Americas, stampeding cabs, Washington Square shaking off Saturday night. Harry takes the path around to an empty bench, waits for the parade of dog walkers to pass and slips the cardboard pipe from his pocket.

Fucking ripped, like you only get in the morning, just like Harry to overdo it. Now he can't move and his eyes are glassy slits, too stoned and Lena coming, Christ. Finally, he pushes to his feet, fires his last smoke and tosses the pack in the trash bin, Lilly Winslow smiling up from the front page Post.

***

"Harry, no, this is no good." Lena takes the bottle from his hand and steers him over to the sofa. "Sit down, we have to talk."

"What happened to you?"

"I hit a pole." She feels for the Band-Aid on her forehead. "It's nothing."

"She's going to die."

Lena pulls a chair around to face him. "You don't know that. Look at me."

Harry stares at the Band-Aid.

"This is the way it is. I don't like it any more than you do, okay? I'd give it all up and go back to our old lives in a minute, but we can't. This is the way it is and we just have to live with it."

"You live with it." Harry slips another bottle from between the cushions. "I need to lose myself for a while."

Lena slaps the bottle away and they watch it roll across the carpet.

"I thought I knew you, Harry. I would have bet my life on it."

"Yeah, well, this isn't my A game."

"So what happens to me, huh? See, the rest I can understand, the poor little kid, it's wrong what we've done to her. But this is me, Harry. You got to care what happens to me. You fucking owe me that!"

Harry hangs his head. "I need you with me, Lena."

"Fine, no problem. I'm here."

"We have to get to Paris."

"Forget Paris." Lena pounds his knee. "You have to pull yourself together, and I'm going to help you. This drinking, it's not you, Harry. Oh, you like to think it is, but it's ugly on you. You know that, right?"

"I do now."

Lena fetches the bottle. "And if you're going to drink, you're going to blow it, so I'm telling you, Harry..." She sets it on the table. "You might as well just kill me now."

Harry groans.

"I mean it. I'd rather you kill me than for me to have to hurt you."

He leans forward, his face pinched in confusion. "Hurt me?"

"I did everything..." Lena's voice cracks. "You said it yourself. The dirty work, the lying and cheating, I did it for you, and I'm up to my neck. You quit on me and I'm totally fucked."

"Oh...that way."

"That way damns right!" Lena revs up. "So from now on it's my way. My way, Harry, or you know what?"

He just looks at her.

"I take the money and disappear."

Her words fade to a ringing silence. Harry looks like she's never seen him, frightened and impossibly old.

"Okay," is all he says.

She takes the bottle to the sink, pops the cork and pours out the contents, pausing more than once for a snoot full.

"You can hate me, Harry, but all this has to stop. We're still in the clear, and I intend to keep it that way."

"Whatever you say."

"Now get changed and I'll take you to lunch."

Harry heads to the bathroom, but Lena cuts him off halfway, hugs him to her without tapping him on the back.

"Hold me, Harry." She feels him squeeze. "You know I love you more than anything."

"You look like someone slapped you around."

"Did you hear me? I love you."

"I know that." Harry holds her at arm's length. "Just stay with me, Lena."

"I will."

They eat outside in a corner patch of sun, and it's almost as if nothing's happened. Sunday in New York, late lunch and the train ride home, like a dozen times before. So long since they've done anything together and it feels good, and instead of worrying, Lena lets it go. Yeah, she threatened him, but if Harry comes around it can only be a good thing. She's glad she said what she said, even if she couldn't really do it. Leave Harry in a bind like that.

"Any damage to the car?"

"Hmmm?"

"When you hit the pole?"

"Oh, just a ding. I must have bounced off the mirror. I was lighting a cigarette." She shows him the bandage on her wrist, so many lies, so much to remember.

"Looks like I beat you up."

"Yes, I know."

Harry turns to the ring of crowded tables, young people of the latest wave. "This is what I needed, Lena, civilization."

"They're young enough to be our grandchildren."

"I was looking through the Village Voice, the ads in the back, for live music? There was a time when I knew all the bands. The ads looked the same, some of the old clubs still cranking, but who the hell are these guys?"

"If you knew you'd probably have an earring and a little gray ponytail."

"Still, it's a blow."

"Look on the bright side. You missed the tattoo fad."

Harry scans the crowd. "Those two by the register, look at 'em. Can't wait to get home and have at each other. How does that work anymore?"

"I haven't the slightest."

He watches as they wrestle each other out the door. "Either you go for it and hope for the best, like always, or you compare your test results and medical records, frequency and number of partners, *their* tests results and histories, or you break out the condoms and hazmat gear and spend the next two weeks crippled with remorse."

Lena shrugs. "Ain't love grand?"

Harry laughs. "Makes you wonder."

A gaggle of drag queens sashays through, showering handbills and tubes of lovey-lube.

"See, you just don't get this in the Catskills."

"Funny what you miss." Lena drops a tube in her purse. "Anymore, I can't go to bed at night unless I know the ball scores?"

Harry shakes his head. "I must have been out of my mind getting you in this mess."

"Lucky for you I don't have the sense I was born with."

"Can you ever forgive me, Lena?"

Her smile is small, all-purpose. "You don't need forgiveness, Harry. You need to relax and set your mind on something. Like I said, we're in the clear."

"You're right." he signals for the check. "Get me a life."

"What about your music?"

Harry stifles a groan. "Not a pretty picture."

"But why not? Get a little singer-songwriter thing going."

"Earring, ponytail."

They pay up and walk the streets for a while. Lena makes him hold her hand and pretends she can charge him like a battery. Maybe it's true. Harry seems more like Harry than he has in a long time. So far, anyway.

"I know a little inn on the Delaware River, an hour from the city. I'll book a room for tomorrow, and we'll start looking for a place for you to live, a real place, not a hotel. It's nice there, you remember. Far enough away but close enough to get to."

"Pretty isolated."

"It's the country, not the boondocks. Rich people live there."

"I still think Paris—"

"When my passport comes we'll talk about it then."

It's a nice day so they take the ferry. Harry fills her in on his Catskill fiasco, leaving out significant details. It's pretty wacky in the telling, and he loosens up, the Meryl Streep stuff, pretty funny.

"Did I tell you I went to Cooperstown?"

"Cooperstown?"

"The Hall of Fame? I drove all the way in a blizzard

and the damn thing was closed. Can you beat that? Lena?"

Silence.

"Hey, what's wrong?"

"Nothing. I'm just...surprised."

"You look pale."

"I feel a little woozy. Must be the wine."

They find an empty bench, and Harry wraps his arms around her as the wind picks up. And she's thankful for the warmth but she wishes he wouldn't. Not with her head spinning and the statue of Liberty drifting by, hollowed out, just like Lena.

***

In the morning, Harry turns in the Caddy, and they hit the tunnel for points west, upriver to the Center Bridge Inn, as Bucks County as it gets with the fieldstone and the walk-in fireplace. Lena sends Harry off for the classifieds then goes through his stuff while he's gone. Finds the reefer and the gun, and it's like there's a soundtrack playing, hysterical violins or the brass section crashing down. But something's not right about it. The news said the guy was clubbed to death. Lena picks up the gun and runs a finger down the barrel. Whatever else this means, it means Harry wouldn't need a club.

When he returns, he's just like he always is, so she acts like she always acts. They circle some rentals and make some calls and a pair of appointments for that very afternoon. And she feels herself absorbing the shock, the name, Cooperstown. Turning it over in her head until it loses impact, and pretty soon she's able to forget about all of it for minutes at a time. And as they turn up River Road and into the trees, Lena pulls the plug on her heart, and something hard fills the space inside her.

"The thing about the Catskills, they're untamed," Harry tells her. "I like my countryside tamed."

"Tamed."

"Yeah, like this. Green and pretty but not, you know, dangerous."

"This is nice, huh?"

"Yeah." Harry smacks his lips. "Maybe I'll write a song about it."

"This place is on the river, one bedroom with a barn, furnished. They said they'd do a month to month lease."

He smiles his goofy smile. "Oh yeah, momma, got those month to month blues down to my shoes."

The first place is as far as they get, a cute little cottage off by itself with a white picket fence and a view to die for. Harry pays three months in advance, and an hour later he's all moved in.

"How about that guy? He didn't even ask for ID."

"This is perfect, small but cozy. See?" Lena pokes his arm. "Stick with me, kiddo. I know what I'm doing."

"I can handle this, yeah." Harry steps over to the bay windows. "Watching the river flow."

"You feel better now, don't you, Harry?"

"You'll stay here with me."

"I'll have to go home to pick up some things, but that won't take long."

"But not today."

"No, not today. But we should go to the supermarket."

"And the liquor store. Don't give me that look, just some wine, to celebrate."

Even food shopping, God, it's been ages. Lena leads and Harry steers the cart like they used to. A week's worth of basics and scallops for tonight, a merlot and a chardonnay, then home to moonlight on the river. Harry builds a fire while Lena busies herself in the kitchen. The silence between them could mean anything. She peeks in once to see him on his knees, reading the newspapers stacked by the kindling. Like an actress playing herself, every movement scripted, the food, this stalk of celery, just props to work with while the silence stretches.

The fire snaps and crackles, Lena's cue to make an entrance, which she does, remarking on how lovely it is, a wood fire. How it makes you feel safe and warm, even though safe and warm is not how she's feeling. Harry tells her about the chimney fire he saw when he was a kid, and Lena says what she always says when he tells her that story, that birds sometimes build their nests in chimneys, though she really doubts it's all that common. So much like a movie scene, Lena ducks into the bathroom for a minute. Not because she has to, because it somehow seems to fit.

Later they make love and even *that* smacks of performance, Harry bucking and moaning, Lena working hard, an intensity that was never there before. When it's over, they collapse against each other and Lena feels nothing. Worse than nothing, like they've lost something they can never get back again. If they ever had it to begin with, which seems suddenly uncertain. Their lives together shaded by what they've done. Not changing it so much as changing her. Not just now, but going all the way back.

"Come here, Lena," Harry calls from the bed.

Then he's at the bathroom door and she can see he sees it. The look in her eyes, gives her away and all his hugging and kissing won't change it. But they hug and kiss anyway and she smiles like that's what she really needed and they pretend everything's all right.

***

Tuesday she drives back to the city. Gorgeous day but she doesn't notice, caught up in lies and more lies and now another one. Telling everybody she's moving, the way they'll take it, more confused than surprised, especially Minna. California. The only place Lena can think of that will explain a long absence. The new job lie, who would question it? But once she breaks the news it sounds like what it is, a big fat lie. No one pins her on it, but it's there, the gaps in logic, if anyone's looking. But no one is, so she throws in some details, the big money, the chance for a new start, the nurse she used to know with an extra bedroom. Once you've told the big lie, the little lies are easy.

"What do you know about California?" Minna keeps asking, as if there's a test.

"I'm just gonna try it for a few months."

"I can't believe you'd do this to me. Abandon me in my old age."

"Oh come on, Rita lives around the corner."

"Imagine, packing up and moving halfway around the world at *your* age. I worry about your judgment, Lena."

"I'm not packing up and it's not halfway around the world and my judgment is fine. I just need to get away for a while."

Her story and she's sticking to it. The kids take it hard and the neighbors fret.

Then there's Alice.

"I'm gonna get Big Dot and we're gonna tie you up and lock you in the closet. Uh-huh, see how far you get with that California business with me."

"It's not like I'm moving away. I think of it as a vacation with pay."

Alice flares her nostrils. "Earth to Lena, I been working with you for twenty years. I never heard of no California girlfriend with no empty bedroom."

"I must have mentioned her. I had a life before General, you know."

"Honey, I was born on a Sunday, but not *last* Sunday. You do what you have to do. I'll be right here if you need me, no questions asked."

"Thanks, Alice, I knew I could count on you."

The last stop is the hardest. Sister M and her turn for the worse. In the weeks since her visit, Muriel has dwindled to nothing. For the last few she's been bedridden, barely a lump in the blankets, and Lena doesn't see her at first.

"You've come to say goodbye." The voice is a whisper.

"Not goodbye, it's just for a while."

"I don't think I'll see you again, Lena. Here." she pulls a small notebook from under the covers and hands it over. "That day at your house, it made me think. If I ever do come face to face with the Almighty, I want to ask him a few things. So I've made a list."

Lena looks at a dozen entries under the heading, Please Explain.

"Eternal damnation, talking in tongues, stigmata, Limbo, Elizabeth Taylor," she reads aloud. "That's a good list. But you're not going anywhere, Sister M."

"It's time." She turns her head but Lena sees the tears. "I should be there to help them."

"But we need your help here."

"Tell me, Lena, do you really think they'll be there, the children? Somehow I still see them as children."

"I wish I knew."

"The closer it gets, the less likely it seems. I know it's just a test, but I'm afraid I'm failing badly. Be a dear and light me a cigarette?"

Lena checks the hallway, fingers one from the pack and fits it to those papery lips. While the old nun smokes, Lena searches for an ashtray, but there's none to be found so she uses her hand. Another sister comes in and opens the window without comment. Muriel takes little puffs and struggles to inhale, but the poor thing hasn't the strength. Lena can't see how she'll hang on much longer. Feels her heart break for the shadow they've cast, a full life's work called into question. As bad as anything they've done, it's a lead-pipe cinch for eternal damnation.

"Sister M, please don't despair. It's not fair to Harry. If he knew you were feeling this way it would kill him."

"Once I saw Harry pick up the Chambers boy and dust

him off after he'd fallen in the playground." Sister looks to Lena. "I mean nobody liked that kid."

"Harry got that from you. See? You've made such a difference to so many people."

Sister hands the cigarette to Lena. "I'm responsible for what they believe. And, if in the end it's all a lie, I'm responsible for that too."

"That's not true."

"You're just gone, like Harry. And you'll never even know it was for nothing. You won't know a thing forever and ever."

Lena can hear her breath go ragged and her hand flutter against her chest. "Sister?"

Someone moves around downstairs. Lena tiptoes over and pushes the door closed. Muriel's eyes follow as Lena pulls her chair closer and leans in.

"Listen to me, Sister M." Lena checks the door. "Harry's alive."

Muriel's brow furrows in confusion.

"I can't really explain it, but we had to make it look like he's dead. He'd kill me if he knew I'd told you, but really, he's okay."

The eyes mist over and the lips move in silent incantation.

"Just remember, when we get to heaven we'll be looking for you. It may seem like a stretch now, but to me it's the truest thing in the world."

"Harry." Muriel mouths the words. "Alive?"

"I wouldn't kid you, Sister M."

The light dims, the features settle, and the old girl takes Lena's secret with her.

***

Harry goes for walk along the river. Half as wide as it is in the city, the banks overgrown then clearing to wide

Murder in Mexico

lawns and some of the houses, Christ! They don't call it Bucks County for nothing, white people with their square footage and swimming pools, their blonde kids and purebred dogs. Here, where money is never the problem. Weeks since Harry's been outside and this, walking, feels terrific. Just cold enough to keep him moving, and he ends up by a set of pilings, stone supports for a washed away bridge. The edges chipped and crumbling, moss thick on the mossy side, like something out of ancient Rome, and he wishes he had a camera, or, even better, a sketchpad. Thinks to buy one when he's in town. Something to get him out and about, take his mind off the nasty business.

He stops at a café. Some old guy going on about the flood of '55, how this very building was under water. An even older guy tells of the inter-urban trolley system that could take you to Montreal, Canada, if you had the time and the transfers. Harry checks to see where the post office is and the bank and the liquor store. Can't get over Lena slapping things together in a matter of hours and how the future doesn't seem so uncertain. How she's more cut out for getting away with it than he is.

Back home, he soaks in the Jacuzzi, piano tinkling through the bathroom door. Harry and the last of the chardonnay, then the fifth he picked up in town, running the jets at lower back level, life is so good when you have all the comforts. And this place has all the comforts, fireplace loft with the big sleigh bed where he'll sprawl après shower through the evening news.

"Police in upstate New York today confirmed reports that Frank Lavin, the man found beaten to death on a Thruway turnoff, may have been lured to his death by someone he knew. A gas station attendant in Cooperstown reported seeing a tall man in a dark jacket chatting with the victim at the station entrance. Investigators are looking into another report that Lavin's death was payback for testimony he provided in a gem smuggling case. Police

released this sketch of the man suspected of clubbing the 46-year-old father of two to death with a tree branch."

Harry can't believe his eyes. Not him exactly, but close enough, and he hears the bottle clunk to the floor. Feels the walls close in as the newscaster babbles. Hears the phone ring with what can only be bad news.

He lets it ring.

***

Lena hangs up and checks the clock on the mantel. Just like Harry not to answer when he's sitting right there. Unless he went out, which would be like him, too. She sits with the sisters for a while longer, not really grieving since Muriel lived a good life. Almost cheerful, with Sister M stories, how she talked that kid down from the ledge or ran the hookers off Front Street, the night she threw out the ball at Veteran's stadium, and on and on. It's dark by the time she leaves and she hits traffic on 95, a mile long gaper grind. So she takes the first exit and ends up lost in a warehouse district. And it's all so ugly she starts to cry, sadness like she's never known, not just for Sister M, but for what it's come down to. Cutting herself off was never part of the package. But what did she think; things could just go on like always?

Then out of nowhere, a sign for the freeway and she follows it to a small ramp that curves into a bigger ramp and just like that she's back on track. Past the jam up point so she has her pick of lanes and she offers up thanks to Sister M. The feeling Lena was giving her something to take with her. The thought makes her smile, then laugh and it doesn't escape her notice, crying then laughing in a matter of blocks. What a mess she's in, her emotions all over the place, and then she's crying again. Misses her mom and the kids on the block, the neighbors needling and feeling safe when you turned the corner. You don't always know the last time around, but you do sometimes. And this feels like one of those times.

It's raining when she hits New Hope, and just north of town something darts across the road then doubles back for no reason, a thump so clear she can't not hear it. Thinks to keep going but there's room to pull over so she pulls over. Walks back along the shoulder until she sees it, a squirrel flattened like a little throw rug and Lena loses it. Throws her head back and howls at the rain until someone comes running, young guy in sweatpants and he sees the squirrel and leads her away. Lena folds herself into him, cries and cries then kisses him once, drives the rest of the way with the heater blasting, her hair a mess and the stupid Band-Aid peeling off. Blinded by the wake from a passing cab, halfway past the darkened cottage. Just like Harry not to be there.

***

He hands her the passport and tries to look as much like Gerry as he can. The flight attendant studies the photo, how he *would* get the diligent one.

"Your boarding pass?"

Harry shows it to her and she waves him by. Window seat over the wing with a view of the takeoff queue, must be seven jets deep out there. Harry badly needs a drink. He's done it now, but still at a stage where it's not a mistake yet. Might turn out to be the only move he *could* make, once the dominoes start to fall. The way cops work when they've caught a whiff. Could be Harry's one of those one-step ahead guys. How would you know until someone's after you? One thing for sure, they can't get him here. Now that he's safe he can think of what to tell Lena. Has to get ahold of her as soon as he lands, let her know, what? That he killed Frank Lavin and they may be after him? If the cops get to Lena they'll put the two together and then they're both in the shit. Not to mention the fact that he's left her flat again.

Paris, like he has the slightest idea. Sticking it all on her credit card, along with the grand from the ATM, like that will last forever, a grand, in Paris. Another thing for sure, how he knew he had to go right away. Once you know, you go. When it's the only chance, you take it, end of story.

What he can't bring himself to imagine is the look on her face when she reads the note, confusion, turning to something else. Rage? Despair? He can't even pretend to know anymore. Now when they talk there's a carefulness, their words tinged with restraint, or reservation. A price they couldn't have foreseen and would never have agreed to. Not Lena, anyway. Their easy life together, what people envied about them.

"Lena, know that I love you and try to forgive me."

That's it. Anything else could be used against him. He'll call her first thing when he touches down. And tell her—

"Flying on business or pleasure?" The guy across the aisle smiles, and Harry realizes he's been staring.

"No, I, uh...business."

"Me too. Nickel's Ball Bearings." He offers his hand. "I'm Nickel."

"Nice to meet you."

"Might be stuck here a while, looks like."

"So it seems."

"Interested in ball bearings?" He waves a handful of pamphlets.

"Only slightly." Harry holds a hand up.

"You might be surprised. This country moves on ball bearings."

And so begins a six-hour slice of the ball bearing life, and lubricants, Christ, Harry wishes he *had* a nickel for every time he says it, machining advances and tolerance

Murder in Mexico

levels, a world of moving parts and lubricants, always lubricants. Harry's attention dissolves in the weird cabin clatter. Snaps back for a second when Nickel stands to take his jacket off, moving just like a guy who takes off his jacket when the talk turns to ball bearings. And much later, when they're finally airborne and the empties are piling up, Nickel conducts a virtual tour of his "little plant" in Pennsylvania. Right through the front door, past Madge, or "the Sarge" as he calls her, and back to the loading dock (three bays, you could eat off the floor) and into production where "the girls" (Mexican, cute as little buttons) off-load and package. Manages somehow to corral the guy on Harry's far side, a guy who actually gives a shit, and Harry can't get away from them, even when he pretends to doze off, even when he *does* doze off, the give and take running through the movie and into the wee hours. Harry's head throbs and his ears track every little sound.

They land in a predawn mist. Security has a go at his bag and he thinks of the gun, wrapped in plastic and hidden in the rocks across River Road. Couldn't figure what else to do with it, but thinking he might need it later. For what, he can't imagine, but he knows he'll know when the time comes. Through the wide airport concourse, down an endless corridor and out into the rain. Asks around for the best way into town, drawing blank stares and impatient shrugs. Finally corners a kid in a Yankees cap who puts him on the train with the address of a small hotel. And it's just like in the movies; the train packed, the steel girdered station with a windowed roof, everyone speaking French, even the black guys. He grabs a cab at the exit and shoves the address through the window. The driver says something in French.

"Sorry?"

He says something else in French and Harry motions for him to drive. They argue back and forth until Harry slips a ten through the window. The cab circles once and pulls up directly across the street. Inside, a man in suspenders tells him, in English, that no rooms are available, but that someone is scheduled to leave in an hour. Harry pays in advance and crosses to an outdoor café where he orders by pointing to something that looks like pancakes, but turns out to be a Danish with preserves inside. Raspberry, if he had to guess. Not what he was after, but he digs in and it's easily the most delicious thing he's ever tasted. When it's gone he sits and smokes, nursing his coffee, watching the people. French people, imagine that.

Back at the hotel, no phone and no TV. Harry recalls a pay phone by the café, but he doesn't have change and wouldn't know what coins to use. Wait until the rain stops. Get some sleep and work out a story, later, when he's thinking straight. Not even a freaking radio, so Harry sits by the window in the dark. Kills the last of the bottle and tries to think. What story? What?

***

"First you're going to California and then you're not. It's your judgment, Lena. It isn't sound. Where are you, anyway?"

"I'm at home. I've just had second thoughts. There's no hurry. I can go anytime."

"They'll hold a job open for you? How can they do that?"

"It's per diem, mom. They always need people."

Minna goes on about her judgment and how Rita wants to move to the shore, as if *that* will ever happen. Lena sees that she should have stayed at the cottage, even though her gut said Harry forgot the phone number. She should have stopped to think things through instead of rushing home and telling lies. More lies than she'll never be able to cover.

"I don't know why you can't just get a job here. The city's full of hospitals."

"I'm trying to get a life going, mom. You could be a little more supportive."

"You have a life, Lena. Why would you throw it away?"

"See, now you're getting mixed up. This is your argument against going. I just told you I'm not going, yet."

"Is this about a man?"

"Don't be silly."

"What's silly about it? You're trying to hide something from your mother. What else could it be?"

"I'm not hiding anything, mom. I'm just trying to get through this."

But Minna won't let up, and Lena feels a tug for the days when they weren't getting along. All the phone calls she didn't have to wade through, the guilt strained through endless questions.

"You know your father hated California, don't you?"

"Listen, I gotta go."

"He was stationed there during the war. San Diego, I think it was."

"I wouldn't go anywhere near San Diego. Listen, mom—"

"And so expensive. I saw on the news where—"

"I'll call you."

The whole night spent watching the phone, but he doesn't call. What if he never calls? Harry's note gave her that feeling, and when she thinks of it her head starts to hurt. Why would he do this to her? He's crazy and he's got a gun, a combination that never ends well. This is about the second dead guy, Lena knows it, which means they're after him, or he thinks they're after him. No matter how she looks at it, Harry's let her take the fall again. What else could explain it? So she can expect guys to come crashing through the door at any time, waving guns, busting up the place. The way it happens when you least expect it. So she goes to the door and peeks outside and sees the Benz parked right out front.

***

It's still raining the next morning. Harry lays in bed, listening to the clank of the radiator. A cozy touch with the windows steamed up and traffic splashing. The feeling that nothing can touch him here and he wraps himself up in it. But then he thinks of Lena and the feeling fades. How she'll never get here without a passport and the nagging suspicion that she never got one.

He rolls out of bed and studies his image in the window. Then he looks down to the top of the marquee next door, a neon sign in French with the time, 12:00 PM. More French across the front, reflected backward in the window across the street, and he makes out *Born to be Bad*, Robert Ryan and some other names. Funny, he didn't notice a theater when he checked in. Must be some sort of American movie retrospective, Robert Ryan's been dead for years. Rain really coming down and he thinks to kill the day at the movies, grab a bite and a bottle and while away the day. *Born to be Bad*, something noir-ish by the poster in the window, Ryan behind a woman in a slinky black dress. The poster clinches it.

He showers and shaves, stops on his way out to reserve the room for two more nights. The girl at the desk looks Indian or Pakistani and her English is weak so they go through it with hand gestures. He thinks she gets it but can't be sure, so he takes the key with him, out the front door and across the street to the same café for the same pancake-looking pastry that's just as delicious as he remembers. He watches someone talking on the pay phone then hits up the waiter for a handful of coins. Christ they weigh a ton. Out in the rain, trying to make sense of the phone, but it's too confusing so he puts off calling. Still time to kill before the theater opens so he walks over to Notre Dame, rain soaks through his jacket as he passes a black guy selling umbrellas. Feels pretty good about the transaction, even if he paid twice what it's worth and it won't last the day. The cathedral as grand as you'd expect, but it doesn't feel right without Lena and he only stays a few minutes. Ends up at another sidewalk café, under the awning with a bottle of burgundy. No label, like they mix it in the basement, but tasty, though he's not really a wine guy. Rain and more rain, as if Paris wanted to look its coldest and loneliest and Harry buys another bottle and hustles across the street just as the man opens the ticket window. At first he's the only patron, but others come drifting in and they spread around like people do in movie theaters. A handful of couples a dozen loners and Harry wonders if they're regulars or just getting out of the rain.

 The lights go dim and they show coming attractions and it's not clear if the movies are really coming or they're just old trailers. Either way, the familiar faces and the black and white work their magic, and by the time *Born to be Bad* begins, Harry's back in the forties, lavish sets and tough talk, the cars and the chain smoking. A world he dimly recalls but rarely revisits, subtitled in French, no less, Ryan, young and handsome, in a dark polo shirt with that sneery delivery. He's a San Francisco writer and he's after Joan Fontaine who looks a bit spinsterish, but turns out to be the "bad" one. Harry sinks so deep into the story he forgets where he is and how desperate things have gotten. And when it's over he has trouble reconnecting and leaves the theater disoriented, passes right by the pay phone to the wine bar where he sits chain smoking and watching the rain.

***

Lena grabs Harry's baseball bat and storms out the front door. Billy starts to get out then dives back inside as the first blow dents the roof.

"Fucking lowlife asshole!" The second shatters the side mirror and then she's all over it, hood, headlights, doors, grunting and heaping curses, giving her all. Lights come on as she takes out the windshield, folding in sections then breaking apart.

"Scumbag stinking Dago piece of shit!" Hand on her arm but she shakes it off, goes at the taillights, a blast of glass and shattered red plastic. In rhythm now, wild and unstoppable, slam banging until the bat splinters in her hands.

"Lena, whoa!" Duffy wrestles her away, still spitting and fuming, but winded now. A final fling and the bat handle bounces down the street. Then she's handed off to Sally who turns her away, and she hears Billy jabbering like an idiot. A dozen neighbors crowd the Benz, men and women barking threats and insults. Billy lays on the horn like that might help, tires crunching glass as he pulls ahead. A bottle clunks off the roof then jeers and catcalls as Billy beats a path.

When he's gone, they mill around talking tough while the kids fill the windows. Someone gets a broom and they sweep up the mess. No one even asks what brought it on.

***

A week of no TV and Harry's climbing the walls. He's gone through half his cash but Lena's card still works, and he hits it for another grand. Moves two blocks to a hotel with a TV, but it's all in French, the shows, news, everything, weather. Lovely sound, though, like music, with the occasional word in English. How un-French they sound, falling from those Euro lips like tasteless crumbs. More on his mind besides Lena and the police sketch, loneliness, for one thing, isolation. He hasn't met a soul except for the fat guy who seems to live at Starbucks and the woman at the jazz joint who beat him for a twenty before ducking out the back. Hasn't even tried to find out about the Thruway killer, as if the French give a shit. And now his tooth is acting up again, feels like it's going to crumble, pain on the way but doesn't want to think about it.

A week without sun, though it does stop raining. He tries seeing the sights, but it's hard to connect, even with the phrase book, which only seems to annoy people. No routine to speak of except sleeping late and drinking, French barflies and women who don't speak his language, crazy to piss his money away.

He sees *Born to be Bad* again and when the feature changes to *Dark Passage* he sits through it twice, stumbling out into more rain and a bone-rattling chain of sneezes. French germs, just what he needs. Harry takes to his bed, watches French TV and stares at the ceiling.

***

Lena gets her credit card statement. Harry's in Paris, and from the looks of things he's found all the watering holes. She tries to picture him there, but all she gets is a shape moving up a crooked little street. The same street that's in the picture above the upstairs toilet, Rue something or other. A picture Harry committed to memory over the years, inventing stories for the little stick figures at the bottom, two in particular, hailing a cab to take them to the racetrack, or a swank café, or wherever Harry wanted over the course of his nightly six-pack. Lena calls the passport bureau, puts her renewal application on the fast track.

She's seen nothing more on the Thruway killer. The police sketch really knocked her for a loop, shave a few pounds and the guy's a dead ringer. And she knows every life has strange twists and turns, but nothing stranger than tracking your man's manhunts over two continents. A sketch of a guy who looks like Harry Watts, if you know Harry and are thinking of him when you see it. Even then it wouldn't mean much, unless you knew what Lena knows and no one does, so no mention is made. Still, late at night it's always SWAT teams kicking down doors or Billy D sneaking in and finally Lena packs some things and drives upriver just to get some sleep.

She dreams that Harry's dead, a dream that chills her when she wakes to the truth. That he's still out there and she still has to worry. What really chills her is she's had these dreams for years, and the relief she felt when she woke beside him was like a perfect gift. The best thing she could ever hope for, a second chance at everything. And this was just the *opposite!* Lena doesn't want to believe it, but she lives in a world of things she can't believe. Lying there, fully awake now, she can see where loving Harry has become too much for her. Amazing, the places her mind will go these days, places she didn't know were there.

Now she's crying, fuck it, and she opens the locket and there's Harry, full of himself. Lena's heart goes out like it always does and she looks to where he should be and it seems so unreal.

The dog comes later that day. Lena sees him lope across the lawn then hears him scratch at the door, nosing his way in when she opens it, slurping at her hand, tail banging the doorframe.

"Whoa, fella." Lena pushes but he dances right back, licking at her chin and up her nose. Big brown dog with big brown eyes and so darn happy to see her, no collar that she can see, but clean, and well fed. Someone else's dog, though it's clear he loves her madly. Follows her into the kitchen where he trots to the corner and scratches at a bottom cabinet. Lena finds a bag of dog food inside and pours a big bowl full. He eats half then circles the rug and curls up with a heavy sigh.

In the afternoon, she takes him for a walk on the towpath, Lena walking, the dog bounding into the brush, crashing over leaves and branches, popping back out a hundred yards farther down. There to sit stock still until Lena calls, then off like a shot, ears pinned back, big, sloppy smile on his face. So much fun he does it again and again, always the mad dash finish, until Lena worries he'll hurt himself. Okay, one more time and that's it, and he takes off, crashes around but doesn't pop out again.

Lena calls down the towpath but the dog doesn't show. Probably took off for home, but she keeps at it until it's almost dark. For no other reason then she'd hoped he'd stay the night, a warm body to curl up and watch TV with. Wishes she knew the dog's name, where he lives, wishes she'd stopped the game when she was going to. They'd be home by now, Lena, the dog and a roaring fire. That which she can't have makes her want it more than ever, and the thought of being home alone hurts more than she can stand.

She gives it a few more minutes then starts back, and halfway there hears him coming on fast. Turns just as the dog blows by, a single pant, a thump of paws, then waiting and wagging at her back door.

The night turns out just how she pictured it, balled up with the dog on the sofa. He's a sucker for belly rubs, a sprinter even sound asleep. The next morning, they walk the towpath in the other direction and it goes the same. More private homes but the dog doesn't mind, ripping through hedges and trampling flowerbeds. She puts him on a leash when they get to the village and the dog is transformed, stepping beside her like a show dog, waiting patiently when Lena stops to shop. Back home just in time for the latest from Oprah central, little Lilly and her brave fight for life. Cameras track the crowd as Oprah runs down the latest setback, calls for prayers and the power of hope. That they must believe, that belief is the key. Then they're cheering for Lilly, cheering and crying for Lilly, and to a lesser extent, God, but mostly for Oprah. All things Oprah and the way the girl gets things done.

Lena wants to believe. But there's an overblown, TV feel to it, Oprah and any damn thing, and try as she might, Lena can't see it ending well. Doesn't want to think how it all could go wrong, or right. Doesn't want to think about Harry at all, not today, with her new dog and how it's going so well. Her dog. She hugs him to her when her thoughts turn to Harry. A thousand hugs and it works every time.

***

"Lena?"

"Yes, Harry."

"Are you okay?"

Lena doesn't know how to answer so she says nothing.

"I'm in Paris."

"I know."

"Please. I don't blame you for hating me."

"I could never hate you, Harry."

"Who's there with you?"

"My dog, Chester."

The last thing Harry expected to hear and he thinks maybe it's the connection. But the dog starts to bark, Lena yells something, and the phone bounces off the floor.

"Sorry, he doesn't like me to talk on the phone."

"I need to see you, Lena."

"What's happened?"

"Nothing's happened. I just need to explain. Something came up and I just had to go."

"Is something coming up for me?"

"What? Why would—"

"Because you know how you'll hate yourself if I should know but you don't tell me. So tell me, Harry."

"No, I don't know."

"Chester, quiet! Tell me what to do if they get me, Harry."

"It's not what you think. You have nothing to do with this."

"Everything you do has something to do with me. I told them you were dead, remember? They paid off."

"Did you get your passport?"

"It's coming."

"Just stay at the cottage until it comes. We paid in cash. The landlord doesn't care who we are. You'll be okay there."

"But they won't send it here. I'll have to go home to get it."

"Have Alice check the mail."

"Forget it. I'm not involving anyone else."

Harry winces. "I have to see you."

Lena wraps her arms around Chester's neck. "Okay. How do we do it?"

"I'll let you know. I have to go now. I love you, Lena."

"Harry?"

**

But there is no way to check the mail without involving someone else, so Lena waits a few days then drives in to check it herself. Less than an hour by car and she thinks what she'll do if the cops get her. Deny everything. They can't touch her for the Cooperstown thing, and if they tie in Mexico, she'll make a deal. Give them Harry like he'd give them her. The thought scares her to death, and as she turns off at Pennsport that hard thing in her heart gets even harder. Her new passport's not there but nobody jumps out to grab her. She waits a few days and drives in again, with Chester. Her passport's there this time, but Sally spots her and drags her into an interrogation. Then the kids come home, see the dog, and the block's all over her.

***

"Est-ce que quelqu'un assis ici?"

Harry turns to a woman in black leather, attractive, but not happy about something. Slips in beside him before he can say a word. Harry looks to the bartender and shrugs his eyebrows. The bartender grins and sets her up.

"Vous etes mignon." She leans her head in her hand. "Est-vous mariee?"

"I don't speak French," Harry tells her.

"Mon mari est un porc."

"Sorry. Can't be helped."

But she doesn't seem to mind, slipping a hand in the crook of his elbow, lighting him up like a hundred watt bulb.

"So, you live around here?"

She answers with a warm smile and a long explanation, in French with coy looks and Audrey Hepburn eyes. Those lips and her hand warming slowly until he wants to—

"Qui diable etes vous?"

They both turn to a big guy with a nasty snarl. The woman spins away and mutters into her drink. The man glares at Harry.

"Ce que vous faites avec ma femme?"

"Sorry pal, it's all Greek to me."

The next thing he knows he's looking up at legs and faces, hears loud shouts and a woman scream. Someone grabs his arm and he knows what's happened, that the fucker hit him. And for the first time in a long time he knows what to do, scrambles to his feet as the guy comes at him. Head butts the asshole, crushing his nose, then a fist to the gut and a picture perfect uppercut. Frenchy folds over then flies backwards, taking out a passing waitress, drinks and glasses flying. Someone blows a whistle and the crush of bodies carries Harry along and then he's out the door and running. Through the streets of Paris. No idea where he's going, but senses when he's out of range, that no one's chasing.

He wanders the streets, trying to find the hotel, finally has to ask for directions. Three, four times until a pair of black women points the way, chattering French and dabbing his face with a hanky. Hookers, no doubt, but tall and lovely, the one blacker than Harry's ever seen. Coal black, so her eyes shine like headlights and he wants nothing more than to lose himself in those eyes. But they have other plans, which they explain to him with much giggling and touching, something that might include him if he only knew what they're saying. But he doesn't know and they wave goodbye and he watches those hips sway into the night.

Tom Larsen

CHAPTER SIXTEEN

Lena's flight is scheduled to leave at 6 AM. She walks two blocks in the dark, catches the 6 bus to Broad Street, transfers to the southbound subway, and takes a seat by the rear doors. Everybody is still half asleep, and it reminds her of Harry. All those bus and train rides, setting off before the sun to one job or another. How he'd tell her about the subway snoozers and the harried moms getting the kids off to child-care and the guy in the fatigue jacket with a bedroll and the three-inch fingernails. Way too early for the world to start up, but here it is and Buenos Dias.

Harry used to say that life runs on habit. If you find yourself on the bus at 5 AM every morning you can't think of it as insanity, so you lose yourself in routine. One of the shitty things you do every day without thinking about it, just to keep going. But if you *did* think about it you'd see that it's madness, so you just nod off. Harry's problem was he could never sleep on public transportation.

She's afraid of what she'll find when she gets to Paris. Harry mailed her the address, Rue de Temple, the Metro Hotel, but when she tried to Google it, she drew a blank. Not that it matters. It's not like they're on their honeymoon or anything. More likely it's near the airport, something small and dismal, close to a liquor store.

The sun's up when the train rolls into the airport and Lena's spirits lift a little. Sure, the circumstances could be better, but she *is* headed to Paris, and it's exciting in a nerve-wracking way. Better to see it like this, she supposes, than never see it at all. That thought makes her feel better too, and by the time they take off, she's considering a different kind of trip altogether. What Harry said, the two of them on the run in Europe, four-star hotels until the money runs out.

The money. It was all she could think about all week. The teller's face when she said she wanted it in a cashier's check. Like it was *his* money! One million, one hundred and sixty-six thousand right in her freaking pocket. At first she was terrified, lose a cashier's check and you're out of luck. But Lena didn't know any other way and she sure as hell wasn't leaving it behind. But she knows she won't lose it and can't wait to see Harry's face when she shows it to him, if she shows it to him. In any case, she's got it on her, folded away in that skinny little pocket she can barely fit her fingers in. Harry doesn't have to know. Not that he's asked about the money even once.

The money. Having it all on her, so if worse comes to worst she can just run. Money's good anywhere, right? American dollars? It's insane and she knows it, but right now it feels good and she sneaks a finger, yeah, there it is. So she can run.

It's just as sunny when they touch down at Orly. Lena makes her way through customs, grabs a taxi and shows the driver the address. He grunts in some language then pulls away. Lena watches out the window, pretty ugly here, sort of bulldozed over then long stretches of boxy apartment buildings with identical balconies too small to use. Nicer as they approach the city, then just what it always looks like on television, older than God and Euro-beautiful. Lena can't help but smile.

She sees a girl walking a dog and flashes on Chester, or Luke, as it turned out. Yesterday, while they were watching her soaps there'd been a knock and Chester charged the door. Didn't bark, just that weepy thing dogs do, and when Lena looked out an older man was standing there, smiling. Chester scratched at the door, the man called out "Luke" and the dog went crazy, pawing his way up the door then dancing back on his hind legs. Lena let him out and while they wrestled around, the man explained that he'd been away and his housekeeper let Luke out by mistake. He's Mr. Hardiman from down the towpath. Sweet old guy, agreed to let Lena come see Luke whenever she wanted, and maybe ride his horses now that they were neighbors. She was sad to see Chester go, but it solved the problem of what to do with him while she was gone, and at least she knows where to find him.

The cabbie drives too fast and they clip a pigeon crossing at windshield level. There's a loud clunk then a smear of blood and feathers. The driver says something then turns on the wipers and laughs. Lena's stunned, by the mess and the notion that you could hit a pigeon. She's lived in the city her whole life and has never once seen it happen. Always assumed pigeons had a sixth sense. Maybe French pigeons were different, slower.

She sees the sign for the Metro Hotel a block before they get there and slips the driver a twenty. He jumps out and opens her door then picks at bits of bird caught in the wipers. Lena passes inside and crosses to the desk.

"Room 6C?"

"6C, 6C..." The desk clerk scans the register. "Ah, Monsieur Watts?"

"That's right."

"Two flights up, second door on the left," he tells her in English.

Emotions swirl as she climbs the stairs. The place is run down but handsome, steps curving around, the cool thickness of the handrail, arched windows at every landing. The door says simply 6C. Lena knocks and listens but she hears nothing so she knocks again, louder this time. Just like Harry not to be there, but then she hears floorboards creak, a deadbolt slides and...

"Harry? My God, what's happened?"

Murder in Mexico

He pulls the door open and she slips past without taking her eyes off him, holding a towel to his swollen nose, still in pajamas though it's late afternoon. She hears a TV and the hiss of radiators behind her.

"Someone hit me." Harry takes the towel away

She sees blood spots. "Who?"

"Beats me." He shrugs and holds his arms open.

Lena hesitates then steps into them.

"I'm so glad you're here," he sobs out.

"Why'd he just hit you? Did he say?"

"He said a few things. They weren't in the phrase book."

She pats his back repeatedly. What she can see of the room is a shambles, clothes strewn around, the bed unmade, bottles lined up on the table. She pushes free and starts picking things up, but Harry pulls her to him.

"Don't." Lena stoops to snatch a shoe. "I'm a little wired from the trip. I need to—"

"It's okay, Lena. I know I've let you down."

"You haven't let me..." She straightens up suddenly. "What do you mean?"

"Nothing, I just..."

Lena sees the strain in his eyes and how Harry's aged. Not just his bruised face, all of him, neck creased in wrinkles, knobby elbows, collarbones like little handles. Poor Harry and what he's done to himself. Lena knows she should go to him, but thinks he might just crumble completely. So she stays where she is, and Harry settles to the edge of the bed.

"What do you want me to say, Lena?"

"Don't say anything. Let's just ease into this."

Outside, church bells ring and Lena goes to the window. The street below is halved in shadows, and the buildings across from them shine in the sun.

"I didn't picture a place like this. You can see Notre Dame."

"All distance in France is measured from the front steps of the cathedral. Did you know that?"

"It's like where the artists would live, Picasso and all of them. Right here."

"They didn't, for the most part."

"Are you in trouble, Harry?"

"How would I know?"

A group of men comes out of a restaurant below, chat for a second by the door then head their separate ways. Farther down, kids in uniforms gather at an intersection, the boys loud and laughing, the girls prim and disapproving.

"I want to go eat in a French restaurant." Lena keeps her back to him. "Coquille St. Jacques and a chocolate mousse."

Harry looks no better in the fading daylight, still tall at least, but wasted and disheveled. The streets are crowded with shoppers and workers going home. As they cross the bridge into Isle Saint Louis, Lena takes his arm, and for the briefest moment it feels like a vacation. Different but not unfamiliar, like Mexico before the ball got rolling.

"Where shall we go?" Lena leans into his shoulder.

"I don't think it matters. There's a French restaurant on every block."

"Where do you eat?"

"No place special."

"Take me there."

"I don't think they have Coquille St. Jacques."

"I don't care. I want to see what you've been doing."

"Right here." He steers her into the Friterie a few blocks from the river. It's busy, mostly young couples and college kids. Harry's never been here, but it's the sort of place he might go.

"This is great." Lena falls in behind the waitress who leads them to a table by a shuttered window. Four other tables are unoccupied, but within minutes the room begins to fill.

"This where you usually sit?"

"I usually eat in my room."

"What do you get here?"

"Soup, usually." Why he's lying about this he has no idea.

The waitress speaks English and they order the French onion, what else? Lena gets a side salad and Harry, an order of fries.

"So, what do you think?" Lena asks when the waitress has gone.

"About what?"

"Anything. Talk to me, Harry. I need to hear your voice."

"I've missed you. Do you mind if I tell you that?"

"I've missed you, too. That's why I need you to talk to me."

"How's your dog?"

"His real owner came for him yesterday, was it yesterday?" Lena puzzles for a second. "Isn't that so amazing? You can be in your yard with a neighbor one day and the next, sitting by Notre Dame."

"He's a neighbor?"

"Um-hmm, sweet old guy, I have dog visiting rights, *and* he has horses."

Harry laughs. "Every little girl's dream, a sweet old geezer with horses."

"Old and rich, every big girl's dream."

A couple in the corner keeps looking over, and Harry tries to place them. Maybe patrons at the bar last night, though he can't recall. Gives them his Pennsport glare, and they nearly knock heads looking away.

"You stopped shaving your head."

"It didn't seem worth the effort. I've lost so much weight no one would recognize me."

"You don't think we'll run into someone we know, do you?"

"Here? Not unless there's a Paris Mummer's club. Anyway, you still look like Lena. We'll probably have to do something about that."

Lena grunts. "Like what?"

"I don't know, do a makeover. To go with your new identity."

"I still have to wrap up things at home."

"What things?"

"Look, I can't just drop off the face of the earth like you, Harry. What do you think, no one will miss me?"

"Call Alice, just say something came up. It's nobody's business."

"Maybe where you grew up."

Harry heaves a sigh. "Okay, but after that we make some changes, both of us. The world isn't as big as you think."

Lena's smile is non-committal. She's put a lot of years into being Lena and doesn't see herself giving it up.

"Have you heard about Lilly?"

"What about her?"

Lena lowers her voice. "You didn't hear? She's making a comeback."

Harry searches her face.

"It was on the news all last week. They don't get Oprah here?"

"You mean she's not going to die?"

"Well, she's still critical, but the doctors seem to think she has a chance."

"A chance."

"It looked bad there for a while. But they showed pictures of her, and Larry King had a telephone hookup with her mom. Everybody's optimistic."

Harry leans in and touches his forehead to the table.

"You haven't been following?" Lena fairly whispers.

"I couldn't take it."

"Maybe that was a good thing."

He looks up. "What do you mean?"

"Maybe you had too much stress invested in her getting well. Who knows how these things work?"

"Am I supposed to know what that means?"

Lena giggles like she thinks he's kidding. "Don't worry, Oprah's in charge."

Their soup arrives. Harry scalds his mouth on the first spoonful.

"Something else, Harry. Muriel died."

"Aww, Jesus."

"I was there when it happened, just me and Sister M. And the last thing she said was the last thing I told her."

"Which was?"

Lena smiles through the steaming soup. "Harry's alive."

At first she doesn't think he's heard, but his eyes well up, and that makes hers well up, and then they're both blubbering.

"Madame, Monsieur?" Their waitress rushes over. "Is something wrong?"

Harry makes a joke about winning the lottery and the waitress claps with delight. So he spins some story no one understands and Lena gets a glimpse of the Harry that used to be. And she cries even harder as he takes her in his arms to heartfelt oohs and ahhs. Then a little man with a walrus moustache presents them with a bottle of champagne to celebrate their good luck.

"Thank you so much, merci, please." Harry nods and smiles.

Moustache bows and blabs away.

"He says the French believe that luck brings luck," their waitress translates.

"I didn't know that."

"My uncle lives in his own little world." She winks.

Closing time comes but no one makes a move. Music drifts up from the street, and Harry leads Lena in a dance, circling the room to the crowd's delight.

"Luck brings luck, you heard the guy," Lena whispers.

"Here, maybe." He steers her to their table. "Let's finish our drinks and toddle home."

"How did you ever find this place? "

"You know me..." Harry lifts a glass. "Monsieur Out and About."

"Vous reveillerez Notre Madame." The uncle points to the window.

"He's saying for you we will wake Our Lady." The waitress leans in, pulls a bolt and throws the shutters open on Notre Dame, centered like a picture in a frame. Jesus! Then a gasp as the moon slips a cloud and the whole sky turns silver.

Harry looks to Lena. "Eh?"

"You sure no how to show a girl a good time."

***

That night she has a dream. Harry's dead again, but she spots him on a passing bus. He gets off after a few stops and she follows him, but it's a part of town she's never been in and she gets lost. Then they're in a bar, that Ninth Street club Riley Prentiss took her to, and Harry tells her that Muriel figured it right, the heaven and hell thing is a crock. And Lena's sorry for M but okay with the rest of it, now that they won't have to burn in hell. When she wakes she feels woozy, the color's gone from the room and everything has a murky look. Like Purgatory, she thinks, cold and clammy.

The temperature dips and Lena makes a wish for snow. It just *looks* like snow, the color clouds get, slate gray and heavy. Lena's always been able to tell the snow clouds. She says nothing to Harry even when it does start to snow. In Paris! Lets him be the first to notice, though she couldn't say why. And Harry can't get over it. Moves the chairs to the window and they sit and watch as the city changes. Later they throw snowballs then trudge to the cathedral to light a candle for Sister M.

Harry takes her to see *The Postman Always Rings Twice*, watching Garfield murder Lana Tuner's husband and the hell they go through. Lena gets a feeling she's never had before. The two of them watching the two of *them* murder for money. Strange too, Garfield with that haunted look and Lana wondering if he's got what it takes. What it is about these hard-boiled women. How they hustle men and work things their way with nothing but the promise of love. And it's over the top, Hollywood style, but Lena sees through to the simple fact. When it comes to crime, the women are stronger.

She comes back from the bakery and Harry's at the window with a sketchpad. He shows her what he's done, their view caught in the winter light, trees and rooftops snow-frosted. It moves her to think he can still surprise her, the sides to Harry she's learned not to see. The sketches are rough outlines, but the scale is right and they might even be good.

"Regarde..." He flips a hand. "Fugitive Artist, the Paris years."

"I like it."

"Here's the good part." He starts on her portrait. "In the unlikely event le shit hits le fan it'll make a splash. With Oprah and the hoopla, see where this is going?"

Lena sets the baguettes on the table. "Your fifteen minutes of fame?"

"Exactement!" He jabs the sketchpad. "Like minting money, whatever happens, hold on to these."

"I rented a video." Lena pulls it from the bag. "Grand Hotels of Europa."

Harry smiles. "Europa. The fugitive years."

"The rules are no Third World, no former republics,

no mullahs or warlords."

"That *does* narrow it down."

"I think we should take notes." She flips him the cassette.

Lena makes sandwiches while Harry figures the French VCR. But the tape looks like 1968 with the washed out color and sappy narration, and by the time they hit Amsterdam, Lena's snoring softly and Harry's on their third bottle of wine. When it's over he goes through the stations but the only thing in English is another stupid tennis match so he switches to the news. Some silver haired anchor forced to banter with the staff, painful to watch in any language. They break for a string of techno commercials then back to the anchor, tight-lipped and grim, the last face Harry sees before the cameras roll and his world spins out of orbit. The podium, the pink dress, the angel Lilly blinking into the flashbulbs, Harry jumps from the bed and rushes over, cranks up the volume but it's still in French.

"What's wrong?" Lena stirs.

He doesn't answer, stands swaying from side to side, eyes glued to a close up still. Lilly on a strip of beach over two sets of dates, the last one today.

"Oh, Harry, no."

***

He takes to walking late at night after everything's closed, favors the river in the mist. Head down and hands in his pockets, unmindful of the danger, if there is any. Lena pretends not to hear him go.

He takes a different route every night, but always returns by Rue du Temple, stopping to catch the light in the old rectory dormer. Soft shadows slanted in the rafters. Something Harry needs but he can't imagine how to get.

They're doing laundry when he tells her.

"I don't want to do this anymore."

"Europa?"

"Fuck it, let's go home and watch real TV."

Lena checks him with a look. "Home where?"

"Bucks County, you know. See how it goes."

She looks at her clothes tumbling. "What is it, Harry. You okay?"

"Stop asking me that, will you?" he snaps. "Jesus, how's that supposed to help?"

"It's not," she snaps back. "But I have to know."

He sags and she thinks again: he won't make it, not Harry, not this time. She's watched him pace away an afternoon and last night heard him sobbing in the shower. Now he wants to go back and it scares her to think what that will lead to.

"I'm tired, Lena. Let's go home."

"It's not a good idea."

"As if we'd know a good idea." Harry feeds coins to the dryer. "Anyway, we have to go back for the money."

Lena's cue to show him the check, but she lets the moment pass right by.

"The money?" Harry leans in.

"I heard you."

"And put the house on the market, still things to do, Lena."

"Okay. But after that?"

Harry looks away. "We wait and see."

On the last night, she takes him back to the Friterie, but the waitress is different, upstairs isn't open and the moustache never shows his face. They pass the cathedral on the way back. Harry doesn't give it a glance.

***

They're home a week when a freeze sets in, so cold Harry's teeth ache, always cold, though the heat's cranked up and the fire's a-blaze. Harry smokes weed and loses himself in movies, days on end without leaving the house. Lena takes walks and tracks her soaps, curled up with Chester through the afternoon. Harry lives in his bathrobe, showers when it suits him, shaves if he thinks of it. Lena cuts down the calls and sees no one, takes to her bed, sleeps the weeks away. They watch the same news on different TVs. No break in the manhunt, the dead still dead.

He finds Frank's gun in the loose chunk of wall, wrapped in plastic and looking like new. Hides it in the basement, high behind the paint cans, where he can reach it when he's sober, but can't when he isn't. Just feels better knowing it's there.

Lena keeps the check in her vanity, pays with plastic or their dwindled savings. Waits for Harry to wonder but it never comes up.

***

"I said 'flag me?' I'll stick that flag up your ass, fucking yokel." The match chases the end of his cigarette.

"That's pitiful, Harry."

"Hah!" He waves the lit end. "See that? Never too drunk to smoke."

They are driving home from the Carversville Inn and a near fracas over comments Harry made. Invited to leave by the owner and butt of said comments, skipping out on the tab, which *had* to be considerable. Harry spent most of the day there after their flare-up this morning. At least before he kept it in house, but now he's always out there somewhere. Has this thing about the old inns and rustic ambience. This makes three where he's no longer welcome.

"So when you blow it, don't look for me, Harry."

"I won't look for you."

Lena pulls over and cuts the engine.

"Listen to me." Her voice goes flat. "I'm through with

this. You can shoot me if you want or bash my brains in, but I won't live this way."

Harry scoffs.

"That's right, Cooperstown. I know what you did. I don't know why but it wouldn't change a thing."

"He saw me. I had no choice."

"You have a choice now."

He wants to explain about Frank, but it's too hard.

"How do you fix yourself, Lena?" He swallows a sob.

"You can do it, Harry."

"It kills me that I can't. When I was a kid, this guy in the neighborhood used to stand on his stoop, ranting and raving. So drunk you couldn't make out what he was saying. But there was rage in it, so we left him alone. Then he died." Harry gives her a look. "It got so I missed it."

***

Back home, and now he's into the weed. She can hear him upstairs, hacking and pacing. Killed that guy, clubbed him to death, wish to Christ she'd never told him. When she goes up to check, he's just sitting there staring at the painting above his desk. The pastel she found in one of the galleries, a lush lawn sloping to a manor house. Harry does this now, disconnects. She doesn't know why and she doesn't care, sick of the sound of both their voices. And it's winter and Lena's sick of dealing with Harry in the cold, thinks of springtime when she can get out of the house and away from him.

***

He drives up to Bowman's Tower, Washington's old lookout point. It's been years but it looks the same, the narrow road up and the tower itself. The shape of it branded in his brain, sort of Gumby looking with the corner turret. He parks in the lot, crosses to the arched wooden door and pulls the handle. It opens like a dream, and it's nothing like it was, the walls plastered over, the spiral staircase replaced by an elevator. He pushes the one button and the doors open. It takes longer than it should, but he reaches the top, steps out and crosses to the railing. The view is all but unrecognizable. Quarries still at it across the river, but whole hillsides are gone. The river and the banks still green and the high sky, but the farms have gone to developments. A thousand patchworks bundled in houses, garish horrors chockablock.

"No wonder the Yanks won the war." A voice behind him.

Harry spins and the woman flinches.

"I startled you." She clutches her collar. "Forgive me, please."

"I didn't hear the elevator."

"Oh, I've been up here quite a while. It's all rather breathtaking." The accent, British or Australian?

"I used to think this was the most beautiful thing you could ever see," he tells her. "I can remember my mom saying I was looking too hard. But I wanted to take it with me."

"And did you?"

"I did."

"And now it's changed."

"Oh yeah, but I still have it." He points to his head.

"A boy with foresight, how endearing." The woman smiles. "I wish you could share it with me."

"Probably I'm way off."

"I'm curious. Did you used to spit off the tower?"

"Every time."

"My boys were forever spitting off of things. I could never see the point."

Harry shrugs. "It's sort of compulsory."

He turns back to the railing.

The woman takes a seat on the turret bench. "When

were you here last?"

"Long time, thirty years."

"Why now?"

"I thought it would help me."

"Can I tell you something?" The woman smiles sadly. "Before you came up here, I was toying with the idea of tossing myself over."

Harry winces. "Bad idea."

"I suppose quite a few have had a go."

"Not that I remember..." *though it seems likely.*

"That said, I should tell you I've reconsidered."

"I'm glad to hear it."

"I wouldn't want to sully the image you carry."

Harry sits beside her. "It would make a mess."

"Yes."

"Are you here by yourself?"

She looks out at the hillsides. "No, Harold's waiting in the car. He has bad knees."

"Can he see you from here?"

"Harold hasn't seen me in years."

They sit for a moment then Harry asks, "Does he know?"

"He thinks I just wanted to see the view."

"The thing is to outlive him."

She doesn't seem to hear, and Harry crouches beside her. "Bury him and move on."

"Yes." She looks up, suddenly alert. "And maybe speed him along a bit."

Harry stands and offers his arm. "Shall we go down?"

"I think so, yes."

***

Chester rolls on his back, paws pawing as Lena rubs. What he gets from it she can only wonder. She's tried it on herself to no effect. They are down by the footbridge.

Chester wanted to cross, but Lena thought back to a Fourth of July, strolling the bridge with Harry. She noticed something moving in the space between the girders. The light caught on a spider's web, massive and perfect, and when she looked around, they were everywhere. And it scared the living shit out of her, so she told Chester no.

"No, Chester." And he understood, even though his name is Luke. Lena wonders how long he can lay like that, balanced on his back with his legs splayed and she decides to find out, rubbing and rubbing until her arm gets tired, switching arms and rubbing some more. Chester uses his head as a fulcrum and shows no sign of getting enough.

"If you were my dog I'd never make you wear silly outfits." One of Hardiman's failings, photos of Luke in chaps and tutus. He makes her call him Hardiman, like some crotchety old boss, just another Rankin to Harry who won't ride a horse and spends his days elsewhere.

In a while they'll go into town, but right now she just wants to rub Chester's belly and forget about Harry, where he is, who he's pestering. The endlessness of Harry-worries seeping into everything, a month now and nothing settled, their lives on hold until he works it out...or blows it completely.

"If you were my dog I'd feed you pizza once a week." Something Chester/Luke can't get enough of, dancing the pizza dance, tail sweeping dust bunnies into the corners.

Lena sees a couple out on the bridge, the girl poses by the rail as the boy works the camera. She watches, horrified, as the girl leans into the space where the spiders live, but then she tells herself it's winter and the spiders are dead, or hibernating, whatever spiders do. When she can't rub anymore, Lena stands up, brushes the leaves from her lap and starts into town. Chester waits until she's far enough away then whirls to his feet and blasts off after her.

"Hello, Luke old boy," Max shouts from the porch of Max' Hardware, but Chester walks right by, and Lena has

Murder in Mexico

to smile. She stops to check the mail and on the way out spots Harry's car coming across the bridge. Lena shoots a wave but he doesn't see, hits the speed bump, head to the ceiling. A few minutes later she sees it again parked in the church lot.

"Come on, Chester," She walks over and checks, keys in it, menu on the front seat, The Fatted Hog, wherever that is. Inside the church, the organist botches Bach's Toccata, and a voice shouts directions to the choir. Harry's nowhere in sight so Lena ducks back out, does her shopping, chats with the woman in the deli then starts for home. Harry's car is still in the lot, so she ties Chester to a meter and passes inside. It's a small church, bright and cheerful and Lena settles into a pew. The organ starts in again, the voices come from above, soft at first, but rising to separate, men going in one direction, women another. Her eye catches Harry in line at the confessional.

Harry?

***

"Come on, boy." She yanks the leash, and they take the stairs to the towpath. Lena walks and wonders what it means. She was raised Catholic but never took it seriously, has her doubts about all religion. Sister M taught them right from wrong, but the rest was hokum and superstition. She'll admit to being Catholic, but thinks of herself as recovering.

There's so much going on in her head she doesn't see the rescue squad out on the river, the lights flashing on River Road, or Chester crashing through the tick-infested brush, only Harry in confession line, the bald spot and spare tire, more of Harry than usual, lately. Then all thoughts circle off, leaving one thing throbbing in the center of her brain. Harry confessed.

***

Oh God, this is bad. This is definitely bad. She hasn't been up here in weeks, and he's got the walls taped with pictures, moonlit landscapes, soft light through frosted windows, sleepy village sunsets, that kind of thing. She tries to make sense but what the fuck?

Lena runs her eyes over. Most of them cut from magazines, but a few old Polaroids she's seen before, the house on Morris Street, a place they rented down the shore, one of the two of them arm and arm in a bathroom mirror. No common thread, but each inviting in some way, a sense of serenity. Hello? Psych Nurse?

Harry's walled himself up in melancholy to counter the pain. And either it will save him or serve as the next step on the long way down. Or a third and better bet, that she's not even close, that trying to think what a loony thinks is, well, loony.

She wants to tear the pictures down, but she can't face the mess or the confrontation. Stares up through the shit splattered skylight and thinks the most amazing things. How love makes no difference. How it starts and ends with Harry, and she's just here to pick up the pieces. Meanwhile, who's connecting the dots and when will they come and why is she just waiting for it. Like the people you read about who get caught because they did something stupid, and no one could be *that* stupid. That's what they'll say about her. But they won't understand, and Lena doesn't either, not anymore. Or maybe she knows too much now, how you can feel love get smaller. How you can be scared out of it.

What she'll do is nothing, for a little longer. But she keeps the check in her pocket and a car in town with her passport locked in the glove compartment. Hardly a plan, but it's the best she can do.

Then she runs into Sue Anne and her husband, out from the city for a weekend B&B. Lena keeps it brief, but the damage is done, and she knows it's crazy to think they can stay here. Sue Anne of the motor mouth, gushing country condos and how they want one. Lena shudders to think they might have seen Harry, though they try not to be seen together. But what if he'd been with her and the thought makes her toes curl.

She calls the post office in Philly, tells them to forward the mail here. Parcels out what's left of their old savings, good for three months, maybe four, long enough, she tells herself. Harry gets the flu and she nurses him back to health. Harry gets drunk she wrestles him to bed. She keeps the check in her pocket. The days pass slowly.

***

What Harry doesn't know, as he babbles on about the rescue squad and the boy in the river, is that someone is listening two tables over. And he's been going on about it for so long he feels like he knows the guy, feels his desperation, too many bills and too many kids. Sees the guy setting it up in advance, years maybe, long enough to establish the birthday ritual with the boat, the booze and the nitwit buddies. Saw where his life was headed and found a way out.

"My guess is Mexico," he says, though he knows he shouldn't. Mexico, a subject he'd do well to avoid for now and forever. But it gives the guy a sort of panache, that he could think of such a thing and have the balls to pull it off. Makes for a good yarn, even if Harry doesn't know what he's talking about.

He stays until the sun goes down then settles up and bids the boys goodbye. It's cold outside so he let's the car run for a while, stands in the lot and smokes so as not to stink it up, hears the scrum of voices as the door opens then footsteps over the ice.

"Ronny wouldn't do that. What you said."

Harry turns to the woman. "Ronny?"

"That's his name. Ronny Petric. He's my brother."

Harry draws a blank but then it hits him, the guy he's been slandering, the boy in the river. "Please, I meant no harm."

"He was twenty-six years old."

Harry wants to run or crawl under a rock or just vanish in a cloud of smoke, but he doesn't move, and she looks at him with the kind of contempt only women can muster.

"I'm just an old drunk with a big mouth. Don't pay any attention to me," he tells her.

She takes a step closer and he can feel the heat. "He had two little girls he'll never see again. Ronny didn't have no fucking insurance."

"If you'll go back in with me I'll take it all back, every word."

"You think I care about *them*?" She jerks her head.

"Diane?" Someone calls from the door.

"I'll be right there." She doesn't turn to look, but waits until she hears it shut.

"This is a small place and people talk." Her eyes sear his face. "My mom heard about what you been saying. Now she thinks Ronny might still be alive. It's all she thinks about and prays for."

"Please."

"And you know what? When they finally fish him out of there, she's never gonna live through it."

Harry can't look at her, has to turn away.

"But I know *you* can live with it. People like you..." She searches for something more to say then simply turns and walks away.

***

He tapes the latest to the wall, a picture of a house. He doesn't remember what the ad was for, but it's springtime, and the trees are in blossom, and there's a cat in the window. That's what caught his eye, the cat sitting in the sun. The house reminds him of his grandparents' place in Rockville Centre, big trees and the sun always shining. The house is the color of butter, but the shutters and front door are deep green. There's a milk box open on the steps with a note stuck in one of the bottles and a newspaper folded on the stone walk. Any minute now the door will open and someone will step out, but not just yet.

***

It snows during the night. Lena lies in bed listening to the plows up on the highway. Hardiman told her that several state bigwigs have homes up north, and River Road is high priority. It's not yet light. The sky has that dead look, the darkness stale and ugly. Lena slips from the bed and into the bathroom, puts on Harry's robe and slippers, then crosses to the landing window to watch. Big flakes falling in slow motion, two or three inches at least, the tree limbs heavy, the lamppost piled in a perfect pyramid.

Harry left the heat on again, and warm air engulfs her as she comes down the stairs. The shadowy look of the place is familiar to her now, the furniture dark and sleeping. She circles the room, pausing at each window, smells the coffee and hears the clink of the crystals she hung above the radiator. 5:30 by the kitchen clock. Some days she's up an hour by now.

She stands at the door and watches the road crew. Thinks of the men as solid types, strong and capable, the bigwigs would see to that. Searches for a word to describe what she's feeling as red lights flash on bare trees. No word comes but it's not a good feeling, this time of day, otherworldly.

Lena's time, the part of the day when Harry's not a problem. Won't be up for hours, here but not here. Nothing can happen to him except a heart attack or stroke or any one of the standard things that come when they will. Things she never has time to think about, which is when they get you. Part of the reason she's fallen into the early routine, if she's honest with herself, to present the opportunity. Though Lena is rarely honest with herself anymore and would be shocked by the suggestion any other time of day.

She sits at the table and finishes the story she's been reading, a guy gets caught in a blizzard on a mountain road. He's a bootlegger with a load of booze and his truck overturns. Lena keeps looking up at the snow out the window, then reading about the snow in the mountains, and it seems more than just coincidence. Snowing like hell now, and already the locals are making their way. Some with chains and she thinks of the sounds that are only winter, the tick of sleet against glass, the scrape of a snow shovel, the different kinds of snow and how it crunches or sloshes or creaks when you walk on it. She makes herself think these things so she won't start crying over the bootlegger and the trouble he's in. The thing you love about men in stories, alone and freezing, everything he has invested in that truck, so it's fix it or die. But it just gets worse, nothing he does works and he knows it's hopeless. But he isn't the sort to give up and with one, last, superhuman effort...

She's taken by the thought of crying over someone who isn't real instead of crying over Harry. How he hardly makes a sound as he comes and goes, except at night when she hears things crashing. Terrified he might hurt himself or burn the house down. Fears for her life sometimes and is relieved to wake and find Harry on the couch, the heat cranking and all the lights on.

The other reason she gets up so early, those predawn raids. The time SWAT teams always come for you. It's why Lena was sold on this place to begin with. The long private drive to give you time. The clothes she keeps on a hook by the back door, the check stashed in a tin above the doorframe. Just a straight shot past the barn to the towpath. If they came right now she'd be long gone.

The bootlegger prevails and the story ends, and though Lena can't know what follows she senses that it won't be good. Still she's inspired by his spirit, his determination to save himself. In the end, he wedged a log against a boulder and pried the truck over with no gloves, or even a warm coat. Thinking Lena could use a man like that.

She counts the empties in the sink. There will be no Harry this morning.

***

Hardiman's in back, tossing hay to the horses. Lena calls to him, pulls carrots from her pocket while the horses yank their big heads up and down, Buck and Tramples, another Hardiman joke.

"They look as happy as children," she tells him.

"They lead an obscenely easy life. And like all animals..." Hardiman leans in and whispers, "They don't know they're gonna die."

"I think Tramples might," Lena whispers back.

"He can't be sure. So please." Hardiman holds a finger to his lips.

"I came for Ches-, I mean Luke."

Hardiman chuckles. "He should be back in a minute. Just went to fertilize Watson's tulip bed."

She takes the towpath up river. Chester's in the plaid jacket that makes him run funny so Lena takes it off when they're far enough away. The fringe of bank ice has widened overnight. If the river freezes over it will be the first time in thirty years, according to Hardiman who knows such things. The snow is ankle deep and the going is easy so she passes the footbridge and keeps going north, to the cleared stretch for the unbroken view. They rarely go that far, but Lena's in bootlegger mode and Chester can't believe his luck.

***

Harry wakes and senses Lena gone. He smokes last night's roach while looking out at the snow then falls back into the pillows as his head starts to fizz. He flashes on the girl at the bar and his limbs lock, sees the drowned boy's mother, white haired and saintly, Cagney's mother in White Heat, top of the world ma. Limbs heavy the rest hollow and empty. His foot tangles in blankets getting up and he tumbles to the floor, cursing and shivering. Dresses in the same clothes he's worn all week, tries to drink the coffee, but dumps the pot and starts another, hunched at the counter as the coffee maker gurgles.

***

Out beyond the ice shelf, thick chunks crunch on the river current. Lena shouts to Chester but he doesn't listen.
"Chester, no! Chest-Duke, here boy."

***

There's plenty to eat, but Harry can't manage, sips bourbon and pages through a coffee table book he picked up at the flea market, color shots of Yellowstone and the Grand Tetons. A tad too flashy, but for one, an alpine chalet lit up for Christmas, a splash of warm and welcome under threatening skies. He can go back and forth, from the warmth to the weather, what he looks for in his pictures, so he cuts it out and tapes it to the wall. But the effect is lost somehow, all that comes through is the storm, and Harry takes it down and tosses it in the trash can with the other rejects. Then he sees that none of them work anymore, and it takes a while, but he tears them all down.

Murder in Mexico

***

The wind picks up as they reach the clearing. The bank drops quickly here, no room for Chester to roam so he takes to the ice. Still cautious, but making adjustments and soon he's running and then he's a blur. Lena yells after him, but it's so wide open he can't resist. More energy than intellect, as Hardiman says.

"Chester! Here, Chester..."

The thing he mustn't do and he's doing it. Heading to the edge, but tentative, looking back, seeing how far he can take it as she yells herself hoarse. Chester draws up and Lena steps out on the ice.

"Chester, come here!"

Sliding her feet, whacking her thigh then cheering him on when he bounds her way. Halfway back when something distracts him, a clump of branches frozen in the ice.

"Chester, no! Chester. Here Luke. Come on, Luke boy."

But he won't come. Sniffs at the clump, wheezing and whining and she keeps calling, but it's no good. She can see the ice is thin around the branches. Chester's paw punches through and he skirts away but goes right back to it.

"Noooooo!"

He doesn't crash so much as sink in slow motion, all four paws at once.

***

Harry slips near the barn and hits the ice like a bag of sticks. But he's okay, except his elbow and the heel of his hand where he landed. Crawls to the drainpipe and pulls himself up, laughing like there's one thing funny. Leaning in so as not to fly backward then face first into the bushes.

Once inside, he cranks up the heat and checks the car

mirror, an inch long chin gash he can press together. Looks pretty deep but it's hardly bleeding for some reason. When he tries to take his coat off, a shoulder socket pops and drops him to his knees. Jesus...Jesus! Like broken glass in there.

"Fuck."

Wind howls out the window and he kneels perfectly still, tries to blank out the pain. He knows depression can be seasonal, and winter fits the bill, even in Bucks County. Especially here with no one to see you fall, frozen stiff and drifted over.

And it wasn't important, what he came out here for, just wanted to make a call from the phone in the garage. Talk in private, out here with the cars and the exercise equipment, away from Lena, except she's not even home and rarely questions him about anything anymore. Just feels more comfortable talking out here. So, who was it he wanted to call and why did he bring the gun?

"Brennan's bar."

Harry listens to Ned's nose whistle.

"Brennan's bar. Anybody there? Hello? God damn."

Click.

Not the number he was after, but he pushed the buttons before he could stop himself. The line goes dead and he's more alone than ever. Then he dials all the numbers he knows by heart, the beer distributor on Washington Ave, Bill the Bookie, Baldini, his long dead mother. All of them ring except his mother's and at first he hangs up, but then he listens. Baldini squawking, Duffy sounding spooked about something. He can't think of any others so he grabs a phone book. And right there in the L's, Lavin, Frank, remembers the time they rode in together when the buses were on strike.

***

Lena's almost to him when she hears the ice crack. Chester churns and paws at the hole, but the edge crumbles and the hole just gets bigger. The way he's honking now, eyes flashing panic, locked on hers as he turns in a circle.

"Luke!" She leans and pounds both knees. "You can do it. Come on, Luke."

She takes a step then another. The ice groans but holds. She tries to make herself light and it really feels that way, closer, ten yards, maybe.

"Come on, Luke. Come on, buddy!" She holds out a branch, as if he could grab it, then sends it skittering past the hole. Chester lunges and a front leg hooks the ice, then both legs and he scrapes and claws.

"Come on! Come on, boy!"

Chester claws and scrabbles but he's not gonna to make it, half in, half out, and fading fast.

"Okay, boy, just hold on, Chester." Lena drops to her hands and knees. Snow swirls in her face and she can see through the ice to the rocks beneath.

"It's okay, boy. Hold on, I'm coming. Just don't—"

Then the bottom drops out.

***

It will make things worse. He knows that. It will double the damage and seal his fate. He knows that, too. But the truest sense of self is to know how far you'll go and Harry needs to know.

He soaks his elbow in a bucket of snow, nips at a fifth from the case Lena hides out here. And she's complicit in this, off with Hardiman's horses while Harry unravels. If she were here, he'd still be upstairs, sleeping off the night.

Harry knows that depression feeds on itself, and the dark thoughts are self-fulfilling. He knows you can cycle out of it, but not forever. It always gets worse until no one can stand you. Harry knows about the downward spiral and self-absorption. He couldn't expect Lena to live with it forever. His elbow throbs in the snow but the pain eases a bit. Outside it's Siberia, the frozen Yukon with the drifts drifting and the wind rattling the windows.

She could be fucking the old goat, Hardiman with the dog, the horses, and all the answers. The guy's a wreck, but what does Harry know? He's a wreck too, but still has his moments. And so what if she is? He should be grateful there's someone to look out for her.

Harry knows about depression. By the time Gerry got to the hospice, he was begging Harry to kill him. Not from pain, though there was plenty, because he couldn't stand for it to end that way, propped in a strange bed, oozing life. But Harry couldn't, even when he should have, even through the screams and curses. The way Gerry looked and the last words from his brother's mouth. "Fuck you, Harry."

He punches the number but gets the message, a girl's voice over rap music. No Lavins home but he has the right number. And now he knows how far he'll go.

***

Lena's first thought is that the water should be colder. That it's not so bad. Then her clothes pull her down and now it's cold and she corkscrews in panic. Tries to tread water but her feet are too heavy. Chester chugs over and pummels her under. Lena bobs up and he rakes her face. The current sweeps her beneath the ice but she catches the edge then he's on her again, thrashing madly for a minute then going under. Lena grabs a handful of fur, pulls him up, but it's all she can do. Hands full, and now she's freezing. Yells for help but her voice is shredded, and no one's around anyway. Tastes blood but can't let go with either hand. And it's almost funny. And she laughs and Chester starts to struggle, catches his foot on her pocket, scrabbles up her chest and out of the hole. Dumb luck and leverage, turns to look but Lena's not there.

***

"Hello?"
"Hi, is this," he checks the obit. "Jennifer?"
"She's not home yet."
"Is this Marie?
"Yes."
"How are you, Marie?"
"Fine."
"Did, uh...how was school today?"
"Who's this?"
Harry hangs up. Enough, for Christ sake.

***

Chester burrows into the bank and watches the hole. Hears Lena thrashing, but she won't come out. It hurts him to move but he pushes up then gives a shake that staggers him sideways. He creeps to the edge of the ice but goes no farther, no more heart for it.

***

Something hooks Lena's foot and spins her around. Her last breath takes her under and her head hits the ceiling of ice. Drifting now, feet dragging, carried under a clump of branches. She grabs and pushes off the rocky bottom. The ice cracks and her head breaks the surface. Coughs up river water, choking and gagging, draining her strength. Ten yards from shore, may as well be a thousand. Pounds the ice with her fist then her elbow, breaks through a few feet but can't let go of the branches. Only way is to swim under and break through again. Lena cries out but knows it's useless. Swim or die, the fact of the matter. Never been this scared, never been this cold. Gathers her strength, lets go of the branches and pushes under. She feels the bottom rise toward shore giving her leverage and she pushes. The ice cracks but holds firm. Pushes again and it gives a little, lungs on empty, one last push and she crashes through. Crawls the last few feet, pulls herself up and into in the reeds. Soaking wet, freezing, alive in the cruelest sense. By the time she coughs her lungs clear, her clothes are frozen. Didn't even know that could happen. Cold like fire, hateful and cruel, save yourself only to suffer and die. And then, in a blinding flash of circumstance, she thinks of the bootlegger, the odds against wizard, not even a good bootlegger, but you just couldn't kill him.

Her clothes crackle when she tries to stand, wet spots freeze but her legs move. She works the muscles though it hurts like hell and the cold is unbearable, rolls to her knees and claws her way up. The wind hits her at the top of the bank and she screams into it. Should be dead. Should be bobbing under the ice until springtime. Bloated, what you always hear about the drowned.

Ringing pain in her fingers and toes, snot frozen, hair stiff with ice. She struggles to stand, searing pain as blood rushes to her feet. The things she thinks, how she'll die standing up and they'll find her rooted to the spot, oh Jesus. Lena closes her eyes, strains to connect to her one remaining function and feels it work, her bladder relaxes and the flow of warmth takes her breath away. One blessed moment and Lena takes a step. And it's like walking on nails and the warmth turns to blistering cold. But she's moving, stiff legged as her pants refreeze, and she thinks what this must look like. The bank curves around and she sees the bridge, feels the thud of her shoes but can't feel her feet. If she falls she'll never get up so she doesn't fall. If she stops she'll die so she doesn't stop. Never stop. The bootlegger never stopped. Fucking bootlegging son of a bitch!

The first time she falls it feels like glass breaking. She

has to make herself breathe, then stand and walk. Every step takes everything out of her. No notion of how far she's gone or how long it's been, but she keeps to the towpath, to the footbridge and past it. No one sees her. Lena falls again and that's it, she's finished. Except here comes Chester, and he nudges and pokes and finally lies down beside her. Lena hears him blubber, feels his nose burrow into her coat.

"No, Chester," she whispers. "Go home."

But he tucks himself in and his breath warms a circle in her shirt. Lena hugs as much of him as she can and they tremble together. Chester squirms to get closer. Keeps struggling with those claws digging and Lena has to push him off, her clothes crack and the ends of her hair rattle. Chester crawls back on his belly and sinks his teeth into her arm. Lena lets out a ragged wail of rage that twists her to her knees. Chester barks and whimpers. Lena staggers behind him.

***

The light hurts her eyes and she hammers blindly at the wall switch. Feeling along the counter to the sink and the faucet, runs her hands in the water. A few minutes until she can work her fingers, lets the sink fill with warmth then she's elbows-deep. The water turns brown but she plunges her head in. At first she feels nothing then a painful warming and she pulls away. It takes her forever to get undressed with all the clasps and buckles zippers that won't unzip. The shoes! Ten minutes with the laces and the joints in her fingers flashing pain. Chester watches like they're still not out of the woods, then checks his bowl, then curls up and heaves a sigh.

Everything burns, skin, muscles, joints. She watches the tub fill, doesn't turn around to the mirror, doesn't look at herself. And Lena knows she'll never tell a soul, gets a change of clothes from the bedroom and it's like it never happened. She turns on the music and it's like it never happened. But her knees are ground meat, hands, legs, scraped and bloody, something happened, all right. The water cools and Lena drains and refills it, washes her hair, ugh, drains it again, stands under the shower until the water turns cold.

And there's no one to tell and it's like it never happened.

Just like Harry not to be home.

***

Lena finds him the next morning. She picks up the gun and feels for a pulse, but Harry's cold and dead. She lifts the phone from his lap and the scrap of paper with the phone number, names she knows. She sits with him for a while: doesn't cry and doesn't say a word. Chester pushes through the door and Lena puts him out again. He scratches and barks so she lets him in and he settles by the door so she lets him stay.

Harry's eyes are open and she leans into his sight line. How can he not see? It's a small hole above the ear and she smells the liquor. Sits with him but she doesn't cry. Then she cries but swears to herself it'll just be this once, for as long as it takes. It takes all afternoon.

***

She drags the painting tarps from the basement and spreads them out on top of each other. Wrestles Harry out of the chair, lays him out on the edge then rolls him up and under his car. For the next hour she scrubs the place down, splatter, bits of gore, walls, the car, the workbench, the stupid Exercycle. Takes short, shallow breaths and keeps at it until it's finished.

Harry spends the night under his car.

In the morning Lena picks up another tarp and a

length of rope. She pulls Harry out and ties him at the waist, knees and ankles, tucking and pulling until he's wrapped tight.

***

She hears them snuffling at her approach, Tramples knocking against the stall. They're happy to see her and she let's them eat while she cinches the blankets and the saddlebags. The snow throws off enough light to see and the horses fidget as she reins them up and leads them outside. Not even worried. Hardiman won't be back until tomorrow.

On the way back, she sees a car pull down the lane, but it's just someone turning around. She leads the horses up their driveway, swings the barn door open, walks them inside then swings it shut. The saddlebags are old but sturdy. She throws them over Buck's back and slips two ten pound weights in each pocket. Eighty pounds, plus the ten she can carry.

Then the hard part, getting Harry up and onto Tramples, not just physically hard, but the rough handling, the bulk, and what she feels through the tarp, his shoulder and knee. Chester gets in the way but she manages somehow and it looks just like in the westerns, head down over the saddle. The horses sense adventure and Lena leads them down the lane. Chester heads the pack around the turn to the towpath. Tramples strains but she pulls him back, and soon they're too far down to be seen.

She smells the river, tastes it, but forces her thoughts away. Buck nudges from behind, his breath hot on her neck. Better to think about horses and it's almost too easy. Not that there's been that many in her life, but she remembers them all. And the picture she saw once of a barn cat sleeping on the horses back and then cats, all the cats she's known.

Tom Larsen

The footbridge is unlit, just a black stripe on the river. The towpath cuts in and she tugs the reins, the horses balk but follow her down.

"Good boys, come on, that's it." She lulls them along.

When they reach the center of the bridge she drops the reins and looks north, the dark side away from the city. Working quickly she lowers Harry down and takes the weights from the saddlebags. Her fingers are clumsy with cold but she doesn't stop. A hundred pounds heavier Harry's too much to pull so she rolls him to the gap, doesn't cry, doesn't say goodbye, sits back and shoves Harry off with her feet. The weight pulls her to the rail but she can't hold on. Harry hits the water headfirst. The rope curls like a snake on the surface then disappears.

Murder in Mexico

So you can plan all you want, but you can't know the future. And when the future falls apart, you either fall apart with it or you make different plans. In the spring, I flew to Puerto Vallarta. Carlos and I lived like lovers for a time, traveled a bit, took it easy. I'd never known the leisure life, and Mexico seemed made for it. Carlos pressed me to marry, but I resisted. He had other women, but that wasn't it. I was Harry's wife, and he was all the husband I could handle.

Two years ago, Carlos was diagnosed with liver cancer. They gave him nine months, but he was gone in two. Before he died he told me about the medical report and the bartender from the Black Sombrero. How he doctored this and tampered with that, my dark sin spoken aloud and it floored me, I'll admit. Not just that he knew, what he did to keep the secret. As a lover, Carlos had his faults, but as an accomplice, he was world class.

With Harry's insurance and Carlos's bequest, I have all the money I'll ever need. I've kept the house in Pennsport, but I live downtown in a co-op with a river view. I see old friends now and again, but the drama in my life lives only in memories.

I miss Chester and visit him when I can. Last summer we went to the bridge on Harry's birthday. I stood at the rail and searched the river, but there was nothing. When I tried to picture Harry, all I could see was the bottom of his shoes as he hit the water. I know he's there but I didn't feel sorry, I didn't cry and I haven't been back since.

I keep his picture in my locket, and part of it's me and part of it's the years, but Harry seems younger every time I look. Not so often, late at night when I'm tipsy and I need to see...long-ago Harry all full of himself.

Tom Larsen

Tom Larsen lives in the Pennsport section of South Philadelphia, home to Mummers, Flyers, and that *'screw you'* slant that made this city great. He and his wife, Andree, lived here for a decade in the nineties, moved away, then moved back again: where the heart is. He's been writing fiction for twenty years plus, and for a writer auditioning characters, the 19148 zip code is a casting gold mine. His novels, *Flawed* and *Into the Fire*, were published in paperback, and his other works have appeared in Newsday, New Millennium Writing, Best American Mystery Stories, Raritan, and the LA Review.

TWB PRESS

http://www.twbpress.com

Science Fiction – Horror – Supernatural – Thriller – Romance – and More

Made in the USA
Middletown, DE
02 July 2024

56576540R00183